D0763389

IN WRATH REMEMBER MERCY

THE REDEMPTION OF TORQUIL DHU

Dedicated to

The Staff Sergeant,
United States Army, Retired
Half the Research Team, the Whole Technical Department, Work
Buddy, Partner in Adventure, Husband, Best Beloved

To the Reader:

"If the foundations be destroyed, what can the righteous do?"
is the beginning of rebuilding a wounded life according to bibli-
cal principles.

Before the characters tell you their stories, I welcome you to
the inside of trauma survival and healing, told in three kinds of
love: man and God, father and son, and man and woman.

The quotations throughout verify the truth of the tale.
Participants and eyewitnesses tell what they knew, planned, did,
saw, thought, believed, and felt. You may be surprised by who
said or wrote these things, so each is identified. Passages from
the Bible bear witness to the Truth and to His love, wisdom, and
blessing.

Opinions expressed by the characters, and nineteenth century
medical practices, are true to the time period and the circumstances. Thus they differ from those of today.

Please feel welcome to share your impressions, questions, or
research corrections, with me at:

AquilaDhu@InWrathRememberMercy.com.

Aquila Dhu

Contents

BOOK III: THE VIRGINIA MILITARY INSTITUTE

PROLOGUE:

IN THE HANDS
OF THE ENEMY

Gloria Victis![1]

For the principle of State rights and State sovereignty the Southern men fought with a holy ardor and self-denying patriotism that have covered even defeat with imperishable glory.

—Dr. Charles E. Stowe, son of the author of *Uncle Tom's Cabin,* ca. 1900.

Lieutenant Drummond

Hands manacled, head throbbing, I came to my senses in a dim cell. Dizzy ... thought I'd vomit. I didn't! Blood oozed from my head, but I couldn't diagnose any other injuries. How to escape? I ran a finger around the top of my right boot. The *skean dhu*[2] was gone.

---

1 Latin: "Glory to the vanquished!"
2 Scots Gaelic: a certain type of long dagger

The only light glimmered through gratings in an iron-bound door. The manacles were chained to the log wall; the floor was rammed earth. The guard would be the only weak point.

I must have passed out again.

Rough prodding in the ribs … blue … Yankees! Brain and skin prickled. Everything in me flamed for attack. I sprang, but the irons caught me midway.

One guard startled back. The other jammed his Spencer into my sternum. "Give up, Reb! You're caught. Get up slow." He kept that carbine on me while the scaredy one unlocked the manacles.

Dizziness and headache were less. Under guard, crossing the parade, I was memorizing everything in view: log palisade, gates, log cabins, North Star, good cover under the edge of a big cistern lid.

Then they nudged me into a stark little room.

"Dismissed."

Silhouetted by the lamp behind him, an officer rose from his field desk, well over six feet tall. Brown hair, a few silver strands glinting. Beneath level brows, intent brown eyes missed nothing. Moustache knifed off at the lines around a wide mouth.

"MacLeod!"

"Good evening, Lieutenant Drummond."

MacLeod

I gave him the dignity he's earned—all he has now—with time to collect his thoughts. Selfless duty showed its cost. He was gaunt, his gray uniform ragged. Blood matted his black hair. He still had the steady steel-blue eyes under winged brows, the eagle's rapt attention, the austere demeanor. Features in balance, nose no longer overwhelming the rest, his beardless face retained the roundness of boyhood. He'd grown. He stood only a couple inches short of six feet now.

I wanted to embrace him for joy he was alive, but first I had to save his life.

"Sit down," I invited.

"Not with a confounded spy!" was the nearest to a curse I'd ever heard him utter.

"We prefer to call it the Bureau of Military Information."

"You betrayed us!"

"Were your men there?"

"No."

"Then you must review your conclusion."

"You weren't in uniform! Why take me now, not then?"

"I have reasons."

"What do you want with me?"

"I want you to enlist in this company."

"I shall not betray my country."

"Lieutenant ... General Lee surrendered in April."

A slight flinch. His face went pale. Tightened mouth showed him choking off emotion.

I drew him past it. "You kept your allegiance, but it's over."

"What of my men!"

"They're safe."

"How do you know!"

"My source is truthful."

"Thanks be to God. They're the hope and future of their families."

"Returning to the subject of *your* future," I continued, "do you know there's a price on your head and a military court ready to hang you in Virginia?"

"What am I worth? To whom?"

"Two thousand dollars, to the general."

"He must have hated the funeral worse than I thought. The court?" He spoke as if the topic mattered less than dust.

"Crimes of war."

"I'll go back. When the truth is established, Drummond honor will be, too."

"It will only get you hanged! The spirit of vengeance is abroad, more so since President Lincoln was assassinated. They won't hear the truth, much less act upon it."

"I shall have tried. Truth has power in itself. If I'm the scapegoat, Abercairn won't be." His expression was anguished.

He still needs to mourn, but not now. Self-preservation never tempts him, so I turned to duty—and made my words barbs.

"Have you ceased to care about your countrymen!"

"I'm willing to die for them!"

"Will you live for them!" I demanded. "Many have lost home and livelihood, so they're coming west. The Army guards their travel. They still need your protection."

I could see the idea beginning to seep in. His hands clenched and his lips tightened with renewed determination.

"I shall call for your decision after supper tomorrow."

I ordered the guard to take him first to the surgeon. I could only pray I'd convinced him. God made clear my duty to foster him, a year ago, but my only powers are reason, and fatherly affection. Those earned his confidence till he heard what he thought was betrayal. Cold rationality isolates him now as it did at first. He might accept military subordination, but my heart still yearns for a son …

* * *

How easily I could get rid of this and be at rest! I have only to ride along the lines, and all will be over. But *it is our duty to live*—for what will become of the women and children of the South if we are not here to support and protect them?
—General Robert E. Lee, Confederate States Army, April 9, 1865

Lieutenant Drummond

The surgeon knew his work and did it with deft hands. He cleansed the wound, swabbed on something that burnt, and gave me bitter medicine. The guard didn't put me in irons again. I sat, leaning against the wall. The physical pain began to fade.

I thought I'd outrun the pursuit, here in the foothills of the Laramie Mountains, but they ambushed me. I downed one before they clubbed me from behind.

How should a Stoic reason out *this*? Set passion aside. Define the decision.

Heart and mind safe from shock in the orderly haven of logic, I lined up the facts.

First point. Enlisting would cost three years. Escape to Virginia would be easy. How to spend the next three years? The Army would be military routine and warfare. I know those too well. In Virginia I'd be hanged ... or set free to carry on life at home. Either would suit me.

Glenlochie is good land. Was it confiscated as spoils of war? Was Abercairn ...

Abercairn ...

Haven and new beginning for the Scots who founded it.
Cradle, matrix, nourisher of her sons' spirits ever since.
Home-place, heart's home, dearer than life to her defenders.
Where I hope my bones will rest with my family's.

Was Abercairn under martial law? A letter to ask would endanger whoever I wrote to. If I were hanged, I'd be free eternally. If the general's thirst for vengeance on me were satisfied, he might leave Abercairn County unmolested.

Next point. Responsibilities. Accountable only to myself and God, no family nor kin needing support, Mr. Ogilvie steward and trustee. My duty to God is obedience to His commandments.

The second Great Commandment resolved the debate: "Love thy neighbor as thyself!"

I couldn't be sure of helping my neighbors if I returned. Worse, the general's malice would make me a danger to them. As a soldier, I could protect those who moved west. I had to agree to MacLeod's demand.

My breath went out in a big sigh. I'd done a soldier's duty but expected to go home when the war was over. I longed for respite. More warfare was weariness heaped upon exhaustion. It dismayed and incensed me.

A few night birds called. A wolf howled far away. Water in a pail smelled sweet and tasted sweeter. The first dipperful never hit bottom. I drank a second. I stretched out on the floor, arms pillowing my head, and gazed into the darkness.

"Dear God," I whispered, "what do You want me to do?"

Into my spirit, in words of power, came commands not to contrive my own death, and to protect my countrymen. I resigned myself to carrying the double burden of life and duty—again.

> When our idolized leader sheathed his sword at Appomattox the world grew dark to us. ... It was as if the foundations of the earth were sinking beneath our feet.
> —Lt. Randolph H. McKim, First Maryland Infantry, Confederate States Army

The Confederacy died the instant I heard of the surrender. Da and Douglas died in her service. The blow stunned me. I'd believed in victory when hope was vain and fought on. In bitterness of soul too profound for rage, this void in my life blotted out the pain of my empty stomach. The battle for Southern independence had been the sinew knitting my life together for a quarter of my years. The cord was severed. I was adrift.

I dozed, but wakened, chilled through, the nightmare haunting my mind. It's as familiar as the chasm that cuts me off from the world around me. Thunder and flash of battle ... carnage of death and wounds ... mutilated bodies ... ground slippery with blood. I was treading around corpses and the groaning wounded, looking for Da and Douglas. Douglas rose laughing from his dead body.

"Come on, wee brither! We'll show the Yankees they can't kill Scots!"

My father didn't rise. Douglas disappeared. All that remained was their bodies ... sacrificed for nothing.

In loneliness too overwhelming for prayer, I kept seeing them fall. "When the war is over, I shall mourn my dead," I'd told Dominie Gilchrist, above their graves. It's over. I walk alone through a life I still don't want.

The Dominie said, "God does not afflict willingly. Remember that. It will bring ye peace."

It's not peace, it's desolation. But the commands to live and protect are clear.

Surely God has some reason ....

The horrible scene repeated itself over and over in the darkness. I felt a sob convulsing my vitals and bit on my hand so I wouldn't howl. I summoned up all the self-mastery Da ever taught us, to choke down sorrow and remember ... before. My father's kindness never failed. He understood us—better than we wanted to be understood, sometimes. He taught us unwavering faith in God, and all our manly skills. He gave steadfast discipline and constant affection. I remembered adventures and jokes I shared with Dougie—he hated his baby name, so I teased him with it—the scrapes we got into, how we sometimes got out and sometimes got caught. Brothers like two halves of a single life.

The truth I fought to bury made me break: they're gone from earth forever. Dry, gasping sobs choked my breath. I buried my head in my coat to muffle my noise. It would shame me if the guards heard.

A big hollow hole in me. Of themselves, my arms clamped around my middle to keep it from spilling out and eating me up.

"My heart's torn out, I miss them so much!" I cried to God.

I don't know how long I wept.

The trumpet sounded First Call at first light. Despite shivering from the mountain cold, I gave dutiful thanks to God for the new day. Using water from the pail, I washed my hands and face, then tried to comb my hair. The wound that downed me was still tender.

I paced the ten-foot square of the cell. MacLeod blindsided me last night. I reasoned cynically that I'd have to make the best terms I could. Food slid under the door so fast I almost stepped on it. The grating banged shut faster than it opened. Do they think I bite!

I savored coffee, warming my hands on the tin cup. Over beef and bread, I gave thanks.

How bad did MacLeod want me to enlist? What could he be induced to offer? The officer corps is the only respectable way a gentleman can live in *their* army. To gain fullest respect, I must earn my commission at West Point. That would be my price.

I was trapped, but I wasn't ready to surrender. I longed to go home to whatever awaited, but I didn't dare disobey God again.

MacLeod

If possible, the boy looked colder, more dispassionate.

"What do you want me to do as a member of your company?" he asked.

"Garrison duties, scouts, Indian fighting."

"That last will help me find my grave."

"Your life is too valuable to waste."

"I don't see it so."

"Not only Southern people need your help. The Indians won't be quickly pacified. We need experienced soldiers to train and lead the recruits. I'll appoint you a non-commissioned officer as soon as I can and promote you when you're ready for it."

"That's not enough." His mouth was taut.

"What is?"

"A commission, earned at West Point."

"I wish that were possible." From a pigeonhole of my desk, I handed him a paper.

> Chapter CXXVIII.—Act of July 2, 1862.—To prescribe An Oath of Office ... every person elected or appointed to any office of honor or profit under the Government of the United States ... civil, military, or naval ... shall ... take ... the following oath ... "I, A. B., do solemnly swear ...that I have never voluntarily borne arms against the United States."

He looked grim when he raised his eyes. The law bars him from the officer corps. I hid sympathy, but I hated it, too. I want to share my occupation with a son who's developed the mind of a soldier.

"It would require a special Act of Congress to award you a commission, let alone an appointment to the Military Academy. If the law ever permits, I'll do all within my power to see that you're commissioned."

"Does your interest in the Information Bureau extend to such matters?"

"I decline to answer. I'm a line soldier now."

"Then how can you secure me a commission?"

"There are factions. Mine is powerful."

"How can I trust *your* word!" he sneered.

I ignored the slur on my honor. He has reason to doubt it exists. "Would you accept my oath sworn upon the Word of God?"

"Yes."

I handed him my Bible and placed my hand upon it.

"I, James MacLeod, do solemnly swear to do all in my power to secure for Torquil Drummond an officer's commission in the United States Army, in return for his enlistment in M Company, Sixteenth Cavalry Regiment, so help me, God."

"How long do you think it will take?"

"I don't know. Till it's possible, I'll put you in the company."

"As well put me in the lions' den." His mouth wryed with contempt.

"Did you think it would be easy! Do we have an agreement?"

"One thing more. Why are you doing this?"

"I'll tell you the full story at a better time. I will not see you destroyed. In that, I am obeying God, using the means at my disposal. Have we an agreement!"

He hesitated, then: ". . . yes . . ."

I took a bundle of papers from the desk. "How old are you now?"

"Seventeen."

"Enlistment age is eighteen. I'll sign as your guardian."

A hard-eyed look. "A legal formality only, I presume!"

"A formality," I had to concede. We filled the blanks. I tried to joke kindly, "You look half dead."

"And smell entirely so."

I gestured toward my back room. "Everything you need is set out."

Torquil

Hospitality from a man I tried to kill? I don't trust it.

Sleeping chamber: bed, cot, table, coal-oil lamp, shelf of books. Clothing and weapons on wooden pegs, washstand and galvanized iron tub, big buffalo rugs on the rammed-earth floor.

Lean-to kitchen east, kettle steaming, door to the outside, north. My saddle pockets and hat on the cot, my saddle and weapons under it—he left me the means to kill him!

Ridding myself of travel dirt and dried blood was a long job of work. I had no spare clothing, but he'd laid citizens' clothing on the cot.

He looked up from writing when I returned, defiantly wearing the clean shirt and my uniform, but he never so much as raised an eyebrow.

"If you want to keep your buttons and insignia, cut them off and put them away," he ordered. "It's unlawful to wear them. Burn the uniform. Put the rest of your clothing in the pot to boil."

"It's not worth keeping."

"If it can be mended, it will save you money on your clothing allowance. I presume you'll want your uniforms fitted. The company tailor can do your mending, too."

"Yankees do everything in grand style!"

"Grander when we're commissioned. You can look forward to that."

A future? Mockery!

Giving up my distinctions grieved my soul and drove home defeat. Broken from gentleman's estate to enlisted servitude! I kept my buttons and second lieutenant's bar. Like making a solemn sacrifice, I folded my uniform and laid it in the flames. My orders went last.

When I emerged in citizen's clothing, MacLeod had more to say, but I ... couldn't.

"Officially, I'm detaining you for interrogation," he began. "Unofficially, you need rest and food before you stand the physical examination. You will lock on that ball and chain when you go beyond these walls." He handed over the key.

My face must have showed I was incredulous.

"We're not all barbarians because we wear blue!" His voice whip-cracked, then softened. "Are you hungry?"

"Yes."

"Go see what you can forage. You're welcome to whatever's there."

"Thank you."

I felt like a pauper invited to raid a treasury. I set beef hash and something that looked like vegetables on the cookstove, tore off chunks of soft bread, and almost swallowed them whole. I chided myself for greed and started frying some bacon.

MacLeod

I wrote:

> Our prayers are answered. I wish I could kill the fatted calf for joy that the lost is found! He's grown a jaw you could wreck a dinghy on, which balances his features very well. There's not much left of him but whipcord and willfulness, but he's here, alive, and foraging in my larder. Continue to pray for him, for I'll soon have to put him in the company and let him fend for himself. But God gives such good gifts! Good night.

I put the partially written sheet in an envelope with its predecessors and went to the kitchen. Torquil ate at the table against the west wall.

"Are you finding enough?" I asked.

Stiff courtesy: "Yes, thank you."

The trumpeters sounded Retreat. The post fell into twilight as the sun set behind the mountain. I'd assigned another officer to command Dress Parade.

"I have some questions." I sat down.

"Ask." His posture tensed, but his voice was even.

"How is Robbie getting along?"

"When I left, he was well." He didn't relax. "He invented a harness so he could ride, and rode with us from Christmas on. He married Miss Carmichael as soon as he could stand at the altar." He tried to swallow a yawn. "Excuse me."

I smiled inside and made soothing conversation. "Are they staying at his home or hers?"

"At Glenlochie." Brusquely, as though to excuse generosity, he continued, "It needs to be lived in. She's with child." He suppressed another yawn and sat up straighter.

"Why don't you turn in?"

"I shall, since you excuse me. Good night."

"Good night. Sleep well. You're safe here."

Torquil

Lying on my back, I thanked God in dutiful faith for the daunting change in my life, and in genuine gratitude for the luxury of sleeping warm, full-fed, and safe. Somehow, my spirit believed MacLeod's word and rebuked the rest of me expecting deadly danger. I floated down into dreamless slumber.

* * *

I ... propose ... to make desolation everywhere.
—General William T. Sherman, United States Army

Sherman made his vastly praised contribution to preserving the Union largely against defenseless civilians.
—Clifford Dowdey, historian

MacLeod

I'd taught about the Regular Army and had him read the *Regulations.* "Questions?"

"What's the name of this post?"

"Camp Sherman."

He looked contemptuous. "What's the strategic situation?"

"The Indians are fighting white immigration and the military presence to guard it. They're seeking vengeance for the massacre of a peaceful village of Cheyennes by a volunteer force in Colorado Territory last year. The Cheyenne have since joined with the Sioux and Arapaho against us."

"How do they fight?"

"When and how they want to, usually by outnumbering us. A war party moves faster than we do."

"What's your strength?"

"One company."

"How do you fill the positions *Regulations* prescribes and still have enough men to take the field?"

"Edicts."

"Like a Roman governor issued when he took command of a province?"

"Exactly." I was glad he retained enough of his schooling to understand the reference. "This isn't a regimental post, so some duties fall to the lower ranks. Do you understand yours?"

"Same as I've done."

"Not quite. You won't have the independence you had in the volunteers. You'll have to toe the mark—right strictly! The *Regulations* are the law by which your life is now governed." I paused. "You're not ready for my cutthroats, so I'm putting you in fourth barracks. There's not a bad heart among them. Most of them enlisted together, from the same county in Ohio." Then I added, "You also need to know Yohanson and DuChemin are here."

Torquil

My insides wadded up. It isn't over. Why is he trying to save my life, but keep me vulnerable to deadly enemies?

"Won't they turn me in for the reward?" I asked.

"They don't know about it. I'm acting as my own adjutant and chose not to reveal those orders. My scouting parties observe all travelers and report to me. I'd intended to ride out myself and ask you privately to make our agreement."

He knew if he tried to approach me, I'd have shot him! What is he plotting?

Salt in the wound, to put on the blue uniform. Departing, I quirked my mouth with contempt to hide apprehension and show him I wasn't conquered. I mocked a salute.

"Moriturus te salutamo!"[3]

"Mortem tuam delenda est! Vale!"[4]

MacLeod

Whether he likes it or not, I have legal backing for my personal authority. For his good, I'll exercise it, but I hope for a stronger bond. Watching him cross the parade—broad-shouldered, long-legged and thin as a splinter, as regally as if going to his coronation—I wondered what he'd make of the farm boys, and they, of a very young Virginia gentleman.

---

3 Latin: "I, about to die, salute you!" (Roman gladiators spoke this to the highest-ranking person in the audience before combat in the arena.)
4 Latin: "Your death must be destroyed! Be well!"

BOOK I
VIRGINIA

CHAPTER 1

VENGEANCE

By sorrow of the heart the spirit is broken. ... So are
the sons of men snared in an evil time, when it falleth
suddenly upon them.
—Proverbs 15:13b, and Ecclesiastes 9:12b

Torquil

Unhorsed, desperate to recapture my family, I was only thirty
yards away, running, my breath searing my throat.

"No! No-o-o!"

In an instant, like a bolt of lightning fuses sand into glass, all
heaven and earth smashed me to pieces and dropped me into a
black abyss. My lifelong Light vanished. My life was turned into
a curse.

Their bodies crumpled to the ground. I marked forever the
features and dead, pale eyes of the big Yankee officer who murdered them after they surrendered. I commandeered horse and
wagon, retrieved their bodies while darkness fell, and drove from
the battlefield to bury my dead at Glenlochie.

Ambulances and wagons carrying the wounded choked the roads. Blood ran down through the bottoms of those that had made several trips. Blood reddened the bandages of wounded men and coated the surgeons' clothing at every farmstead I passed. Blood soaked the ground, stained the creeks, and threw a veil before my eyes that made the Potomac a river of blood as I brought my revered burden across the ford from Northern into Confederate territory. I didn't know, then, that my unseeing expression and the dead determination in my manner prevented all from interfering with me.

The household tended me as when I was growing up. I heard them talking but couldn't answer. A chasm seemed to fall deep between me and them. Keir alone blessed me with silence. In the morning, Mr. Ogilvie, my father's steward, brought a sheaf of papers and summoned me to the library-*cum*-office.

"According to the customs of Drummond inheritance, the estate of the Drummond passes to the eldest surviving son. Until you meet the conditions your father specified—adulthood and graduation from college—it is held in trust. Captain Murray and I are the trustees."

Their bodies lay in state in the parlor, in the old way of clan chieftains, hands folded over the hilts of swords which lay upon their hearts. I stood beside Keir as honor guard. I'd eaten nothing. Sleep deserted me. I stared through the front window at the night sky, willing the hours to pass, so I could pass this ordeal of ceremony and return to war. I wouldn't see their faces again, so I studied them, fixing their still features in memory that will have to serve till I enter the eternity of joy they now inhabit.

Mrs. Grieg

I found Torquil Dhu—I think of him as my last lad—at first peep o' day, standing straight at the foot o' the coffins, face white as ashes and still as the grave, eyes seeing naught they looked upon. But he saw me and spoke.

"Mrs. Greig, please ask Mr. Greig to have the team and wagon ready at the cemetery, with Thunderfoot on lead, saddle and equipments packed. I shall return to the lines as soon as the service is over."

"Aye."

"Thank you."

Soft, soft, I coaxed him into the library and directed the Dominie to him there.

Torquil

As chief mourner, I sat closest to the coffins. It was like a sheet of glass fell between me and them. I heard not a word of the funeral service. Ewen, face stained from tears, was in the front rank bearing Douglas's coffin. Following the coffins out the front door and along the lane to the family burying ground, I stood before the open graves through the ritual and the final coronach the piper played.

> Unto God the Lord belong the issues from death.
> —Psalm 68:20b

> For the wrath of man worketh not the righteousness of God.
> —James 1:20

Dominie Gilchrist

As the last of the congregation passed through the gate, I turned to Torquil. I'd baptized this boy, witnessed him giving his life to Christ, answered his solemn questions, watched him grow in grace, and blessed him along with the rest when he rode to war. Black crape mourning band on his left sleeve, he stood straight, dry-eyed, gaze fixed on the open graves. During years of ministry, I've seen many such still faces by gravesides. My heart aches for each one.

I laid a hand of comfort on his shoulder. "Ye may grieve, Torquil Dhu, not for their reward, but for your loss."

"Tears are for the women. When the war is over, I shall mourn my dead."

"Our Lord has told us there is a time to weep. Be not ashamed of the honest tear. God doth not afflict willingly. Remember that. It will bring ye peace."

"Ashamed I am not. Now is the time for war." A flame of fury flashed in his eyes. "They were not killed in battle, Dominie, they were murdered, against the laws of God and man! My duty is to avenge them!"

"No! Vengeance belongs only to God!"

He turned away, scooped up loose earth in each hand, stepped to the foot of the graves. He cast earth onto each coffin.

"For Da. For Douglas."

He took a step backward, stood at attention, and lifted his face toward heaven. "Before Your throne and judgment seat, Almighty God, I swear I shall not rest until I have shed the heart's blood of the murderer. I shall hunt him to the ends of earth and time, and by my hand and sword I shall send him to hell. Amen!"

He turned to me. "Goodbye, Dominie."

Then he drove away, never knowing he had pronounced a doom upon himself. I knelt in the grass by the graves and beseeched God to spare his life. He will pay dearly if he commits the sin he vowed.

* * *

Why is my pain perpetual, and my wound incurable, which refuseth to be healed?
—Jeremiah 15:18

Torquil

'A man maun dree his ain weird,'[5] I told myself, and did my duty. The sorrow was unbearable, so I buried it and sealed it off. Knowing there was no remedy, no consolation, nothing but irreparable loss, drove it deeper. I had no hope and desired no future. I walked alone, in company with the shades of my dead. I'd rather be with them, but I'd sworn my oath. I felt like God had forsaken me.

> I realized the fierce infatuation of matching life with life.
> —George Alfred Townsend, *Campaigns of a Non-Combatant*, 1866

In battle, I fought with unquenchable fury till no target was left. I slung a captured carbine and pistol, with ammunition, from my saddle, and carried in my boot a razor-edged *skean dhu*, to fight hand to hand. In every Yankee, I saw the murderer and tried to destroy him—till I could no longer think.

Then every fight was a glorious, fiery haze. My strength was a lion's might, my aim was pinpoint accurate, my perceptions intensified. I felt neither pain nor weariness nor fear. I had ultimate senses and extra-wide vision. Following battle and its after-duties, when all my powers were used up, I fell insensate till I could fight again.

I ate little, learning to forage, and choosing to despoil the Northern enemy rather than the already depleted Confederate countryside. Sleep evaded me, so I scouted at night into the Yankee camps, searching for the murderer. Sometimes our camps and theirs were but a mile apart. Perfect in ability to move

---

5 Scottish: "A man must suffer his own fate."

silently and unseen, I disdained disguise. I'd die or escape as a soldier, not a spy!

We of the cavalry were in action all winter. We guarded the Confederate rear and flanks, picketed the Rappahannock River, scouted across on the enemy side, and attacked their communications. I helped drive the Yankees out of Jeffersonton, past the academy where I got my schooling in a former, better world.

We suffered increasing scarcity of remounts. Forage was scarcer still. By turns, detachments took leave to rest and heal their horses. Those same men became the couriers who brought letters, food, and clothing from Abercairn. I stayed with the army, but Mrs. Grieg always knew, and sent, what I needed. The home I'd looked to as the source of all good things was only a shadow now. I was chained to my vow of vengeance. Willingly.

Men whose horses were killed or disabled marched on foot at the rear of the columns, carrying their saddles and equipments, hoping to capture remounts for themselves. We derided them as "Company Q." When Thunderfoot was killed, I marched among them. Extra weapons and ammunition made my load too heavy, but I slogged through sleet, snow, and bottomless mud with all of it slung on my shoulders. Often, I lagged behind. I was disburdened only in camp or to serve as a sharpshooter. Once I was ordered out of line to help serve a gun.

> A sharp, venomous screech, clap of thunder, right over our heads, followed by a ripping, tearing, splitting crash, that filled the air … a bursting Parrott shell from a Federal gun! … Another shell, and another, came screaming over us. Then they began to swarm; the air seemed full of them—bursting shells, jagged fragments, balls out of case-shot—it sounded

like a thousand devils, shrieking in the air all about us
… and the ground … was furrowed and torn.
—Willy Dame, First Company Richmond Howitzers,
Confederate States Army

Assigned to the No. 4 position, I placed the friction primer in the vent hole at a nod from No. 3, moved to the outside of the wheel, and watched the gunner in charge of the piece for the signal. Then I pulled the lanyard to fire.

No sooner had the gun boomed forth its load of death than No. 2 twisted the worm down the tube to remove any burning matter. No. 3 cleared and stopped the vent. No. 1 dipped the sponge on its long staff into the water bucket and swabbed the bore. No. 2 plunged the dry sponge down the tube so the charge would stay dry and turned to receive the load from No. 5 advancing from the limber chest well behind the gun. He placed the charge in the mouth of the gun, No. 1 rammed it home, and No. 3 punctured the bag of gunpowder and nodded off to me. We fired three shots *every minute.*

While we let the gun cool, the artillerymen piled fence rails behind the wheels, to save the exhausting work of running it back into battery after the recoil from every shot. When fired, it jerked back only a little and rested against the rails, saving our strength for prolonged firing.

I placed the primer and pulled the lanyard again. And again. And again. Amid gun thunder and billowing smoke and the demonic screech of enemy shells, the lightning-paced work and short pause were hypnotic. Motions and watching were part of my eyes and body and brain. When the battery commander ordered the crew to elevate the gun and pivot it left oblique, it was an annoying interruption to the perfect flow.

But it meant the Yankees were beaten.

"Cease fire!"

"Secure the piece!"

"Limber up!"

In waning daylight, cavalry galloped in pursuit. Bleary-eyed from smoke, deafened, unnerved by loss of vital senses, exhausted, I recovered my weapons and followed. I didn't receive Victory, the horse I sent home for, till February, when the First Virginia moved to the upper Rappahannock. I reckoned cynically that I'd walked the length of the river at least three times.

Vengeance was my life and combat a glorious blaze. I knew of it only from Greek literature, so I called the battle fury my daemon. I spoke of it to no one. I lost my dear Thunderfoot without mourning. I had to send twice to Glenlochie for remounts. I forgot Da's admonition to be concerned for enemies' souls. I discarded mercy.

I didn't notice my heart withered. I didn't need it. I could quell most men with an unwavering look of determination. Trust destroyed, I never thought of God. To kill Yankees, I needed only my weapon and myself. Darkness grew inside me. I felt neither that nor anything else. I didn't notice anything was wrong. This was my fate, the way things had to be.

> The United States Army deliberately targeted Confederate civilians and prisoners of war in a war of vengeance … it is a story which reveals a policy decision reached by the United States government to kill without mercy.
> —Michael R. Bradley, "In the Crosshairs."

The Yankee War Department issued General Order No. 100. Like much else published at the North, it was soon well known to us in the South. Written by a merciless Prussian who believed all the States were morally wicked and in need of regeneration by bloodshed, it was analyzed, and its true purpose discerned, by the keen minds of the Caledonians. County officials serving in our company joked that they were the Ultima Thule Subcommittee for Abercairn Public Benefit, but they took their advisory role seriously.

"'Military necessity does not admit of wanton destruction of a district'—indeed! Do they call Pope's trail of ravages 'a rearrangement of residences'!" snapped Mr. Loudoun.

"'Military necessity' is all through it, to excuse every atrocity." Mr. Airlie looked up from the page. "They say killing defenseless citizens is '*necessary*'!"

"Hang our scouts, retaliate on unarmed prisoners, desecrate our churches, 'starve the hostile belligerent, armed or unarmed,' execute citizens defending their homes—they're trying to outlaw manhood itself! What man won't defend home and family!" Good-natured Mr. Kendrick was angrier than I'd ever seen him. He handed the document to Mr. Menteith.

"Call women and babes their enemies!" Aidan Mor MacHugh worried for the fate of Aidan Beag and Nannie and the rest of his family at home. "They're saying wrong is right! It *isn't* right, no matter how they delude themselves. It's God we're answerable to—and so are they."

"They published this to make Europe think they conduct war virtuously. Europe won't be deceived!" Jock Menteith, Abercairn's Commonwealth Attorney, brought his expertise to bear. "They covet the higher stance, legally and morally, which in truth they do not merit. What they intend to do—as blatant a statement of criminal intent as I ever saw—shows where the guilt lies!"

"Nevertheless, we now know their intention, and it behooves us to defeat it by all the means in our power. A *levee en masse*, which they claim to respect, consists of all the men enlisted by the general government. Thus we must make sure all our Home Guards, Defense, Reserves—every man and boy in Abercairn!—are regularly enlisted."

"They won't respect it!" sputtered Mr. Kendrick. "Look how they ignored the evidence on Captain Burke's dead body—uniform, orders, commission—and still called him a guerrilla!"

"That's their sin," Mr. Menteith said. "On their heads be it, and on their hands be the innocent blood! 'Whoso sheddeth the blood of man, by man shall his blood be shed.'"[6]

I agreed.

* * *

At Brandy Station in June, the fight began at four in the morning. My new horse, Victory, was the fleetest of a stable known for speed. I broke from my place in the charge and rushed upon the enemy. I rammed through three ranks of Yankees, yelling like the fiend I was becoming, dealing destruction and confusion, opening a gap through which my comrades followed. Riding through the Yankees again and again, I turned their lines into useless, milling knots and killed as many as I could. The battle raged till about five in the evening, when they retreated from the field.

We were fought-out and exhausted nigh unto death, with horses blown, disabled, or killed. I rubbed down and restored Victory till I could give him water and feed before I dropped under a tree to restore myself. I'd fought too hard to stomach food. I emptied my canteen and was still thirsty. The daemon was slow to release me. I ached all over … drew long, shuddering breaths . . . .

"Captain Murray says they're looking for you." Jemmie's voice woke me. "Cavalry Headquarters. Report right away. An aide's waiting at the captain's tent."

---

6 Genesis 9:6.

Overawed that I'd be in the presence of a general, I washed enemy blood off my face and tidied myself as best I could. I saluted and stood at attention before the Chief of Cavalry himself.

General J. E. B. Stuart, Chief of Cavalry, Army of Northern Virginia

I studied a slender yet well-formed boy about five and a quarter feet tall. His beak of a nose had grown faster than the other features of his face. His large blue eyes couldn't seem to focus—I suppose from weariness. He was but a child.

"Caledonians? The company with the pipers?" I asked.

"Yes, sir."

"A valiant company, Private Drummond. You do them proud. I sent for you to present you the commission your own valor earned you today." I had to smile. "The formalities of approval and confirming will take some time. Richmond has a few other things to attend to!" I paused. "But I want you to assume your rank and begin its duties tonight."

"Yes, sir."

I beckoned to a young aide-de-camp, a second lieutenant. "Give your coat here, Addison, and I'll replace it for you. Lieutenant Drummond will need his insignia before a tailor can catch up."

Torquil

Captain Murray would have made me an aide-de-camp, but I pleaded to fight. "Please, sir, I'm called to protect Abercairn."

"Ye weel still be part o' the work. Ye are Young Drummond, the last of your name. I owe my best friend, your faither, to keep ye by me and, if God so will, unhurt."

"How better may I honor my father than by taking up the sword he left?"

41

"By preserving the name he left!"

"Sir, if I could obey you, I would. In truth, I can't."

"How say ye!"

I had to tell him how it was with me when we fought. He paced a couple of turns like he always does when he's agitated. For seconds that seemed centuries, he studied me, but he believed me and gave me a squad under Aidan Mor. Assigned to reconnaissance and sorties, I led as furiously as I fought and kept the advantage of surprise. All but one escaped as unharmed as I. I feared I was invulnerable.

CHAPTER 2

GETTYSBURG

1. Fifty Miles from Gettysburg

[Every Southern soldier with whom I spoke] has his tale of outrage committed by our soldiers upon their homes and friends in Virginia and elsewhere. Some of our soldiers admit it, and our own newspapers unfortunately confirm it. If this charge is true, I must confess that we deserve punishment in the North.
—Philip Schaff, theologian, Mercersburg Pennsylvania; diary entry June 30, 1863

The commanding general considers that no greater disgrace could befall the army, and through it our whole people, than the perpetration of the barbarous outrages upon the unarmed and defenseless … that have marked the course of the enemy in our own country.

It must be remembered that we make war only upon armed men, and that we cannot take vengeance for the wrongs our people have suffered without lowering ourselves in the eyes of all … and offending against Him to whom vengeance belongeth.
—General Robert E. Lee, Confederate States Army, General Orders No. 73, June 27, 1863

The regiment had not at any one time taken more than an hour or two to rest, consequently when we arrived at Gettysburg on the night of the 2nd of July, the men were worn out with hard service and for want of sleep.
—Sergeant C. Chick, Second Virginia Cavalry, Confederate States Army

Yankee Sharpshooter

Born and raised in the Maine woods, I been shooting squirrel for the pot since I was five, through the eye so's not to spoil the meat. My good aim means they post me to take first crack at 'em. I been in this-here tree since afore daybreak, watching for Rebel cavalry. I'm used to artillery, like slamming giant doors in the sky, but this cannonade sounded like the Day of Judgement. I jes' let all them shivers of earth and tree pass on through me.

The day's so hot, even birds'd wilt if they hadn't flown off. Powder and percussion cap was dry in my .52 rifle. The Rebs sent skirmishers on foot down the ridge for'ard to my right. I swung my rifle up, took a lazy sight—out of range. Can't hardly believe I ever called it murder, to aim purposeful at a man and kill him.

Horsemen was winding through the trees, down the ridge, with sabers shining at the carry. In the open, under murdersome fire, they lined up their ranks and did a slow half wheel like they was on parade. I never seen so many cavalry at once. No matter. They die one at a time.

Trumpets blew the Charge. They broke for'ard. Trot a quarter mile, gallop a quarter mile, and they're on us. When they come in range, I aimed and shot from left to right, among the 7th Michigan gallopin' to meet 'em. The lines met with a crash like trees fallin', so fast and hard, some horses was turned end over end and crushed their riders under 'em. Amongst the spin of blue and gray clothes, glaring blades and rarin' horses, I led my target and downed an officer. Beyond the left of the Reb line as they pushed the 7th Michigan back to where they begun, a Reb officer on a tall, powerful black horse I wisht I had charged full bore. Saber in right hand, revolver in left, reins on pommel, he rode like he an' that horse was one. I set my sights on his scrawny body and squeezed the trigger.

Torquil

Battering ram! Red-hot picket pin right into me! Hurled to the ground before the impact touched my mind, weapons ripped from my hands. A horse jumped over me. Hooves thundered and were gone, Victory's among them.

Pain broke into the right side of my chest and flooded all through it. My right arm was paralyzed. Blood frothed from the wound. I tried to sit up ... felt faint ... lay on the earth and gasped. Used my left hand to clamp the nerveless right hand over the wound.

Crack of pistol shots against deep boom of field pieces. Hot sky blazing. Blood welled up in my mouth ... had to push myself over on my right side to let it drain so I didn't strangle.

Night. Never so thirsty. Cold. In and out of consciousness. Where was Victory? Would the Caledonians find me?

"This one's still breathing. Bring the stretcher, Gilmore."

Picked up, loaded into an ambulance. Every bounce racked me so bad, if I'd had breath, I'd have yelled. They laid me on still-warm ground.

Daylight. Shrill whine of flies. Shooed them but they settled again. A fog of groaning, low around hundreds of other wounded. Terrible scream. Men shaking or writhing in pain. Some way in front of the toes of my boots stood an open-wall surgical tent

… more screams. In between, a pile of arms and legs. It all smelt like death and corruption.

Chest too full for my ribs to contain … thunder … cloudburst … soaked to the skin. I made my hat shield my face for room to breathe. Warm rain turned icy cold. Relief from heat, then I shivered all night. Thirst parched me … thin streamers of delirium … fever. Pain. Away from myself.

Roused at night … lifted. Lamps, candles, flickering shadows over prostrate and writhing men. Groans and cries and screams. Blood-smeared men, tall as columns. Low lights cast shadows up over haggard faces of … demons! I'm in hell! Cone over my face … peculiar odor … smothering . . . .

> The surgeon should examine the patient *thoroughly*. Omission to perform such an examination properly is an act of injustice to the sick. Their span of life, as far as human efforts go, is in his hands.
> —Francis Peyre Porcher, M.D., Confederate States Army, Surgeon in Charge of the South Carolina Hospital, Petersburg, Virginia

Union Army Surgeon

Plastered with blood from neck to knees after more than twenty-four straight hours of work, I knew that this, the irritative stage after injury, was the worst during which to operate, but I had no choice. Compelled to work quickly—hundreds more to treat!—I probed, found the bullet, levered it out with my finger, and removed the cloth it had injected. I jerked my head to my assistants to carry the Rebel boy elsewhere for dressings and bandages.

"Next!"

Torquil

Something like sleep but for hurting hurting hurting hurting that beat like a slow drum ... worse when I drew breath ... less when I exhaled. Shallow breaths couldn't get me enough air.

Mouth and throat felt lined with dry, sharp crystals of sand that rasped against each other when I tried to swallow. When I coughed, a dozen daggers stabbed my lungs. I thought toward God and met only the dark, empty desert where I am when I've sinned.

White far overhead. Green haze. Moaning. Whisper like wind. I shut my eyes, trying to will the pain away.

Points of light hurt my eyes. Swishing.

A kind-faced, gray-haired woman brought me the water I longed for, and broth with salt that soothed my throat. Days till I had strength to sit up. She had to help me.

Sick when upright ... bowed my head to ease dizziness.

"There, slowly now, and it will pass."

"Thank you, ma'am."

"Ah, you've been brought up well. Your mother would be proud to hear you so polite even now. Where are you from?"

I raised my head a little at a time. "Virginia, ma'am."

"Why, you're fifty miles from home."

On another day, Yankee soldiers collected Confederate prisoners and loaded us on railway cars. The train lurched out of the station. I'd eaten a lot of bad cooking, inflicted on worse food, but what I had at midday was the worst. Add the stink of sick, unwashed, close-packed bodies: my stomach heaved. Hands to my mouth, I nodded toward the platform between the cars. The guard jerked his thumb that way.

I got out just in time to hold onto one of the uprights and the chain that barred the platform steps before I vomited. Into my mind came the woman's words, *Fifty miles from home.* And

Da's command, when I was captured before, *I don't want you in a prison, Son.*

I unhooked the chain, gathered myself in a crouch, protected my head with one arm and the wound with the other. I jumped sideways and thumped and sprawled down the steep embankment.

Shaken, battered, I crawled out of sight and leaned against a tree and drew long, shallow breaths. The wound had opened, but I'd broken no bones nor lost my hat. Free! I thanked God in case He might hear me. Gritting my teeth, I stuffed the dressings into the wound to stop the bleeding. The mourning band was torn and dusty.

Fifty miles, point to point. Beyond Pennsylvania, only Maryland between me and Virginia. A straight line southwest would be correct. It might be farther than fifty miles. I gathered strength, looking to the sun for time and direction. I wanted water to wash away the taste of vomit. I went southwest, looking for some.

Fifty miles, point to point. Foraging for food at isolated farmsteads, I avoided towns and roads. I kept to cover, aiming for White's Ford, where we crossed the Potomac on the way to Sharpsburg last year. The water level was down from a freshet that'd left debris twenty feet up in the trees, but Yankee pickets stood guard.

Fifty miles, point to point. Watching took all my energy. I floated across the Chesapeake and Ohio Canal bordering the river, like a corpse … let a canal boat nudge me aside. In darkness, I used the bloated carcass of a drowned sheep for transportation and cover across the Potomac, the wide, wet boundary between the Yankees' country and mine.

Fifty miles, point to point. The breeze chilled me as I waded into Virginia, but I couldn't risk a fire. The wound trickled a warm fluid. I stanched it with a strip torn from my shirt. The pain made me wince. I might be thought a deserter, or blunder into Yankee lines, so I crept into the underbrush.

Slow. Slow.

I wasn't hungry. My mind didn't warn me I needed food. Thirst drove me to streams.

Fifty miles, point to point. The wound closed, but it was hot and tender to the touch, the skin and flesh around it inflamed, shiny and swollen. It never stopped hurting. It stole my strength. The Blue Ridge loomed to my right front. Cough got worse. Fever dreams stalked through my mind.

Fifty miles, point to point. Homing blindly through the foothills, I couldn't tell whether blue-clad columns marching were real or phantoms. I spotted the top of Raven Crags. Some other time, I half crawled, half pulled myself up Chieftain's Hill. From the top, the little loch glinted to my left. Directly below were the roofs and chimneys of home. Holding to trees to stay upright, I slid downhill and at last staggered onto the back porch. I was too far gone to wonder why so many people were there.

"Ye weel no' set foot in this hospital in such filth and stench!"

Arms akimbo, she barricaded the kitchen door against the straggler confronting her.

"Aye, Mrs. Greig. Weel ye summon Keir—" My strength gave out. My knees buckled. The hard jolt when I landed shot pain through all me and into my head.

Later, slumped half-awake in the wash house, I submitted to Keir scrubbing off dirt, blood, and vermin. The wound broke open again, and gushed pus and blood.

"Lieutenant, I weel send for the surgeon."

> As for those cases with injuries unattended well beyond the twenty-four hour primary operative period

and in an exhausted state, they should receive no an-
aesthetic at all.
—J. Julian Chisholm, M.D.[7]

Dr. Gask gave me an opium pill and spoke to Mrs. Grieg.
"Anaesthesia could kill him. Keep these hot in the fire." He handed her a pair of cauteries.

The portent escaped me. I craned my neck to see an awful
hole in my right side, but I was given no time to contemplate
it. Keir's steely grasp held my arms aside. Greig and others were
heavy weights when they pinned me to the big kitchen table
and put a chunk of leather between my jaws. Every touch, every
probe, raged through body and brain in red assault. Tears started. I clenched my teeth hard.

Dr. Gask

I searched the wound till all contaminants, foreign matter,
and splinters from the eighth rib were gone, excised necrotic
tissue and took the hot iron to cauterize. The kitchen reeked of
scorched carrion.

Mrs. Greig

I gave the doctor a hot cautery for the cold one. I cleaned it wi'
boiling water and set it in the flames. Tears came o' themselves, I
did no' bid them! Torquil Dhu is for aye my littlest lad.

Torquil

When the iron seared living flesh, I writhed with all my
strength but couldn't tear free. The fire went on. I ground my

---

7 J. Julian Chisholm, *Manual of Military Surgery for the Use of the Confederate
States Army*, 1863.

teeth on the leather … the fire went on. Bolts of lightning on blood red field … the fire went on. Gasping for breath … the fire went on. Roaring filled my ears … the fire went on … and on … and on. Consciousness was ruthless talons that clung fast. My whole body shook and I couldn't stop it.

Dr. Gask

I painted the wound with tincture of iodine inside and out and applied powdered morphia topically to allay the pain. I had them sit him up while I applied a poultice, dressings, and bandages.

"Put him to bed," I told Keir and Greig. I dropped my instruments in the boiling water and turned to Mrs. Greig. "The critical feature of his case is exhaustion. The demands on his body were greater than it could meet. It's used up from hard exertion and nervous strain and lack of food, besides the wound. Beyond a certain point there is no recovery.

"Keep him completely quiet. Preserve his vital powers by every means you have. Support his system with stimulants and all the light nourishment he can take. He must absorb and assimilate more than he loses, or he dies."

From my scant stock of opium pills, I gave some to her for the pain. "Give him one of these every twelve hours if he can swallow. If he can't, I have other ways. Paint the wound with iodine three or four times a day. Lay him on his right side so any fluids can drain. I'll call again tonight."

Torquil

Keir and Grieg carried me upstairs, still shaking like a leaf in the wind. I blinked, but my eyes wouldn't focus.

Mrs. Greig fixed everything soft around me and put pillows to raise my head and shoulders so I could breathe. She held my head up and fed me a cup of cool, thick cream laced with maple syrup—and about half apple brandy that settled my shakes right down.

I collapsed. My old chamber spun past when I laid my head on the pillow. Let out my breath ... eyes fell shut ... pain going away ... drifting into silent darkness. ...

I wouldn't waken. The shore I'd left held only fury, pain, and sorrow. My weary spirit revolted from it. It seemed if I allowed the soothing darkness to carry me, I'd reach the Farther Shore where Da and Douglas are alive. There I'd submit to purification by the Light, and be my own, unstained, true self again. The yearning lingered when their efforts brought me back to the unwelcome light of day.

> Somebody wafted his name above,
> Night and morn on the wings of prayer.
> —Marie Ravenel, "Somebody's Darling"

Mrs. Grieg

'Twas the lung fever. I feared and prayed. I'd cured both the laddies' sickness wi' the medicines I learnit from my mother, who learnit them from her mother before her, and healed the hurts of a' the hoosehold, but he did no' rouse.

I could no' get him to swallow the pills, nor sips of beef tea. It fashed him when Dr. Gask treated his wound and used his ain ways to nourish him and ease the pain, but 'twas naught but his body acting.

I'd ne'er seen him so low—but death will no' rieve my last lad!

Torquil

Sleep ... hazy, short periods of waking ... night or dawn, bewildered not to find Douglas in the bed we shared all through boyhood.

I asked the shadow by the bedside, "Where's Douglas?"

"He's wi' your faither." It was Keir.

"Then he's all right?"

"Aye, lad, he's all right."

Delirium ... crying, "No! No-o-o!" Hot plasters on my chest drove the daggers away on a wave of warmth. The cough loosened. Half roused, I swallowed soothing syrups, a peculiar tea, tinctures and opium, beef tea and broth, cream-and-brandy. I'd never been so sick, for so long.

"Am I going to die?"

"Ye weel no'! Ye're Young Drummond, and ye alone to continue the line. Sup this."

I grimaced at a vile-looking concoction. "Mrs. G-r-e-i-g ..."

"Do no' fash me, laddie! Drink it doon, the noo!"

"Yes, ma'am."

The contradiction between what Keir said and Mrs. Greig said didn't register. I drifted back into dreams.

* * *

Thought forced on me the memories of my world before the war. Mockery! War had buried everything I loved, under blood and death.

Home. I'd cut myself off from it to bury the pain, but fought my way here by instinct. I was home, but the home that nurtured me ... wasn't. Or I wasn't ....

2. Glenlochie

Robert Bruce Drummond

"I'm truly sorry, Robert Bruce. There's nothing more I can do," Dr. Gask condoled.

Dread words! I'd heard them before our firstborn died—but now ... this babe lived, but, oh, Mary Elizabeth! From then on, I never left her side.

Mrs. Greig

He volunteered for the war wi' Mexico after she was awa', and campaigned wi' General Scott—the hoose was too still withoot her. He saw his bairns nae mair till he returnit.

Puir wee bairns! I cuddled them together. Wee Dougie would no' be comforted, he missed his mama so. I taught him, when she went to heaven, she left him a wee brither, her last giftie to him. His nature made it fare weel—he was like her, ye ken, a soul of sunshine. He took up Torquil like his ain pet. Wi' loving-kindness, he won him. None could fash Wee Brither and no' be scoldit!

Lady guests at The Drummond's table wi' their husbands would say, "Torquil's such a serious little soul."

"Still waters run deep," I said to myself, nor was I e'er disproven.

Torquil

Feet of furniture ... polished wood floor ... Dougie's heels leading into baby frolics. The tall column lifted us into his embrace. We always called him Da.

Mrs. Greig

He was scarce home when he took up his laddies. 'Twas sweet to see them cuddle doon in his arms while he read the Scripture at morning worship, eyes bright like they followed every word. A' too soon—for me who loved them—he had them out o' frocks and into breeches. He gave them new names, Torquil Dhu for his black hair and Douglas Aureus—I learnit that it means 'golden'— for his red-blond color.

But, being hoosekeeper o' Glenlochie, long and oft were they mine to cosset.

Robert Bruce Drummond

We firstborn sons carry in gratitude the name of Robert Bruce, first king to unite and rule all Scotland, who decreed lands to Clan Drummond, our sept included. The fourth of my name in America, I knew my character would live beyond my death, in my sons. I strove to embody the godliness and honor I want them to emulate. I read the Bible to them and taught them to pray. I breeched them as early as possible, to define them as male and bring them under my discipline. They couldn't act like babies any longer and had to meet a stricter standard of behavior.

> Introduced from my infancy into the society of men, while yet a boy I was accustomed to think and act like a man.
> —Joseph Allston, antebellum planter[8]

Torquil

Da taught by example and ruled with justice. We learned what the result would be if we didn't obey—he always made the penalty fit the crime—but mostly, we obeyed because we wanted to be exactly like him. As long as we lived, that desire never changed.

Robert Bruce Drummond

After my sons were breeched, I took them with me when I rode about the Glenlochie holdings, teaching them and answering their questions. They loved to ride on wagonloads of straw from field to stack. They learned by watching and imitating to drop seed corn in the exact cross of marked furrows.

They learned the rhythms of the days, the seasons, and the crops by constant use—not by hours and minutes, but rather the

---

8 Joseph Allston, quoted in the *Atlantic Monthly* CXXXV, p. 664.

time to plant or harvest being determined by the fall of rain or the amount of heat and length of daylight. Hog-killing time came in cold weather, after the hard frosts began. Cows came to be fed and milked when sunlight was low, and roosters crowed at dawn. They learned how all depended upon what the Lord provides—food for man and beast—and that good stewardship of God's gift of fertile soil was their duty.

Torquil

The memories went on like they had a will of their own, bringing my blesssed former life to my mind, like the acts in a play.

When I was little, the glowing colors of October told me my birthday was near. But they reminded Da my mother died of bearing, that year of 1847. He never found her like, nor did he remarry. Douglas told me she was warm and soft and happy, and she sang the old lilts to him.

Mrs. Grieg made sure we looked like "gentlemen, no' ruffians!" when we went to school to Mr. Stafford. He was from Ohio, but he was a Menteith on his mother's side. Homely as a mud fence, good natured, and excellent in sports, all the big boys and girls liked him. Aidan Beag's twin, Nannie, and all the other girls, had to go to Mrs. Heywood's school.

Mr. Stafford had to teach us proper English, because we spoke the Scots like Mrs. Grieg and the household. I still use it when I'm too far gone. When he started us in Latin, I liked the martial Roman authors, but … the rise and fall of empires? I'd never seen a nation fall nor been trapped in the ruins. I loved our federation of States, her independence and liberty, and, most of all, her ideal of justice. To me, justice was truth and righteousness, parts of the character of God.

Learning primary philosophy, I admired the Stoics. They taught that one must accept all that life brought, with courage, honesty, dignity, and grace, and coolness under duress. Virtuous living, free from excess passion and rational in all things, suited my nature.

I succeeded pretty well in self-disciplined stoic manliness—I didn't complain, I reasoned things out, I stayed silent when I got hurt—till one day, when I'd got hurt so bad I couldn't go to school. Douglas went, and that day was a week long. I pined for him. I hardly knew my own self from his. I missed him like I'd miss my right hand.

I was called very early to truth and righteousness, by a Spirit within myself. When I failed to live them, by folly or disobedience, I felt desolate inside, like I'd lost His shining Light.

Though I'd received from my Creator a sense of what was true and what was not, sometimes in spite of what people claimed, I also quested for God's truth stated in the Bible. (Da had given us each one). Righteousness, I discovered, was summed up by Jesus the Christ pointing out the First and Second Great Commandments. On the flyleaf of my Bible, I inscribed them:

> I. "Thou shalt love the Lord thy God with all thy heart, and with all thy soul, and with all thy mind, and with all thy strength."
>
> II. "Thou shalt love thy neighbor as thyself."
> —St. Mark 12:31–32

When I was ready to commit my life to Jesus, Da took me to talk with Dominie Gilchrist. I confessed my sins and my faith and explained about the Light.

The Dominie prayed, "Holy Father in heaven, graciously be pleased to receive this repentant soul into thy kingdom, and to write his name in thy Book of Life for now and all eternity. In Christ's name, Amen." And then God's Holy Spirit spoke through him. "Torquil David Drummond, the Lord our God says, 'Ye are pure in heart. "Keep thy heart with all diligence; for out of it are the issues of life.""""

Into me flowed the Living Water. It was to my spirit as sweetness is on the tongue. I was awed and delighted by what my spirit understood even when my mind did not.

* * *

Our next-neighbor Ewen Murray was our best friend. In summer we swam in the icy waters of the little loch till our lips were blue and our backs sun-scorched. In winter we raced our sleds over jumps that set us flying, and skated on the loch and saw fish beneath the ice. We competed in skill and speed, strength and style.

Mr. Murray taught us swordsmanship and wrestling. To us, he was more than a man. Tall, muscled like a blacksmith, he was an elemental force all in himself. On his land, in the kirk Session, in Abercairn affairs, he radiated a power for good that swept all before it. He couldn't be resisted, nor did he entertain the idea he might be. Ewen had the power, too, but he exercised it calm and unmovable.

Da required bold riding, gentle handling, and sustaining a distinctive style when we traveled. After he taught us to jump, Douglas and I took it farther. Our favorite competition was a point-to-point race over or through any obstacles in our way. Getting hurt didn't stop us. Bearing the name of a coward is worse than bearing pain.

We learned from Da to use and care for firearms. He gave us each a boy-size Colt revolver. We taught ourselves to drop reins and use legs and seat to control our horses, and shoot at targets while galloping past them, right- or left-handed. We hung targets from tree branches and thrust or slashed at them with our little swords while riding full tilt, bareback, just like Light Horse Harry Lee!

Robert Bruce Drummond

Although Abercairn was now far removed from the frontier it had been when my sons' great-great-grandfather settled here, excellent horsemanship and marksmanship were still necessary. In bedtime stories, I told them how their ancestors had to protect themselves against Indians and the French, wild animals and wicked men, till a measure of civilization had been established. The large predators lived higher in the mountains now, and outlawry was rare, but the chance remained of having to defend themselves. The extensive forests could still be hideouts, and the terrain was a challenge to horsemanship. I made sure they were prepared. I told them of their ancestors' long escape from the English, too, when the "butcher of Culloden" was razing the glens, and the Scots had to use all their combined woodscraft to elude their pursuers and survive. To teach my sons the skills I'd learned as a boy, and still practiced, I turned their instruction over to my ghillie, Keir.

Torquil

We invited Ewen to join us. We learned complete observation of our entire surroundings, the animals and plants in them, the connections among them all, and how to track and know perfectly anything that moved. Keir taught us to go everywhere without being seen or heard, and how to become so still and blend so well with the cover we were in that we were invisible to all but his practiced eye.

We watched him shape his body to conform to the shapes of stones or bushes around him. He really disappeared into shadows and places where the light wavered. He looked for lines of advance or obstacles to them, twisting his body around bushes or under branches to progress without leaving sign of his passage. His every motion flowed into every other and blended with the motion of the natural world.

Douglas, as usual, learned quickly to perform the new skills. I resolved to master them and practiced diligently. Ewen practiced with me, calm and patient till he could elude even Keir.

We liked knowing the quiet things of the world. A perfect habit of observation became second nature—an instinct that informed us of minute changes in the atmosphere, of the pulse of sounds otherwise inaudible, of increase or decrease of light undetectable by ordinary seeing.

From explorations afoot and on horseback, we knew the country for twenty miles around. How swift all the creeks and rivers were, and where they could be forded; where hunting was good; where all the animals passed from their lairs to feed and water; where useful plants grew; every lane and road and the homeplace of everyone along each; and where every trail penetrated the mountains and if it was passable for man or horse or only a rabbit.

We were keen hunters. Overcoming weakness was the prize, so the more difficult and dangerous a hunt, the better it was. Hunting taught us to conquer over-eagerness with patience and endurance. After a long, hard stalk and hot anticipation, it demanded strong will power and self-control—mental and physical—to aim the gun and hold it steady. Da exemplified it and helped us achieve it.

Hunting also protected the flocks and herds that provided income and sustenance, by reducing the number of foxes, bears, panthers, and other predators. When a panther raided our tenant Iain Grieg's sheepfold one night, we tracked and shot it. Da had the hide tanned with the fur on. It took up a big space on the library floor.

I saw the panther rug in my mind's eye, but it wasn't there now. The library was only another ward in the hospital. Home served the needs of war. When I was little, home was the center of everything.

> To be a gentleman, you have to learn your table manners before seven, your social manners before twelve, and your moral obligations before twenty-one.
> —Mrs. Mary Berkeley Minor Blackford (1802–1896)

Our lives were born at home, lived at home, and went out from home. Home was a circle of beloved, familiar faces and surroundings. When Da entertained, we and the guests' children were included at table when we were old enough. When Nannie was present, gladness was part of the feast. Sometimes we had music and dancing after dinner.

To be acceptable as gentlemen, we had to present erect posture, a firm mouth, and cleanliness, with coats buttoned and cravats straight. We learned good manners from Da, reinforced by Mrs. Grieg. We learned to think before we spoke, to converse without shyness and with care not to offend.

Conversation ranged over weather and crops, advances in medicine, legislative matters, literature recent and ancient, and many branches of natural science. Our shared experiences were discussed in terms of threat and security, life and death, love and hate, mercy and cruelty. We were to listen to our elders, reflect upon what they said, and respond properly when remarks were addressed to us. We heard and thought about the reasons men live, why they love or hate, why and for what they fight, and why they must die. Douglas answered amiably and with ease. My ideas were framed in few words.

The Son works as well as the Servant, so that before
they eat their bread they are commonly taught how
to earn it.
—Dixon Wecter, quoted in *The Saga of American
Society*

[My father] trained his boys to work and the necessity
for it. We were taught and required to do every kind of
farm work the slaves did and consider it an honor in
stead of disgrace.
—T. J. Howard, Confederate States Army

Determined that we shouldn't grow up to be idlers, nor ignorant of how our living was produced, Da required us to work.

"You must know, when you direct it in the future, how work
should be done. You'll be respected when you know about crops,
animals, implements, soil, and all it takes to run a farm.

"A man's work in itself is a virtue—but when it's done only to
pile up material wealth, rather than to serve others, it's no longer
noble."

By the time we were twelve, we'd become fair plough hands,
driving teams, and doing some kind of farm work every day (except Sabbath) since we were little. Da worked, too, with God, to
make all eight thousand acres of Glenlochie the best it could be.
He studied soil and plant chemistry. He went to the first State
Agricultural Fair in Richmond in 1853 and took us with him.

While we watched new machinery operate, he drew diagrams
of the operations he could connect to his mill. They all depend
on a turning wheel, so, with proper gearing and a great enough
head of water, he could use his power source. We boys thought
Nightfire, Glenlochie's stallion, or Sachem, Mr. Murray's best
horse, could beat the winners of the horse races. The big boys
and girls attended balls and parties. Da let us listen to the talk
about crops and animals he held with planters from all over the
State.

The bustle in the house, the hum and tramp of people helping win Confederate independence, disturbed me sometimes, but it sounded like the gatherings at Abercairn Court House.

3. *Abercairn*

Yea, happy is that people, whose God is the Lord.
—Psalm 144:15b

Da and the other justices and officials—most of them were our friends' fathers—governed Abercairn County by the God-given moral law. Everyone except maybe the criminals found their decisions fair and right. Court Day was a holiday, especially after Da put us to work. We rode past neighbors' gates and barns and Dick Murchison's forge. Dick's family had been Glenlochie's blacksmiths since before they were emancipated, after the Revolution. My great-grandfather had given them a plot of land and set them up in their own business then.

We went about with Ewen Murray and Robbie Kendrick, David Airlie, Alex Menteith, Duncan MacCammond, and Donald Loudoun—and Aidan Beag MacHugh, even though he wouldn't leave his twin behind. Nannie was often distracted by things like orphan kittens, which she took home to care for.

In the forest with Keir, we learned the ways of God's creation: Court Day taught us the ways of men. We observed the temper and characters of our equals and superiors, citizens of all classes, some of whose ways were strange to us. We were cautious about men from the backcountry and mountains, lean men with a look of wariness and of fight ready to break loose. We respected the land-owning farmers and noticed the difference between men like our fathers, who served their neighbors, and pompous pretenders. We punctured the latter's self-importance, as if accidentally, by crowding them into mud puddles or knocking their hats askew.

Long lines of wagons, pulled by stout horses with bells on their harness, hauled produce and goods from the Shenandoah Valley and all of Abercairn to the railroad at Culpeper. Drovers trailed herds of cattle, sheep, hogs, and turkeys. We thought it a great adventure and reveled in the mayhem of wagons clogging the streets and animals milling through the lanes. But we had to mind the rough, swearing waggoners and drovers who threatened us if we got in the way. They meant it! Donald was once picked up and carried halfway to Culpeper, and left to walk back, because he tried to boss them.

We bought gingerbread from the vendors, or pickles, peanuts, and candy at Mr. Mitchell's store. Nor did we ignore the other tradesmen, artisans, and professional men. With friendly ones, we got in trouble by curiosity, excess energy, and accident. With the short-tempered, we made a game of how much we could annoy them before they chased us off. Nannie knew before anyone, when we had to run.

Douglas burnt holes in his jacket getting too close to the blacksmith's forge. Alex climbed onto the driver's seat of the stagecoach and had unwound and lifted the reins when the driver caught him and gave him some lashes with the ends before he let him go. Robbie and I battled, with spokes for quarter staves, at the wheelwright's. Sometimes he let me win. Crowding too close while he watched Mr. Menteith affix a wax seal to a document, Ewen knocked over the inkwell. Aidan Beag and David dipped their fingers in the pigments while the chemist was tinting a pot of paint and smeared the colors on each other's faces. They wore their warpaint many days. Duncan fought. Head down, fists flying, he could whip boys a lot bigger than he was. He didn't attend Mr. Stafford's school, but was taught at home by harsh parents who berated and whipped him too often, so he always had a headful of resentment to work off.

We had to respect greater size or strength among ourselves, but that didn't always make leaders. We honored skill, style, courage, endurance, and ability to endure pain without flinching. Loyalty to each other was a—what did Mr. Stafford call it—*sine qua non.*[9] We called Donald "Overseer" for his dictating attitude. Douglas was "Thumbs," a left-handed compliment to his dexterity. He built us toy water mills and boats that worked like real ones. Ewen became "Oak," for the same good power his father had. We could never move him from a position taken. Aidan objected to being called "Dan," but we said he'd sound too agreeable if we called him "Ai." Robbie, with his great good nature, answered to "Shakes," because he followed his father in quoting the Bard of Avon on all occasions. David, our fastest runner, was "Speed." Duncan was "Dunk." To acknowledge her possession of all our boyish virtues, without admitting it, we dubbed Nannie "Lady Ann." Though he thought up the most comical and most dangerous mischief, Alex was "Snort" for no reason at all. I, the youngest and smallest, was "Owl," because I was bookish and held to what was right.

We learned we had to keep our names honorable when we squeezed into the court one day and saw a trial for larceny with assault. The accused man bore the name of a good family but had fallen so low that he robbed and hurt a widow lady. We heard people despising him. The justices sentenced him to be whipped—the worst shame and disgrace there could be—and didn't back down though the fellow begged not to be. The public whipping was so awful we didn't watch but the first of it.

---

9 Latin: "without which, nothing."

We waded in Maple Run and tried to catch fish with our hands. We used short slabs from the sawmill for rafts in the mill race, to see who could come closest to the mill wheel before he had to jump in the water. It was a tie between David and Robbie. We tried to walk around a bateau, balancing on the gunwale. Only Ewen completed the circuit.

I grew up in a quiet, peaceful world that moved in the gentle cycles of God's creation: summer and winter, seedtime and harvest, tallied by the Christian calendar.

The War didn't explode into being at Fort Sumter. It stalked us step by step.

CHAPTER 3

THE SERPENT IN THE GARDEN

1.Initial Hisses

The South is ... a distinct nation in the United States;
but the North has to thank ... itself for this distinction,
in sacrificing the interests of the great mass of the population in other sections of the Union to a fatly protected class of Northern manufacturers. Disaffection is
fostered ... by this blind and heartless policy.
—Robert Somers, Scottish social and economic author

Torquil

Without the newspapers, we'd never know what happened
beyond Abercairn. Da subscribed to the *Central Presbyterian*,
the Richmond papers, *Leslie's*, and the *New York Herald*. Douglas
and I read them to learn about events and changes that could
affect life here. Da understood that Northern citizens threatened
the Constitution itself.

"A frenzied mob of abolitionists attacked the courthouse in Boston and killed one of the guards, trying to kidnap an enslaved man from custody."

"But slavery's a sin! Why shouldn't they?" Douglas favored direct methods.

"Because federal law requires he be returned to his master. I don't agree with laws favoring slavery, but rather than law being broken, it should be changed, to reflect moral truth."

Because industry grew, Northern cities grew, he told us, and so did their crime rates, disease, riots, and apostasy. These were an alarming departure from the natural course civilization had followed through all time past. Most countries were based on agriculture, which stabilized society.

Too many at the North rejected the pure, holy truth of Christianity to follow spiritualism or universalism, both rooted in paganism but wearing the mask of religion. In Abercairn, no false beliefs tainted the teachings of Christ. Northern apostasy, protected by an aggressive political majority, was a threat to the sacred highest we believed in.

"We could even say industry in the North has become its own god," Da went on. "It writes its own commandments, and it bribes too many legislators to worship it by passing laws setting high tarriffs on manufactured goods, which give it unfair economic advantage. We produce raw materials for the North to manufacture and grow rich on!"

"That's like the colonies doing the same for England, before the Revolution," I said.

"Yes. That's why I've been enlarging the mill. We now manufacture nearly all Abercairn's fleeces into finished woolen goods, besides grinding grain."

"The Richmond paper says we ought to do the same for all our raw materials, or trade directly with Europe, and boycott Northern products," Douglas added.

"We've been doing the first two, here, since before the Revolution," Da told us. "But the high tariffs increase the cost of what we import from overseas and thus steal from us! I sorrow to see the country our family helped establish, taking such a divisive course."

I'm the last of us, alone living the chaos that division of the country brought. It never occurred to me, then, what Muster Day prepared us for.

* * *

> Along with our rights there must coexist correlative duties—and the more exalted the station, the more arduous are these. … the character of the *real* gentleman … consists not of plate and equipage and rich living … but in truth, courtesy, bravery, generosity, and learning.
> —John Randolph of Roanoke, letter to Theodore Dudley, February 15, 1806

Da's example proved manhood the best of prizes, well worth the effort to win. He taught us to revere and obey God and Christian truth. Within that framework, we must be independent in spirit, action, and conscience. He required us to practice self-mastery and restraint of passion. He must have thought we were ready for Muster Day.

Mustering the militia brought together all classes of men, who understood their social ranking and showed their mutual political allegiance. Officers' titles were prized, and their holders honored, because they showed the ideal stance of a man toward his community: fulfilling the duty to protect.

Douglas and I thrilled to the martial music of fifes, drums, and bagpipes, and citizen soldiers marching and performing drill. While Da enjoyed conversation with his friends after supper at DeVique's Inn, we were allowed to go out. Noise soon drew us toward the tavern by the river, where boatmen and other wayfarers, and men from the mountains and backcountry, gather to drink.

Two men fought while the others stood back, shouted support or threats, and made bets. The fighters hit, kicked, bit, and gouged. Someone shouted insults at one. Both turned on him, others ran to his defense, and the fight exploded with fists, feet, teeth, and nails, to wound and maim. If a man went down, he wasn't spared, but kicked and stomped.

A boy about our size, roughly dressed and smelling of strong drink, flew at Douglas with fists and feet, daring us to both fight him at once. I leaped on him, and we all tangled on the ground. He about had us whipped, when Robbie's father broke his hold and pulled him aside. We got up.

"Dare you attack The Drummond's sons, Joe Beecham!"

"We was all fightin', Mister, an' I was gonna whup 'em!"

"'Rude art thou in thy speech / And little bless'd with the soft phrase of peace!'" Mr. Kendrick paraphrased. "You'll go before the justices for assault! Now it's off with you to 'durance vile'!"

"What?"

"Jail."

"It's our fault, too, sir. We accepted the challenge."

Douglas, handkerchief to his bleeding nose, nodded agreement.

"I'd a-whupped yew!" Joe brandished a fist.

"You hadn't yet!" mumbled Douglas.

"Want to try again!" I scowled.

"Gamecocks all!" Mr. Kendrick kept hold on Joe's collar and looked at us. "Your father is waiting."

We turned toward the inn.

"Jes' yew wait till—!" Joe shouted after us.

Robert Kendrick, County Surveyor

"That will be a long while. Court Day isn't for weeks."

"Mister, yew heerd what they said. We was all agreein' to fight!"

I heard the plea behind the bravado but started marching Joe toward the jail. "Didn't you know better than to pull gentlemen into your brawl?"

"I didn' know who they was!"

"Very unlikely!"

"Cross my heart an' hope to die, Mister! I never seed 'em afore in all my days!"

"That's a serious oath."

"I mean it!"

"If you give me your oath not to attack gentlemen again, I'll let you off this time."

"May they hang me an' dig out my guts with a shovel an' then drown me, if I ever do it again."

He sounded solemn as if he meant it, but I know the vindictiveness of him and his kin.

Torquil

Riding home, Da heard our story.

"Brawling with inferiors is not becoming for gentlemen." He raised a hand to stop Douglas's protest. "Hear me!

"It is your duty, Sons, in the station in life you're born into, to become public servants. You will work for the good of Abercairn as county officials or farther afield, for the preservation of order and the well-being of all. Thus their government will suit them, and they will consent to being governed.

"You're being prepared by education, for these duties. Jesus said, 'Unto whomsoever much is given, of him shall be much required.' If you're elected to public office, men have committed the goodness of their lives to you. You cannot fulfill your calling unless you command due respect."

We saw every day, the respect people gave Da.

"To engage in a low brawl with any over whom you will preside, causes them to disrespect you. Disrespect leads to contempt. Contempt for superiors and the rule of law leads to anarchy. Anarchy is lawlessness. It produces a society as barbarous as the fight you saw."

"But, sir, doesn't God's Word say all men are equal before Him?" I asked.

"Yes. It states clearly, however, that we are to obey those whom He appoints to rule over us. His Word thus recognizes the different positions men hold.

"You are born into a station wherein truth … faithfulness … courage … courtesy … responsibility … are moral absolutes. We treat others decently and are true to our convictions. To be truly free, we must, under God, possess ourselves. We must be masters of our acts and our thoughts, not impulsive.

"The men you saw fighting have a society different from ours. They don't try to restrain passion. They expect sinful behavior and human evil. Rather than trust in the justice and protection of the law, they settle disputes with the violence you saw.

"That's the difference between the low, inflamed passions of the mob … and the restraint and careful search for truth, of Christian justice. Order produces protection for people and their property, so they can live in the peace God calls for. Law is the written form of order. We are on the side of law.

"A man may improve his station by honest effort. In the meantime, differences exist. A gentleman does not engage in fist fights with his inferiors."

"But we had to, sir," said Douglas. "He challenged us."

"Challenges are answerable only between men of equal position, moral as well as social. Nor need the *Code Duello* be resorted to by Christian gentlemen. God's Word teaches us His ways of resolving grievances."

It was the first time Da spoke at length about our future. Under his generous, kindly rule and protection, we hadn't thought beyond home to the places we'd hold in the world. We had to consider the idea of ourselves as men and leaders of men.

Robert Bruce Drummond

In 1859, I enrolled my sons in the academy at Jeffersonton, to be prepared to enter the University. To be established in the world, they needed to mingle with more of Virginia society than Abercairn contained, and establish their presence in it. Their good characters would be polished and tested. Since the academy pamphlet claimed Jeffersonton was "free from the haunts of vice and dissipation," I trusted their exposure to evil influence would be limited. The course of instruction included algebra, geometry, surveying, natural science, geography, logic, rhetoric, Latin and Greek, as well as English language and composition, which my sons needed to learn. At Jeffersonton after the harvest was in, I got them settled in lodgings and arranged stabling for their horses. I blessed and embraced them and gave them some pocket money before I returned to Glenlochie. I missed them before I'd gone a mile.

> At a period of life, from twelve to fifteen, when the intellect hungers and thirsts after knowledge, I could have devoured a library.
> —William John Grayson, Beaufort, S.C. (1788–1863)

Torquil

We had to bid farewell to Ewen till Christmas, but Robbie, Aidan Beag, Donald, Alex, and David came to the academy, too. The food was plain but sufficient at our lodgings, and I was interested in my new studies. The older students, however, considered new boys their special prey. We banded together and defeated them.

"I reckon they've learned not to meddle with us!" David crowed.

"Abercairn's a clan. If we stick together, we can whip anyone!" First among us to state the ideal, I became its proponent.

That term we studied algebra, geography, and Greek literature. We learned to construct rhetoric, with pure and complete English, and accuracy in language that made knowledge a force for good or evil. Learning to deliver a speech led to debate, a serious business in society and government. Proving the stances I took were right and true drew me into deeper Bible study. I found truth faster when I asked Da for a copy of Cruden's *Concordance*, to give me word-by-word reference to all the Bible contained.

* * *

The New Englander had also learned to love the pleasure of hating.
—Henry Adams, grandson of President John Quincy Adams

Autumn had shown and shed its glory when all Virginia was stunned by John Brown's attack on Harper's Ferry. He was the same abolitionist who'd led a gang that murdered and mutilated suspected Southern supporters in Kansas. We were horrified at the abolitionists' intention to arm black men and goad them to kill white citizens. Rumor said men, women, and children were being slaughtered all over the countryside. Three counties away, men were cleaning guns, barricading houses, and preparing to assemble and resist.

Brown was captured by a company of United States Marines, legally tried, and hanged in December for several murders, including that of a free black man. The fanatical Northern abolitionists proclaimed him a martyr. This was another warning: at the North, some hated Southerners so much that they thought wholesale murder a good thing!

> For the last five years the air of the North has been surcharged with envenomed assaults upon the South. Every insulting epithet that malignant ingenuity could invent, has been applied to the Southern people ... They can be uttered for but one object, and that object must be to exasperate the South to the point of withdrawing from the Union.
> —Chambersburg, Pennsylvania, newspaper, *Valley Spirit*, September 12, 1860

> The aggressor in a war, that is, he who begins it, is not the first who uses force but the first who renders force necessary.
> —Henry Hallam, *Constitutional History of England*

The summer of 1860, Da allowed us to drill with him in the Caledonians, Abercairn's volunteer cavalry, formed to defend the South against the fanatics' threat. All were friends, neighbors and equals, men who'd shared the hospitality of Glenlochie. Da was elected first lieutenant and Aidan Mor MacHugh, second lieutenant. Mr. Stafford served his adopted home as company clerk. No one but Mr. Murray was ever considered for captain: in spirit, manner, and physique, he was a cyclone for good. Ever at the head of it, he made his command a part of himself and forged us into a single blade for the single purpose of defending all we held sacred.

Severe tacticians—some were veterans of the Mexican War, some were graduates of the Virginia Military Institute—drilled us. "You're a martinet!" one uncle serving as a private called his nephew in jest. "Tyranny's not in fashion, these days!" another man chaffed his brother. But we all learned military discipline. Douglas and I thought we had to be twice as good as our elders at everything, to earn and keep the privilege of membership.

Each man furnished his own horse and weapons. Our carbines were the most up-to-date we could purchase, but many sabers had been carried by ancestors and handed down through generations. Our veterans convinced us to wear uniforms practical for field service. Ours and some others' were from fleeces grown, spun, woven, and dyed gray on our own property. We were a crack company, especially since we marched to the pipes. The Great Music had come to America with the first Robert Bruce Drummond and flourished since.

Furor about the fall elections was arousing everyone when we went back to the academy, Ewen with us. By Christmas, Lincoln was elected President, and South Carolina had seceded. In January and February, seven more Southern states and the Choctaw Indian nation joined the Confederacy.

But Virginia was circumspect.

Our state convention favored staying with the union of States my own family and many other Virginians had created and molded over the eighty-five years of our republic's life. Abercairn sent men pledged to preserve a government of limited powers, protecting the rights of citizens and property. The States had existed beforehand, had created the Union, and had equal political power. Would the Union violate the terms upon which it was created, as stated in the Constitution? Now that the country was controlled by a passionate majority at the North, would the

Constitution protect the rights of the Southern minority? We prayed and trusted it would.

The Virginia convention called a peace conference from all the states, but their plan of reconciliation for the country was rejected by a Congress now dominated by Northerners.

Douglas was eager to fight: he embraced Southern rights and wanted adventure. I hated to jeopardize the country our ancestors had won, nor did I want to bring fire and sword to home and loved ones. He was convinced that Southern military expertise and martial spirit would overcome all the odds, that the war would be a short one with the North giving up quickly, and that England, needing cotton, would join the conflict on the Southern side. I recognized that we had a much smaller population than the North and lacked the industrial capacity to provide materiel for a prolonged war.

Drummonds had fought in every war Virginia did. The only question was which side we'd fight for.

The Virginia convention sent a party of delegates to urge upon Mr. Lincoln and his Congress a policy of conciliation, and another party to Mr. Davis and the Confederate Congress to plead for the same. Both sides rejected Virginia's calm, conservative counsel. Lincoln wrote, and gave to the Virginia representatives, a paper stating his intention to coerce the seceded States. The New York *Herald* said a country pinned together by bayonets would be military despotism.

* * *

There is no power under the Constitution to coerce a seceding State.
—Edwin M. Stanton, Secretary of War of the United States, 1861

April 12, 1861: The armed fleet sent by Lincoln into Charleston Harbor menaced the city. Charleston opened fire on Fort Sumter. Still Virginia did not secede.

April 15, 1861: Lincoln called for 75,000 troops to put down the response to his provocation, later admitting he had manipulated the South into firing the first shot, in order to generate war fever in the North. Still in the Union, having tried every means of making peace, we learned *Virginia would be invaded.*

April 17, 1861: Virginia enacted her Ordinance of Secession.

April 21, 1861: Governor Letcher called for volunteers to repel invasion and protect Virginia citizens. The Caledonians were ready.

* * *

"Da, may we come with you?" I asked.

"Would you not rather be defenders closer to home?"

"We want to be in the first lines of defense, sir." Douglas was firm.

"I'm always glad to have you with me, Sons. But in this venture, you will be subject to my orders at all times."

Robert Bruce Drummond

My sons were the envy of their schoolmates, but Ewen Murray and the other boys organized the Abercairn Shield. To be the military arm of the home defense, they drilled as rigorously as we.

Abercairn boiled with preparations. Men streamed from hills and glens to the Court House, where militia officers formed them into three companies—who named themselves the Blue Ridge Rifles, Abercairn Guards, and Rapidan Panthers—and began drill. The court met in special session. Though civil officials were exempt from military service, most of us were already in it. We planned defense and provision for the county.

No less industrious were the women and children. Mrs. MacHugh and Mrs. Murray taught Amelia, Nannie, and Mary to knit socks, while women stitched uniforms and shirts and ransacked their linen closets so each soldier would have a blanket. We were their soldiers: they felt responsible and did everything they could for our well-being, comfort, and cheer in the field. Madame DeVique gave the inn as venue for a bazaar to raise money for soldiers' accoutrements. Mrs. Heywood would be the children's sole educator, because Mr. Stafford had closed his school to fight for his State.

The rest of Mr. Stafford's family were en route to Abercairn. In a rush, before the Potomac frontier was closed, Virginia's sons returned to share her destiny. Those delayed in homing found their ways blockaded and resorted to many a stratagem to reach their destinations.

The evening before the Abercairn companies left, the ministers joined their congregations to hold a solemn service of dedication. Abercairn sang the old hymns and heard sermons on courage and the soldier's Christian duty. The Caledonians dedicated their sabers, and the infantry companies, their muskets, to their new country's service. Mrs. Murray presented the flags the ladies had made, one for cavalry, one for each infantry company, and one for the Abercairn Shield. Dominie Gilchrist and Brother Cheswick, the Baptist minister, prayed blessings upon Abercairn's defenders and God's protection upon us. They, like other Southern ministers, believed defensive war was just, and men's protection of their families a sacred obligation. They preached against hatred because too much of Christian character would be lost if men held personal hate against their enemies. They decided to take turns shepherding both congregations at home, in camp, and in the field. Doctors Gask and Wilkins made a like agreement.

Ewen the Elder and I met in the lane between our houses. We rode out together on a last circuit of our holdings, noting final instructions to give the men we were leaving in charge, in my case, Keir, Mr. Ogilvie, and Grieg.

My best friend spoke hesitantly. "My wee lass fears for your lads."

"Douglas will run away to the army if he's left behind. Torquil won't let him go alone. It's better to keep them myself."

Abercairn's defenders departed on a morning early in May to join the army of the Southern Confederacy, pipes skirling and flags snapping in the breeze. Those flags symbolized ourselves: the insignia of Abercairn, the emblems of defense of all we treasured in heaven and earth. Citizens treated us generously all along the road. At Harper's Ferry the infantry companies joined Colonel T. J. Jackson. We marched down a hillside to Lieutenant Colonel J. E. B. Stuart's First Virginia Cavalry camp at Bunker Hill amid the dread black skirl of "The Campbells are Coming." We paced our horses in time to the threatening swell and dire phrasing of the music, then pranced them over a little grassy glen and up a hillock to the strains of "Killiekrankie," and drew rein in a stamping halt before the headquarters tent, to Stuart's delight.

I kept my sons in my own care, kept them to their studies, and taught them the rules of civilized warfare. With Christian mercy for our enemies, I instructed them to disable, not to kill. Their marksmanship is good enough to practice that distinction. On the march and on duty, they rode in place with their comrades.

* * *

For freedom alone, which no good man loses but with
his life.
—King Robert the Bruce, founder of Scotland as a
nation

The First Virginia Cavalry went into action at once, screening
General Johnston's withdrawal from Harper's Ferry. Only three
hundred of us held a fifty-mile front along the Potomac until
Johnston's army was secure around Winchester. Stuart took us
on sorties that brought us under enemy fire and taught us not to
fear it overmuch.

Torquil Dhu learned to fear it so little that he was captured in
a skirmish. He was overmatched by a Union regular cavalryman
who pinked my son's throat before he stayed his hand. I blessed
the man before God, for showing mercy, in my prayers the night
my son returned safe. Though he lost his weapons, he'd kept his
wits about him and used Keir's woodscraft instruction so well
that he rescued Thunderfoot, too! I nevertheless instructed him
to accept parole if it were offered—I don't want my son in a prison!—and required him to perfect his sabre technique before I
allowed him to carry a blade again. Since the sabre is the heart
and spirit of cavalry, he learned quickly.

The very last public and general act of the men at the
opening of the campaign ... was, of their own account,
to gather for a farewell religious service—Bible reading, singing of a hymn, prayer, words of exhortation
and cheer—and this meeting closed with a solemn
resolution to hold such a service daily ... we held that
prayer hour nearly every day, at sunset. ... And some
of us thought and think, that the strangest exemption
our battery experienced, our little loss in the midst of
unnumbered perils and incessant service ... was that
in answer to our prayers the God of Battles "covered
our heads in the day of battle," and was merciful to us,

because we "called upon Him." If any think this is a "fond fancy," *we don't.*
—Willy Dame, First Company Richmond Howitzers, Conffederate States Army, italics original

The Caledonians forged tighter bonds by fighting and en-camping together. We who'd served in Abercairn, were servants still. We were consulted upon matters ranging from our opinions as public officials, to how the soldiers' wives might best maintain the farms at home. Ewen was a colossus. Indomitable, always leading in person in front of the battle line, he inspired the men with his benevolent energy. He was also a force for the kingdom of God. As an elder of the kirk, he conducted daily prayer, devo-tions, and hymns.

2. First Blood

The soldier ... falls as the sparrow falls, speechlessly; and like that sparrow, I earnestly believe, not without a Father.
—B. F. Taylor, September 20, 1863

Torquil

We had to wait.

When the call to battle came, the First Virginia marched for thirty-six long hours to Manassas. Riding into position, we saw infantry like palisades marching, and roads choked for miles with wagons and teams, artillery and caissons, and still more infantry.

We had to wait.

We were reserves, grouped in fours, positioned too low to see the battle. But we heard. Crashing volleys of musketry, a nev-er-ending crack of thousands of rifles blending like the roar of a huge waterfall and drowning out all but the deep, echoing boom of artillery, all crowned overhead with the terrifying, demonic howl and shriek of shells. Flying bullets hissed and whizzed and whispered of death. If their flight wobbled, they seemed to buzz around our heads, sounding so much as if they circled to hunt us down, that Andy instinctively tried to bat them away like bees. The sound of battle was the earth being torn apart, rocking beneath us: a rumbling, a grinding, a splintering.

We had to wait.

Our four—Douglas and I, Andy, and Jemmie—kept position.

A terrified horse burst through the brush and careered madly off toward the left. Wounded men limped between the cavalry, to the rear. On a stretcher was carried a man with part of his jaw shot away. A demoralized man ran headlong, blundering blindly against the horses.

"Colonel Stuart, General Beauregard directs that you bring your command into action at once and attack where the firing is hottest!"

Stuart galloped us at a Zouave unit. We charged into the volley intended for General Jackson's men. Andy was shot from his saddle.

Kill or be killed, horrible and glorious all at once! We rode through them, scattering and felling—men. They tried to stand. Some stabbed our men and horses with bayonets.

I fired to wound one and saw him reel to the ground. Instantly, another was before me. I shot at him. Shouts and cheers, commands and furious curses, crack of weapons, hiss of shots, swish of sabers—the fight consumed all else. Groans, prayers, screams, and threats merged into a roar. When the squadron reversed to ride through them again, I thrust and slashed with my saber, but the enemy scattered. Their retreat became a stampede for safety. Crowds of thrill-seekers out from Washington City to watch the battle were entangled with the routed Northern army, all running in panic.

Colonel Stuart called us back from the chase and divided us into squads of ten and twenty. "If there aren't officers enough, let anybody command a squad. This is business. Attack any force you find! There's no cohesion left among 'em."

Squads of ten, carrying only sabres and pistols, captured whole companies of fully armed infantry by mere threat. "Throw down your arms, or we'll put you to the sword!"

At our tent in bivouac that night, excitement gave way to numb shock. Shock, when we remembered distorted corpses and terribly mutilated men still alive, turned to horror. Douglas and I leaned on each other for support, huddled close. We noticed an overwhelming thirst for the first time but were too exhausted to help ourselves. The night was hot: we were shivering. We climbed to our feet in respect to Da.

Robert Bruce Drummond

I went to my sons with arms open. Both fell into my embrace. I lifted up my voice.

"Holy Father in heaven, thank You for sparing my sons to me and me to them this day. Heal, we pray, those who are wounded, and comfort all who have lost comrades in death. In Christ's name, Amen."

I tightened my arms around them, looked into their faces. Douglas was close to tears. Torquil's lips quivered. I surveyed the untouched food and turned my trembling boys toward it.

"Come, Sons, what have we for supper? We must all stay strong."

It rained most of the night.

Torquil

Garish dawn drove away night's merciful veil to reveal carnage more pitiable for being sodden, spread farther than Douglas and I could see. A howitzer with carriage broken leaned aslant near the crater of its exploded limber. Bodies of horses lay in grotesque contortions or relaxed sprawls. One whole team of six, killed by concussion, lay where they'd dropped.

No leaves, no saplings—all shot away. The Yankees had left cannon, horses, wagons, tools, medical supplies, muskets, accoutrements, clothing, and thousands of blankets.

Corpses mangled beyond all semblance of humanity ... parts of bodies ripped apart by shells ... dead men looking like they slept in peace. Stiff arms raised as if in prayer, muskets still clutched to the breasts of some, ground torn up by hands and feet still stretched or flexed where death throes had brought and, finally, released men tortured by their wounds. Blood clotted on the earth around them. Some mortal remains were blown high into trees, some were tumbled in heaps where death had reaped by handfuls, some lay in rows for burial.

Hospital details and citizens searched for the living. Farm carts, elegant barouches, and army ambulances moved about, surgeons directing, to fill each with suffering men. We recognized Abercairn carriages and saw wounded men taken home to be cared for—and Andy's body to bury.

Death defiled the wind that brought the fetor of decaying flesh of man and beast, till the air became a solid, smothering, sickening cloud of stench. Flies swarmed on bleeding wounds, on bloated or stark pale bodies. Carrion fowl squawked along the ground and hovered in the sky.

The pity and the horror were unspeakable. We didn't speak, we wept. Dry, choking sobs, heads on each other's shoulders.

* * *

Besides doing picket duty, the cavalry escorted troop movements and guarded supply trains. We were scouts and couriers:

neither night nor foul weather released us. No matter how sick or exhausted we were, we had to care for our horses before we could care for ourselves. Rations were often missing because we moved too fast for supply wagons. Men and horses were much used up by ceaseless work. Douglas and I learned to sleep when able and be always on the lookout for food. Though we'd proven ourselves in battle, we still wouldn't show weakness, lest we be excused or accused or, worst of all, sent home, because of our youth. That would shame us. We were determined to show we were men.

Robert Bruce Drummond

The First Virginia didn't build winter quarters until the end of January. My sons and I settled into a log hut with our tent for a roof.

We had time to write more than the brief missives reporting survival after battles. I wrote Mr. Ogilvie about Glenlochie business, and other leading men of the county about affairs of public concern. We Abercairn officials serving in the army joked about being the Ultima Thule Subcommittee for Abercairn Public Benefit, but we were often consulted. We advised that the court purchase and store emergency provisions, especially salt, which the county doesn't produce.

Torquil

To Ewen especially, and our other friends, we wrote accounts of battles and what we saw and did. Our friends wrote about the Shield, suspicious-looking strangers who turned out to be someone's distant relatives, the capture of a deserter, or their families and farms. Most mail and packages were delivered by friends and acquaintances passing between home and the army, even during active campaigns, but they were a feast-or-famine event.

Stuart was Brigadier General Stuart by February. His defense line extended west to Jeffersonton, with the Rappahannock between the two armies. Da got permission from Colonel Fitz Lee to go home and exchange our exhausted horses for fresh ones. Grieg had our remounts "up to the touch," as he put it. I received Grey Lobo. Mrs. Grieg had prepared us whole new outfits of clothing.

3. In Memoriam

> I have been reading the *New York Herald* of the 7th. ... I wish all our people could read more of the Northern papers. They would see a malignity which is absolutely fiendish. ... The people, the genuine native Yankees ... cry to their army ... to give no quarter ... and they offer them unlimited spoiling of a rich empire for reward. ... Probably the true source of hate peeps out in their bitter allusions to "Aristocracy," ... and how they hate a gentleman.
> —Private Lewis B. Blackford, Confederate States Army, December, 1861

Torquil

The Northern newspapers we received through the lines were a source of keen interest.

"If we'd made good on all *Harper's* fears, we'd have 'great steam guns' and 'masked batteries' threatening their very press!" Da said.

"Wonderful how they exaggerate the least breath of rumor into an all-encompassing threat," Mr. MacHugh agreed. "They must have their own people cowering in cellars."

"'Are there no cellars in Boston, that McClellan hath taken them away to quail in the wilderness'!" Mr. Kendrick paraphrased as usual.

"If their War Department obeyed the *Herald's* orders, they'd have captured both Richmond and Charleston by now!" Mr. Airlie grinned.

"Remember how Andy used to say our best weapon would be a Southron editor there?" mused Mr. Menteith.

When our elders all went silent at the mention of Andy's name, Douglas and I remembered too well the first of our company to die, and the horrors of the battlefield after the fight. They all returned to tear at us. In our minds, we built walls between the bloody glory of battle, compassionate care of the wounded and sick wearing either gray or blue, and ordinary camp life. Though blooded many times over, we still had vulnerable hearts. We refused to let them show.

Battle was a blazing, raging thing apart: a fight for our own lives and Da's and those of neighbors who, sharing mortal danger, had become brothers. Battles ended. War did not. The Yankee invaders' destruction did not. Nerves strained to respond to every alarm did not. We lived in the never-ending-ness of war and learned to hold horror at bay with wry epigrams. But it was never at bay for long. It was the substance of nightmares.

I couldn't reconcile the eternal meaning of our friends' deaths with the matter-of-fact manner all the company maintained. We had to "shed a soldier's tear upon a soldier's grave" and fight again. We couldn't mourn our dead, we couldn't honor their well-lived lives, but only keep our vows to fight to protect the loved ones at home. I buried my sorrow deep within.

Dominie Gilchrist

"I mean no reflection upon ye, Captain, when I notice the company seems melancholy." I spoke my concern apart from the camp.

"We are. Meseemed, with food and rest, we should gain good spirits again, but we have no." The colossus identified himself with his men.

"Ye've nourished them well. They look in better flesh than when I visited last."

"'Tis no' meat we hunger for, but solace of the heart," said the elder of the kirk.

That night in prayer, I laid the weary spirits of the Caledonians before our heavenly Father and prayed for a way to minister to wounds of the soul. They could not and would not give up the fight. Their mourning was mute and unacknowledged. It seemed I'd barely fallen asleep when I was roused by God's answer to my prayers. I got up and sat at the captain's makeshift table. As though I only held the pen, God's Scriptures and words of consolation and counsel poured out upon the page.

I began the service with hymns. The holy music of our faith drew men to congregate. I invoked God's presence and stated the memorial purpose, called for names of the fallen, and began, "Jesus said, 'Blessed are they that mourn ...'"

I evoked their memories of their comrades' appearance, words, and actions; I evoked their feelings of gratitude and guilt toward them; I gave a pause for reflection and sorrow. I saw their tears.

I presented the hard truth of physical death and underscored its finality. I saw them eye each other in mutual sorrow, some clasping the hands or gripping the shoulders of others.

"Jesus said, 'Blessed are they that mourn ... for they shall be comforted!'

"Though some of our friends and brothers may not have had the outward seeming of salvation, we cannot be certain they were condemned.

"Only God knows the hearts.

"Some may have been passing through that dark night when sometimes God withdraws the light of his countenance—living all the while in deep despair. Some may have been on the threshold of repentance.

"Only God knows the hearts.

"Jesus said, 'I am the resurrection and the life.' He assures us that the bodies we have committed to the ground shall be raised in a perfect form, and united with the spirits which have already gone to God.

"Friends and brothers, our true consolation is the knowledge that their souls are now purified in heaven. By faith, we believe our departed friends are there—some we are sure of, and for the others, we have hope. At the hour of death, if they called on Him to save them, they did not meet the last enemy alone.

"We shall see them again in glory, all of us who believe, forever with the Lord. Our Lord Jesus Christ, the Lamb of God, by the shedding of his blood, in the sacrifice of the cross, redeems us.

"We are but sojourners here. We are journeying through this world on our way to a better country. Though the path lead through a wilderness, fear not to follow. There are provisions for the way till the promised land is reached.

"There, we know, that for the loved ones who have gone before, and for us who follow, the inheritance on the Farther Shore is sure. And it is a blessed portion. In that fair land there is no more curse. There beside the crystal river grows the tree of life, whose leaves are for the healing of the nations. There God and his Lamb are in the midst, and the redeemed of the Lord see his face. There is no night, no darkness, for the Lord giveth them light—He is Light. Let us pray:

"Holy Father in heaven, we who remain on earth now breathe 'Farewell,' and commit unto Thee the souls of the men who have gone to Thee before us. By thy grace, we expect to see them again and rejoice together in heaven, in thy salvation, in thy forgiveness, and in thy purification, which restore us for ever to the creatures Ye meant us to be: created in thy image, loving and worshipping Thee in the beautiful land upon the Farther Shore, for all eternity."

As surgery is only the beginning of healing wounds, so my service was only the first step. Relieved of a bitter burden, the men had received the means of healing, but the scars of healed wounds always remain. I pray God will give them strength to bear them.

Torquil

I thought about the glorious future presented. God's deliverance from earthly troubles to the perfection of the Farther Shore ... my own soul being purified in heaven ... never being without the Light again. Our departed friends were enjoying it now. On a day I supposed would be far in the future, I'd see them there and enjoy it, too. Douglas and I imagined meeting our mother and baby brother.

* * *

I strive to inculcate in my men the spirit of the chase.
—(then) Colonel James Ewell Brown Stuart,
Confederate States Army, May, 1861

General Stuart was now Chief of Cavalry for the entire Army of Northern Virginia. In June, he took us on a ride around McClellan's whole army. After a hair-breadth escape across the flooding Chickahominy, we brought back information General Lee used to drive the Yankees away from Richmond, and hundreds of prisoners, horses, and mules. I got a revolver to replace the one the Yankees took when I was captured.

Horses and men were so worn down by five months and hundreds of miles of hard marching and fighting that we had to rest. But on August 4, we were ordered to protect General Lee's Confederate communications from depredations by the Yankees' latest commander, General Pope.

> Our men know every house in the whole country, and they now believe they have a perfect right to rob, tyrannize, threaten and maltreat any one they please. ... Satan has been let loose.
> —Brigadier General Marsena Patrick, United States Army

> Frightful ... war conducted upon the principles of Attila ... a desert. ... On every side were ruins of houses, wantonly burned by the troops of General Pope; fences were destroyed, the forest cut down, the fields laid waste; woe and desolation; ruins from which women and children had fled to escape plunder and insult. ... I felt for the enemy a hatred a thousand-fold greater than any which could have been produced by blood spilled fairly in open fight, and ten thousand others felt the same.
> —Captain John Esten Cooke of General Stuart's staff, Confederate States Army

Robert Bruce Drummond

Keir got through the enemy lines, bringing us letters from home, folded into his plaid. Sigel's column of Pope's criminals had plundered in the Thornton Valley, but the rest of Abercairn was safe.

"I hate it that they're suffering like the people have here." Torquil looked miserable.

"You can't tell where the plantations were at all, except for the chimneys!" Douglas scowled. "Not a landmark left, only the streams and the lay of the land to tell where we are!"

"There will still be the land," I told them. "Your great-great-grandfather started with the land, and if we must, we can do the same. I pray God everyone will be able to keep his holdings."

"Why shouldn't they, sir?" Torquil asked.

"If they have to borrow to buy seed or breeding stock, their land is the only security they can pledge. If crops or animals fail, they will lose it. I work and pray against such an outcome.

"Life is a matter of overcoming obstacles. Nothing in it is certain except God's wise plans and his care over us. Thus, I have ground for faith. We've obeyed His word by helping our neighbors through hard times. The spirit that sustains us is a spirit for each other's good.

"So long as we have the land, and that spirit among us, we shall survive."

Pope never suspected he was facing only part of the Army of Northern Virginia until General Lee loosed the other two-thirds of it upon him. We rolled up his left flank: defeat became rout when demoralized soldiers fled and created panic in the rest. My boys were elated.

"We're free of the Yanks! Every last one's across the Potomac!" Douglas crowed.

"Let's wash them out of Washington City, too, now our flood's come this far!" Torquil grinned.

General Lee took the offensive by invading Maryland. He'd lose the advantage gained if he didn't pursue and engage the enemy on his own ground. He allowed his famished, exhausted infantry what rest he could.

As always, while the infantry rested, the cavalry worked, creating a diversion. One sharp and bloody action after another cost us sore, but our screen never failed. When we reached Sharpsburg and went into bivouac among knolls at the extreme left of our line, we knew where our enemies lay.

"Maybe tomorrow," Torquil speculated. "They know we're on their soil."

"They're honor-bound to defend it," Douglas agreed.

"They have no honor! Pope made war on women and children!"

"Without honor, they're not worthy enemies! We should slaughter them like cattle!"

I made my voice rap hard. "Sons! Remember ever: they are souls for whom Jesus died! We may neither hate nor despise them."

They were silenced by the eternal truth.

"What's the good of honor, then?" Douglas asked.

"It stems from goodness. It begins with character. Jesus said, 'A good man out of the good treasure of his heart, bringeth forth that which is good.' Your words and deeds are the fruit of your character, by which men judge whether you are worthy of honor."

"But how does a man gain honor?"

"By warring against what's base within himself. If he defeats greed with generosity, for example, or fear with courage, he wins honor among those worthy to bestow it. The opinion of the unworthy counts for nothing, though their voices be many and loud. If your honor is rooted in Godly virtue and irreproachable character, it will be established and need no defense. We must live so it will not be called into question."

Torquil

I repeated Da's words in my mind and heart: a benediction upon my striving to live righteously, and a charge I intended to keep all my life.

That night, Captain Murray led us in prayer and singing a Psalm.

* * *

The next day, September 17, the armies battled across Antietam Creek. Both sides fought desperately for every inch of ground. It sounded like all heaven and earth were falling out of place and into one another, or like the mountains were ripped apart, from dawn till night.

The left end of our line was bad ground. General Stuart tried to mount counterattacks, but cavalry couldn't maneuver. We met a barrage from thirty-four Napoleons parked hub to hub, firing right in our faces. Stuart called it off.

Later, the Caledonians were sent out by squads to scout for ground and opportunity to attack again. When we came into the open, Yankee cavalry attacked us.

Then my cynical, distrusting nature was forged. I saw my family murdered.

CHAPTER 4

REPENTANCE

Torquil

Even the home I'd longed for couldn't erase the catastrophe. Nor ease it. Its contrast with the peace of home made it more outrageous. I denned like a wounded animal and refused to have visitors while confined to my chamber. Mrs. Grieg, knitting a sock, said Glenlochie had been a hospital for a year.

I didn't answer, only stayed silent. The yearning to be purified, to be as I was, and things to be as they were, before— My mind felt the thunderbolt ... took me far away from the graves where my world lay buried ... filled itself with the blank blue of cloudless heavens, where I felt suspended from earth and time, still hoping I'd be carried to the Farther Shore.

"... and Miss Nannie's running a hospital. Ye may see Aidan Beag. He helps here when she and her mother can spare him."

I nodded like I'd been present all the time.

Soon after, Dr. Gask arrived. He dressed the wound and announced, "Granulation tissue is forming vigorously." He said it was a landmark in recovery. But it killed my hope for the Farther Shore.

* * *

When I was well enough to dress and go downstairs, the chasm between me and other people still gaped. As if watching from a distance, I felt like I was hearing myself from far away. Few came to visit: too much work and too few hands to do it. Mrs. Grieg made me go to bed so soon after supper that I missed those who came after nightfall put an end to their outdoor work. But my first visitor was Ewen, my best friend.

"I came over as soon as I heard you were out of hiding! How are you?"

"All right. What are you doing?"

"Trying to keep the farm running and save a couple of brood mares from impressment. I gave the agent Flossie and Star instead. I hear the army's horses are worn out."

"They are, and hard to come by. I lost Victory at Gettysburg."

"He's found. Mr. Kendrick is riding him. Blaze didn't survive his wounds."

"That's too bad! Did they find my sidearms?"

"Papa didn't say. He said they're all praying for you, but stay home till you're well."

"What else do you hear?" None of the household had given me any war news.

"Vicksburg fell, so we've lost the entire Mississippi. We can only communicate with our States beyond by dodging the blockade in the Gulf of Mexico. You knew General Lee got safely across the Potomac after Gettysburg?

"Everybody thought they'd have to fight Meade's whole army north of the river. It was in flood when they got there. General Imboden brought away the train of wounded—seventeen miles long!—and the First Virginia had to fight to keep them from getting captured.

"Some places in Maryland, Yankees came out and axed the spokes of the wheels to stop them. What blackguards! Hurting wounded men! The Caledonians are picketing along the Rappahannock, and the Yankees are on the north bank.

"I suppose you'll be going back as soon as you can."

"I haven't thought so far." Before the—I'd have thought of nothing else!

"Well, if you want to, the Shield could use you. The Yankees keep coming closer, and we're spread thin, trying to keep body and soul together and keep a lookout, too."

"How're you handling the defense?"

As he told me the details of their attempts to keep Abercairn safe, I could see it was ineffective.

I retired to my chamber after supper, resolved to reconquer reason. Wandering away in my mind was an awful state to be in! The yearning to be with my family, and the sweet longing to be pure and unstained again, filled my heart, but I refused to let them carry me away.

My thinking and my spirit lay in ruins. I felt hollow inside. All my days had been bleak since I saw the big Yankee murder Da and Douglas. The honor of receiving my commission from General Stuart himself was dust and ashes. My heart was dead. I existed only in what was left of me ... didn't care whether I lived or not.

Murder was violation of justice itself—justice, my ideal since boyhood. I felt overpowered by boundless, unstoppable wickedness. What could I have done but mend that breach of justice?

But it poisoned my life.

The revelation startled and confused me so bad, I set it aside in favor of the other question: what to do next? The Shield weren't putting up an effective defense, but farm work was equally important. Too few men were left.

Da had talked about Drummond duty, riding home after Muster Day: "Jesus said, 'Unto whomsoever much is given, of him shall be much required.' You are prepared by education for the duties you're called to … public servants of Abercairn … so citizens may live in peace, in security … the goodness of their lives is committed to you."

I changed my question. My duty is to Abercairn. Where am I most needed?

The Farther Shore must be postponed. Duty chained me to life.

Mr. Ogilvie

My ward looked less than robust when I entered the office, but his expression was firm. I outlined Glenlochie's and Abercairn's situations briefly: barter, domestic production of necessities, emergency uses of the land, shortage of labor, horses and draught animals.

"I'm thankful Glenlochie is still productive, but I'd like to do more for our neighbors. What resources can you give to help them, rather than gain profit beyond what's needed to retain my father's holdings? I've no idea how, but I trust you do."

"I shall study the matter." I thought how like the family their last remnant was.

"I can't do heavy work yet, but I'll help with clerking or whatever will serve you best."

"It's time for you to know the business of the farm. We'll begin this evening."

* * *

The man who comes back from the lines has lost his original self.
—Dixon Wecter, *When Johnny Comes Marching Home*

His eyes are in mourning for the loss of his character.
—Captain J. McEntire, United States Army

Torquil

Mrs. Grieg thought I was in bed that night, but I sat up in the morris chair, pondering. My wound ached like it always did when I got tired.

My spirit was dead—why? Deadness and legitimate vengeance were connected, I was sure, like a white beam of truth had pierced the darkness. Why should my oath to execute a murderer cut me off from God? Dominie Gilchrist had warned me vengeance is against the law of God. But in the Bible, God said that for willful murder the just penalty was death! Did it matter how the penalty was exacted, or by whom? I sighed. Evidently it did.

* * *

For mine iniquities are gone over my head: as a heavy burden they are too heavy for me.
—Psalm 38:4

Flora was in foal. Next morning, I rode her gently to the kirk. I could approach God on my own, but I wanted Dominie Gilchrist's counsel. At the chancel, I knelt on both knees and bowed low before the presence of God.

A wordless lament rose in my throat ... voice low, keening Godly sorrow. Thoughts and words I didn't originate came to my mind. I prayed them reverently: confession and repentance, pleas for forgiveness, sometimes quotations from Scripture or phrases of such fresh and holy beauty that I knew they were from God's Spirit. I wept. The floor was hard and cold, and my legs grew stiff; but I was in the grip of holy power that wouldn't let me move, agreeing to pray as the power directed. Forgiving the big Yankee officer was the hardest.

I had to receive the devastation of my soul and my world, like it was a gift. I had to take the punishment of his wrong, like I'd done the wickedness instead of him, like the guilt was mine.

But I was innocent! I'd never seen him before in my life, let alone done him any wrong.

But to really forgive, God's Spirit taught me, I couldn't ask God to judge between us, or cry to Him for vengeance, or even pray for justice. I had to let the murderer off, scot-free! I had to take his sin upon myself.

Like Jesus the Christ took mine!

"Oh, dear God ..." I faced the Infinite.

"Dear God, I *will* to forgive him. I place this sacrifice of forgiveness on Your altar, in the Christ's name. ... and on his behalf."

What! Sacrifice on behalf of the one who destroyed my world—and me! My ravaged soul still cried out against it. It was like saying wrong was right! The Holy Spirit urged me, won for me the fight to make the sacrifice in the same spirit my Savior made sacrifice for me. It was like He carried me over an impossible barrier. When it was done, I knew in my spirit that I was cleansed, and restored to God's side of the eternal battle between good and wickedness.

I couldn't understand it. Nor could I lift my head, or rise, or unclasp my folded hands until God's power was done with me, though I tried. At last, my mind clicked back to ordinary consciousness from the holy place it had been.

Dominie Gilchrist was kneeling at the front bench. He opened his eyes. "Welcome home, Torquil Dhu. Ye've been far and long away."

Dominie Gilchrist

Returning to ordinary consciousness, I looked with joy at the returned prodigal. He sat at my feet and told his soul's journey.

"I grieve I was away so long, sir, in such a wicked place. I never want to be there again! I should do penance."

"Ye will."

"How is it so? I renounced my oath and forgave him! I never harmed him!"

"Did ye not live long with hatred and vengeance in your heart?" I felt sad. "Harboring them corrupts the soul. In the intentions of your heart, ye sinned, against both God and your own soul—in deeds almost to murder."

"I want my heart to be right so I can be with Him, not away in the dark," he mourned.

"Likewise King David was called a man after God's heart, but he chose to do murder and adultery. Yet after God punished him, He restored him. He restores ye also, just as your father on earth restored ye to his heart after ye did wrong. Your heart is cleansed and pure again."

"So swiftly? But … it feels like … it can hardly breathe."

"Great wrong was done to ye, which crushes the heart. It was not your fault, but it overset your reason. Ye did not seek God for remedy, but turned to sin.

"The evil ye did will overtake ye, and ye will have bitter warfare before ye win free. But I shall pray your 'daemon' will not vanquish ye again. Ye are at great risk and must guard against it.

"The day ye swore your oath, I prayed God to spare your life, but I have known ye will be grievously punished. God has forgiven ye, but men must suffer the results of what they do.

"Ye walked in the path of sin instead of in God's law. He who ordained that law does not spare ye from its due process. 'Whom the Lord *loveth*, he chasteneth'—'even as a father the son in whom he delighteth.' He has loved ye as his son through the sacrifice of

Jesus Christ since ye were a little lad and gave your life to Him. Do ye think He will deprive ye of chastening?"

"No, sir." He looked at the floor.

"Ye have been directly before Him since ye were left alone on earth, and now He himself attends to your discipline and your glory. He does not afflict willingly, any more than your earthly father did. Ye will find chastening grievous, but know it is needful."

He lifted his chin. "I'll pray for courage to bear it bravely, sir."

"Pray also for grace to thank God."

"Thank Him!"

"Aye, for loving ye enough to prepare ye for His service, rather than cast ye away as reprobate and unworthy of correction. Gratitude, in submission to the process of His law, is the penance ye will do."

His shoulders drooped. He gazed unseeing at the far end of the bench, but soon he lifted his chin.

"I think I understand. It's justice, isn't it? I'll pray for grace to thank Him."

"Justice is more than punishing sin, Torquil Dhu. It also honors righteousness. What ye enter upon now is more. 'Tis how God will use past evil for future good, and your suffering to bring His plan to fruition."

> Let them that suffer according to the will of God, commit the keeping of their souls to him in well doing, as unto a faithful Creator.
> —I Peter 4:19

Torquil

I left the mourning band on the altar as a symbol of my repentance and rode home gloomy. I felt like a sentenced criminal. What would my chastisement be? When and how would it come?

I didn't know, then, it would hunt me out. I didn't know how many more years my life would seem a curse. I prayed for courage and for grace to thank God for whatever He chose to inflict.

I found solace in being able to pray again.

* * *

I wasn't fully recovered, but I'm the only Drummond now. I can't rest while Abercairn is threatened. Every soul in Abercairn was spending every ounce of strength, every scrap of material provision, every minute of time, to defend ourselves and fight for independence. How could the need for soldiers, Army provisions, and defending Abercairn, be met? In less time, with fewer men? The only answer I knew was raids. I'd ridden many. We'd captured horses or armament or supplies the army needed. Abercairn's needs could be met the same way.

I rode Flora on a scout around the county borders. At the summit of the Blue Ridge, I climbed a tree and looked far east into the Piedmont. Dust clouds marked the roads where Yankees moved soldiers and materiel. Thin rooster tails of dust followed dispatch riders. By night, campfires revealed picket posts and encampments. I noted gaps in their lines and observed their daily routines. The wound ached.

I made notes on endpapers torn from books. Sketching a map, I noted Yankee positions, roads and trails, dense cover, watercourses, landforms. Propping it against some books on the office desk, I slumped back in the chair to study it, matching it with the exploring we did as boys. The enemy were still outside Abercairn. They must be kept out!

I had to convince Ewen to take the offensive.

* * *

"I've scouted where you can attack and what you can raid. It's better than them raiding you."

"We've got all we can do to get the crops in, let alone raising the Yankees against us!"

"Not if you put them to such confusion that they couldn't."

"Maybe you could."

"If I led the Shield, I would."

"Well, are you going to?"

"Not like it is now, waiting for them to march in whenever they please! You don't have enough men for armed resistance. But you can carry the war to wherever they are and draw their attention away by keeping them engaged there."

"But we'd put others of our own people in danger!"

"They already are! The Yankees think they're prey!" I remembered the wickedness that made "laws of war" out of false excuses for atrocity. "There aren't enough men left here to both provide and protect. If raiding's part of your offensive, you can capture food and horses and other supplies from their stores or supply trains."

"How, with so few?"

"Scouting. You know the country! You know how to move unseen. Find small detachments you can defeat.

"Make your escape away from the direction of the county, so they'll think you came from ... our lines, for example ... scatter and return by roundabout ways. It'll help the army if you keep some of the enemy amused, so fewer will be against General Lee. The law states partisan companies can keep whatever they capture, except ordnance. You can distribute it as you will."

"That'll make us brigands!"

"The difference is your objectives. If you capture materiel, you deprive the enemy of its use. You can sell captured ordnance to the army, to buy what you can't grow."

"What about the crops?"

"They won't be as critical if you have other sources of supply."

"I won't lose what we've worked so hard for! We should be able to finish harvest in the next few weeks."

"If you're left in peace."

"How close are the Yankees?"

"Culpeper."

He whistled. "Any other ideas?"

"Keep all the men together in a well-hidden bivouac elsewhere, so homes won't be targets. Remember the fault cave we found?"

"It's an awful risk."

"It's your decision."

"It's everyone's. I'll call a meeting. Will you lead, if we choose raiding?"

"'Everyone' includes my captain, your father. I must have orders for detached service. I'm willing if I get them."

The Abercairn Shield voted in favor of offensive tactics and chose a party of twenty-four to meet for training when I returned with the necessary orders.

Captain Murray

"So you see, sir, it's like what we've been doing since the war began."

"The difference is strength. Yon Northmen respect the large force raiding, but condemn the sma'. They name them guerrillas and use them for dishonor when caught."

I saw protest rising and lifted a hand. "Nae more, lads, the night. I weel ponder, and speak wi' men o' wisdom, and give ye an answer the morrow."

In the clear light o' next morn, I saw the bloom o' health in my son's face, but I sorrowed, my best friend's son had it no'. 'Tis a matter I've authority to correct. But I'd observed the lad's dour demeanor. I took him aside.

"Young Drummond, I fash myself ye are too reckless to command the other lads. Ye've had no care for life syne a year agone. Can I trust my firstborn to ye?"

"Yes, sir. I repented before God, of vengeance. My father said the Yankees are souls Jesus died for. I've come to see it so, and repent of hunger for blood. I hold my friends too dear, too vital to Abercairn, to put them in any but necessary danger. I'll teach them to protect each other, as well as the county."

"Aye weel. I trust your troth. I weel speak for ye among the fathers."

* * *

Verdiersville, Sept. 15, 1863

Dear Judge Carmichael:

The "Ultima Thule Subcommittee" have approved detaching twenty-four members of Ewen the Younger's Abercairn Shield to Lieutenant Drummond as Rangers; Captain Murray styles them vedettes. We authorize scouts around the county borders, restrict the boys to a ten-mile swath beyond it for offensive actions except when in pursuit, and order them to perform military duties rather than capture enemy goods except as part of such duties, to wit: reconnoitre enemy movements, report information gathered, disrupt enemy patrols and scouts, and their supply and communications lines. Like other Reserves, they will join larger operations when ordered out. We exacted their promise to abide by these rules of engagement. Lt. Drummond is answerable for the portion of the Home Guard detached to him and is required to obey the orders of the Army of Northern Virginia.

We send you one qualified to command, whose good faith we trust, and whose early dedication to Abercairn we approve. Would you please meet with him to relay the citizens' views in the matter of defense.

Respectfully, your obedient servant,
Jock Menteith, Commonwealth Attorney

By hand of Ewen Murray the Younger

Torquil

I was exhausted from the long rides, but my idea of duty, formed in the cavalry, required me to go till I could go no longer. I told Ewen to call the Rangers to report at Glenlochie next morning. I read my sealed orders and scowled.

Army of Northern Virginia
First Virginia Cavalry, Co. S, "Caledonians"
Verdiersville, September 15, 1863

2nd-Lt. Drummond
Commanding Ranger Company of Abercairn Shield

I. Ye will commence training your command, at the home farm, upon the morn following your return.

II. Ye will immediately return the muster roll. Submit reports twice a month to me, for transmittal to higher commands.

III. Daily, for four weeks, from dinner until supper-time, ye will lie upon your bed, that ye become fit for duty.

IV. During these weeks, ye will confine yourself—except for Kirk attendance—to the borders of the home farm unless orders from the Army of Northern Virginia command otherwise.

E. W. Murray the Elder, Captain

After dinner, expecting not to sleep, I took *Stratagemata* from the classical section of the library. This collection of military ruses was the language thesis Da presented while a student at the University of Virginia. He'd translated Frontinus's original Greek into Latin, proving his mastery of both languages. I put it on the morris chair by the bed, pulled off boots and coat, lay down, and shut my eyes. When I woke, it was night. I threw off the blanket Mrs. Grieg must have laid over me and went looking for something to eat. At first light, I wakened again and gave thanks for the new day and prayed for wisdom for my new duties. With Da's example before me and harsh lessons of war in mind, returning to the reserved and thoughtful nature of my boyhood, I took up my new post. I didn't know I was fighting for a love already lost.

CHAPTER 5

RANGER COMPANY OF THE ABERCAIRN SHIELD

Their war cries were the names of their places.
—Alistair Moffatt, *The Highland Clans*

Torquil

I bestrode Flora to receive my detachment when they rode into the stable yard, careless and laughing, some in uniform, others not. My schoolmates, as young as ten and up to seventeen, they were like Douglas was at first, eager for adventure, heedless of danger. I was responsible for their lives, and to Abercairn's future.

I looked at them so long they became restive. They trifled among themselves as an antidote to the direct, silent gaze I couldn't change. I kept my voice low with authority.

"Men."

They quietened at once and tried to look like men.

"Collect your horses."

I wished I had the eloquence Tacitus put into the mouth of his Caledonian warlord before the battle of Mons Graupius, but tried to remember some of the rhetoric they taught us at the academy.

"We are going to take the war to the Yankees, to distract them from attacking Abercairn. We'll serve with the army when called upon. Our great disadvantage is our smaller numbers, but we have surprise and speed and our knowledge of the country.

"We'll intercept their couriers and attack their rear guard and destroy their communications, and we'll do it all so that they think we're coming from somewhere else.

"We'll travel light, move quietly and unseen until we attack. We won't stand and fight them, but disengage and be gone at will."

Aidan Beag, like his father Aidan Mor, worried about his family's safety: "Won't they follow us?"

"They will. I intend to make them glad to see the last of us."

"How're we going to get away, Torquil Dhu?" Robbie, at seventeen summers, was the oldest of the would-be raiders.

"Confusion. Capture their horses so they'll be afoot, or start a fire and be gone while they're fighting it, for example."

"What about getting back here?" David wanted to know. "Won't they trail us and find our base?"

"Whenever we can, we'll go to the army lines, to make it look as if we came from there. It will prevent them from taking vengeance upon citizens, or us being thought guerrillas. We can turn over our prisoners to the provost and receive fresh orders, too. In some cases, we'll scatter. They're used to fighting in a body, not going in twenty directions at once. Then we each take a roundabout route and cover our trails and meet elsewhere."

"What about signals? A fight will be deafening," Donald pointed out.

"I can blow a trumpet!" claimed Willie MacCay, the ten-year-old.

"Can you sound the regular commands?"

"Yes!"

"You'll have to stay right by me, so I can tell you what to sound. Can you do that?"

"Yes!"

"I'll depend on you."

I turned upon them all the matter-of-fact voice and unyielding gaze of rightful authority.

"You will become an effective fighting force because you will be trained soldiers. I shall drill you in the work you have to do. Some may not match your present ideas of what wins victory in war. You will learn otherwise, and swiftly, because the safety of Abercairn depends upon you.

"You will address me as Lieutenant, or Sir. You will be silent when I speak. You will obey my orders without delay or be dismissed from this Ranger company to make place for a man who will. None whose obedience I cannot rely upon will ride with me again.

"You will do this ... because a company must be disciplined to strike successfully.

"You will do this ... to protect your families and each other's lives.

"You will do this ... to save everything we mean when we speak of ... *Clan Abercairn.*"

I turned my gaze upon each in turn and watched them take possession of the idea. The wound pulled at my side muscles, but I raised my right fist overhead and snapped it high. "ABERCAIRN!"

"ABERCAIRN!" they answered.

"Hear now the orders from the First Virginia Cavalry, by which we are bound."

They disdained the safeguards and showed disgust that they wouldn't be raiders, with sneers and scowls, but—obeying their first direct order—kept silent.

"We have not only the protection of Abercairn to perform, but the honor of Abercairn to uphold. We shall therefore fight as Christian soldiers, bearing in mind that the Son of God sacrificed his life for the souls of our enemies as well as for ours. We shall not commit murder, but, rather, wound them sorely enough to put them out of the fight and protect ourselves."

I could see them agreeing to Abercairn's Christian stance.

"Neither shall we rob or abuse prisoners, but treat them humanely. We may capture the enemy's materiel of war, or be entertained by citizens, but we shall not plunder.

"You will report each morning except Sabbath for training, properly uniformed. The uniform is one mark that sets us apart from the lawless marauders called guerrillas. Another is discipline, under which we all must come as soldiers. Another is legal enrollment in the regular army of the Confederate States. I shall muster you all in today.

"Now, a few maneuvers …"

* * *

Attila, King of the Huns, adopted the only method that can exterminate these citizen soldiers. A policy of extermination alone can achieve the end expected. I can clear this country with fire and sword, and no mortal can do it any other way. The attempt to discriminate nicely between the just and the unjust is fatal to our safety; every house is a vedette post, and every hill a picket and signal station.
—Colonel Horace Binney Sargent, United States Army, September 2, 1863

Recovering, I slept less, and spent the time after supper studying tactics and making plans. Mrs. Grieg had a new uniform tailored for me and, herself, transferred to it the buttons and insignia from the old one. I carried my army orders in an oiled-silk packet in the breast pocket. I took Da's sabre for my officer's sword, bought a strong black gelding from Lachlans, named him Nightwind, and trained him for duty with the other horses.

To shorten training time, I dispensed with sabres for the men, but distributed the Glenlochie firearms among those who had none. We marched first to the cave below Raven Crags, where we established our base.

I took them a long time scouting. Crossing and recrossing our border, to the ten-mile limit, quartering the ground, they memorized landmarks and watercourses, open ground and forest cover. Through chill nights, we camped without tents and, when close to the enemy, without fires.

I showed them how to cover all kinds of ground quietly on foot, and how to play with the reins or hold a horse's nostrils to keep him from neighing, and how to take advantage of all available cover. I warned against over-eagerness betraying our presence too soon—much like hunting—to put us needlessly in harm's way.

Teaching them to recognize picket lines, camps, and movements, I showed them how close the enemy were. From old campfires, they learned to estimate how many had been there and, by the condition of embers and hoofprints, how long ago they had left and in what direction.

From citizens' information and from observation, I kept a complete picture of the enemy's location. I read the pulse, the ebb and flow of their movements, and felt the pressures from far away.

Aidan Beag

Torquil Dhu and Nannie and I were like siblings since we were babies. The stern, terse commander he became, was a cold and distant stranger. He taught us army life in all its rigor. He kept his promise to dismiss for insubordination: we received MacCammond in Fraser's place. Duncan hadn't lost a bit of his anger, but he kept it under—till we were in a fight. So we wouldn't miss the adventure, we all obeyed, to the letter.

We didn't like that part.

When we were growing up, he was Douglas's shadow, except a couple of times. When he wouldn't lie to save himself a horrible whipping, we learned he was strong, even if he was Owl to us—bookish and too well-behaved. Then at the academy, when he persuaded us to skip Saturday recitation and ride home. And when, after we'd banded together to punish some rotten bullies, he called Abercairn a clan who could whip anyone if we stuck together.

We saw he was uniting us like a clan. Our birthplace, our homeplace, our lives together, our heroic ancestors who'd saved us from Cumberland the Butcher after the 'Forty-Five and brought us to America in their loins, gave us of Abercairn a spirit different from other people and other places.

We saw that his moral strength gave him the right to lead us. We followed better after that.

He made us scout the nearest Yankee picket post till we could identify individual voices. In twilight, when visibility was decreasing and they were settling for the night, we surrounded and overcame them in a short, sharp fight. Our first of many.

Torquil

MacCammond and I—the harshest—silenced the sentinels. Willie sounded the Charge. We plunged through the camp, shouting, riding over tents, scattering embers to set canvas on fire in the brisk wind, downing soldiers. Blair and Galbraith cut the ends of the two picket lines and led off the resulting strings of horses. We countermarched to surround the camp, dueling till we'd disabled so many, they could only surrender.

We put the prisoners under guard, tended Aidan Beag and the enemy wounded, and reaped a harvest. Each Ranger became well armed, well mounted, well equipped. After we collected all their weapons, I allowed the prisoners to retrieve their belongings. We marched to Major Willis of the infantry, the field officer nearest Abercairn. His provost took charge of the prisoners. His ordnance officer received the ordnance we turned over. We kept the horses for remounts.

Dr. Gask

In dressing gown and carpet slippers, I stood on no ceremony when a wounded Ranger was brought to me after dark. Young Drummond half carried Aidan Beag, whose left hand was clamped to his right shoulder. I made him drink plenty of water with an opium pill.

"It's well you could get him here so soon. During the first shock is the best time for the first surgery." After washing my hands and the wound, I handed Aidan Beag a chunk of leather to bite on and removed the Minie ball and contaminants.

"You're blessed it didn't break a bone or sever an artery. I'll let you have your memento when I get you bandaged. This next is going to burn."

I shook bromine onto a sponge. Since bromine cures gangrene, early application prevents it. Young Drummond held him down, body across body, right arm on his neck and left hand immobilizing his arm. When I swabbed the powerful antisepsis thoroughly into the wound, Aidan Beag yelped and by reflex, kicked. I dusted the wound and surrounding flesh with powdered morphia for an analgesic.

"I want a meeting with you tomorrow, Lieutenant." I applied dressings and bandage. "You and your men need to learn how to take care of yourselves when I'm not available."

"When shall I be here, sir?"

"Late evening." I folded seven opium pills into a paper and handed it to him. "Give them at twelve hour intervals." To Aidan Beag, "These should get you through the worst of the pain. Are you still riding Auld Aidan's Clio?"

"Yes." His voice was weak.

"Good. She's got the smoothest gaits in the county." I put the Minie ball in his hand.

Torquil

Dr. Gask made his proposal while I repressed a shudder at the sight of his cauteries.

"I'd like you to assign some of your number to me, to learn the treatment of wounds. Neither I nor Dr. Wilkins can chase about with your Rangers! I won't leave you at the mercy of each other's ignorance. You need to know what to avoid, such as severing arteries or damaging vital organs, as well as how to treat."

"I'll be your first student. When do you want to begin?"

"Now. First, you must discipline your mind. You cannot let your natural sympathy for another's pain negate your ability to *observe* what the case, in *reality*, presents. You must think and reason from the facts and what presents itself before you. Using the judgment you thus make, you must act boldly and independently upon it. You are responsible.

"You need to know how to use and take care of the instruments. I learned from Doctor Terrell—he's at the Lynchburg hospital now—that if they're boiled after use, you have a lower incidence of post-surgical diseases. A man can die from a massive inflammation even if the wound is slight to begin with. You need to wash the wound and your hands, too.

"You must first know something of how the human body fits together. You and your chosen men study this." He handed me Gray's *Anatomy*.

Breaking communications is the chief work for a partisan—it defeats plans and starts confusion by destroying supplies, thus diminishing the offensive strength of an army.
—Colonel John S. Mosby, 43rd Battalion of Virginia Cavalry, Confederate States Army

Satisfied with my men's obedience and developing skill, yet I repeated the need to do the most damage while suffering the least loss before I led a foray to a supply train in Yankee territory—within the prescribed ten miles! We cut out six wagons of ammunition and five Autenreith medical wagons without alerting the rest of the train. And captured a sutler's unauthorized wagon and team weaseling through the woods in hopes it'd be protected!

I kept Airlie with me and scouted toward the Yankee lines. We intercepted a courier. His dispatch told me if he and the sealed message didn't arrive, the Yankees would know their plan was discovered.

"Dismount and strip."

"You Rebs going naked?"

Fuming, he obeyed, and stood red-faced in only his linen. I copied the dispatch and resealed it. Impersonating the courier, I scouted the Yankee camp while I delivered it. At Glen Ness, where I'd sent him with Airlie, I swapped uniforms and returned his belongings. Airlie turned him over to the provost while I asked the ordnance officer about payment for captured munitions delivered. It was authorized and would be expressed to me.

* * *

I held my hands up and tried to look scared. I wore clothes that would shame a beggar, but the captain commanding the Yankee column kept his revolver pointed at my heart like I was dangerous as a Cossack!

"Boy, do you know how to get to Benton's Corners?"

"It be yon way." I pointed right. From here, both roads looked equally well traveled.

"You just march along ahead of us!"

I marched beside the off leader of the first team: when we came to my ambush, they'd shoot at me first. Around the bend was a boghole. Rangers hid on both sides.

"When I give the signal, make enough noise for a whole regiment!" I'd ordered. "*Watch!* I'll raise my arm high. *Disable the Yankees first!*"

I raised my arm, then pulled the mules toward me to create cover. When the team bolted, I dashed for the roadside. Shots whistled over my head.

The first team pulled to the right of the boghole; the second dodged left. The third crashed into both, plunging and squealing. I dived into the underbrush and grabbed my revolver.

In four shots, it was over. A solitary horse ridden at a dead run ... shouts of its rider urging it on. "Dunk! Bring him back!"

He wheeled away. I assigned guard and capture chores. "The rest tend the wounded."

I tightened a tourniquet onto the captain's leg. The knee was smashed and gushing blood.

"Is there an officer to whom I can surrender?" he croaked, gritting his teeth

"Lieutenant Drummond, sir, at your service."

"You! You hayfoot!"

I showed my orders.

"A craven deception! Nevertheless, sir ..."

He presented his straight sword hilt first. I raised it in salute.

We saved fifteen mules and all the harness. MacCammond brought back the horse with its rider lying dead over the saddle. I pried open a crate.

"The Yankees' experiment. Repeating breechloaders!" I displayed one. "Henrys. Sixteen shots, one in the chamber, fifteen in the magazine. And ammunition enough!"

I resolved never to take the field out of uniform again.

CHAPTER 6

UNCLE JAMES

1. The Spy

A republic, however free, requires the service of a certain number of men whose ambition is higher than mere private gain, whose lives are inseparable from the life of the nation, and whose labors and emoluments depend absolutely upon the honor and prosperity of the Government, and who can advance themselves only by serving their country.
—President James A. Garfield, speaking of Regular Army officers

MacLeod

When the blindfold was removed, a lieutenant leaning against a tree was studying an anatomy text. Three fingers in the book, turning pages, he recited softly to himself. "The abdominal aorta divides into the interior and exterior iliac arteries. The exterior continues"—he turned the pages—"as the femoral artery which divides to run along the inner side of the right and left thighs."

"He says he's from General Ewell's camp, sir," the shorter guard reported.

The lieutenant was about a hand shy of six feet tall when he stood up straight. Level gaze. Large, bright eyes the color of blued steel betrayed indelible pain. Aquiline nose and singleness of attention made me think of an eagle stooping upon its prey.

"Your reason for arriving here, sir?" Pleasant low tenor, patrician accent.

"I want to join you, sir. We need all we can capture to supply the army."

"You must be exempted."

"I've been serving elsewhere." That was true! I told a story of blockade running and bringing munitions to Virginia.

"You might be of better service to the army than to us, Mr. ..." The beardless face didn't soften.

"MacLeod. James MacLeod." My real name. If they mark my grave, my family might find it, and lay me to rest at last beside Eleanor and Davie.

"To whom did you deliver your munitions?"

"Colonel Thorpe of the Rappahannock Rifles can vouch for it."

The lieutenant penciled briefly on a scrap of paper and handed it to a guard. "This is for Overseer."

A nickname. It could belong to anybody. I was captured.

The taller guard's easy, swinging stride carried him speedily up the hillside. The other replaced the blindfold and led me back where we'd met. The guerilla was wary, but such precautions must reduce his fighting strength. How? I'd find out! Since March, when the "Topogs" were discontinued, I'd belonged to the Corps of Engineers, but, trained as a topographical engineer, I'd long practiced thorough investigation. I was ordered to capture Black Drummond and make a map to guide a force to destroy the gang. I hated the tacit order to lie. I've lived by West Point honor since entering the academy as a boy. But I've sworn to obey my country's orders: deceiving the enemy is part of them.

I made idle-seeming conversation into the muzzle of an ancient horse pistol.

"I've heard this command is making a lot of trouble for the Yankees."

"It's like firing a shotgun at a big flight of ducks: it's hard to miss.

"Not that you're a bad shot, of course."

"Middling compared to some. The lieutenant and his brother, now, their father taught them till they never missed. He still doesn't."

"He? They?"

"Douglas was killed at Sharpsburg."

"A sad loss. I suppose they were close."

"Like hand in glove. I haven't seen him smile since, but he doesn't seem to mind if the rest of us skylark a little. Ment—Snort fooled me the other day when he said he'd brought me a prize mount from the Yankees. It was an ornery mule, and he put my saddle on it. I had to chase the fool thing a mile to get it back." He grinned. "It was probably because I put nettles in his bedroll."

"You must often go on raids."

"They don't always oblige us by coming close, but that doesn't bother the chief. He makes ways where none are, and no one sees or hears him. Keir's even better."

"Another of your company ..."

"The chief's ghillie ... personal attendant, these days also his forester."

"You seem to keep the old ways. How does a Scottish chief happen to be in Virginia?"

"He's chieftain of one sept—part of a clan. We escaped here after the 'Forty-five."

"Bring him here now, Kendrick!" The patrician voice descended from midair.

We climbed the steep hillside to a level space where faint light from the cleft of a fault cave silhouetted the boy lieutenant.

"Colonel Thorpe confirmed the delivery you made and said you'd been helpful in pointing out some of the mechanical quirks."

"The British manufacture things somewhat differently."

"Raise your right hand and repeat after me: I—say your name—do solemnly swear ..."

"... that I will bear true allegiance to the Confederate States of America, and that I will serve them honestly and faithfully against all their enemies or opposers whomsoever ... so help me God."

I thought I'd choke on "Confederate!" I'd perjured myself— but I had to play my role as believably as possible. To God alone I added: 'As long as I have to, to obey my country's orders!'

We filled and witnessed enlistment blanks.

"Private, is your expertise greater in munitions or logistics?"

"Logistics, sir." To learn the region of the guerrillas' operations!

"You'll go with Mr. Lachlan tomorrow. Come in to supper."

A passage lit by couple of candles led deep into the side of the granite ridge. I observed with scientific interest some offshoot faults, apparently with special uses, before the main fault widened and rose to form a high, rhomboid-shaped room. A couple dozen boys were eating, talking, or trifling among themselves. An old man and one wearing a kilt chatted near the cookfire.

On the other wall were stacks of equipment. By each stood a Henry rifle. Consternation at the War Department when they captured that shipment had sent me hotfoot after it.

"Help yourself."

I filled a cup with greens and bacon from the kettle over the cookfire.

"Men."

The chatter ceased.

"This is James MacLeod. Introduce yourselves."

A brown-haired, bright-eyed little boy scampered up to me. "I'm Willie MacCay. Come sit over here!" I took the place he offered, among the boys.

"Alex Menteith." Sergeant's stripes, auburn hair and greenish-brown eyes. He offered his hand.

"Donald Loudoun." Another sergeant. Eyes so dark that the pupil wasn't differentiated from the iris assessed me. His hair was black, his handshake quick and firm.

"Aidan MacHugh." Red hair and fair, freckled skin he had, and blue eyes. White edges visible at the neck of his coat showed the right shoulder bandaged. He apologized for offering his left hand.

"Robbie Kendrick." The guard I'd conversed with was broad built, blond, blue-eyed, with a good-natured smile below an attempt at a moustache. His handshake was warm.

None of the boys looked old enough to be in the army. Where was the rest of the gang? After I tended Redspeed and brought my traps inside, I found my saddlebags had been searched.

* * *

The boys were away before dawn. I put on the gray uniform issued. Mr. Lachlan, the old man I'd seen last night, summoned me to hitch up.

"Aye, Jems, we've a few stops, the day. Whooaa there!" He stopped a frisky mule with one bend of the harness around a gnarled brown fist and backed the mules into position.

Returning late at night after having delivered captured military stores to Confederate camps, we came upon the lieutenant. Seated on a wooden bench by the entrance to his quarters—one of the side-shoot faults off the main passage—he was studying by the light of a candle set in a tall brass candlestick on the bench beside him. Engrossed, he didn't look up until I spoke.

"I never heard your name, sir."

"Drummond."

I noticed his book was Frontinus's *Stratagemata* at the same instant I made the connection between his raven-black hair and his name: Black Drummond! I covered astonishment by attempting conversation.

"You must read Greek."

"A Latin translation."

"Perhaps the ancients can teach us something about warfare."

"Some useful subtleties."

"Which may have been overlooked in today's preference for European tactics."

"Even so. You must be hungry. Portions are set aside. Mr. Lachlan, may I have your report, sir."

Dismissed, I sketched an awkward salute, trying to act non-military.

What a contrast between what I'd been led to expect and the actual guerrilla! Any ferocity in him was hidden under unsparing attention to duty. He had only to speak to be obeyed, yet none of the boys seemed afraid of their somber chief. I'd never seen such serious demeanor in one so young. By the roundness of his face, he could barely be sixteen. His sober reserve seemed a shield. None of the boys joked with him or about him.

* * *

On my fifth day at the cave, the guerrillas didn't ride out. When the youngster nearest me roused, yawning, to roll up his blankets and straw mattress, I asked, "What are the orders for the day, David?"

"Clean-up, inspection, and divine service afterward. Excuse me, I have to be taking my turn."

Conducting inspection, the lieutenant paced down the line and back up, scrutinizing each boy. He himself was neat and clean as a new pin. I'd never seen him otherwise.

At "Present ... arms!" the lieutenant inspected each Henry minutely.

"Well done, men. Sergeant, march the company in."

The lieutenant entered behind us and stood next to a fine, small table on which was placed a Bible. He prayed confession and invocation. I carried the bass line of the first hymn, appreciating how the acoustics of the cave enhanced yet didn't distort the music. The boys read the Old and New Testament lessons. I'm Methodist; at West Point, divine service was Episcopalian. Whatever this was, I thought I could follow along.

"Let us pray."

The guerrillas knelt, closed their eyes, and bowed their heads.

"Dear God, holy Father in heaven, we thank Thee for preserving our lives this week and for your providence for all our wants. Please continue graciously to watch over us and help us and all our fighting men, and cover our heads in the day of battle, and heal the sick. Please bless and grant wisdom to President Davis, General Lee, and General Stuart, and all who rule our country and lead our armies. Comfort those who mourn. Bring back any who have gone astray from Thy commandments. Grant us the Light of thy Holy Spirit, to cheer and guide us. Let us now pray silently the petitions of our own hearts."

I prayed, 'Holy God, grant me wisdom and strength, that I may do all my duty to my country and unto Thee, according to Thy perfect will.'

"In Jesus's name ... Our Father, Who art in heaven..." I knew them for Presbyterians when they prayed "debts" instead of "trespasses."

"Our closing hymn is 'How Firm A Foundation,' verses three through five."

> Fear not, I am with thee, O be not dismayed,
> For I am thy God, and will still give thee aid;
> I'll strengthen thee, help thee, and cause thee to stand,
> Upheld by my righteous, omnipotent hand.
>
> When through the deep waters I call thee to go,
> The rivers of woe shall not thee overflow;
> For I will be with thee, thy troubles to bless,
> And sanctify to thee thy deepest distress.
>
> When through fiery trials thy pathway shall lie,
> My grace, all-sufficient, shall be thy supply,
> The flame shall not hurt thee; I only design
> Thy dross to consume, and thy gold to refine.

"The Lord bless thee and keep thee ... Amen."

* * *

After the midday meal, I climbed into the crags. Miles of mountainsides clothed with autumn leaves looked like vari-colored tapestries. East, the Piedmont: farms and villages—and army encampments. I wished I'd brought my field glasses. I noted the lieutenant's sentry points and sentinels walking their beats.

I made rough triangulations and committed the terrain to memory, for the map I'd draw when I returned to my own lines. Had Colonel Long recommended me to Secretary of War Stanton for this assignment? I knew them all, since the "Topogs" had reported directly to the executive branch of the government. But why detach an engineer for espionage?

I glissaded down the other side of the summit to a rock ledge and followed it south toward the cave entrance. In a shaded niche, the lieutenant sat leaning against the rock wall with wrists resting on bent knees, looking into the little glen below. There stood the cow shed, and the horse herd grazed on sere autumn grasses beside a tumbling rill.

"The service this morning was a fine devotion, sir."

"Thanks be to God. He arranges it." Neither his gaze nor expression changed.

"The last hymn was especially appropriate."

"He put it in my mind at that moment. I've been reasoning out why today, since we can expect such trials at any time. Perhaps it's because war is a daily trial of all that's in us." He sobered even more.

I knew now that the next-to-last verse—"the rivers of woe shall not thee overflow"—was God's gift of comfort to me. Respect for my taciturn young adversary increased.

* * *

High spirited and friendly, the boy guerrillas were as intent on their practical jokes as unconcerned about the privations of their life. Cheerfully they rose in cold darkness to ride out; gleefully they trumpeted their successes. I was getting to know them. Fergus Blair, Mr. Lachlan's grandson, was the best hand with horses. Gareth Dunnachie, a piper's son, carried the flag. Robbie named me first.

"Now there're miles of line down and we've got the iron, and the Yankees won't hear from Washington City for *days*! What do you think of that, Uncle James!" His eyes shone with mischief and his grin showed all his strong, white teeth.

"The poor fellows won't know what to do." I was sure my compatriots would have the telegraph repaired by this time tomorrow.

The rejoinder sent them all into fresh laughter as they jostled toward the kettle. "Brunswick stew!" crowed Alex. "Three cheers for Mrs. Greig!"

My journeys with Mr. Lachlan soon brought me to the redoubtable Mrs. Greig. She pushed a crock of pickles aside to make room for the small keg of whiskey I set on the table. Less than a foot shorter than I, strong and trim of form, tidy coiffure setting off wise and kindly brown eyes. Mouth both stern and ready to smile, and the dignity of a queen.

"I'll see it gets to the doctor. Ye maun be Mr. MacLeod."

"Yes, ma'am." I removed my hat. "Have I the pleasure of meeting Mrs. Greig?"

"Aye."

"I hear of much you've done to aid the company."

"Och, the braw laddies! 'Tis but right to do all we can, wi' them in daily danger for our sakes." She handed me a squarish bundle. "Take this to Young Drummond and mind it does no' get dirty! And yon basket. Mayhap 'twill cheer him, for 'tis a man's burden he bears on a lad's shoulders. 'Twas aye his favorite, from a bairn."

"You must know him well."

"I brought him up, as much as his faither could no' do, widowed and a'."

"This is his home."

"Aye. Glenlochie o' the Drummonds." The basket smelled of fresh-baked bread. "Lest ye an' Mr. Lachlan be temptit, there's bannock and a wee pot o' preserves for ye twa."

"Lachlan's ready for the crates, the noo."

An older man entered the kitchen. Exiting across the porch, I heard him say, "Lachlan's seen bluebirds this side o' the Hazel." A code word for Union soldiers? Remembering the lieutenant in conference with Mr. Lachlan, I was sure the web of observation was widespread.

At supper, the contents of Mrs. Greig's basket were set out on the wide bench next to the kettle. The lieutenant's "favorite, from a bairn" was bread, butter, and strawberry preserves. Mrs. Greig must have known what he'd do with it. There was enough for everyone.

* * *

The scarred bodies of the wounded will be trophies of
valor and patriotism
—General Francis Henney Smith, 1864[10]

"Where's Willie?" I asked.

"Oh, he finally caught a bullet," said Donald. "The chief's patching him up."

"How bad is it?"

"Slight. Dunnachie's assisting."

"Now you're a real soldier!" said Robbie. "Show Uncle James where you're wounded."

We made room between us. Willie smelled of whiskey and looked pale, but he showed the bandaged right forearm with a proud little smile.

"It's my trumpet arm, but Caesar will let me hold the rein high and I can do both with my other one."

"Yes, but will Caesar like the trumpet blown right in his ears?" I smiled at his pride in being initiated.

"You smell like a still!" teased Aidan. "Did Torquil Dhu get you drunk?"

"He wouldn't! He hoards it like gold!" snorted Robbie.

"You'll be glad he does if *you* ever get shot!" Aidan was proud of being the first Ranger wounded.

Willie tried to stand up.

---

10 General Francis Henney Smith, report after the Battle of New Market, 1864. VMI Archives.

"Ye stay put," said Gareth. "I'll fetch ye a bite, the noo. Loudoun, fetch Menteith, Mr. Lachlan an' Keir, an' some o' yon food for Torquil Dhu. He wants to talk wi' ye."

David, the lieutenant, and another boy who came and went, attended medical instruction. They recited to one another till they had it by heart and practiced surgical procedures on the corresponding pieces of meat while studying directions from a manual. No one objected to the meat in the kettle next day! They often detailed me to assist with the wounded, for my strength to keep them immobile during surgery. After harvest, a score more of the Abercairn Shield joined the camp, including their captain, Ewen Murray, the other medical student.

The boys considered me a reference for mechanical knowledge, a judge of factual arguments, or a source of practical knowledge. Willie considered me a comforter.

"He was the only horse I had all my life, and now I'll never see him again!"

My arm around his shoulders, he lost the battle to be brave, buried his face against me, and sobbed. The other guerillas pretended not to notice. I let him settle his bedroll next to mine. Persistent rustling next to my ear wakened me later. Willie tiptoed into the passage. I followed, for fear that in his distress he might come to harm. When he came abreast of the lieutenant's quarters, the older boy spoke kindly.

"Trumpeter MacCay, report."

"I'm going to bury Caesar, and you can't stop me, Torquil Dhu!"

"Come in. We'll plan how you can do it." Candlelight glowed from the doorway. I heard Willie sit down.

"How big a grave will you need to dig?"

"Well, Caesar's about fifteen hands, and about the same length, I reckon, but there's his head. But his legs bend ... and I guess he could be lying down. Maybe with his head tucked around his shoulder like when he'd nuzzle my foot." Muffled sniffs.

By the time the lieutenant led him gently to the conclusion that granting his wish was impossible, Willie was yawning.

"I have an idea what you could do to honor Caesar. You could make a memorial stone with his name on it and set it up where everybody can see it."

"Then they'd think of him, wouldn't they?" The sound of a lightweight body lying down.

"Yes." A voice as soothing as a lullaby. "Early, early, before we report to the army, we'll go to Lachlans' so you can choose the horse Caesar would like to do his work. I can't take the field without my trumpeter." The voice stopped on almost a whisper.

Soft, regular breathing, then susurration of clothing. The lieutenant, coatless, in stocking feet, appeared in the doorway with an expression of tender pity on his face, carrying Willie. He didn't seem surprised to see me stretch out my arms.

"If he stays with me, I might waken him again. Good night, MacLeod."

* * *

Robbie considered me a source of advice.

"Uncle James, there's a girl ..." He blushed, ducked his head, gave full attention to kicking a stone.

I resisted the temptation to tease, *Only one?* His manners were handsome as his looks.

"... and I'll see her on Sabbath, 'cause it's communion and we're all going to kirk and I want to sit with her and I'm not sure whether to ask her or her mother or ask if she'd sit with me, and I was wondering whether she'd like to see me better in my Sabbath clothes or my uniform and. ..." He gave me a sidelong look.

"Are you sure the young lady will welcome your company?"

"Yes! That is, I'm mostly sure." His face flamed. "I think she would … I hope."

I was reminded of courting my Eleanor, but I couldn't indulge sorrow now.

I quoted etiquette and gave him West Point instruction and inspection for his uniform and accoutrements. Polished till he shone, he adorned the column. Even the incipient moustache looked handsome.

I could no longer think of the boys as guerillas. Dismissed at the kirk, they scattered to join their families. I took a seat near the back and looked over the congregation, surprised at how many I knew. Robbie sat self-consciously next to a girl wearing a modest bonnet.

The service was crowned by Holy Communion. I opened my heart and spirit to the memorial of Christ's sacrifice.

"Give us grace, O Holy heavenly Father, to consecrate ourselves to Him who has bought us with his own blood. Heal any backsliders … restore them to the joys of thy salvation. If there be strangers among us that love our Lord … may they come with glad hearts and unite with us in celebrating the love of Jesus, at his table."

Keir and the minister served the bread and wine. I joined the communicants, heart smitten by the deceit I was practicing. I confessed it silently and prayed for forgiveness.

"Let us, O Lord … experience spiritual refreshment and comfort. Impart to us, we beseech Thee, some fresh tokens of thy gracious presence. Quicken our faith … *let not one soul go unblest away.*"

I was blessed: I recognized why the boys had created me their Uncle James. They were lending me the place of all their fathers, dead or at war, who weren't here this morning. I was humbly grateful.

After the benediction, going toward the door, Robbie's girl rested her gloved hand in the crook of his arm. Fair and blue-eyed as he, she raised her eyes shyly when he spoke.

"Your sermon gave me much to think about, sir," I said to the minister.

"May your thoughts bring ye blessing."

Willie ran up, stopped in one step. "My mother would like it if you and Miss Gilchrist would come to dinner at our house, and you, too, Uncle James."

* * *

"Though their methods are appalling, from a strict Christian standpoint, the abolitionists are right," declared Miss Gilchrist.

Younger than her brother, she had not a thread of gray in her auburn hair, but the same blue eyes, full of light. Her fair, fine-grained skin was unaged except for tiny laughter lines around eyes and rose-lipped mouth. Her color heightened becomingly with the ardor of her statement.

"The Epistles recognize slavery as a natural part of society, and St. Paul makes no suggestion of abolishing it, ma'am." I congratulated myself for what I thought a proper response.

"My reasoning goes closer to the source. Jesus taught, we're to love our neighbors as ourselves, and that all people, in a sense, are our neighbors, even those who are very different. I should never subject myself to slavery, therefore, I shouldn't subject anyone else. That seems to me what the abolitionists are saying."

"With the addition of venomous hatred, and their purpose to destroy us all by the vilest means they can invent!" I feigned fuming. "While doing business at the North, our family noticed they don't practice what they preach! Black people there are despised, and kept degraded—hovels for housing, only menial labor. They're barred from many public places.

"But I haven't seen any slaves around here. Are they all hired out to the army, or run away to the Yankees?"

"In the spirit of the Revolution, liberty being the first principle, some of us took action," Dominie Gilchrist explained. "The Virginia legislature granted the right to manumit slaves. The General Assembly of the Presbyterian Kirk reinforced us in 1787, ordaining that we should prepare the slaves for freedom and then abolish slavery.

"By then, Abercairn had already done the work. We had before us the example of some of the first families of Virginia, Randolphs and Carters who freed their slaves and made provision for them to earn their livings, by deeding them land and other help. We did much the same. By unanimous sanction against it, we rid ourselves of it entirely—and keep it out."

"But that's not lawful!"

"That's so. In the 1830s, with a bill before the Assembly to emancipate all slaves within the State, our legislators were considering a number of plans, keeping in mind the welfare of the enslaved people as well as compensation for their owners.

"The Northern states had begun vilifying the South, most unjustly. I do *not* say there was no economic or political motive! Our citizens and legislators took such umbrage at the hatred and false accusations that the plans were tabled. It was a tragic failing of human nature, not to persevere in the good work. After the Nat Turner massacre, more stringent laws were passed.

"In practice, however, laws concerning black people are enforced according to the perceived degree of danger. We have chosen here to annul the danger and do without those laws. Would it were so throughout Virginia!"

* * *

Robbie returned to the cave last, minutes before the sunset deadline, interspersing his usual modest swagger with a few dance steps, hat at a jaunty angle, a bemused expression on his face, humming "Lorena" to himself. I didn't see who started whistling "The Girl I Left Behind Me," but in a trice, the Rangers all took it up. Several bars were required to pierce Robbie's reverie.

"Oh, pshaw!" He made a dismissive gesture, but grinned, did another dance step, and bowed.

Only he could have carried it off. He dipped out soup and poured it back into the kettle. The nearest Rangers hooted, but it didn't register. When he sat down, he realized he had no soup. He grinned foolishly and pretended to empty the empty cup over his head.

* * *

I am a pore harted sinner and got no chance to be no other way, for I ain't got no Bible. Yankees want us to lose our soles, same as our lifes.
—Joseph Cowan, Confederate soldier, letter to cousin, December 1, 1862

. . . the side which possessed a navy shut out from the other as contraband of war the medicines necessary to the saving of human life . . . the blockade was to this extent a part of that savagery which makes war upon the sick and wounded . . . .

But none of this availed against the untiring pluck and audacity of the inland blockade-breakers. Daily the lines were forced, spies evaded . . . . Such ventures brought small supplies of much-needed medicines, surgical instruments and necessaries for the sick. They braved the roughness of camp and the long, icy rides to the river—often through hostile lines that caused hiding by day and progress only at night—to what was known as the 'Potomac Ferry.'[11]

As sentinel one piercing cold night, I heard hoofbeats ringing on the frozen road below. The rider came at a perilous gallop. Just as I sensed hoofbeats of others following, the first whirled up to me.

"Halt! Who goes there!"

"Never mind that nonsense!" gasped a girl's voice. "I've got to make them think I took the wrong road! Turn your back!"

"Friend or foe?"

"Friend, you ninny-hammer! Turn your back!"

I took the chance. Rough, hasty rustling of garments. The rider's hat fell at my feet.

"Here!" A tousled slip of a girl adjusted her balance in the sidesaddle. She thrust a petticoat at me and grabbed her hat from my hand. "It's medicine. Give it to the boys!"

She wheeled her horse, jamming the hat on her head as she urged the animal to descend. The other hoofbeats had reached the foot of the road: I couldn't call very loudly.

"Corporal of the Guard! Post Number One!"

I heard the girl leave the road to shortcut between its hairpin turns and intercept the other riders. She cried out as though surprised, and fled. The others gave chase. They'd almost passed out of earshot when Gareth arrived. He was away before I finished reporting.

Within minutes the lieutenant, teeth clenched amid the desperate expression on his face, led a party of a dozen crashing through the brush to cut a diagonal to the girl and her pursu-

---

11 George Cary Eggleston, *History of the Confederate War;* Thomas Cooper De Leon, C. S. A., *Four Years in Rebel Capitals,* respectively.

ers. Gareth showed me bags of precious medicine sewn into the petticoat.

"Yon lass is Nannie, MacHugh's twin. She tellit us Communion Sabbath, she and her aunt would run the blockade. The Bibles are at her Aunt Bess's hoose."

"Bibles?"

"Ken ye naught! The Yankees made God's Word contraband, too!"

* * *

The Rangers rode with the army or made attacks of their own, returning with coats, warm clothing, boots, shoes, and blankets for the county, the army and themselves. Their prize capture was a Union sutler's wagons carrying festive food and merchandise for Christmas.

I walked outdoors after supper wearing a Union greatcoat. Mrs. Greig had worked with homemade dyes till the coats were no longer blue but a brownish gray. My breath billowed in the light of the half-moon. Snow from past storms lay drifted among the crags. I smiled over Robbie mimicking the despoiled sutler's threats. My heart warmed to his generous heart and unfailing good humor, but I liked all the boys, especially since I'd realized why they took me to their hearts. I'd gladly have been Uncle James till the war was over—and beyond—but it was threatening my mission.

I had enough information. I need only capture Black Drummond, who'd no doubt bear prison in the same stoic manner he lived—if he weren't executed out of hand. I'd do it tonight, before I became further enmeshed in this likeable little company and their web of friends and relatives.

Had the Rangers been the vicious guerillas I was told they were, I'd gladly help destroy them—but they're children! My conscience revolted against making war on them: earnest partners in the quarrels of their elders, innocent of any intention beyond the adventure of their young lives while protecting their homes and families. I cut off paternal thoughts.

The lieutenant, on the other hand, studied the enemy, made the plans, kept discipline, and, though courteously deferential to Ewen, led. He was the spirit and backbone of the company. Command seemed natural in him. He trod precisely the line between familiarity and the respect necessary for effective command, seldom appearing among his men and having no easy dialogue with them. Only Ewen seemed close to him.

He had no spark of cheer. All that was light seemed consumed by his calling. Too wise for his years, never an emotion tempered his icy rationality. Yet I remembered his sympathy and patience in turning Willie back from a passionate but perilous errand, and his desperate concern to rescue Nannie.

It wasn't awkward calling him "sir." He's a gentleman; unfeigned young dignity merits the courtesy. Like him I did not. His curt manner kept him isolated and unknowable.

The capture must be at gunpoint: by surprise, alone, in the dead of night, in his quarters, while the others slept. I arranged horses. Later, by the faint light of cookfire embers, I belted on my revolver. I'd stop the sentries by threatening to shoot their chief. The candle in the passage deepened rather than dispelled the darkness. In the lieutenant's quarters, I drew the revolver.

"The earth will move soon." Patrician voice just outside the entrance! "I think its strength varies with the phases of the moon, like the tides do, but I haven't devised an accurate way to measure it. The exact timing may vary likewise, but it's always between two and three in the morning."

I tried to level the revolver, but I couldn't raise my arm. It was paralyzed!

"I thought I heard something, sir."

The eagle gaze took in my hat and greatcoat.

"It's possible. Sounds are different in the clarity of darkness. Thank you for your vigilance. Dismissed."

I catfooted down the passage in wonder. My arm had refused to move, regardless of intention and strength! Now I could level the revolver unhindered. I'd failed to do my duty, but was not guilty. Angry, I was: I felt foolish and ineffectual. I couldn't have deceived the lieutenant. Why hadn't he put me under guard? Back in my blankets, I prayed silently.

'Holy God, You know I serve my country. Yet tonight I obeyed my orders and was prevented! Did the power that stopped me come from You? I don't pretend to know your ways. I place this confusion before You. Please lead me to resolution. Show me what You would have me do! In Jesus' name, Amen.'

2. Granite Bend

Reveille sounded in a cave should be unlawful! was my first thought when Willie blasted us out of our blankets. I jumped up to release the horses while it was still dark, shrugging into my greatcoat while long strides carried me around some Rangers and over others.

"Private MacLeod, report," the patrician voice snapped.

I snapped— to attention, and saluted in the entrance. The boy stood at a high shelf fastened to the wall, pen in hand and a partially written report before him. A hand-drawn map hung above the shelf. His bedroll was folded beside a wooden chest with a well-read Bible lying on top, next to a few books and the candlestick on an ammunition crate. It was a wonder I hadn't knocked something galley-west—loudly—last night!

"You are assigned to the field. See Sergeant Loudoun for your equipments. Dismissed."

* * *

In the open instead of confined by the cave, I'd have a better chance at him. The Rangers were to support recovery of a section of the railroad from Union control. They reported for orders to a major who seemed to know them well.

"I want you to scout into Granite Bend. We're going to occupy it. That'll give us a link with our camps along the Rapidan and draw the enemy away from your position. It's a supply depot. You boys are welcome to all you can use.

"Lieutenant, go. Send word of their strength, positions, movements, guns, and all."

The lieutenant gestured, Forward! to someone I couldn't see and put his horse ahead at a lope. Riding along a wooded lane parallel to the rail line, I heard only hoofbeats and jingle of accoutrements till a train of cars rumbled and clanked to where Union control ended at a barrier of logs. It stopped with a squeal of driving wheels and clouds of smoke and steam.

From boxcars poured hundreds of Union soldiers. Their commander deployed them, anchoring his center on the log barrier. We were within Union lines, but Ewen increased the pace. The chuff, clack-clack, and roar of the returning train blotted out all other sound.

Gunfire ahead! The column drummed across a wooden bridge over an ice-edged stream dancing around an outcrop of granite, before we passed a straggle of weather-worn cottages. Town center was blurred by powder smoke. Shotgun blasts punctuated the crackle of musketry.

> It is very desirable to arouse the people, and to induce as many as possible to come forward and meet this special emergency, and with such arms as they may have.
> —General Thomas J. "Stonewall" Jackson,
> Confederate States Army, May 3, 1862

From behind a high sledge of dilapidated wagon boxes and broken fence rails tied together, and pushed by a couple of oxen, a little crowd of old men and young boys, wielding the widest assortment of weapons I ever saw, advanced across iron-frozen ground toward a Union skirmish line holding the entrance to a wide road leading north. In our front, beyond the town, cannoneers on a high knoll pivoted their pieces to bring them to bear on the citizens.

> A plunging fire is of all others the most inaccurate, especially when the target is moving towards the guns.
> —Jennings Cropper Wise, *The Military History of the Virginia Military Institute*

Ewen sent the left half of the column with Gareth and the flag to attack the Union right flank and rear, in support of the citizens. He led the rest of us galloping in a rank of drumming hooves, tossing manes and tails, and crescendo of yelling. We jumped fences and dodged outbuildings, into the face of black cannon mouths fast-firing solid shot from above. Surprised by a coherent idea in the midst of it, I thought my countrymen should be using double-shotted canister if they hoped to break a charge at such close range. The ground trembled from concussion, but the horses adapted to the shocks. The guns' muzzles weren't depressed enough, or we'd have been annihilated. Solid shot thumped through the air and shattered structures behind us.

Willie sounded, Halt!

"Ready ... aim ... fire!" Not a gun crew remained intact.

"Fire!" Scarce a cannoneer was left standing, but remnants of crews gathered in a frenzy to a couple of the pieces.

Willie sounded the Charge: we burst to the Gallop. The rounds landed behind us. We overran the battery before the cannoneers could reload. The Rangers gathered prisoners and hitched cannon to limbers.

"Follow me!" Ewen led off at the Trot.

Billowing black smoke showed the locomotive keeping steam up. The lieutenant and an old man herded the engineer and fireman out of the cab. With a metallic, explosive hiss, the safety valve blew off steam. The old man left all but four boxcars on a siding and backed the train to be loaded.

"We're going to carry four guns to the front." The lieutenant pointed. "Look in the freight houses for rope to tie them down. Load a dozen of those railroad ties in each car."

While we steamed to the front, the Rangers knocked boards off the sides of the cars to make gunports. The train shuddered to a stop a couple hundred yards from the barrier, sand applied to the tracks making the driving wheels grind and stutter. The Confederate infantry had pushed back the Union foot. Fighting was heavy all along the line.

"Aim the gun left, at a twenty-degree angle to the car, and leave room to serve it."

"It'll recoil completely back in, sir! It could break through the opposite side! The ammunition's too close!" I protested in alarm.

"Pile those ties behind the wheels to absorb the recoil. Move the limber chest away."

Each boxcar carried a twelve-pounder Napoleon howitzer. The lieutenant supervised gun emplacements, directed crews, and saw the pieces cleansed, then loaded with canister—"canned trouble," the soldiers call it. He set the elevating screw to fire point-blank, a level trajectory. The muzzles could have been elevated a degree to good effect, but I didn't say so.

The Rebels charged the barrier and took it, driving the Union line of battle in upon its left. Their commander re-formed his men to meet the onslaught. The lieutenant studied the action through field glasses. I saw the Rebel signal.

"Cannoneers! Post on the piece!" He shouted the order down the train. "Fire!"

The report boomed and reverberated. The gun leaped high against the pile of railroad ties. We cleansed and reloaded while the lieutenant surveyed where the shots took effect. Windrows of blue lay where canister had mown down men.

"Fire!"

As slowly as I could, hoping to retard the rate of fire, I soaked the sponge and thrust it down the barrel. The gun in the next car fired before I had to ram the charge. Again the canister, twenty-nine small metal balls in each case, scythed swaths out of the Union lines. The lieutenant ran from gun to gun, directing the fire to avoid hitting the Rebels closing in. At last the Union commander waved a white flag.

Robbie

"Those poor fellows are going to have a bad Christmas." I looked out at the file of prisoners marching past under guard. Beyond them, hospital details cared for the wounded.

Torquil Dhu opened the splintered door. "We're going to load the wounded into the cars. Secure the guns and make room. Kendrick, pass that order along."

I did, jumped off the final boxcar, and sauntered to where Major Willis met with his officers.

"My aide tells me you have an idea, Private Kendrick."

"Yes, sir. We captured all the Yankees' stores, didn't we?"

"I'm told we did."

"Well, sir, all those Yankees are going to prison, aren't they?"

"Yes."

"It's going to be a mighty unhappy Christmas for them, sir. Could we give them a good meal before they go, and maybe some food to take with them?"

"Those are excessively kind thoughts about our enemies!"

"But sir, the Lord's word says, 'If thine enemy hunger, feed him,' and it's almost Christmas, and if the lieutenant agrees, we'll take it out of our share of the stores. You said we could have all we could use."

"Very well! Tell your scheme to your captain. If he agrees, tell him to report to me."

MacLeod

The Rangers were reserves who could be called to join with Imboden's Shenandoah Valley army. Major Willis was their link to the larger force. I stored these facts in my mind.

In full dark, going to care for Redspeed, I counted Rangers returning: I'd be alone with the lieutenant. In the middle of the Rebel encampment, but in the dark, I could escape with my prisoner. I know the country fairly well by now. I was unarmed, but a man. A boy's strength could be no match for mine.

"Sooooo, laddie. ... Whiiisht noo ... whiiisht."

The lieutenant, holding a pot of ointment, was intent upon a fidgeting, bullet-grazed gelding. To preserve silence, I snapped my right hand up to deliver the punch that will kill a rabbit or stun a man—and the gelding reared, kicking. The lieutenant backstepped right into me.

"Hold his head!" He recovered the little pot from soft straw where it hadn't broken.

Robbie

The prisoners were marched away next day. When they passed our cookfire, they cheered. "Three cheers for Kendrick! Hip, hip, HUZZAH! HUZZAH!"

My friends jostled me forward and made me acknowledge. I ducked my head and muttered, "Oh, pshaw!" but watched the bluejackets trudge along. Near the end came a fellow who had no coat. I shed my greatcoat as I met him and handed it over.

MacLeod

The lieutenant and Ewen took it in turn to command their base on Christmas Eve and Christmas Day, giving half the Rangers home leave on each. I accepted Ewen's invitation.

Murrays' stout house was of the local granite, with tall windows and a massive front door. Ewen's father, an auburn bear of a man wearing a kilt, was on leave to subsist himself and his horse. With a brawny arm around my shoulders as if I were a long-lost friend, he drew me to the fireside and settled me with a cup of eggnog in a comfortable chair.

"This," he said, still standing as he raised his cup, "would hae been a stirrup cup. Lang syne, meseems, we went a-hunting on the morn o' Christmas Eve. But we a' have our hearts-full o' hunting Northmen noo, so we weel cherish the fireside until we hunt again.

"To the season o' the Christ, and to a', His salvation!"

Ewen and I stood. "To all, His salvation!"

"'Tis no' usual for a man o' your years to be wi' our sons, Mr. McLeod."

I told my blockade-runner story. "I hoped to join this company because they're active and successful. I didn't expect to be the eldest."

Ewen sat back and let the conversation flow over him. He seemed to be basking in the strength and warmth of father and home.

"It's struck me this is the only place in America I've seen Scots wearing kilts. You must take pleasure in keeping our traditions."

"Och! Did ye no' ken the Queen made it the fashion! In her castle at Braemar, she hath the plaids e'en o'er the windows! The

Sassenach wi' the olive branch, mayhap! I like the freedom. I would no' wear the kilt to war, but on his ain lands, a man may have his ain weel!"

"A great will and a good one it is, that keeps the land and all of us in heart!"

We rose as Mrs. Murray entered. She was fair and slightly freckled, with fine blonde hair and brown eyes. I saw where Ewen got his looks. *"Clothed all in green, O,"* I thought, for so she was, with a sprig of holly tucked into the smooth coil of her hair, and the slender grace of rushes in her movements. A little boy and girl came with her.

"Mother, this is Mr. MacLeod. Mr. MacLeod, my mother."

I bowed over her hand. This was the kind of house and the kind of company where it seemed right and not outmoded. At home, I'd merely have shaken hands.

"It's a pleasure of pleasures to meet you, Mrs. Murray."

"I'm happy to meet you. Children, this is Mr. MacLeod. This is Mary."

A small replica of her mother dropped a graceful curtsey. I bowed to her.

"This is William."

Auburn-haired and tawny-eyed, he gave a gap-toothed grin and offered his right hand. I shook it ceremoniously. Mrs. Murray embraced Ewen. The children came to me like iron to a magnet.

"Are you really a pirate?" asked William. "You don't look like one."

"I wear my gold earring and carry my knife in my teeth only at sea."

"Do you have a parrot that talks?"

"I had to leave him on board ship. He's afraid of horses."

"Which one is your wooden leg?"

"Wulliam, be no' impertinent! Pirates maun hae a secret or twa!"

"I think you're really Uncle James, not a pirate."

"I have that honor. You've found me out, Miss Mary."

"Oh, I'm so glad. The big boys all say you're very clever and kind."

"They may speak a better opinion than I deserve."

* * *

Alex had taken the Rangers' flag home to have their first battle honors recorded. At the top edge of the blue field, beside the St. Andrew's Cross, was embroidered: "Granite Bend."

CHAPTER 7

"THE BRAVEST ARE THE TENDEREST, THE LOVING ARE THE DARING."[12]

1. Compromise

Defeat was one thing for the volunteer soldiers in the ranks, but for the regular army men who had gone in with the Confederacy it was something more dire. And especially if those army regulations dealing with officers who deserted and took up arms for the enemy were to be applied.

—Gerard A. Patterson, *Rebels from West Point*

MacLeod

Every time I tried to capture the lieutenant, I was prevented by the power beyond my own. Only God would stop me so consistently and harmlessly—why? On the next Communion

---

12 From "Song of the Camp" by Bayard Taylor.

Sunday, I used the rest of the day's leave to call upon Dominie Gilchrist. Miss Gilchrist sat in a wing chair at a little distance from the fireplace in the parlor.

"It's good to see you again."

"The pleasure is all mine." I bowed over her hand. "I hope you're keeping well and warm, these frosty days." I chose the chair nearest hers.

"All the earth is like stone, isn't it. It's hard to imagine that when the year has half turned, we shall feel too warm."

"Yet every year we take it on faith. God's faithful to tell us what we can expect, though it's not always easy to be sure what He expects of us, in the minutiae of living. Perhaps you've had the experience of trying to do what you're sure He wants you to do, and being prevented."

"I once had words of advice in mind, but when I spoke, I said the exact opposite! Later I learned it was the right thing to say. I still marvel over it."

"Thought-provoking! I'm having some similar experiences, and I'd like to consult your brother about them."

Dominie Gilchrist

"Come with me. In a hundred years, our manse is become a maze!" I led him around the unexpectable corners and closed the study door against chill drafts from the hall.

"My sister says ye have a spiritual puzzle to solve."

"I've tried a dozen times to carry out a certain order and, every time, been prevented by power beyond my own. I think God may be preventing me, but I don't know why He should. It's reasonable and just, and I've sworn to obey and do my duty."

"Perhaps your duty is beyond what ye know. Your order may not be in accord with his will. He tells us to obey civil and kirk authority, but He is above both. Ye know 'His ways are higher than our ways, and His thoughts than our thoughts.' Perhaps He wants ye to do something else. Is it an either-or matter?"

"Yes."

"What would be the opposite? We are to obey God, not men, if commands conflict."

"But ... that would mean I don't have to do it."

"Does that agree with your conscience?"

"Yes and no, because I've sworn to obey my superiors' orders."

"Which is your higher allegiance—God or man?"

"God, of course."

"Then ye must expect to suffer at the hands of men."

His expression softened, as if the stark fact began to bring him peace.

"But other things hinge on that particular action."

"Ye might ask what conscience bids ye do."

His countenance brightened as though a lamp were lit behind it.

"Its bidding would be pure joy!"

"Ye hesitate only because of your orders?"

"Yes."

"What is the penalty for disobeying them?"

"Loss of my occupation, death, dishonor."

I honored the gravity of his decision by a long silence.

"Ye are called to risk much to obey God. Are ye willing?"

"Yes! I must be sure, however, what is His will."

"Think ye not that your conscience reveals it?"

"It must."

"Are ye Presbyterian?"

"No, Methodist."

"Calvinist doctrine—I am not sure of the Wesleyan—declares the right to resist unjust rulers, and to rebel against immoral policy. Some consider it a duty. 'Tis a matter for your conscience, whether disobeying your superiors, in this case, might come within that providence."

"That must be the precedent." He relaxed his tense posture. "Thank you, sir. I believe you've pointed me toward correct conclusions."

MacLeod

I stayed chatting a while with Miss Gilchrist—and letting my thoughts sort themselves out!—while I enjoyed her conversation.

"If your countenance is an indicator, your heart must be lighter than when you arrived."

"Yes. There are matters to refine, but my general direction is clear. Your brother's mind is keenly honed."

"'Iron sharpens iron,' Scripture says. Your own is no less so."

"I shouldn't have suspected a minister's sister of flattery!"

I smiled to allay any suspicion of insult. She smiled, showing a dimple next to her rose-pink mouth, but hardening her lips the smallest bit for emphasis.

"None was spoken."

* * *

The only privacy I had was behind closed eyelids, under my blankets, after the Rangers settled to sleep. That the army could be wrong was an alien idea. It demands obedience of its soldiers to lessen chaos on the field of battle. The idea of higher law— easy to misuse—was anathema. If I were to act contrary to my orders, why God had brought me here? He must have used us all—myself, the intelligence service, and Sharpe who plucked me out of the Engineers for his lying, underhanded spy system—to accomplish a purpose I didn't know.

No more attempts to capture the brusque lieutenant. But too late, now I'd served the howitzer that mowed down my compatriots, to do no harm to my own side.

Even so, I smiled because the battle with my conscience was over. It was a simple matter of choosing the right. Man's retribution might take away my life. If I were spared, my name would be reviled by brother officers in the service to which I'd given twenty years of my life. I'd dare both for the children's sake.

The first duty of a prisoner of war is to escape, but the lieutenant didn't trust me alone in the field. The Intelligence Bureau should have put a roving scout in the vicinity, for me to pass information to, but I'd met none. How could I protect these ardent children and yet report so as to satisfy the Bureau? Showing I'd performed my duty was crucial to keeping my occupation.

When the lieutenant sent away all his men and stayed alone to delay the enemy, I worried about the Rangers' welfare. They'd be easy prey without his direction. Perhaps his danger was how God intended, all along, to remove such a nuisance to my army. The Almighty didn't need my help to accomplish it: that must be why I'd been prevented. I was persuading myself with that line of rationalizing when Willie came to me.

"Uncle James, where does it fit? I got it all back together but this."

He opened a grease-grimed hand to display a curved bit of steel. I tested the actions of the pistol while he leaned closer to watch. I smiled, glancing down at his tousled brown hair, reminded of Davie watching intently when we worked on guns together.

The horror I thought was banished exploded in my mind: Davie's body, mortally torn by the train wreck, lifeblood gone, yet my child's face untouched. I froze in midmotion. My face must have mirrored my anguish, for I woke to the present only when Willie spoke.

"What's the matter?" He looked worried, almost frightened.

I pretended to misunderstand. "That piece you have is the sear and bolt spring. The trigger won't work without it. See here."

I reassembled the mechanism, swearing to myself that none of these amiable children would be torn and killed if I could prevent it. I found the lieutenant returning to the cave and stepped into his path.

"May I speak privately with you a moment, sir?"

He gestured a way that would keep us within sight, but out of the sentinels' hearing.

"I'm concerned, sir, that you risk yourself too much. It's a detriment to the command."

"Why?"

"They depend upon your direction for success and survival. Without it, they would be vulnerable to defeat and destruction."

"They have another commander."

"Yes, sir, but if I may make the observation, he is staff, while you are line. Field operations depend upon you."

"You know how a command is organized. Regular Army?"

"Yes."

"Then you will appreciate the weighing of risks. The danger in being last to quit the field is least for me. It is therefore the rational course to take."

"But—"

"Private, the probationary period of your service is not ended! I shall send you to the provost if you are guilty of insubordination. Dismissed!"

* * *

Called upon twice to drive off destroyers coming ever closer, the Rangers suffered greater casualties, but recruits straggled in during the cold weather. By the end of February, the company numbered about sixty. In March, General Ulysses "Sam" Grant came East to take command of all the Union armies. If he followed the same strategy he'd used in the West, the war might soon be over: he battered at his objectives till he won them. With the coastal blockade, control of the Mississippi, and keeping the Confederates out of the North, the Union was tightening its noose.

I failed several times to escape. Was God's will in this, too, the opposite of my orders? I had to play my part as convincingly as lack of guile permitted, but without killing my own countrymen. If ever forced to it, I could not. If I didn't, the Rangers would know me for a spy, and the lieutenant would have me shot.

So be it.

There's more than one way to die for one's country. If I killed Union soldiers, I'd have broken my oath and be guilty of their deaths. If I ever crossed that Rubicon, I'd be a traitor.

'Holy God,' I prayed silently, 'what would You have me do? You have shown me what You forbid. Show your servant, I pray You, what action to take, what course to follow, to accomplish your will. In Jesus' name, Amen.'

"Wait on the Lord!" came in instant answer to my prayer.

I scowled. I'd obey, of course, but I hated blundering forward with no specific goal in view. I gave obedience silently: 'I commit my way unto thee, O God.'

2. *Crossing the Rubicon*

> Our life is a sad struggle;—our material nature … tethers the soul.
> —General Philip St. George Cooke, *Scenes and Adventures in the Army*

Black Drummond, eagle stooping on his prey,
Today in one place,
Tomorrow west of their expecting,
Again where least they looked for him,
Rapt prisoners here,
Rifles there,
Wagons of supplies in other places—
And was gone
As though a vapor distilled into the air,
As though his hills had swallowed him,
As though clear water plunged down canyon rapids.

While initiative was his,
He eluded their snares as quicksilver,
Leaving behind the sprung trap
With cruel-toothed jaws still starved.

They caught sight of him but rarely
When he toyed with their traps,
But he advanced, young solid flesh,
From woods that hid his men's escape,
White handkerchief in thin up-pointing fingers,
Forward, slowly,
Saying,
"I am the one you want."
Thinking,
'They've gone free.'

"Do with me as you please."

They bound him in irons,
Then paraded through the camp
A creature soaring still
Through ranks of plodding foes

Whose hunt had always failed
Till he gave himself to them.

Wearing ferrous fetters as he would
Gold bracelets of Viking days,
Gold ankle jewels of Pharoah's age,
He stood surrounded by his enemies
To face the highest of them all,
Calm confidence in
Face and stance and voice.

His life was forfeit by no treachery,
Nor skill nor power of theirs,
Nor by mistake of his,
But by his sacrificial choice.

Serene smile scarcely touched his lips;
Eternal joy glowed warmly in his eyes;
For he could go to his true Home,
And live with his best-loved.

Torquil

I'd expected to escape, but I was too closely bound, too closely guarded.

I was barefoot. Leg irons bruised my bones and gashed my feet and ankles. Handcuffs, tight iron bracelets connected by an eight-inch bar, forced me to move both hands at once, or a sharp jerk would cut the flesh again. In the hot April sun, my sweat stung the raw spots. They'd kept me chained to a post like a dog, for two days now. Why were they waiting? I thought I'd be hanged or shot immediately.

No matter, only a delay on the way Home. I tried to fight off the allure, but I was eager to go, and be purified, and see Da and Douglas again. It wasn't much sacrifice, laying down the burden of temporal life to enter eternal life. I hoped God would consider it acceptable. I trusted my Creator knew I hadn't sinned by throwing away His gift of life. My life for my men's lives seemed right. The commander must be not only servant of all but sacrifice for all if the need arose. Two days ago, I had no other means of getting them safe away.

"I have fought a good fight, I have finished my course, I have kept the faith," I quoted from Saint Paul. 'And I've done my duty in the last opportunity.'

'Dear God, I want to come Home! O, Lord, how long?'

MacLeod

Garbed in a Union brigadier general's uniform, in a War Department carriage rolling into a Union encampment, I startled when drums thundered. Infantrymen poured into company streets to form up. Officers before them, they awaited two ruffles of drumbeats, when the colors dropped, officers saluted, and the men presented arms—to me!

The lieutenant, chained to a post beside the commanding officer's tent, sat upright, with dignity, watching the disguised Rangers from under lowered brows.

Returning the salutes of the colonel and his staff, I adopted a haughty demeanor.

"Colonel, we're from Secretary Stanton, to conduct the prisoner to him. Captain, the orders."

I shot a gauntleted hand at Ewen without looking at him. We did the business of transfer.

"Will you join us, sir, in a toast to celebrate this long-awaited event?"

"With pleasure, sir, but the Secretary's train has steam up. We shall conclude without further ceremony. May I trouble you for the prisoner's effects and the keys to his bonds."

We were escorted out of the tent while the guards bundled the lieutenant roughly into the carriage. At the Trot we cleared the camp and pickets, turned onto the depot road, followed it to the obscure trail that led to Abercairn Court House. From there we galloped.

As Ewen unlocked the handcuffs, I saw sadness in the lieutenant's eyes. With the eerie feeling that I was seeing into his very soul, I turned my mind away from the intrusion. I sighed within myself with regret for insignia of rank I might never wear. But I was grateful, having recognized no one in the Union camp, that I could be almost sure no one recognized me.

The lieutenant set his hat on his head, stretched and worked his arms and legs. Then he stiffened back into the seat and demanded, "How dare you risk the whole command!"

"Unanimously." Ewen was calm. He took a flask and a roll of bandage from his pockets. "Hold out your hands and feet."

"It's not significant!"

"If gangrene sets in, they'll rot off. Hold out your hands and feet ... *Lieutenant!*"

He scowled. "Yes, sir." When Ewen washed the cuts with whiskey, he scowled harder.

* * *

At the cave, the lieutenant thanked his men sincerely and followed it with a dressing down that failed to damp their jubilant spirits. He reminded them of their duty to Abercairn and thanked God they hadn't all been hanged, before he went outside. I followed, kicking loose stones to warn of my approach, to the niche overlooking the glen.

"State your purpose!"

"Again I petition you to guard yourself better, sir. The men without you are like the proverbial sheep without a shepherd."

"It's the commander's duty to lead, which puts him in the forefront, where only God decides whether he will fall. He offers himself as a sacrifice for his country. What matter how it be slain?"

"I beg to differ, sir. This command depends upon you." I felt like a schoolmaster repeating the lesson for a dull pupil. "As an example, see how foolhardy an action they undertook in your absence. Do you not see that all your lives are entwined? Without you, they operated rashly. Sufficient losses among them would leave Abercairn in worse danger. Is it not your duty to preserve yourself for all their sakes?"

"There are factors in my decisions you know nothing about. When your knowledge increases, so will the worth of your counsel. Thank you for your concern. Mine is no less. Dismissed!"

I burned to brave the dismissal and try again. Behind the artless eloquence of his words, the lieutenant's emotion was held in check by only the thinnest thread. Again I had the unearthly sensation of seeing into his soul. The boy was near to breaking.

Then a flash of revelation told me I had to stay at this camp with him! It was more real than blood and breath! If I provoked him into sending me away, I'd fail to accomplish my Maker's purpose.

"Yes, sir." I saluted and strode away.

I'm a rational man, accustomed to solving problems by mathematics or straightforward logic. Personal direction from God was still new. If I chose—even at God's command—to stay with the Rangers, I became a turncoat, an object of contempt in my own eyes. Never mind the joy of being Uncle James, never mind growing friendships with Abercairn citizens, never mind my increasing hatred of being a fraud among them: those were temptations luring me from the path of duty.

To my previous plea for direction, God had answered, *Wait on the Lord.*

Was I to go on as before and see what I'd be forbidden next? It was galling to my sense of purpose, but, determined to trust God, I obeyed.

Torquil

MacLeod had an awful stomp when he was crossed, but at last I could be alone. Was he right about the Rangers' survival depending on me? Was it my duty and no one else's? I had to admit their foolhardy rescue made it look that way, but it was my duty to take the risks on their behalf. They all had families who loved and needed them, and would need them more once the war was over: I alone had no one. That the whole Shield was dependent on me was too overwhelming to believe. Was it as necessary to live for my men and neighbors, as I'd thought, three days ago, it was necessary to die? I surrendered.

'Here I am, dear God. Do with me as You please.'

MacLeod

Precipitous terrain. The lieutenant had dispatched most of the Rangers downhill, out of sight. Only he, Robbie, and I held the sharp ridge crest against the pursuit. My countrymen were a small detachment, but tenacious, fixing bayonets and forming for a charge—acting like hunters closing on their quarry! The back of my neck prickled. I reloaded with care and precision.

Robbie shoved cartridges fast into the magazine beneath the barrel of his Henry and balanced himself on a tree root; his feet were slipping on a slope slick from recent rain. The lieutenant held the left end of the line; I was about ten yards away, Robbie a few feet to my left. We could just see over the crest.

The Unionists charged at a run. The lieutenant downed one, then another. Robbie hit his man with each shot. I aimed to miss and succeeded. The last few were within eight paces. First the lieutenant, then Robbie, downed an enemy. Then the rest were upon us.

Two taking long strides raced at Robbie. His magazine jammed. He was desperately trying to ram cartridges past a dent when they drove their steel straight at him.

I leaped in a diagonal, shouldered Robbie tumbling down to safety—and shot to kill.

I'd crossed my Rubicon before I knew my feet were wet.

* * *

That night I lay exhausted while my mind refused to release me to slumber. I saw my countrymen run upon me, fall contorted, run upon me again. Joy at saving Robbie was subsumed in horror at killing them face-to-face. I went outside, paced up and down the rock ledge.

However they punished me, I deserved it. They couldn't condemn me worse than I condemned myself: I was a traitor. Throwing off my hat, I dropped to my knees in the lieutenant's niche and raised my hands in supplication.

'Most Holy God, what have I done!'

I confessed my sin, with tears for all I'd destroyed: honor, righteousness, colleagues' and country's good opinion, my whole life's work.

A choice between those strangers in blue and defenseless Robbie: I made it by instinct. Faced with the same choice, I'd do the same again.

I pleaded with God for forgiveness, until—all in a rush!—my spirit and all my being were filled not only with forgiveness, but absolute, perfect knowledge of God's individual care for me. I didn't deserve such blessing and never would. He showed me that the course He led me in was part of His plan. I was pardoned, forgiven, my faith reinforced and made new. I stayed on my knees praising and thanking Him till dark thinned into dawn.

CHAPTER 8

PENANCE: NEMESIS

This Expedition of Hunter's. ... I must say that I am ashamed to belong to such an army under such a tyrant. Loose rein was given to the soldiers in all kinds of vice, robbery and murder. Every house was plundered of everything, women & children driven to starvation, their persons violated; many were murdered after homes lain in ashes. I saw many inoffensive citizens murdered in their own yards. I saw many dangling from limbs of trees as I passed along. Villages were destroyed after being plundered, hundreds of private mansions were laid in ashes and great black smokes were arising at all times in the day in all directions. Truly Hunter's path has been one of blood and ashes. ... He is tyrannical to his men. I have seen him horse whip poor wounded soldiers, for some little misdemeanor, with his own hand, until the spark of life had about fled.

—Alexander Neil, Union Army surgeon, letter, June 29, 1864

Torquil

After Sigel's defeat at the battle of New Market on May 15, 1864, Grant replaced him with General Hunter. The host camping at Cedar Creek engulfed the surrounding Shenandoah Valley.

Ewen and I rode unseen on its eastern flank when they started up the valley. Through my field glasses, I recognized the badges of the VI and XIX and another corps, saw flags of two cavalry regiments. I didn't need the glasses to see miles of supply wagons.

"I can't believe my eyes. Torquil Dhu, we're not going to win, are we?" Ewen's voice was dreary.

"We have to win." It was work to keep my voice steady. He'd never seen such a huge army, and I'd never seen one so close to home. "And we're going to save Abercairn, so don't despair. If I catch you at it, I'll ... I'll tie your toes together!"

His ghost of a smile came and went too quickly. "I reckon I knew it, but I didn't really believe it before. Now I've seen it."

"You're going to go right on like you hadn't. This horde may not touch us. But in case they cross the Blue Ridge, we need to be sure everybody has seed and enough food to stay well till it's planted and harvested, every year."

"This year's looking ill. It's way too dry for a good yield."

"All the more need to bring in what we're allowed to, from the Yankees. We can plant what they feed their horses! When it darkens, we'll leave our horses concealed close by and separate to reconnoiter. Leave at Meridian and get through the Gap before dawn."

"Wait for each other?"

"No. Pass the information to Major Willis immediately, by separate couriers if need be."

* * *

I hid among the thick-leaved branches of a tree as Retreat sounded. Enough light remained for them to see me. Directly above the picketed horses, I touched the hilt of the skean dhu. It'd make short work of the picket rope. Four Yankees brought a deck of cards and sat at the base of the tree. They dealt the cards and lit pipes while they played out the hand.

Smoke rose straight into the still air. I fought a sneeze, wrinkling and rubbing my nose till the urge passed. Turned my head away, breathing through my mouth—the sneeze exploded! The Yankees startled. I jumped on a horse . . . jerked loose the knot of its picket rope . . . used it for a rein, then wheeled toward the camp perimeter. Before I could draw my revolver or spur forward, they pulled me off its back. Guards with muskets leveled marched me to an officer's tent.

> Honorable men, when captured, will abstain from giving the enemy information concerning their own army, and the modern law of war permits no longer the use of any violence against prisoners in order to extort the desired information.
> —U.S. War Department[13]

"Bring 'im in."

The murderer! Heavy features and pale, dead eyes were etched in my mind. I froze with shock.

"Wa-a-al. A little lieutenant. Lookee here, DuChemin."

The big blond Yankee wearing the blank shoulder strap of a second lieutenant handed my revolver to the other, who laid it on a table among bottles of liquor. A slender, foppish first lieutenant

---

13 War Department of the United States, General Orders No. 100: Instructions for the Government of the Armies of the United States in the Field. [Laws of War], Section III, paragraph 80.

of medium height, sallow-complexioned, wearing a waxed black moustache turned up at the ends, strolled out of the shadows.

"Who are you, boy?"

"Lieutenant Drummond, First Virginia Cavalry."

I gathered my wits, resolved to say no more. I'd forgiven this murderer! I quelled rage trying to invade me. Why was I meeting him now? 'Dear God?' I asked.

God seemed gone, replaced by red, black, malevolent evil, solid as my own body. Was my punishment for vengeance to be inflicted by my quarry? Then the hatred I'd poured out on him would be turned back on me, like I'd filled him with it! I knew its demonic power too well. Terrified, I prayed for courage.

"But zees, Yohanson, is Black Drummond, *non*?"

DuChemin knuckled my chin toward the light. I jerked my head away.

"Izzat so, boy? Answer me!" Yohanson backhanded my face and surged toward me.

"Wait … an easier way." DuChemin cocked my revolver and backed me to the tent pole till I was square against it. "Hands behind ze pole!"

He passed rope around my neck and the pole, tied a noose, pulled it tight. I choked.

"Now you see, struggle ees useless." He wound the rope around me and the pole and looped a Prussik knot on my wrists. It tightened when he pulled the loose end. Yohanson lumbered a circle around me.

"Black Drummond, eh? Not so pert now, are ya? What're ya sneakin' around here for?" He punched me hard in the belly. I doubled over … strangled … raised my head, gasping. He punched me again … tent pole an anvil my backbone was hammered on. Staccato jabs bent me forward.

Yohanson was holding my head up by the hair when I came to, strangling. He rapped my head hard against the pole.

"Who're ya spyin' for?"

Anything I said might tell them something they wanted to know.

Yohanson tapped the left side of my face with his open hand.

"Where's Imboden? How many men's he got? Where's Breckinridge?"

He hit me full force with the open hand, snapping my head aside, then did the same on the right. My head rang. My vision skewed. Yohanson questioned, hit like a piledriver—head, chest, midsection, belly—and hit, and hit, and hit.

My soul hurt. The pain was no worse than when I was wounded, but that was a clean fight. I'd been free to defend myself. Beaten while helpless was an outrage! The wickedness hurt my soul worse than the blows hurt my body.

"Perhaps eet ees not enough pain."

DuChemin made his suggestion languidly, sitting at one side of the table.

Yohanson growled deep, raised a bottle, and poured its contents down his throat. He stropped a Bowie knife on the heel of his hand, then shaved the thick blond hairs on the back. Another large draught. He fixed his blank eyes on my eyes ... approached with the knife held very low, aimed centrally, edge up. In horror, I shifted my weight to my left foot, to kick with the right ... fought terror and pain all alone.

"Not yet, zat cut—but later, later. Start weeth one like ze Indian sun dance."

Yohanson growled again. He slung a piece of rope over his shoulder. He grasped my left elbow and plunged the knife through my upper arm, distal from the bone. I grimaced. Agony ... then worse. Twisting the knife, he forced through enough rope to tie a hard knot. He tugged on the free end ... sat by the table ... tugged harder.

Tears of pain welled in my eyes. Rough rope rasped raw flesh. Blood flowed.

"Where'd ya come from, ya sneakin' little spy? Who sent ya here?" He took another long swig, pulled on the rope, held it taut. My triceps muscle felt torn loose from its insertions.

"Tell us, enfant. Ze entire plan. Eet will stop ze pain." He smirked, swallowed liquor, and nodded. Yohanson jerked the rope sharp.

Question, silence, more pain. Demand, silence, sharper pain. Offer of relief, silence, pain. Taunt, silence, pain. Threat to cut me more, silence, longer pain, the knife brandished as if to disembowel.

The torturers imbibed and interrogated. If I so much as groaned, they'd harry me, like wolves, to the kill.

"How many men ya got?" Seesaw on the rope. Grinding pain.

"Where ees ze army?"

"What's Imboden's plan?"

"Talk, enfant. Where ees ze First Virginia?"

In the wee hours of morning, vital force wanes before the power of night. Mine was ebbing, but I noticed questions less often, words slower. They'd each consumed a tremendous amount. I breathed deep through every respite. Pain and my will kept me tensed.

The rope slackened.

"Zey will not rescue you," DuChemin mumbled into his goblet. "You are prisonaire. We cut you to ze death."

They possessed my body, to mutilate at their pleasure! Fear of being carved to death gnawed at my courage. I begged God to keep me from surrendering.

Yohanson rumbled in his throat and jerked the rope hard. He swilled liquor, set his bottle down with a thump.

I waited till lethargy siezed them again. I didn't know, then, that slaking their lust to inflict pain relaxed them as much as liquor did. I raised my leg to touch the skean dhu ...caught the running end of the rope with my fingers ... worked the Prussik knot back in upon itself ... slipped my wrists free while the torturers snored. Yohanson's hand let go the rope. DuChemin's goblet rolled on the ground. Never taking my eyes off them, I grasped the skean dhu.

Clenched teeth ... cut the loop ... pulled it out of the wound. Blood gushed. I freed myself, holding the long dagger in my teeth, tasting the saltness of my own blood, listening.

Horse on the picket line stamped ... horse guard paced by ... sentries called the hour of three. I noted their positions. Slid an unopened bottle of liquor into my coat pocket ... cocked the revolver ... took the lamp. Slit the tent wall closest to the camp perimeter ... crawled into darkness. Shielded the lamp with my body ... levered off its chimney ... placed it under the ragged slash to set the tent on fire.

Eluded the horse guards ... through the sentry line ... heard the dry canvas go up like a torch. Silhouettes quenching the blaze. Yohanson bellowing.

"I swear to God I'll kill you, Drummond!"

Sheltered in the woods, I opened the wound ... poured liquor ... worked the flesh till it burned into every crevice. Rinsed my mouth with the last thimble-full ... swallowed it blood and all. Ebbing fast ... had to get through the gap. ...

* * *

Dunnachie hailed me from the sentry post atop the crag.

"What happenit to ye?"

Roused with a start ... made myself speak with pretense of strength.

"The Yankees wanted my company, but found my conversation wanting." Hard work, keep tongue … thoughts … words … connected.

MacLeod

I was on guard when Ewen returned alone in the wee hours and sent Aidan posthaste with a dispatch. Later, his urgent shout roused me from a nap between guard reliefs.

"Airlie! MacLeod! Wounded here!"

He supported the lieutenant to the bench next to his quarters. The boy could hardly stagger. His left coat sleeve was soaked with blood, his face beaten and bloodied. Rope burns encircled his neck.

"What did they do to you?" Ewen demanded. "None of your Stoic tales this time!"

He mumbled a report of a brutal interrogation. Ewen took off his coat and shirt so we could wash him and examine his injuries.

"French one … talk' … 'bou' pain. Din' know … Yankees torture."

"I've never heard of it before!"

I scowled while I rubbed yellow soap on a sopping wet cloth. Furious … sickened. The army I belonged to committed this crime! It hurt: they'd betrayed my trust in their righteousness. I washed the lieutenant's face and body, frowned with concern as I passed the cloth over a dull red scar on his side.

"Who were they? What rank?" I snapped.

"Firs' lieuten' DuChemin, sec' lieuten' Yohanson."

I stored the names in my mind. "What did they want to know?"

"Ev'thin'."

"What did you tell them?" Ewen examined the wounded arm.

"Name, rank, reg'men'. No more."

"Airlie, whiskey." Ewen didn't even look at him.

David filled a cup and gave it to his chief. "They laid on a thrashing! You can see where all your buttons were. You'll be a beauty tomorrow!"

"Mus' I wai' tha' long? I'm no' ... tha' ba' hur?"

"That's what you always say!"

Ewen worked whiskey liberally throughout the wound and examined the other injuries. The lieutenant clenched his teeth and kept silent. Slight pressure on his backbone made him wince and draw a sharp breath. He took a few mouthfuls of the whiskey. Ewen palpated his own abdomen and then compared as he palpated the other boy's.

"It's swollen, but I can't find anything else unusual."

"Have you passed any blood?" I asked.

"Haven' pass' ... an'thin'?"

"Be sure to notice, next time you do."

I held a dipperful of water to his mouth till he drank it all. Ewen bound the wounds and broken ribs and bade him finish the whiskey. We helped him to his bedroll. I was still enraged. Assigned to tend him, I took station at the entrance to his quarters.

Torquil

My backbone and middle hurt so bad I could only curl up on the edge of my back. I laid the wounded arm on my side and turned my heart toward my Creator in silent prayer.

'Dear God ...'

Hazy ... started over.

'Dear God ... the Dominie said I'm supposed to thank You.'

Mind drifted off ... tried again.

'Dear God, thank You, I didn't surrender. Was that what ... he said would come? Strange. Man I tried to kill. I deserved it.

Vengeance isn't right, and I tried to kill him anyway. Thank You for punishing me and not … casting me away. I want to be with You. In the Christ's name, Amen.'

Relieved I'd done the penance I owed, received the grace I'd prayed for, my spirit was at peace. By and by, whiskey eased the hurt, and exhaustion overcame the last of consciousness.

* * *

I woke in the dark, hurting all over, inside and out. Bandages pinched. Coatless, shirtless … shivering. Drew my blanket closer … curled up tighter. I wriggled, trying to make myself less miserable.

CHAPTER 9

"LIKE AS A FATHER PITIETH HIS CHILDREN ..."[14]

MacLeod

Roused by the cornshuck pallet rustling, I lit a candle and dropped to my haunches by the lieutenant's side.

"What do you need?"

"Go ou." His words were almost unintelligible.

"Can you get up?"

He rolled onto his knees and pushed himself up with his right arm. The effort made him gag. I helped him out to the sink, where he took the candle and turned away.

"Any blood?"

"No. Get me milk ... half to half with whiskey."

He was still shivering when he finished it. I covered him with his coat over the blanket.

I settled at the corner of his quarters and frowned into the darkness. Keeping vigil was the least I could do, after what some of my own had done to this resolute boy.

---

14 Psalm 103:13a.

'You'd hate being called a boy! You or any of your "men!" You're fighting to protect your families, when you should be protected, yourselves! You should be at school instead of studying tactics to save your lives!

'Holy God, such manner of war is accursed! My orders are loathsome! It's right to preserve the Union—but not by torturing a child! If You'd left me a son instead of a grave, I'd want him to be valiant like this one.

'Holy God, what would you have me do? In Jesus' name, Amen.'

For some reason in the will of God, I had to stay here. My mind refused to confirm the calling my spirit knew: the reason lay asleep a few feet away.

Torquil

"No! N-o-o-o!" I wakened screaming from the nightmare, sitting bolt upright, seeing in the darkness my family die and my world blown to pieces.

Candle lighted ... arm around my shoulder ... soothing voice and words ... I spilled it all.

MacLeod

He trembled when he spoke. It made me heartsick ... angrier. "I'm ready to vow vengeance on him myself!"

"It will only come back on you."

'You don't know I'm the proper authority in this case!' I thought.

He was still shaking, so I kept my arm around him. "You often have nightmares..."

"I don't sleep much. I'm always on guard for attack I have to fight to the death. It's like having the earth fall out from under your feet. You can't trust anything when there's no justice."

Wrath and pity strangled speech, nor could I think of any comforting answer. I tightened my embracing arm a little.

Torquil

By instinct, like a bairn, I leaned into an embrace that felt like Da's embrace, absorbing comfort I'd scorn, any other time.

"But God's different. He's constant. It's right to trust Him whether you understand or not. It's not this. I sinned, I had to be punished, I'm not complaining.

"If they'd been killed in battle, it would've been expectable. We all might be. But he shot them in cold blood after they surrendered, that's what I don't understand."

"You mourn them."

"I went all empty inside. When the war is over, I shall mourn my dead.

"How much longer? I don't know how we'll win. They lose a thousand and replace them with two thousand. If we lose one, he's one the less. We don't have any more. I didn't know how bad it would hurt our hearts. ...

"We have to win, or we'll be destroyed. We can't let them into Abercairn."

I let out a long breath and relaxed against his shoulder. The whiskey relieved my pain as it had loosened my tongue. I felt heavy with sleep.

"Don't tell them I fashed myself about winning. They'll get discouraged."

"I won't. Are you ready to sleep? I'll be on guard, so you can."

He laid me down with care and put covers over me. I roused only slightly when the earth moved. As if God rocked me in everlasting arms, it soothed me to sleep again.

MacLeod

I pinched the flame out and resumed my vigil. I understood his coldness now. He simply hadn't strength enough to fight his sorrow and the vultures that tore his soul all alone—except for God, from whom he expected only punishment—and do his all-consuming duty. It was no wonder he had nothing left for everyday social niceties. It was no wonder the pain never left his eyes.

He was walking righteously upon an earth that teetered under him because he believed justice was dead.

Likeable? No. Not in the cheerful way the others were. But of them all he had the strongest, deepest character. He'd come through the fiercest fire and still done all his duty, and kept his faith. In his mind and heart, the protector's mind and heart had a life and will of their own. They possessed his wounded and exhausted body and kept it striving to guard his neighbors and his men. It seemed God had created him a living sword for the purpose. I was awed by the terrible singleness of his devotion. His faith in God and constancy amid bitter suffering tore my reluctance to pieces.

'Holy God, grant wisdom to Your servant! Did You send me here for this one? Give him to me, and I'll try to set things right for him. In Jesus' name, Amen'

A merry heart doeth good like a medicine.
—Proverbs 17:22

Torquil

Something was tickling my nose. Eyes swollen shut, I could barely see Kendrick bending over me, twitching an ostrich plume.

"I brought it for you from the Yankees—grabbed it right off an officer's hat!"

I was touched by the gesture but had to reprimand the needless risk. I curled up to ease the pain in my middle and growled, "D'you thin' you're an Indian coun'ing coup!"

Unperturbed, he looked closer. "They really hurt you bad."

"It was a pleasan' social call!" I tried to snap but my mouth wouldn't let me. "Tha's wha' they mean' to do, you halfwit!"

"Tch, tch! Temper, temper, Torquil ... *Beau*! That's right! The Yankees took your beauty, but we'll give it back to you! Where's your hat." He tucked the plume under the hatband and flourished the hat before presenting it, on one knee in mock ceremony.

I softened. An attempt to smile didn't hurt much. "Thanks."

He set it on my knees. "Your servant, Beau!" He swept off his own hat and bowed.

"If you're *quite* finish', jester ..."

He crossed his legs and scissored down beside me, assuming a mournful expression.

"... get me some milk and whiskey. Half and half, and full."

"I'm on my way!"

I looked at my decorated hat. Every company needs one like him to cheer their hearts.

"Here, you sour old souse!"

I saluted him with the cup. "To you, Sir Good-heart!"

"Oh, pshaw!"

MacLeod

While the Rangers ate supper, they talked about their enemies.

"My mother's cousin wrote that they're taking all of everybody's food and forage, over in the Valley, and killing citizens and burning down houses and barns and mills." Aidan looked miserable.

"I reckon some armies live off the country, but it isn't right to take everything and leave women and children to go hungry!" declared Alex.

"And attack them when they're defenseless, the cowards!" Duncan scowled.

"Why don't they fight like men!" demanded David.

"It's their policy to make war on non-combatants," Donald lectured. "For example, they support the Swamp Dragoons. They give them weapons and horses and everything to help them attack and plunder citizens!"

"And now they've tortured Torquil Dhu! What kind of people are they!"

Looking at me, Willie tried to appear fierce instead of frightened. I masked fury and shame and disillusionment.

"I used to think they were like us, and it was a political battle. Now I don't know."

Torquil

Ewen confined me to quarters to heal. I protested, but his calm power overruled me. Injury exacted a worse toll than I expected: my energy would all of a sudden give out. I prayed at greater length than duty allowed before, for each of my men … their success in the field … the safety of Abercairn. MacLeod, detailed to tend me, argued tactics with me. We fought whole campaigns with Napoleon's or Caesar's armies represented by stones and twigs.

MacLeod

"So while my left and center are amusing your assault force, I send my reserves from back here to circle around and take you in the right flank. Then while you're meeting that, I wheel my right"—I fanned a whole line of sticks together—"pivoting where they adjoin my center, and attack your left flank. That's called a mobile defense—as opposed to a static one from behind earth-works. It was a favorite maneuver of Frederick the Great."

I wasn't sure whether, still recovering from his ordeal, he comprehended the strategy. His eyes were half-closed.

"It would work if you had the reserves, which probably means superior numbers initially. With those, your plan might matter less than your strength. But a lot depends on how determined your enemy is. If his line has gaps, or you see his men wavering or hesitating, you know you can whip him. But if they're full of fight, they can run right over you before any of your tactics avail."

He sat up.

"You once said the pattern of our engagements is too predict-able. How?"

"First, because the objective is too often the same: acquiring materiel. They could bait and trap us with it."

"Not if I knew it—and I would. Ever since ... murder ... I've had extra sharp senses and vigilance. What else?"

"Insolence. We seem to spring from nowhere, right among them. Humiliation only makes them furious—deadlier—more determined to destroy us."

"Surprise is one of our best advantages. They don't know where they'll be struck next. That unnerves them so they don't fight as well, and we clean them out—if they're a small force. The only tactics I can use against large forces are attack-and-with-draw, like what George Washington used against the Indians and French. I can't offer battle, nor make a stand, with so few. We'd be annihilated.

"Virginia is fighting a defensive war, and I'm doing it more so, to keep my men alive, too. I'll defend my home and neighbors with the last drop of my blood, but I won't have theirs wasted. I know of brigades that are the size of a company now! With losses like that, the country's survival will depend upon a small remnant. I can and do vary the objectives, but the tactics must remain."

"What's your strategy?"

"To keep the Yankees away from Abercairn. It's the best protection. Now that Hunter's making war on defenseless citizens, my neighbors are in worse peril than before."

"So are you. You saw they were willing to let the rest go, and take you alone. Not only do they consider this war an insurrection and the army mere lawbreakers, but they count the Rangers in the same category as Colonel Mosby—guerrillas. They hate your methods and hate the success of them even more. They'll hunt us down the way they're hunting him. They could detach a company like Blazer's Scouts any time for the purpose."

"Why haven't they?" He slouched to the right and let the wounded arm lie easy on his body.

"Our force and its effect, though infuriating, are too small, and they evidently haven't learned where we come from. They will, because our return trails are becoming clearer, and the wagon road leads nowhere else."

He lay down, eyelids drooping, and fell asleep again.

I looked over his books. *Stratagemata*, Tacitus' *Agricola*, Caesar's *Bello Gallico*, Cooke's *Cavalry Tactics*. Shakespeare's *Othello* made me wonder if he read for pleasure when he couldn't sleep. He must sometimes need to give over his single-minded study of war. I was absorbed in the tragedy of the Moorish soldier and his lady love when I heard a murmur.

"'She loved me for the dangers I had passed, / And I loved her, that she did pity them.' A pleasant hope."

"I'd have read aloud if I'd known you were awake. Would you like it?"

"I couldn't concentrate, thank you. I've been less sleeping than dreaming, but for once, not about my own Iago. I think I created

Iago in him with my hatred. He poured it back on me double. I don't think I'd be … whole … if DuChemin hadn't delayed him.

"It isn't over." A tremor riffled the low voice. "He swore to kill me."

I countered the tremor with logic. "It's not likely he'll find you."

"In all my hunting, I didn't find him, but I was delivered to him for chastisement."

"Which is completed. The guilt will be on him if he tries to carry out his threat."

"But it's two lessons: not to hate—even unto murder—and not to seek vengeance. I've only been punished once."

"If you've learnt the lessons, once is enough."

"Dominie Gilchrist said evil will overtake me."

"It has. If it does again, that's because of its nature, not your deserving."

"But men might be alive today if I hadn't seen him in all of them. I'm forgiven, but their blood is on my hands, as in Genesis, and I'll have to bleed to pay for it."

"You have."

"But I doubt enough."

"To the death?"

"I don't know." His half-smile was wistful. "But if it is, it's all right. Except for this duty, I don't hold life tightly. That's why a lady's love is only a pleasant hope. I won't live long enough to win it."

"Why do you liken Yohanson to Iago?"

"In the play, I don't find any reason for Iago's wicked deeds, and I don't know any for Yohanson's. He hates me now because I escaped, but till then he didn't know me.

"He didn't know Da and Douglas. I deserved punishment, but they didn't. He's Iago because both do wickedness for wicked-ness' sake alone."

He seemed relieved to confide the things that troubled him. I answered from a father's heart, but without the authority of a father's position. I'd have to wait till he accepted it.

* * *

With leave to go to Abercairn Court House, I walked Redspeed down the hairpin bends of the wagon road, enjoying spring sunshine and the fresh scent of grass and burgeoning leaves. The glen echoed with the sound of rushing water. At the Manse, the maid showed me into the parlor.

"Mr. MacLeod! What an agreeable surprise!"

"I came to consult your brother, not expecting your company. It's a pleasure."

"I hope you'll enjoy having it a while! The Dominie's calling on a sick congregant, but I expect him home to tea. Please stay and take the meal with us."

Dominie Gilchrist

I brought Mr. MacLeod into my study.

"'Tis good to have ye call on us again. Miss Gilchrist and I enjoy your conversation. 'Tis more than a social call, however."

"Yes. The matters I consulted you about last winter have become clear. My mind has a more logical inclination than I was allowed to indulge, but the Lord is teaching me to trust him rather than rely on my own understanding."

"So must we all. 'Tis difficult to reach from human to spiritual wisdom. When we walk in His ways rather than merely know of them, the journey is full of surprises."

"Some have been disconcerting and some joyful. Without tracing the process *ad taedium,* I'm certain now, He sent me here for Lieutenant Drummond's sake."

"May I know in what office?"

"Foster father, presumptuous as it sounds, since many here are zealous for his welfare."

"Many who are zealous do not replace one who is called."

"Then you think such a thing might be."

"Does he speak freely with you, confide in you?"

"Until he did, I had no notion of such a calling."

"Confidence from him is rare. He's been reserved all his life. I believe trust originates in his spirit, which overrides the wariness of his reason."

"From such a noble-hearted boy, trust is an honor ... of which I hope to prove worthy. A father's joy carries with it grave responsibilities. Saving him alive is the gravest now. Much as I'm dedicated to it—and that's what brings me here—I have yet to establish the means."

His face hardened with angry resolve.

"I want to stand between him and all harm, and prevent such a crime ever being committed against him again!"

"If this is of God, He in his wisdom will provide the means."

"A remark he made troubles me. He doesn't hold life tightly nor expect to live long."

"In one sense, it's a logical conclusion. His is not a long-lived family, from the hazards of life, however, rather than constitutional weakness. His expectation could stem from seeing the murder of his family. The shock, and the inferred threat to his own life, act upon the soul.

"I shall speak more openly than I might otherwise, so soon, because we know not what the events of war may bring. Ye have good character among us, which makes it reasonable that ye be called here to foster one of our own. I shall therefore set forth the charge that falls on ye as a father's duty to him, so ye may choose, in full knowledge of its weight, whether to undertake it.

"Ye are called to protect a pure heart. Though he sinned grievously, Torquil Dhu has a heart after God. Since he was very young, his greatest desires have been to do right and to speak the truth. When he does not, he feels he is in the dark alone, instead of in God's presence and light. That Light and Presence are more precious to him than anything else. They must continue to be.

"He lives now only to perform the duty God calls him to, not for any allurement of earth. He's more willing to give his life than to keep it."

"I've seen that, and it's very dangerous! I've remonstrated, but he hasn't heeded."

"There is a greater threat. Since for him it is not a sacrifice to die, but to live, if his soul is overthrown again, he will be as deadly to himself as to others. The 'daemon' will drive him to destruction. Ye may be called upon to turn him back from such a course, not only for others' sakes, but his own soul's sake. Ye may find that even with your Godly intentions, only God's power will avail to redeem."

"I've recently lived a number of examples of God's power to accomplish his purpose."

"He prepares ye to exercise greater faith. It will be needed. Knowing now the gravity of this calling, will ye embrace it?"

"I will."

"Let us pray." We knelt.

"Holy Father in heaven, Ye have heard your servant's promise to guide and guard your child Torquil to manhood, in the nurture and admonition of the Lord. I pray Ye, consecrate him to this service.

"Grant him wisdom, that the precepts he sets forth and the example he lives will be pleasing in thy sight. Grant him strength in heart and spirit, that his discipline over himself and the lad will be firm and unwavering, and just, yet compassionate. Grant him constancy, to address patiently the faults and foolishness of youth until they are overcome. Increase the greatness of his heart, to make the sacrifices of fatherhood.

"In thy Holy Name we pray, Amen."

MacLeod

I undertook the charge in reverent fear.

CHAPTER 10

DARK DAYS UNDER THE SUN

"The Yankees are coming!" The words meant war, the fall of loved ones, the burning of homes, the wasting of property, flight, poverty, subjugation, humiliation, a thousand evils, and a thousand sorrows.
—Brevet Major John William De Forest, United States Army

MacLeod

Wearing gray, anchoring the center of a Rebel skirmish line! Either side would eagerly hang me if they discovered my true identity and purposes! We scouted around the south end of the Massanutten Mountain until Ewen and Torquil returned from in advance, running. Ewen had strapped Torquil's wounded upper arm to his body, coat and all, so his gait was awkward.

"To the rear! The road's black with them ... from Harrisonburg," panted Ewen.

We galloped back to rejoin Major Willis through prosperous farmlands along the main road through Page Valley. Torquil sent riders lancing to each farm and crossroads shop.

"The Yankees are coming! Only a few miles behind us!" I shouted to an old farmer.

"Ach, you dey vill be fighting, nicht uns." He took up his hoeing again.

"This is Hunter! He makes war on citizens, too!"

"Denn ve vor him vill be retty. Danke, Herr Soldat!" He started at an arthritic jogtrot toward his farmyard.

I wheeled Redspeed and dashed back to the column.

> On that field he found, in a soldier's duty and with a soldier's glory, a soldier's death.
> —Captain Charles M. Blackford, Confederate States Army

The Rangers were only one of the hastily summoned local companies. Some were boys, some were men over fifty. Most carried shotguns or hunting rifles and were otherwise ill-equipped. General Lee, needing every soldier to defend Richmond against "Sam" Grant's massive armies, had to require Imboden and his few small regiments to defend the Shenandoah Valley and its vital supplies of foodstuffs and forage.

The Confederate line numbered less than five thousand men, worn and weary with hard marching, sharp fighting, and scant rations. A thousand were mounted. We had fourteen guns. The Unionists bearing down upon us were a fresh, vigorous, well-equipped nine thousand, including several cavalry regiments and twenty-two guns. Major Willis and the Rangers were held in reserve till the squadron was ordered forward against a brigade of Thoburn's infantry.

"Captain Murray! Charge their left flank!"

"ABERCAIRN!"

We crashed headlong into Thoburn's flank, yelling at the top of our lungs. Torquil and Ewen, sabres in right hands and pistols in left, guiding their horses with legs and shifts of weight, dashed into the midst of the Union files. Men shouted defiance. Orders unheard in the melee! "Thuk" of lead smashing into flesh, prayers, cries ... told of wounds received. Hundreds of pistol shots! Duncan bayoneted in the thigh, but his horse's momentum wrenched him free. I aimed high instead of low ... parried bayonets ... didn't bypass infantrymen. Redspeed knocked down several, trampled at least one. My hat carried off by a bullet ... a recent recruit struck from his saddle. A horse went down, spilling its rider, who held tight to his weapons as he jumped to his feet.

"Sound To the Colors!"

Torquil re-formed the Rangers and led us in another charge, but it was too late. All we could do was feint to screen the Confederate retreat. Alternately attacking and falling back, he brought us away. As we countercharged the pursuit, Ewen was knocked back against the cantle of his saddle. He rebounded onto the pommel.

"MacHugh! Take him to the rear!"

The Confederates preserved the rest of their army as best they could. Imboden with his mixed force drove back the Union pursuit.

Ewen drooped on his horse's neck, face white. Blood that had pumped, and coated horse and saddle, now only trickled from the wound. We eased him to the ground.

"Get my saddle pockets!"

Torquil

I knelt and cradled him against my shoulder.

"I'm all … empty." Only a whisper. "I'm … going."

"Let not your heart be troubled: ye believe in God."

"Tell … my family good-bye … I'll tell … yours … hello."

He looked beyond me to someone I couldn't see … smiled, lifted his hand reverently.

"My Lord … and my God!"

His breath left him, together with his spirit. Only his body collapsed into my embrace.

MacLeod

I returned as Torquil was tenderly closing Ewen's eyes. His face was frozen in such a rigor as would soon grip Ewen's body. Delaying intrusion, I got Ewen's blanket, praying before I knelt and put my arm around Torquil's shoulders. They were rigid.

"He's Home now."

"I saw him arrive." His soft voice was cold as death itself. "I shall take his body home. I shall not take vengeance, but the highest of them all shall know what he has done."

Was my lad turning to me, needing to justify himself? How did he mean to inform "the highest of them all?" He surrendered his burden reluctantly, tightening his embrace for a second, a tear escaping from eyes squeezed tight shut. I held the foot of the blanket. He covered the beloved face.

"I'll come with you to the Murrays."

"No. The men need you. You'll stiffen them up and comfort them at the same time."

Willie came up, hat in hand. Torquil gripped the trumpeter's shoulder briefly and turned to see about his wounded. When they'd all paid their respects to their schoolmate's death on the field of honor, the Rangers bade Godspeed and turned away.

"May I have a word with you, sir?"

"No. You're needed here."

"But—"

"Private MacLeod, I warned you of the penalties of insubordination. The army is convenient for you to receive them."

I strode to Redspeed, fuming. But as a command decision, my being left here was irreproachable, the same I'd have made.

* * *

Torquil rode into the funeral procession leading a mounted, blindfolded Union general in full dress uniform. I beseeched God to ameliorate the situation the boy had created. That general was ruthless with personal enemies.

Inside the church, he motioned me to sit on the general's other side. The Federal officer sat frozen, eyes front. I, too, kept eyes front and hoped not to be noticed. When Dominie Gilchrist called for the pallbearers, Torquil rose with the others. Amid the movement, he replaced the blindfold and handed me a Derringer he'd concealed.

"If he moves or makes a sound, shoot him."

I could feel his tension as if sparks danced about him, but his face was grave and still. Hoisting the coffin, he and Robbie, Aidan, David, Alex, and Donald carried Ewen's remains to their final resting place. When the piper began to skirl the coronach, he returned, took the pistol, and gestured to dismiss me. I had no chance to speak to him alone till a few days later.

* * *

"You are perhaps unaware, sir, of the general's repute as a vindictive man. It behooves you to practice great caution from now on, so you don't meet him again."

"He knows my face and the interior of the kirk, no more. He will see neither again."

"He will use the considerable means at his disposal to learn all the particulars. You made him a laughingstock. He will not forget or forgive. I solemnly warn you, he will stop at nothing to avenge himself." My composure disintegrated.

"You've broken your own cardinal rule of not calling attention to the county! You put your men, your neighbors and yourself into needless jeopardy! Such bravado can do nothing to further, and everything to destroy, your purpose!"

Though his eyes narrowed, his face was still, his voice quiet.

"I need not explain myself. For the sake of your usefulness, hear. I disabled the sentries and other staff, wakened and removed the general, blindfolded, from his quarters. We passed unseen to the horses and thence through his lines. I brought him to the procession by ways known to me, then returned him in like manner."

"You created exactly the provocation I warned you about! It will only infuriate them the more!"

"Let them match my wrath!" Anger instead of honest guilt.

I was superior in the contest of wills. In the voice of dominion possessed only by successful career officers, I added, "You deserted your post of duty."

Torquil

Truth rang through the accusation and pierced my exhaustion, my grief and rage and desolation, like a clarion of pure light. I sorrowed.

"I accept rebuke. I won't need it again. Dismissed!"

* * *

A few days later, when we left their supply and ordnance transfer depot, Yankee gunners were still finding their range. A shell bursting behind our column spooked the mules drawing wagons full of captured stores. Blair and Galbraith each grabbed the headstall of a leader while Mr. Lachlan fought the wheelers and swing team to a trot. Kendrick and Airlie supported Greig's team.

"Take them to the rear!" I directed with extended saber. "Sound To the Colors!"

We gathered in the cover of a thick stand of elderberry bushes.

"We're going to take those guns. They're unsupported. Two volleys. First squad, cannoneers. Second squad, drivers. Don't hit the horses.

"Then we'll charge and surround them before they can reload. Bring down gunners and drivers as you go. Sergeant Menteith, first squad, west. The rest of us, east."

We deployed into a single rank as the next shells fell short of the fleeing wagons and Blair, Galbraith, and Airlie came pounding into their places. Forty-one rifles blazed twice, downing crews and drivers.

"Forward!"

We burst from cover, disabling Yankees who could still resist. A shell fired point-blank by a falling cannoneer burst where we'd been a few seconds earlier.

"MacLeod, take the first squad, limber up, follow to the rear as fast as you can."

The rearguard rode north to draw the Yankees' fire in the wrong direction … withdrew slowly. We found Kendrick where his dying horse had carried him.

"'Tis not so deep as a well, nor so wide as a church-door; but 'tis enough, 'twill serve'!" he quoted, through clenched teeth.

"Airlie! Ligatures! My saddle pockets!"

Kendrick's left knee hung by tendons. The shell fragment had shattered it and the end of the femur. I tightened the tourniquet till it bit into the flesh … pinched the femoral artery shut … looped and tied the silk threads around it.

* * *

We went over the procedure in the surgery text. Then we knelt in prayer. Kendrick lay on the stout wooden bench we'd moved outdoors for better air and light. I knelt by his side and took his hand in both of mine.

"My dear old friend, it's got to come off."

Sad faced, he could only nod.

"Help him sit up, MacLeod."

I held a cup of whiskey to his lips and made him drink its contents quickly. We'd run out of captured anesthetics long ago.

MacLeod

Torquil tightened the tourniquet to compress the artery against the femur. As they held his legs down, Robbie looked up to me, whispering.

"Uncle James ..." He swallowed hard, quoted, "'Our doubts are traitors.'"

"Yes, they are. Cross your arms and grip my wrists." I straddled the bench and held him, shaking, tight against my chest.

'Holy God, how many more torn and broken children will I hold?' I prayed in silent misery. 'Grant this go right, I pray You! Spare Robbie! Guide my lad's hands and strengthen his heart for this terrible work. Comfort them all.'

David put the chunk of leather between Robbie's teeth. Torquil picked up the longest catling knife. He cut and slipped back the skin, then cut the flesh. While David retracted and held the flaps that would cushion the stump, I felt Robbie's body stiffen. He clenched his teeth.

Torquil finished separating the bone before Robbie fainted. The medical corps smoothed the edges, removed all the bone splinters and ligated the blood vessels, carefully separating them from accompanying nerves. They cleansed, sutured, and bandaged, and laid Robbie on a thick, comfortable bed near the fire. David decided to give the amputated leg a decent burial.

* * *

Torquil sat in his niche, folded hands resting on bent knees, head bowed upon them. I sat down beside him. When he raised his head, I saw anguish great as my own.

"It had to be done." He seemed to be trying to convince himself.

"He'd have died if you hadn't." I confirmed it.

He looked into the distance past the little glen below … slammed a fist onto his knee. "I hate it he'll have to go through life like that! No one ever had a better heart."

"You may be surprised how well he'll get along. Today's surgery aside, how are you?"

"All right. The arm needs re-dressed. I'll get one of the medicals to do it later. They've had all they can take for now."

"I'll take care of your arm. When we were surveying in the West, we had to be our own doctors." In the medical niche of the cave, I unwrapped the wound. "How does it seem?"

"All right. Washing wounds with whiskey right away seems to make them heal faster."

"I'll do that again."

I washed it with water first. The flesh was uniting cleanly. I applied whiskey, sweet oil, fresh dressings, and new bandage.

"Bind it tight. I've got to be able to use it."

"Have you noticed any failure of use, beyond the effect of the injury?"

"No."

"Extend your hand and fingers, and then make a fist."

He did.

"Are there any parts that don't have feeling?"

"No."

"Then there should be nothing to worry about." I tied off the bandage. "Your old wound doesn't seem to hinder you."

"I breathe all right now. I'm going to check on Kendrick. Come along. I want you with him when he wakes up. It will comfort him."

* * *

Torquil

Flash of bayonets through trees and underbrush! Ambush! We wheeled breakneck in thirty different directions. Two Yankee horsemen doggedly pursued MacLeod. They took him at gunpoint and galloped him away.

MacLeod

I didn't resist capture. For all I knew, they thought me an enemy and would shoot me without ever knowing otherwise. It shocked me to realize that in my heart, I was their enemy. My oath hadn't changed, but their despicable crimes against inoffensive citizens had roused my contempt even before they tortured Torquil. I hoped I'd taught my newfound fosterling enough to protect himself.

Torquil

I cantered along my escape route till I was sure I wasn't pursued, before I reversed to attempt recapture. I quartered back and forth till I picked up the trail.

MacLeod

My captors confirmed my notion that the Bureau was in it when they slowed to a trot and holstered their pistols.

"We thought you'd deserted, MacLeod!"

"How do you know me?" I began to be careful what I said.

"An ambrotype of you with Sharpe and some of the others. Remember the meeting when Russell was showing off his techniques?"

"Has he pictured any valuable information?" I stalled for time to choose my statements. My mind was not producing any.

Torquil

They'd slowed to a trot, south toward the railroad. I followed at a canter. The train whistled to signal the railhead. When I came within earshot of the shanties at the end of track, I slowed to a walk, weaving through cover.

MacLeod

"We're just in time," one of my captors announced. "They don't turn around here, only pick up freight, mail and passengers, and back up for water and wood."

From the platform next to the tracks, I watched the approaching train. How to balk when they questioned me? I'd obeyed God rather than men. Now I'd have to answer to them.

'Holy God, I pray You, put Your words in my mouth!'

Torquil

Guards patrolled around the railhead. I spotted MacLeod and two bluecoats. Strange—he had his sidearms, and neither had a pistol trained on him. I concealed Nightwind and advanced, revolver in hand, to crouch among barrels on the platform and cautiously peer around.

MacLeod

"We thought you were going to stay with the Johnnies till the war's over, long as you've been gone!"

I thought I saw a flicker of motion. I laid my dear hope on the altar by raising my voice.

"I thought I was, too. What became of the messenger you promised me?"

The muzzle of a revolver.

"Henderson was killed. Two others failed. You'd better have a pretty detailed report on those guerillas after all this time!"

"I'll give you chapter and verse!" I almost shouted.

Torquil

Betrayal—a knife in the heart. I was a prize fool! That I'd trusted him made me feel defiled. I aimed at the furrow between the spy's brows and squeezed the trigger.

MacLeod

One of my colleagues stepped past me. A shot! The man sagged to the platform just in time for me to see Torquil jump off it. He'd heard it all, including my warning. His shot was meant for me. The son of my heart was now my enemy.

Torquil

Torn between fury and sorrow, I'd almost reached Raven Crags before I could recover stoic dispassion. My base and my company betrayed, Abercairn in terrible danger. My men's spirits would sink at losing their beloved Uncle James. I wouldn't tell them he was a spy.

'Dear God, I beg you, forgive my weakness! I let sentiment stand in the way of reason! I thought he wasn't what he said he was, and now all's in worse danger, and it's my fault. Dear God, I'll give my life for theirs, but I don't know how to stretch it far enough. Please show me what to do! In the Christ's name, Amen.'

Betrayed! Another curse on my life. Expect nothing good. Hope for nothing except for it to end. But endure, to do my duty. Da did, after my mother died.

Ewen.   Robbie.   Betrayer.

I buried sorrow. It needs a bigger grave now, and a heavier cairn of stones.

CHAPTER 11

COVERT CORRESPONDENCE, JULY 2 TO SEPTEMBER 29, 1864

Willard Hotel, No.18-M
Washington, Dist. of Col.
July 2, 1864

Dear,

Let us not use names. In this time of peril and enmity, interception of a missive might endanger us or those we hold in affection. I regret being unable to keep my promise to attend you at dinner Thursday last. On Wednesday last, I was captured. The line of communication through which you received this is safe for you to use, should you wish to respond.

You may wish to discontinue our acquaintance, when, as I tell you the worst first, you learn I was sent to betray my late hosts. I hope you will believe me when I vow to you that I have not, nor shall I do so. Though subsequent events may seem proof to the contrary, I am greatly concerned for their safety.

The memory of my association with you, especially, is the aurora that illumes the darkness of separation from you all. I pray daily that God will bless and guard you.

I remain, though not in outward seeming, respectfully, your faithful and obedient servant.

* * *

Abercairn C.H., Va.
July 5, 1864

Dear,

Receipt of yours of the 2nd inst. emboldens me to trust the means by which it arrived, and, though timorous lest the means ever be endangered, to respond.

Though you make no mention of your condition, we pray you are in good health and that they are not treating you badly. I share your low spirits caused by separation.

All here go on much the same. A number have had to travel upon learning of their uncle's condition, and we pray they will continue safely. The fighting has come within a day's journey of here, but we have had none "within the gates."

We pray for you, too: God's guidance and protection and comfort.

I remain your sincere and faithful friend.

* * *

Washington, Dist. Of Col.
July 4, 1864

I take pen in hand in haste, for events are moving swiftly. I hope this finds you well, as it leaves me. I would not intrude upon you again so soon except to impart the following news. The past two days have been a whirlwind, but it has cast me upon a more hospitable shore than I expected. I am being sent West to build a new post to protect our people there against marauding Indians,—transposed from the Corps of Engineers (and my— thanks be to God it is over!—former assignment), to the line. Since the post is to be garrisoned by only a single company of cavalry, we shall have our work cut out for us, to put ourselves under shelter by winter. I am meeting with the contract surgeon in a few minutes, to ask his advice on measures I can initiate to keep my soldiers in good health.

If you wish to correspond, you may use this same direction for a while. I will let you know when it changes. Mail may not overtake me on the journey, but it will catch up when I arrive. I shall take the liberty of sending back a few lines whenever I have opportunity, in the earnest hope I shall not offend you.

I continue in prayer for all of you. May God ever watch over you.

* * *

Pennsylvania

July 7, 1864

Please excuse the unevenness of my hand! The railroad is rougher, the farther west it goes, hence the occasional blot or unintentional serif.

The whirlwind continues. I go by rail to St. Louis and once there, board a steamboat to Fort Leavenworth, Kansas, accumulating parts of my command there and at Camp Dennison, Ohio. I am also authorized to enlist suitable men along the way. The changes in transportation, and composition of the command, will certainly prove my sergeants' ability! Having learned ill of their characters, I cherish no hope of the same in my lieutenants.

Please forgive me if I have discoursed at too much length upon my own situation, when there is so much danger in yours. I would prefer to be there to protect you, but the choice was taken out of my hands. It is surely another plan of God's. I go forward in faith, trusting in His direction. I pray His blessings upon you and yours, in the place which, for all too brief a while, became the home and center of my heart.

* * *

> Kansas
> July 23, 1864

I take pen in hand upon dry land again, to scratch a few lines tonight. We accomplished the riverine part of our journey without loss, in spite of partisans firing upon our steamboat. My seasoned veterans set the example of steadiness which I am pleased to say my green recruits took up, and we drove them off. I had half feared they would set an ambush to damage our vessel, but the "Missouri Star" arrived unscathed.

We stop here to draw rations, shoe horses, and otherwise prepare for the five hundred miles' overland march to Fort Liberty, Dakota Territory, which will require at least a month. I shall send back word from each stop, hoping for your favorable reception of the same.

As each day takes me farther from you and yours, I become more grateful that there is no distance in prayer, and that our heavenly Father keeps the spirits of His children in close communion. With continued prayer that He will keep all of you safe and well, I remain, respectfully, your very faithful and obedient servant.

* * *

Abercairn C. H.

August 7, 1864

Please excuse the inferior quality of my ink! I have watered it down to make it stretch farther. All of our men and boys are in the field now, and the fighting is concentrated around Petersburg and Richmond and in the Valley. We are still spared, but my soul pities those who are not so blessed. With great joy, I thank God you are still safe. I am writing this to send on the morrow, in hopes it will reach you before you begin the final portion of your journey.

There were a terrible cannonade and explosions west of us within a week after you left, so powerful that some features of the landscape were altered. We feared the inhabitants must all have been killed, but all survived and are now in the field, I don't know with what regiment. Should I gather more specific information, I will dispatch it immediately.

My own employments, compared to the stirring deeds and noble sacrifices of our men, and to the adventures of your journey, are mundane. We knit socks and sew clothing and send food to our brave soldiers. The most and best we can do is never too much, for they are pouring out their lives and strength for us every day. This year has been so dry that the crops are not as bountiful as usual, but we shall preserve all we can for the winter's needs.

My brother sends his greetings and pledges his prayers for your continued welfare. He expresses admiration for the courageous stand you have taken in obedience to God rather than to men. We both pray the result of your sacrifice will be blessed as only He can bless.

I long for the day "when this cruel war is over" and all our dear ones can be re-united in, as you call it, "the home and center of my heart." Sad as was your "exile" at the beginning, your duty's distance adds bitterness to it. I take courage in the thought of the communion of our spirits "in Him." My prayers are with you and for you morning, noon, and night.

I remain your constant and faithful friend.

* * *

Fort Liberty, Dakota Territory
August 21, 1864

It was great happiness to receive both your letters upon my arrival here, and even greater happiness that you do not, now that you know my former deeds and my true position in life, reject my friendship. Though I am taking time from the brother officer who is my host here, I had to draw apart to receive your greetings, as it were, and begin to write to you on this evening of my arrival. It's almost as though I were able to converse with you in person, now I have your letters before me, after so long a time apart. I had not realized how much I had come to look forward to "taking sweet counsel together" (as it says in the Psalms) and to your ready wit and thought, until I was torn away from you, and from all who lighted my days and lifted my heart there.

Thank you for news of the younger citizens. I am grateful to God they are still alive. All things considered, the army is probably the safest place for them now, as they had become dangerously conspicuous. I must ask your indulgence not to mention me or my whereabouts, as it might result in increased danger.

For now, I must do my duty to my host. I shall write more and answer your letters at my first opportunity tomorrow. Good-night.

Continued August 22, 1864: I shall answer your letters line by line, even word by word, for each deserves attention. You conveyed much meaning through them.

When my captors discovered themselves to me, I tried to think what to say in order to accomplish God's purpose (which in heart and conscience is my own) without compromising my honour nor any of my sworn duties. Our holy God put the truth in my mouth in such a way as to please Him and lessen their condemnation at the same time. I cannot, for my life, remember exactly what I said!

They did not mistreat me, and now, as then, I am blessed to be safe and in good health. Thank you for your intercession. Please continue, as I shall for you and yours. I am sorry to cause you distress by distance. I share in the same, if that be any consolation.

I thank God the fighting has not come too close to you. However strange it may sound, considering the color of the coat that covers the heart from which it comes, I bear deep gratitude to and for those who protect you. It is strange to think, as I have caught myself doing more than once, "all I can do is pray," when there is nothing I can do materially; for prayer is always efficacious, answered as it is, according to the will of our all-wise, all-powerful, all-merciful God.

The sincerity and faithfulness of your friendship is rich treasure to me. (See! I respond even to your valediction!)

I am sorry to hear of your shortages. Should you need to save your ink for more important documents, I shan't mind receiving letters in pencil, just so I continue to receive them. You may direct letters here, and they will be forwarded: Co. M, 16th U.S. Cavalry.

I had some hints beforehand about the explosions you mentioned, hence my allusion to potential danger. I was counting on one's sagacity to bring the others away, in time and unharmed. Though Providence may have decreed that our short association be the only one on earth, my concern for his welfare, and my paternal affection, continue. I shall be glad for whatever you can report.

You speak of my "sacrifice," but God has left me my occupation and my life. That life has taken on dimensions I never dreamed of when first I came to the "home and center" of it. Since it is His gift, I am resolved to use it in whatever service He calls me to perform. The only real sacrifice is separation from many who are dear to my heart.

We traveled through Nebraska along the immigrant trail, a broad road beaten smooth by the passing of thousands of wagons and teams. They tell me here that as many as five thousand wagons <u>per month</u> pass the fort during the season. We kept a strong guard posted, for the Indians in this region have been troublesome.

This is a major post, where the process of supply will take a few days, during which we shall enjoy the "fleshpots of Egypt" before we make our way into the wilderness again. The march should take about a week. We shall be occupied with patrols to locate and possibly engage the Indians, woodcutting for construction and fuel, cutting hay if any nutritious grasses remain at this season, construction of the post itself, perhaps some escort duty, and the day-to-day routine and administration.

Continued, August 24, 1864: We march on the morrow, having packed supplies, tools, rations, &c. My surgeon has brought equipment and medicaments from the east and had an easy time convincing the commissary here to part with a large amount of the dessicated vegetables he insists we shall need if we are to survive the winter without scurvy. Strange to say, he has bought a flock of chickens! He and I have become good friends during our journey, as well as consultants for the health and hospital practices we intend to establish. I respect his dedication as a surgeon and scientist. He's an Englishman named Barnes.

I suppose I am rambling, with the intention of postponing my farewell, for it seems like yet another parting to be going still farther away. I shall try to scribe a few lines each evening, and send the accumulation when the post is dispatched.

God bless you and all there. Please give my warm regards to your worthy brother, and my thanks for his prayers, which I reciprocate.

* * *

Abercairn C. H., Va.

September 13, 1864

This leaves me well, as I hope and pray you are, but, oh, such scenes of battle and destruction! (No, they have not come here.) The Kirk and our public buildings at the Court House are again in use as hospitals, and some soldiers are being nursed in private homes, including your lad's. (He and his command are somewhere in the Valley.)

Oh! The horrors! The enemy make war on women and children! We have received refugees whose stories tear our hearts. Barns and mills burnt to the ground, some people's homes burnt, all the year's crops stolen or destroyed, all horses and livestock stolen. The citizens are left with nothing. Some of the soldiers killed people in their own dooryards, while their officers did nothing to prevent it! Whence such vicious hatred? It is as if the very imps of the enemy-of-souls are loosed upon the helpless! I really cannot—trying to think objectively and from a military point of view—see that robbing, hurting, and killing old men, women, and children achieves any military goal! But they must answer to God.

I thank Him that you have come so far, safely, and hope you and your men will succeed in sheltering yourselves before the winter. Your surgeon must be a wise and provident man who anticipates many calls upon his skill. Chickens are not a strange thing for a hospital. The meat and broth are very nourishing, and easy for the sick to digest.

Your warm reception of my words is pleasing. I shall adopt the same practice as you, of writing a bit each day. On, then, to news of home.

We grow and manufacture nearly all we need to nourish and clothe ourselves, but salt is hard to obtain. Wool being necessary for uniforms and blankets, we spin only a bit of it together with rabbit fur for knitting socks. Little boys snare the rabbits and trade them for things their families need. The older men still at home gather from farm to farm to help bring in the harvest. We take satisfaction in doing so much for ourselves, not depending upon the frivolous things that used to be part of our lives. Our crisis draws forth the strength and ingenuity of us all. We only wish we could do more for those who have lost everything.

My brother teaches us to count our blessings in the midst of adversity. They are many, and the good will among us is the best. So you see that though we lack some material things, we are rich in spirit.

With continued earnest prayer for you, who face so many dangers in that unsettled place, I remain your constant friend.

* * *

Camp Sherman, Dakota Territory
September 29, 1864

Would that I were there to comfort you and, insofar as my powers extend, alleviate the suffering you recount! I condemn such vicious means of prosecuting war. I pray the county will be spared a similar fate. Were it not for my sworn oath, I would come to you. The purest of emotion allures me. Believe me when I say I am torn in two!

We have been ordered out several times to chase and punish Indians for attacks upon emigrants or isolated "ranches." We have lost only one man killed, but a number are wounded. Dr. Barnes has set up his hospital in a tent. The rest of us are still in tents, too. All work hard to fell sufficient timber for a palisade, living quarters, stables, &c. A clear, year-round stream is our water supply, so we are constructing what in the West is called an <u>acequia</u> to channel water to a cistern (already dug and lined with the granite which forms the substratum and outcrops here) within the palisade. As I am told we can expect the first snows at any time, I am setting a fast pace. I presented the need to survive, to convince the men their construction work is of vital importance, and I am happy to say that except for routine grumbling, they are working with good will. I create competitions and offer prizes such as membership in a hunting expedition for most logs ready to build with, or best marksmanship, or most hay made. I conduct divine service and give the men what rest I can for the Sabbath.

Line command is new to me, so the *Regulations* are my vital guide, besides discussions with brother officers and what I learned of company discipline at the Military Academy. All these have so far kept us from disaster! My Ohio volunteers are very independent-minded, but they are learning from my veterans to yield to discipline and do their duty well. They can, I think, be led to excellence by justice and compassion in the application of discipline.

I drill the men thoroughly once a week, keep a guard mounted, conduct inspections, and hold target practice so their fighting skills will not wither. I have to buy extra ammunition out of the Post Fund, but I think training them to defend themselves effectively counts as benevolence! Other than that, we are all engineers, of one level or another—and farmers!

I am called now to lay out a line for the palisade,—before the mail leaves in a few minutes. God bless you and all there, and protect you from harm.

I remain, your true and faithful friend.

CHAPTER 12

OH, SHENANDOAH: WINTER

The South must yield at last. Taxed to her utmost, her strength is not yet failing, but ... her fall may be coming. Not that her brave spirit will be broken, but that the chains of her oppressors are too heavy for her, and she must sink a struggling victim to superior brute force.
—Horatio P. Batcheler, 73rd Regiment, British Army, 1864

Torquil

My heart was so heavy my voice had no life. The dreary monotone sounded like a calf bawling through dense fog. I ordered our base evacuated, to answer the army's call for defense of the Valley.

Next morning, I took Sergeant Loudoun and four others back to Raven Crags to reconnoiter. We made conspicuous, bold demonstration, with polished buttons and weapons flashing in the sun. By evening, we saw signs of troop movements. That night, we fetched ordnance stores. Next day, the enemy bombarded our position.

* * *

This summer the war grew vicious and bitter. Yankee generals intensified their war on citizens. With his massive armies arrayed against diminishing numbers of our defenders, Grant spent soldiers' lives mercilessly, knowing he could replace them. He ordered that the Valley be destroyed. General Sheridan began The Burning.

> The people must be left nothing but their eyes to weep with.
> —General Philip H. Sheridan, United States Army, advising Chancellor Bismarck of Prussia

> That an order so desperately wicked, so contrary to the spirit of Christianity, and so revolting to the civilization of this age, should have been issued and executed by officers commanding the armies of a free, civilized, and religious nation, is, indeed, almost too incredible for human belief.
> —Chambersburg, Pennsylvania, newspaper, *Valley Spirit*, October 26, 1864

> The conduct of the Federals to the distressed Confederates has become the scandal of Europe. Every expedition is undertaken in a spirit of vicious malice, and their whole line of conduct is marked with cruel destruction of life and property, and wanton tyranny. Houses, barns, villages, engines, railroads, stations, they destroy ruthlessly. … Their craving is now for blood.
> —Horace P. Batcheler, 73rd Regiment, British Army, 1864

Citizens were helpless against armed men robbing them of everything they had, destroying all their means of supporting life. Houses were ordered to be spared, but some were not. Our ranks were so thinned, we could only attack isolated portions of the destroyers' rear guard.

General Early, sent to the Shenandoah Valley to create the impression that his force was much larger than it really was, was ordered to put on a bold front and do the best he could in holding Sheridan at bay. As part of Early's Army of the Valley, we Rangers rode with General Imboden in the Northwestern Brigade. The fighting was ceaseless. In ten months, our army marched 1,670 miles and engaged in fifty-three battles and skirmishes. The ruin of the Valley was complete. More than four hundred square miles of prime farmland was laid waste.

We had no chance for independent forays. Our horses grew worn and weary. Only twenty-six of us remained. I grieved for the losses but maintained command distance and kept the men on their mettle. I led divine service each week. I prayed.

General Early left cavalry pickets at New Market and a signal detachment on Three Top, and took the rest of his force to Staunton to winter. But when Sheridan sent General Torbert with 6,000 cavalry to destroy the Virginia Central Railroad, Early sent the Northwestern Brigade to Gordonsville. We stopped Torbert just short of the town on December 23. He withdrew.

* * *

"What's the condition of your command?" Major Willis set my reports on his table. He stretched his hands toward the scanty fire and motioned me closer to it.

"Much reduced, sir. Our effective strength is nineteen, including myself. The men and horses are badly worn, a number are sick. I request to subsist them at home for the winter when the present campaign is finished."

"This part of Virginia is too important to lose. I desire you to follow Torbert, observe him, and report his movements. Stragglers or prisoners could give us the information we need.

"Follow them till they cross the Blue Ridge or encamp on this side. Establish an outpost, observe the enemy, and send word if he stirs. Keep post till you receive new orders."

"Yes, sir. May we expect to be supplied?"

"If you do, you'll be disappointed, unless you can recapture the cattle they stole north of Gordonsville."

We marched north the next morning, Christmas Eve. My sick begged not to be left behind, so I ordered them into the wagon for shelter from the freezing snowstorm and had Blair hitch their horses with the team. I could locate the wagon in the dark by the sound of coughing.

Warfare was my life. It plugged the void left by loss of dearest human love. It consumed all my energies. It had filled a quarter of my years, till the ways of peace were a dim memory.

In Virginia's first war for independence, the Continental Army's cause sometimes seemed lost. This bitter winter must be the Valley Forge of my State's second fight for government by the consent of the governed. Defeat was unthinkable.

> [At] grandmother's ... I saw about a hundred lights moving around, and such a row as I heard ... planks were being smashed up, doors broken open, oaths and glassware flew like hail ... premises were stripped of everything ... what could not be carried off was broken to pieces. The yankees ... took hold of her collar and demanded her money which they did not get. Everybody within three or four miles of the road on which the Yankees marched was treated just as

bad as Grandma and in a great many instances much worse for in some cases they beat the women and men who remained at home. ... [at Moreheads] the ladies said the yanks had slit all their ears getting out their earrings and ... destroyed everything that they could get hold of and carried what they could ... [at] Mr. Tutts where we found a Yankee ... whose days were evidently numbered and whom the ladies of the house although they had been robbed and plundered of everything they had, had taken into the house and taken care of.
—From the diary of William Nalle, Culpeper, Virginia, age 15, eyewitness, December 24–25, 1864

This demoralizing and disgraceful practice of pillage must cease, else the country will rise on us and *justly* shoot us down like dogs and wild beasts.
—General William T. Sherman, United States Army[15]

Torbert's trail led to Culpeper Court House, where as school-boys we'd savored the novelty of a large town. We bivouacked in its abandoned buildings. Some who'd survived the wicked marauding told us that citizens shooting from their own houses had accounted for some of the pillagers, and armed, mounted men were hunting for others.

On Christmas Day, the trail led to Abercairn. We Rangers were the only Confederate regulars in the county. I raised my sabre above my head and my voice above the storm.

"We are Abercairn's Shield! Eighty-eight years ago today, a Virginian led his men to victory over the British at Trenton! Today our duty calls us to rid our neighbors of the Yankee

---

15 General William T. Sherman, United States Army, General Orders No. 49, July 7, 1862, italics added.

wolves and save the women and little ones from harm! As we go, we shall invite the county to take up their arms and join us, and raise the alarm till all men hear! The Court House is the rallying point and the time is tomorrow morning's light. As we go, we shall capture all the destroyers we find.

"For the honor of Abercairn and of our own names as Christian men, we shall not murder them. They alone will bear the foul name of villainy. As we have always done, disable them. Kill only in defense of self or each other or the lives of our neighbors, *no matter what the provocation.* There are courts to hang them. God is our Judge. Our hands must be clean.

"May God bless our hunting!

"*Abercairn!*"

"ABERCAIRN!"

* * *

I brought my detachment into the Glenlochie stable yard late at night. No one was trying to sleep. Rangers and neighbors about the barn and yard, enraged at the brutality, anticipated tomorrow's hunt.

"Didn't you find any, sir?" Menteith greeted me.

"They're in the jail, fourteen of them. How many here?"

"Five, and a few killed east of Willow Run."

"Casualties?"

"MacHugh and a Yankee, taken care of."

"How bad is MacHugh?"

"Flesh wound in his leg. He's in the kitchen, sopping up sympathy."

"Take the men to the house for something to eat, and prepare five days' cooked rations. We'll continue after Torbert as soon as we finish the hunt. Camp in the house tonight."

At the Court House in starlit, biting cold, I met with the gray-haired Abercairn leaders. Judge Carmichael, Mr. Ogilvie, and Dominie Gilchrist stood in the porch; Sheriff MacKeith and Mr. Lachlan were riding up. We divided into parties to cover each watershed and ascertain the welfare of every family. We'd hunt down the marauders and bring them as prisoners to the Court House to be tried and sentenced.

* * *

"Reporting for duty, sir."

"Kendrick!"

"In the flesh, Beau!"

"More of it than there used to be!" His uniform coat strained its buttons.

"My wife's good cooking!" He'd rigged a harness to keep his balance one-legged in the saddle, and slung a crutch below it.

"That's quite an invention!"

"I've been using it a month now."

Married! Thinking he was able to fight!

"Take MacHugh's place in the column." I gave my half-smile and meant it.

The Rangers burst into cheers. Robbie shook hands with everyone as he passed.

We soldiers took the eastern section, the most dangerous part of Abercairn today. We cut Torbert's track and followed all the side trails the criminals made along MacKnight's Run.

Heart-sickening, ruthless destruction at MacKnights' farm: household goods and furniture, covered in snow, smashed and strewn around the dooryard; women's and children's clothing, for which the robbers could have no use, torn and scattered about. The farm dog's body still guarded the path to the front door. The Yankees had tried to burn the house, but cold and snow prevented the fire from taking hold. They'd broken down doors and smashed out windows. Bullet holes in the walls told of attempts to murder the family within.

In the farmyard, Mr. Case, the elderly hired man, was salvaging animals wantonly killed. Carcasses hung on tree branches. In his hands were saw and knife, by his side a flintlock musket, polished with use. Pigs and chickens lay where they'd been shot by the ruthless plunderers. A wounded cow lowed piteously. Barrels with their heads knocked in were fouled or their contents spilled broadcast. A home and a year's work and thrift lay ruined.

"Fan out and make sure they're all gone. Airlie, see about Mrs. MacKnight and the children." I dismounted to question Mr. Case.

David Airlie

I found Mrs. MacKnight and her four small children in the dimmest reach of the cellar.

"They've hurt Andrew."

She held him in her arms, wrapped in her shawl, while the other children, warned to keep quiet to save their lives, clutched at their mother's skirts and stared at me.

I was shocked. "How bad? Let me see."

She uncovered the little boy's head. Along the left cheek and into his hair, a deep gash had now quit bleeding, but Andrew was unconscious.

"How did it happen? When?" I palpated along the wound and found serious swelling.

"He ran in front of me and shook his baby fists and said, 'Don't you hurt my mama!'" she sobbed. "One of them hit him with his gun. Yesterday evening."

Andrew's eyelids fluttered, but when he opened his eyes, they only stared unseeingly.

Torquil

Mr. Case's account showed we'd already captured this gang of destroyers. I received Airlie's report with gravity that covered rage.

"So it's concussion for sure, and maybe a depressed fracture of the skull, like McClure had after Cedar Creek. He came around all right."

"McClure has a harder head! There's bound to be swelling inside the skull, too, that needs to be relieved. We haven't the skill. Escort them to Glenlochie, and send to the Court House for prayer and a surgeon. Then catch us up. We've got to get the rest of them."

* * *

In bitter wind, we reached Ashby's Gap, where the Yankees had crossed the Blue Ridge. It was so cold, and the horses so worn out, that we had to walk to keep from freezing and make the march possible for them. Clouds were thickening on the third day when I led my command into a hollow, where knives of wind were deflected by forested heights to the west.

"Sergeant Loudoun, set up camp in the best place you can find. Post sentinels. I'm going to reconnoitre while there's any light."

I clambered straight for the crest and climbed a tree. Deep white snow was slashed by the Yankees' back trail. A last ray of sun shining under thick storm clouds cast thin, long shadows behind the enemy column marching west.

Nine days later, the wagon I'd sent for supplies reached us. I'd ordered my men to half rations the day after we arrived. My woodscraft had produced only a deer and a few rabbits. We tied our horses to trees so the hungry creatures could eat the bark. Loudoun had cobbled our ragged tents together to make one thicker, warmer shelter. Wet or green wood made a minimum of heat, but it encouraged us and warmed our scanty rations. I brewed a tea of evergreen needles and required everyone to drink it to stave off scurvy.

The enemy had evidently gone into winter quarters. Any picket posts they might have established were beyond our view.

Every soul and hoof depended on me for survival. I was worn to a shadow, but I forced my tired, cold, and hungry body to serve. I had to be stronger and more enduring than my men, but it was hard to think and order duties. They looked drawn and weather beaten. The bitter cold took a harsh toll on their bodies and put grim expressions on their faces. Their eyes were sore; their lips and fingers chapped and cracked and bled. The cold fatigued us so we moved like sleepwalkers. We wore all the ragged garments we possessed. Our boots and shoes were thin and broken. We slept huddled two or three together for warmth, under our combined blankets and greatcoats.

Though I shortened the reliefs to thirty minutes, men came off guard stumbling, with cognition and reason impaired. Willie shivered as if to shake himself to pieces. MacCammond and I gathered his little body between ours and drew our blankets tighter. I took Willie's relief after that. Robbie's leg pained him. He tried to massage it only when no one was looking.

So worn out we could move only at half speed, we built a hut and a shelter for the horses. When the weather broke enough to make travel less perilous, I sent Loudoun to the army.

"My report, with requisition for supplies and any new orders." I handed over the scraps of paper. "Then go to our telegraph station at New Market. Here's my request to them.

"Learn how to use the telegraph and how to connect a pocket relay set to the wires, anywhere. If they can spare a set, bring it back. If they can't, we'll get one by other means. If the Yankees start to move, the army must know immediately."

On hunting trips, I scouted farther and located an isolated, badly guarded Yankee telegraph station. Till Loudoun returned with his new telegraphy skill, I gambled dwindling stores of food and forage against the possibility of capturing more, ordering extra portions for man and beast before I led them to the attack. We appeared like wraiths out of the storm to capture pickets, horses, food, munitions, and an entire supply-and-repair train of wagons. I put Loudoun in charge of the telegraph and left four others for guards.

I kept one new wagon, medical supplies, rations, and clothing. I reclothed my men, but ordered them to wear their tattered uniform coats outermost. Keeping all the horses for remounts, I sent our own starvelings home, along with wagon loads of rations, tools, spare wagon wheels, and other goods for the court to distribute. The Yankees owe the county much more! I armed my men with the Spencer carbines, which were now the regulation arm for Yankee cavalry. They had only a seven-shot capacity, but we'd captured plenty of the cartridges. I kept my Henry and all the ammunition: I was still the best marksman.

When the Yankees recaptured their telegraph station, and Loudoun and his guard escaped safe, I sent him, with a guard and the captured telegraph relay, to intercept the Yankees' messages. Thus, in late February, we learned about Sheridan's march from Winchester up the Valley, with ten thousand sabres in his command. We informed Major Willis and received orders to rejoin him and the army to resist the Yankee advance.

* * *

War is evil, war is horrible, war is a plague. But there is one thing worse than a war, and that is the loss of a war.
—Colonel R. Ernest Dupuy, United States Army

Human virtue must be equal to human calamity.
—General Robert E. Lee, Confederate States Army

General Early's Army of the Valley now consisted of less than two thousand men of all arms. He made his stand on the ridge west of Waynesboro. On March 2, a day of bitter cold, biting wind, and steady fall of heavy sleet, Sheridan attacked. One of his mounted brigades assailed our left, while the other two overran the center and right. General Early had made the boldest front he could with the valiant Valley Army.

Abercairn fought to the end. Reading the battle by its currents of sound and through field glasses, I withdrew the company just before we, too, could be overwhelmed. We regrouped among thick timber on a steep hillside north of Rockfish Gap, where we'd left our wagon. No one was missing. Dunnachie furled and cased our flag.

"Sergeant Menteith, post pickets and set up camp. No fires. No noise. I'm going to find out who to report to."

I scouted all night and found no one.

The Army of the Valley was no more.

My original commission to defend Abercairn must, therefore, remain my purpose. I divided my men into two squads—eight and nine members—to scout east and west of a crow's-flight line to Abercairn and gather information. Loudoun was ordered to wire into the telegraph lines.

* * *

"I got it from Winchester. Their operator always pauses before a J. The General's hunting you," Loudoun reported when we met.

"Where?"

"Culpeper to Blue Ridge, Wolftown to Flint Hill, searching houses, questioning citizens—with force!"

"Do they want me alive or dead?"

"Alive."

"Good. I'll draw their fire. I'll meet them and make them chase me west, through the Gap and across the Shenandoah. They can't do more harm there! If they lose me, I'll double back and engage them. That'll lure them away from Abercairn!"

"What's the Shield to do?" Menteith asked.

"Protect the citizens. Visit everyone and tell them to tell the Yankees I've gone to meet them. Coordinate your strategies with the home defense."

I took provisions for a journey of unknown length and borrowed all the money in the command. Each Ranger knew his word to Mr. Ogilvie would be honored with repayment. My final orders commended their courage and fidelity, and formally turned the command over to Menteith. I took the strongest horse and rode to meet the enemy.

It was a fox chase. I was Reynard.

* * *

COVERT CORRESPONDENCE, March, 1865

Abercairn C. H.

He's drawn off the Yankees and they're chasing him west ...

WESTERN UNION

Horseshoe Creek Station, Dakota Territory

Pray daily 2 PM God send him to me .. stop .. yours

BOOK II
DAKOTA TERRITORY

CHAPTER 13

IN THE PRESENCE
OF MINE ENEMIES

1. Alone

[The *Code Duello*] brought constantly to a man's mind, not as a menace, but as a principle, the belief that his words were part of his character and his life. False or cruel speech was to be answered for, as was an evil act; it, therefore, was held *to be* an act, not mere empty breath.
—Harriot Horry Ravenel

Torquil

Fourth barracks was a powder keg with match held to fuse, since I'd wounded "one of theirs" before they captured me. I got the wall behind me and touched it off.

"My name is Drummond."

"'Dumb 'un', did he say?" someone sneered.

"We-ll, boys," drawled a backcountry voice, as its lanky, red-haired owner unfolded himself from his bunk, "let's give the Johnny a wel-come."

"Teach a traitor his lesson, you mean!" A fair, stocky young soldier joined the advance.

"Sure an' I've been hearin' a Reb can whip ten Yanks. Let's be afther findin' out!" A wiry Irishman stalked up, a forward jerk of his head drawing the others with him.

"Where I'm from, only cowards fight many-to-one." Disdain made my words a purring goad.

"Begorra, the sauce o' the man!"

A thick-built blond stepped belligerently close. "Not a dog, only a pup."

"If you think you're the best, be the first."

"We are the best. Licked you Rebs, didn't we?"

"Only by larger numbers and acting like the Huns!"

"Yew all was whipped to pieces, puppy! 'Fess up now." The redhead's drawl equally patronized and goaded.

"Not him! Too pert by half! Guess we can fix his flint!" A soldier with shaggy blond eyebrows and a clenched fist came closer.

"Where's your slaves to help you now, Secesh?" jeered another, who looked like his twin.

"My family never had any."

"An' afther bein' a liar, too!"

"Take back your lie or answer for it!" I closed the distance to the Irishman in a half a step.

"What answer would ye be havin'?" Safe among numbers, he gave a tight little grin and tapped my shoulder with his right fist. "Me right answer"—he tapped with the other fist—"or the one that's left?"

I drove a fist into that grin, and the rest closed in. The broad-built blond, on my right, looked dumb as an ox and strong as one. The Irishman staggered to my left. In front, the lanky redhead and the fair, stocky soldier were backed up by the lookalikes.

They rushed me.

"Cowards." I sneered the patent verdict.

My daemon took over at the first blow. Last I remember, I was fighting.

* * *

In solid darkness, I revived, body armored in pain that shattered to a thousand spears that stabbed me when I moved ... gritted my teeth and diagnosed a molar loose, face damaged ... hoped a couple of stabbing ribs were only cracked. I washed off the blood before I rolled myself in my blanket and catnapped till First Call, then forced my protesting body to respond to Reveille. At roll call, looking as blank as I could, I saw I'd given a good account of myself.

"Sure an' it's a pretty bouquet o' mugs ye've brought to me this mornin', ye brawlin' scuts!" Sergeant O'Shea, tall and gray, burly and battle scarred, stalked along the line. "Wid such inergy to spare, ye'll be wantin' more to do, an' I've just the thing. Ye will be carryin' the log for two hours." He stopped in front of me. "Ye led me bhoys astray. Ye will carry it four hours, and be on the chines another four."

At Stables, I was assigned an awkward, rangy Chestnut mare who rolled her eyes and stamped nervously. I got a halter on her and approached closer. She tried to back away.

"Sooo, lassie ... sooo, then," I soothed, close as possible to ears now pricked to listen.

I talked soft while I examined her for defects, injuries, or signs of ill treatment. None.

I murmured assurances while I groomed and fed her. At mounted drill, her gaits were as awkward as her appearance. I collected her and began, with legs and reins, seat and voice, to retrain her while we performed the drills. She had the build for stamina and speed. I named her Severa.

Carrying the log meant, carry a forty-pound log in any chosen manner, but forbidden to put it down or get off my feet. It's one of the lesser punishments, but it felt like more than four hours when the guard dismissed me. "On the chines" was to stand half a day on top of a barrel with the head knocked out, so, on the ends of the staves. Standing alternately knock-kneed and bow-legged to ease leg muscles and feet, I was jeered by all who passed by. The laundresses' brats threw dust and stones till the guard—after some time—chased them away. I surveyed, beyond the palisade, pine forest, granite outcrops, a few aspens, and ground cleared for half a mile around. When the guard released me, I leapfrogged down from the barrel to pretend it'd all been a lark.

> Then ever I awake with a convulsive sigh, which comes unbidden – like an echo. 'Tis the answer to the summons of the REAL.
> —General Philip St. George Cooke[16]

It took all my faith to thank God for each day. Worse than continued hostility, fourth barracks ostracized me—acted like I didn't exist. Still stunned by loss and feeling kicked into the Yankee army, I kept my face blank and never spoke, but I began to feel like I had no *right* to exist. It took all my reserves just to live and not believe that.

To the rest of the post—contract waggoners, citizens passing through or trading at the sutler's store, the laundresses and their legitimate or illegitimate husbands and families, soldiers from other barracks or posts—I was fair game. My manners, speech, and fitted uniform provoked jibes about "the little gent." Birthplace and Confederate service made me a target. I'd fought

---

16 General Philip St. George Cooke, *Scenes and Adventures in the Army*, p. 299, emphasis original.

to protect my home and neighbors, I said, and maintain the government by consent of the governed my forefathers had created. I'd done nothing dishonorable. We'd been defeated in battle *only*. They heaped scorn on that.

Some, determined to humble me or make me recant, goaded me till I had to fight or be shamed. I usually lost. Pain made my temper short, and so did the punishments I got for fighting. Sergeant O'Shea sometimes put me in the guardhouse. He had me on his bad list: I was told off for all the hardest, dirtiest, and lengthiest fatigue details.

When soul and body hurt too much, I took refuge at night in the post library, a room in the headquarters building holding a lot of old books and some military manuals. Because my desperate act after losing Ewen made home a deadly trap, I was cut off from my own place, my own home, my own friends. Desperate for news, I read the papers. All the Confederate States were under military rule. Citizens in some places were forced to surrender all firearms. My dear devasted Virginia was visited as a curiosity by self-righteous, gloating Northerners who exhibited my people and their poverty like a raree show in the public press. One, Whitelaw Reid, wrote with cruel greed that Northerners could easily exploit impoverished Southerners to make fortunes for themselves, by buying their lands or businesses for a tenth of their real value.

MacLeod had been kind, but my trust, once broken, can't be restored. Had I wanted to visit my only link with home, I couldn't. Unlike the easy mingling among ranks of Southern volunteers, in the Regular Army an iron line lay between officer corps and enlisted men. First Sergeant Dunahan was the only intermediary.

The victors sentenced me to third-rate status in the army I thought God had ordered me into. I could never marry a lady, never meet other gentlemen on an equal footing, never receive the respect I'd earned, as long as I was an enlisted man. The highest I could rise was regimental sergeant major. Just to amuse myself, I might as well try for it. I playacted what I supposed I should do. With my clan motto, *Fidelis*—"faithful"—in mind, I met MacLeod's dismissive challenge, "Did you think it would be easy?" head-on.

Sorrow that Da and Douglas were gone kept me awake after the nightmares, but rehearsal of the hopeless truth blunted its power. Emptiness and sorrow remained.

> There's not a comrade here tonight
>> But knows that loved ones far away
>> On bended knees this night will pray:
> "God bring our darling from the fight."
> But there are none to wish me back,
>> For me no yearning prayers arise.
>> The lips are mute and closed the eyes—
> My home is in the bivouac.
>> —William Gordon McCabe, Confederate
>> States Army, "Christmas Night of '62"

I patched my life together with iron thread.

* * *

MacLeod led divine service every Sunday after inspection. I attended because I wanted to be with God. Waiting for worship to begin, I bowed my head to beg forgiveness and enter into His presence. I sat in the back, never opened my mouth, and departed unseen after the last amen. One Sunday, the text included Jesus' admonition, "Love your enemies, do good to them that hate you, bless them that curse you, and pray for them that despitefully use you." Reminded of what my Savior desired, I obeyed.

I covered for Smith when he slipped away from a work detail, but I'm not sure it fooled Corporal Graham. I did the lion's share of kitchen fatigues when Woods, despondent because his sweet-heart had married another man, stared dejectedly at the work instead of doing it. Though I had to pray in strict obedience and blind faith, when I heard or thought of ways my squad mates might wish to be blessed, I prayed for them. Thus I took an aggressive position toward the enemies around me. I saw no sign that my obedience to God changed their stance.

In the longest-lasting spiritual discipline I'd ever undergone, I had no earthly satisfaction, but my spirit was satisfied in my Lord alone. It was not happiness, but it had the clarity and purity of the Light.

After reading my Bible by dim candlelight in the barracks each evening, I observed my squad mates' characters.

Corporal Graham kept his squad under discipline by pungent reproofs delivered in his deep bass voice, and rough kindness. Competent in many things, he'd been one of the lead artificers when the fort was built and now led in maintaining it. I learned a lot when assigned to his work details.

Maguire, the Irishman, was from the port of Marietta on the Ohio River: riverfront roughness tempered by sincere Catholicism and concern for his mother and younger siblings. Barely tall enough for the army, he was tough and wiry and had a sardonic twist to his mouth.

Smith, the tawny-eyed redhead, found a lot to hoot at. From his lanky height, he looked down on the foibles of his fellows and punctured them. While he honed his verbal barbs, he whittled wooden animals so lifelike, a man'd expect them to scurry from his hands. He'd be a good man to have on your side in a fight.

Grey, my bunkie, was well brought up but trying to act rough. He embarrassed himself with his watered-down version of risqué language. His anger at traitors was from principle, not spite. In the simple fairness of his heart, he thought everyone should do right and take their licks if they didn't. Ash blond hair, gray eyes, round pink cheeks—he looked like a cherub in a painting. The others chaffed him because he was the youngest.

Woods and Anderson were half brothers who looked like twins: tall, square-shouldered, lean flanks, long legs, small hands and feet. Sun-bleached blond hair, shaggy eyebrows to match, long, thin noses. Woods had brown eyes, Anderson's were blue, the only difference I could see. They were bunkies and did everything together.

2. *Commandant*

> With the men of his troop ...[the] commander all too often had to be priest, physician, lawyer, banker, friend or tyrant.
> —S. E. Whitman, *The Troopers*

MacLeod

Military life requires order. Without it, men are set on edge and erupt into chaos. I'd set up the post for maintaining order. The new recruits lived in one barrack, the incorrigibles in another, and the Old Issues, men serving their second or third enlistment, in two more.

Convinced that a commission is a solemn contract, requiring stern duty as well as bringing privileges, I worked for my soldiers' welfare. I kept up their morale by providing enough warm clothing for the bitter winters and plenty of the best food available. The post garden was planted to hardy, scurvy-preventing vegetables suited for the dry climate and 6,000-foot altitude. I was unyielding about cleanliness—the Old Issues said, "finicky as a woman!"—and was rewarded with healthy men ready for action. In battle I never sent them where I wouldn't lead. Thus I conquered their hearts—and their obedience.

On nights when duty allowed, I stopped at the hospital to visit my sick and wounded. I wrote letters for those unable to do so and brought books and periodicals from the post library. The books were from my family and friends, to save the Post Fund for other improvements.

When military polish was equal, I chose the more sociable man for orderly. While the trumpeter was watching the clock in the orderly room next to my office, to sound the calls at the precise times, he and the orderly would chat. I'd designed the two rooms for transmission of sound, but made the adjutant's room, behind my office, with thick walls and door behind which confidential business could be transacted. While I did administrative work, I heard the news of the post. I built the reputation of reading minds and having eyes in the back of my head, to prevent trouble before it began.

My word established in the post regulations was law. I was strict, permitting no trifling about duty or discipline, but as fair as my information could make me, and had no favorites. As the only representative of government within fifty miles, I was called upon to adjudicate citizens' infractions and disputes, too. I made justice evenhanded, to the point, and swift.

Without basic honesty, or faithfulness to duty, from the heavy-drinking lieutenants, I took much of their work upon myself to save time. I suspected them of worse, so I collected evidence to substantiate the charges I would bring, to have them cashiered for the good of the service.

3. Proven

Torquil

Independence Day was celebrated with games and races, the artillery's National Salute at Meridian, and a target-shooting contest. The best-placed three shots with our Spencers would win. Though the best marksmen were seldom effective beyond two hundred yards, the targets were now at two hundred fifty. Only Smith and I succeeded that far.

He stepped up to the mark, laid the buttplate of his rifle into the hollow of his shoulder almost lazily, sighted, and fired.

"Three in the bullseye!" shouted Sergeant Powell, the down range judge.

I fired three shots.

"Three in the bullseye!"

Powell moved the targets to two hundred seventy-five yards. Smith fired quickly.

"Three in the bullseye!"

I fired three deliberate shots.

"One in the bullseye!"

The soldiers cheered, crowding around Smith and clapping him on the back.

"Ask the sergeant to see how many are in the hole."

Powell dug out a bullet, a flat second one, then a third mangled by the impact of both.

Smith shook my hand. "That was some shoot-in."

"First time all evening I could make it work. I thought you had me at two fifty, when you made them all touch like a cloverleaf."

He grinned. "Took me all eve-nin'!"

* * *

Sun baked the earth in the foothills next day, where I was one of a wood-cutting detail. On the other side of the clearing a hundred yards away, Maguire was fastening a clanking chain to haul a log. Beyond him, a black bear stalked purposefully out of the woods at a pace I didn't know a bear could sustain. It was almost upon him.

"Maguire! Down! On your face!"

Too late. The bear tore him, spinning him to the ground. Arterial blood pumping—in three minutes, he'd be dead. Grabbing my Spencer, I chambered a round, counting seconds.

Fifteen.

Firing on the run, I hit the bear's hindquarters.

Twenty-five.

It looked around. Roaring at the top of my voice, I ran closer, dropped to one knee, and fired a lung shot.

Fifty.

I ran on.

Seventy.

Incredibly, the bear shook itself and charged me. To the knee again, aiming with great care: a head shot.

Eighty-five.

It kept coming! I emptied the magazine. The bear fell within a pace of me.

One hundred and twenty.

Tossing the carbine aside, I sprinted to Maguire, who was writhing on the ground and holding his abdomen with both hands.

"Shut your eyes and hold your hands behind your head." Low, flat voice to command confidence and compel obedience.

One hundred and thirty-five.

Straddling his legs, I grasped the peritoneal artery and pinched it shut.

'O dear God, spare his life!'

O'Shea and the rest of the detail arrived.

"With your permission, Sergeant." Command voice.

"Ye hev it!" O'Shea growled, furious.

I rapped out precise orders.

"Anderson, pull a thread from my coat. Grey, grip wrists with him."

To Maguire, as I searched the wound and picked out shreds of cloth with my left hand, I crooned, "Bide wi' me, laddie, bide wi' me. Are ye wi' me, noo?"

"Yes." His whisper was weak.

Peritoneum torn, muscle layers and skin in broad ribbons, blood pooling in the wound. From the ribcage past the center of the abdomen, it gaped ten inches wide.

I took one end of the thread in my teeth kept it taut. With my free hand I wound the other end several times around the artery, tightened it, tied it off. I sank back on my heels, drawing deep breaths, looked nowhere, and commanded, "Whiskey!"

A flat bottle fell next to my leg. I didn't see or hear the donor. O'Shea didn't seem to.

"What're ye scuts gawkin' at! Cut some poles and be makin' a travois!"

I poured whiskey throughout the bloody damage, wet my shirt, and laid it over the wound. Left the bottle to its owner and helped load Maguire onto the travois. O'Shea told off an escort.

"Graham, Smith, be dressin' that meat to haul! The rest o' ye, cut wood!"

We returned with a full load. On my way to the mess hall, O'Shea called me into the orderly room and shoved the door shut.

"If Maguire lives, 'twill be your doin'. 'Tis why I let ye hev yer head." Then he roared, "If iver agin ye speak to me as ye did this day, I'll break ye in two wid me own hands!"

I lifted my chin—made him madder.

"Hev ye more orders ye'd like to be givin' yer betters!"

"No, Sergeant." My face felt hot.

"Hev ye iver heard the word 'respect'!"

"Yes."

"What is it!"

"To give proper honor."

"Then *honor* me words wid yer full attention! Ye may've been Jeff Davis hisself, ye arrogant Reb, but ye're now the least! Keep a civil tongue in yer head accordin'ly! An' to be sure ye've learnt your lesson, ye will be at hard labor with the prisoners tomorrow. Dismissed!"

* * *

"Still think you're too good to talk to us, you high-nosed Reb?" Grey hailed me when I brought my supper to the table.

"How's Maguire?" was all I could think of to say. I'd missed human fellowship, but now I was tongue-tied. The chasm gaped.

"I stopped to see," Graham rumbled. "Sawbones fixed him up. He was asleep."

"Did he give him ary chanst?" Smith looked like he cared.

"He wouldn't predict. He was the color of his blanket." A nod to me. "Good thing you got there when you did. Hunt many bear?"

"Only panther. He was the hunter. I didn't know they stalked like that."

"Generally they don't."

"Yew fixin' to keep the hide?" Smith probably had plans for it.

"Is it here?"

"In the wa-gon."

In the wagon park, we rescued it from a couple of stray dogs and spread it on the ground. Smith said he'd show me how to tan and cure it. We were scraping the fat off the underside when Grey came up.

"Maguire's asking for you. Sawbones says you can go in for a minute."

Dr. Barnes pointed me to the small ward, where the walls were whitewashed and the smell of bromine bit my nostrils. Maguire opened his eyes.

"You asked for me?"

"To give ye me thanks. I owe ye me life."

"You'll return the favor some day. How are you feeling?"

"Like a mewlin' kitten."

"You bled a lot."

Then we didn't say anything. Maguire stretched out his right hand to break the silence.

"I'm John Patrick Maguire, Johnny Pat to me friends."

"I'm Beau, to mine." I grasped the hand.

Doctor Barnes beckoned me to leave.

"Good-bye."

"Only good-night. I'll pray you recover." Walking to the barracks, I did.

* * *

At hard labor with guardhouse inmates—MacLeod's "cut-throats"—I parried profane and obscene taunts about my late allegiance, parentage and character, but I had to defend with my fists. Since that first Muster Day, I knew I had to stay on my feet or jump up quick, or I'd be stomped to pieces. Incensed by the prisoners' baiting, I pitched into Biggs with brain full of red fire. I battered him down and kicked him till the others beat me away.

CHAPTER 14

NEMESIS: *FINIS*

1. Yohanson's Revenge

It is a sin peculiar to man to hate his victim.
—Cornelius Tacitus, *Agricola*

Torquil

Grey could be counted on to blunder into territory where angels feared to tread. "What got into you when you were attending O'Shea's play-party?"

"I don't know. It comes on me, don't know what's happening till it's over."

"What you do is go berserk." Graham's grandpa was Norwegian, he said. "He yarns about old-time battles when men 'ud throw off their armor and helmet and shield, and go rampagin' into battle with only their weapons, like they couldn't be killed. They was battle crazy."

Next day when MacLeod had departed to serve on a court martial at Fort Liberty, DuChemin led out a scouting party, and Yohanson was acting post commander. Fourth barracks had garrison duty. I was helping position an artillery piece when the orderly bounded up the steps to the firing platform.

"Lieutenant Yohanson wants you right away."

My insides knotted up so bad they felt like stones. The night of torture wasn't the end of it! "To the ends of earth and time," I'd vowed. Dakota Territory wasn't the end of the earth, but it was far enough. Would this nemesis stalk me all my life?

Yohanson rose slow, lumbered in a circle around me, breathing loudly, saying nothing. Standing at attention, I kept eyes fixed on the wall, so afraid I couldn't think what to pray except: 'Please! No!'

The little room filled with wicked red, black darkness.

"Yer goin' on a scout thet won't attract no attention from the redskins. Alone, not a noisy herd scarin' 'em off. Yuh'll leave here after dark. Meet me outside the sally port with yer horse and field outfit right after Taps fer final orders."

Orders to be murdered! If he didn't accuse me of desertion—with my horse, weapons, and all to prove it!—and have the guard shoot me "while trying to escape," he'd kill me himself. I was forbidden to seek death. Whatever punishment he chose for insubordination might not be fatal.

"With all due respect, sir, I refuse."

"Refuse to obey a direct order?" A sly look settled on his heavy features.

"Yes, sir."

"Guard!"

They locked me in a cell. I had to acknowledge God had justly abandoned me to the result of my sin. I'd hated, hunted, and tried to murder. The commander of an isolated post like this had absolute power. He could abuse it with impunity. I was delivered to nemesis—again.

When I didn't get dinner, I supposed no one had drawn rations for another prisoner. With no supper, I wondered if I'd be fed at all. Anderson moved me out while Smith filled the water bucket that night.

"What became of my supper?"

Neither answered. Then I saw the notice by the cell door.

No food. No talk.

By order, Lt. Yohanson

Day after day, I had too much time to fear what worse vengeance he'd take. It would be more than confinement and starvation. He loved to inflict pain.

* * *

Without my blanket, I shivered through cold, high-altitude nights. Hunger left no energy for pacing. Was he going to starve me to death? Late one night, the grating eased open.

"Ssst! Reb! Here!" I could barely hear Grey's whisper.

"Go away! You'll be up the spout if you're caught!"

"I'm the guard. I'm supposed to be here. Here!"

In the faint light, I siezed a tied-up rag, forgot thanks, slavering to devour the beef inside.

"What're ya doin'!" Yohanson bellowed.

"Overseeing the prisoner, sir."

"If I'd a-wanted 'im seen, I'd a-said to! What's thet I smell? Guard!

"Lock 'im in there! Mutiny, aidin' a prisoner."

Woods put Grey in the other cell. Yohanson lumbered into mine and caught me gulping the last of the beef.

I'd have tried guile to fight a massive opponent—I could've used the water bucket—but *Regulations* prescribes death as the maximum penalty if a soldier strikes a superior officer. Yohanson would revel in exacting it! I dared not raise a hand to defend myself.

He hammered me with his big fists. One blow at a time, pause, another blow. He didn't hit hard enough to knock me senseless, but kept me conscious to feel all the pain, all the time. He held me up by my coat collar when I'd have fallen, and hit and hit and hit. It was almost dawn when he left me on the floor.

I stifled a groan. Total helplessness. He hurt me at will. I had no power to prevent it. I felt bruised clear through. It hurt to move. It hurt to swallow. It hurt to breathe. My soul hurt.

More days passed.

One evening at Recall, Yohanson entered. My muscles and viscera tensed when I stood at attention. All my senses flared high.

"I'm orderin' ya ta go on a one-man scout."

"With all due respect, sir, I refuse." To me, the usual phrase meant "no respect at all."

"I'll hev ya whipped fer thet." He left.

Whipped! It was for low criminals! For moral outrages! I'd rather be killed than disgraced like that, my name trampled in the dirt, my honor destroyed. If I pleaded for death, he'd enjoy shaming me the more. I'd acted honorably, obeyed God the best way I could. I deserved punishment for vengeance, and insubordination, but not this! Not this!

> This evening our Brigade is ordered out to witness a horrible sight. One … condemned to be whipped publicly. … tied to a pole … hands stretched above his head and his shirt stripped to the waist. The executioner being likewise a criminal who is to earn his release from punishment by inflicting this disgrace on his fellow man. The word being given, the executioner began his disgusting work, the wretched man wincing and his flesh shrinking neath every blow which one after another were delivered in quick succession until 39 were rec'd. by the culprit. In truth it is a horrid sight,

and the executioner was so overcome by his feelings that as soon as his work was done his eyes filled with tears and he wept—wept!
—Captain John Dooley, First Virginia Infantry, Confederate States Army

The guards marched me to where the garrison was formed on three sides of a square. My insides were roiling like cats in a tow sack. I braced up and marched with dignity, mouth set tight and eyes looking far away. I couldn't look at my squad mates or my control would break.

Yohanson uncoiled a three-tailed whip and snaked it on the ground.

"Insubordination. Fifty lashes on the bare back Twenny five t'day an' the rest t'morrow. Spread eagle 'im."

My face went numb, my heart dropped out of my body. To resist would make me look like a fool, or, worse, a coward. Against dishonor, I presented dignity, and drew it to me like a shield. The guards stripped off my fatigue blouse, cap, and shirt. Half naked like a felon! They made me lie facedown on the ground. They stretched out my arms and legs. They drove stakes and tied my wrists and ankles to them.

Yohanson counted, "One!"

The brute force thrust my body aside. I gritted my teeth and hoped not to flinch while he laid on hard lashes. I gasped. I'd been holding my breath.

I didn't cry out under his torture before. I will *not* to do it now! I clenched my fists. I took my lower lip between my teeth and started to bite down. I tensed my muscles. I bit down, cut my lip … forced myself not to wriggle … spat blood.

"Thirteen!"

The whip hit previous cuts, but outcry was strangled by the slam of the next blow. Red crept through my brain. All agony melted together; the whip only punctuated it. It took all my self-respect not to yell.

"Nineteen!"

My head was reeling. I opened my eyes to fix them on some point to make it stop, didn't remember closing them. I tried to draw a long breath.

"Twenty-two!"

I shut my eyes and opened them again.

"Twenty-seven!"

Where … was I … too many. …

"Dismiss the formation."

Everyone went away. Flies swarmed on my back. Some of them bit. I writhed to dislodge them. No use. Gnats whined around my head. They all bit. I shut eyes and mouth, snorted to blow them from my nose, but I couldn't keep them out of my ears. The hot sun scorched my skin—none but my face and hands had been exposed to it. My back burned.

'Uncle James will sort this out when he gets back,' my spirit mused. 'I wish he were here now!' My mind recoiled—I'd never thought of MacLeod the way my men had! Thought reprimanded my spirit's wish: 'The *captain* will sort things out!'

I tried to ease arms and legs, but they were held fast … muscles ached and burned … trumpet sounded Water Call, Drill, Recall. …

Battle. Charging into a countercharge of Yankees. Yohanson. I shot him. Yohanson. I shot him. Yohanson. Yohanson. Every one with the form and features of Yohanson. Exactly so had it appeared to me then.

Now, instead of rushing upon the next identical enemy, my dash was arrested. Each Yankee became himself again. Youths barely older than I or men in their prime, fair or dark, looking afraid or looking enraged, they fell from their saddles. Some fell into open graves surrounded by mourning wives and children, mothers and fathers. Now I knew what happened when I was berserk. My soul grew heavy within me. Bitter sorrow pierced me through and through. What I saw was real, but at the same time I knew I was dreaming.

I didn't know, then, the tragedy was also my own. Mind overcome, soul devastated beyond all human power to heal, neither could withstand the catastrophic, wicked loss of my family. Both had given way.

* * *

Dinner Call … close by. Burning heat, cramping arms and legs, torment of insects.

'O dear God, have mercy on me!'

Vicious kick in my ribs. Wrists and ankles released.

"Put 'im on the firewood detail the rest o' the day so's he earns 'is supper."

Woods and Smith hauled me to my feet. Yohanson stood facing me. I fought to command tormented muscles … staggered. Then, with all my strength, I shrugged away the guards' support and stood to scornful Attention.

"Learnin' ta mind yer betters now?" Yohanson snarled.

"Yes … sir."

My voice conferred contempt. I lifted my chin, kept expression wooden and eyes forward, giving the lie to submissive words.

He backhanded me across the face and knocked me on my back in the dirt. The cuts broke open, with gravelly dirt ground into them.

"Yer gonna learn a lot more before I'm done with ya!" He lumbered away.

To hands and knees … one knee up … both hands on it … pushed myself upright … spat blood. Head rang … eyes wouldn't focus … back burned … body felt swollen and weak.

"Come on." Smith took me by the arm.

"We'll go the long way." Woods picked up my clothing.

"'s Grey a' righ'?"

"He's out, wasn't no or-der to keep him."

"We're keepin' him out o' sight, best we can."

They took me behind the barracks to a horse trough by the stables.

"Strip off."

"Hold your breath!"

They lowered me into water that stung the raw flesh. Flies and gnats floated up. I scrubbed more out of my nose and ears and hair as I surfaced. Took a couple long, deep breaths before I ducked my head again. Woods gave me all the fresh water I could drink, and they let me revive as long as they dared. Smith smeared something greasy on my back when I climbed out.

"Keeps the shirt from stick-in' to yew."

* * *

Prisoners from the guardhouse at hard labor were cutting and splitting logs.

"Well, boys, if it ain't the little gent!"

"Nobody'd know by the company I'm keeping, Biggs!"

"Or by yer back! Took ya down a peg, dint he, 'Yer Honor'!"

"He may think so!"

Folly! If my words were repeated to Yohanson, he'd make matters worse. Disrespect to officers was another punishable offense. *Regulations* penned me in.

"Shut yer mouth an' keep it shut!" ordered the guard. "Shuck yer coat an' stack wood."

"Lookit thet! Jes' like one o' his slaves!"

"Know what it's like now, don't ya, Secesh!"

"If he wasn't a sorry Reb before, he is now!"

Sweat stung and burned. My suspenders rasped raw flesh. All determination to move naturally and walk upright failed. I was so hungry and weak I could barely move at all. My shoulders sagged. I plodded. My arms and legs ached. I let my body fall from one motion to another, momentum of one to push me through the next.

Why was I ordered to Stables instead of kept with the prisoners?

Smith

The ol' Bull was a-showin' the Reb fer a threat to ary one as got acrost him. Some uns in our barracks was a-skeert if they took his part, they'd catch it like Grey did. Some blamed the Reb. One er two on us did what we could.

Torquil

Getting ready for Dress Parade, I found my shirt hadn't stuck to my back. I cleaned up as well as I could with unsteady hands; appearing dirty at parade was punishable, too. Graham, looking stern, inspected me before I went out. In silence he corrected what I'd missed.

> Give strong drink unto him that is ready to perish.
> —Proverbs 31:6

Orders at Parade published that Private Drummond would be whipped after Parade the next day. A whole day to dread it! I faltered back to the barracks. Smith stepped noiselessly from beside the building and caught my arm. Startled, threatened by being touched, I tried to jerk away. He tightened his grip.

"Come 'long now. Ah've got some-thin' fer yew."

He steered me to a concealed niche in a storehouse, uncorked a bottle and passed it under my nose. Potent fumes. Smooth, no bite … big swallow. We sat on kegs.

"Tha-at's the way. We ain't a-leavin' till it's gone." He stiffened, scowling. "Ain't no-body ought to do to a man what he done to yew!"

Long, slow swallow. "What …?" I gestured with the bottle.

"Double-run. Pa makes the best in Kain-tuck. He taught me."

"You're from Kentucky."

"By way o' Widefield Coun-ty, a-visitin' cousins. We decided to go see the ele-phant."

"Your cousins are . . .?"

"Anderson an' Woods."

Whiskey warmed my belly and relaxed my body. How long till it killed the pain? I drank more. He sipped from another bottle.

"Yew shore got crossways o' the ol' Bull. He ain't done that since we been he-ah."

"You wouldn't believe it if I told you."

I swallowed a big mouthful. My head drooped to my chest and I snapped it up again with a start that woke me. Smith handed back the bottle that'd slid from my grip.

"We ain't a-leavin' till it's gone."

"I do no' want to." Sketched a salute with the bottle. "Your faither taught ye weel."

"He knew yew befo-ah."

"Aye."

"It be an old grudge."

"Aye."

Despite the haze, I knew I'd said enough. "Your faither also taught ye to shoot?"

"An' all. In the woods, Ah'm an In-jun."

"I learnit the same, mysel'."

"Then why don't yew leave befo-ah . . .?"

"The Drummond's word is aye guid, an' I hae gi'en it!"

"Yew could hide till the cap-tain's back."

"An' be accused o' desertin'. Yon is … what I refused him."

"Is he a-tryin' ta kill yew?" Smith's tawny eyes drove his question past my silence.

"Aye." The bottle was half empty. "He swore to."

Smith

A heap more to this scrawny Reb than I thought.

"He's a-makin' it a ha-rd death."

"He kens naught else."

"Waal, Ah'll see yew have more o' this jes' a-fore he tries."

"An' bring worse on mysel' for drunk on duty?"

"Yew be a-chewin' on some o' these." I showed him the dried leaves. "Ah ain't been caught all the time Ah been he-ah." I raised my bottle. "A man wants a dra-am betimes."

"'Tis guid … betimes. I thank ye." He looked like fallin' asleep.

"Ain't no-body ought to do to a man what he done to yew!"

He finished the bottle. We chewed the leaves. Tattoo sounded. He staggered to stand. I took his arm an' got him in line, an' we kep' him upright. O'Shea pretended not to notice nothing.

Torquil

I wasn't grateful for next day, so I didn't give God thanks. My spirit darkened. My insides knotted hard. The clotted cuts on my back were hard and stiff. Using my back muscles on firewood detail tore them open. More bleeding. Tried to quit thinking. Counted the axeman's blows or pieces of wood I stacked, but the whipping overwhelmed everything. I told myself it was only pain, only surface injury.

It didn't work. I knew better. The tormentors last year meant to cut on me till I died of it, or dishonored myself by betraying my men. How much more, before the merciful hand of death opened the gate to eternal life? My earthly life is a curse. I shook with fear.

My hands shook, getting ready for Dress Parade. My insides were trying to fight their way out. Smith had no chance to give me whiskey. I'd have prayed not to tremble visibly, but I was afraid God wouldn't hear me. I forced my step steady when the guards marched me to one of the flagpole supports ... stood straight, chin up, eyes front, while they removed my cap and jacket. The shirt was stuck. Yohanson tore it off.

Smith

Loose hide an' threads of meat come off with the shirt. Blood all over. We was all sickened and looked some-wheres else. I clenched my fists.

They tied his wrists 'way over his head to a flagpole brace.

"Insubordination. Fifty lashes." Half agin what the sentence was! Ol' Bull looked like the devil hisself.

We was supposed to face for'ard, but me an' my cousins looked slant-wise at each other. Seein' that miserble excuse for a two-legged creetur tormentin' that boy agin was givin' me the horrors. Mad as all blazes—and couldn't do nothin' about it! Curse them *Regulations*!

Torquil

"One!" I'd braced, but the force made me stagger.

When the whip ripped flesh already raw, it felt like red-hot iron. My head jerked back all by itself. Yohanson growled low in his throat like an animal. I bared my teeth, eyes squeezed tight shut, counted backward to the number of lashes remaining.

"Eight!"

Forty-two.

"Sixteen!"

Tried to draw a long breath, control my body.

"Nineteen! Twenty!"

Buffeted from side to side, lost my footing.

"Twenty-one!"

I got one foot under me.

"Twenty-two! Twenty-three! Twenty-four!" Yohanson tried to keep me down.

"Twenty-five!"

I clutched the flagpole brace and pulled myself upright … planted my feet wide.

"Twenty-six!"

The feral growl raged in a higher pitch.

"Twenty-eight!"

What's twenty-eight from fifty?

"Thirty!"

That's easy. Twenty.

"Thirty-one!"

Clear rippling water, between me and everything I could see … edges of vision all gray.

"Thirty-seven!"

The feral snarl deepened again.

"Thirty-eight!"

Couldn't see anything … whole world was fire and slash of the whip.

"Thirty-nine!"

Spinning … down and down into a black vortex.

Smith

"Forty!"

The Reb's body jerked.

"Forty-one!" Ol' Bull's face fired like a demon. He kep' on, hit harder.

"Fifty!" Then he hit agin and agin, for'ard and backhand like tryin' to cowhide him to death!

"Guard!" Dunahan bellered. "Arrest him and lock him up!"

The guards had to rassle him down. Me an' Graham an' my cousins broke ranks to help. Ol' Bull cursed … writhed like a stomped snake … struck at us. His eyes was red an' crazy.

2. Dishonor

MacLeod

I returned from the court after dark, grim in mind. Two of my escort were wounded and Sergeant Powell killed. Dunahan gave me the garrison report. I ordered him to prepare for Powell's funeral and dismissed him.

I raged. The shame would've cut my lad as hard as the whip, but he hadn't yielded an inch. I stalked several turns between my office and the adjutant's room. That my orders about the scout detachment were flouted was infuriating, too, but there's military law to redress that. No remedy for my lad's ordeal. I could have taken him as part of my escort, but, avoiding favoritism, I'd left him with the rest of his squad. Fury, barbed with grief and sorrow for failing to protect him, racked my soul.

Dr. Barnes

My proper English speech amuses the Americans. A firm follower of Florence Nightingale's dicta for hospital procedure and sanitation, I also have outlandish ideas of my own. Or so my colleagues think, though my procedures are consistently successful. Whether they'll answer for Drummond's case, I can't be sure.

"How badly hurt is Drummond?" MacLeod asked me.

I shook my head. Tightening of facial muscles beneath his calm expression told me the boy's welfare was of unusual concern, but I couldn't soften the facts.

"Three-strand whip, eighty-some lashes—the skin's shredded. The superficial fascia is torn, some muscle tissue lacerated. The viscera are much contused. He was enfeebled at the outset. Nervous shock has passed off, but stimulants have failed to restore consciousness."

"What's the prognosis?"

"I've cleansed the wounds, removed foreign matter and used strong asepsis. If the irritative stage progresses naturally, or the tissues unite by first intention, he'll survive. In cases of extensive destruction of the skin, however, the cure is very tedious. If there's necrosis and sloughing, over such a large area, or pyaemia ensues, it will carry him off. He lies, so to speak, in the hands of God."

> The effectual, fervent prayer of a righteous man availeth much.
> —James 5:16

MacLeod

They'd drawn the blanket only up to my son's waist and laid his arms above his head. Ugly, dark bruises everywhere, skin sun-blistered and speckled with gnat bites. He breathed out a soft moan.

'You wouldn't let that escape if you were awake, would you?'

I laid my hand on his head, blessing him. Weary, anger's energy gone, I sat down and set elbows on the table between the beds. I bowed my head onto my folded hands.

'Holy God, have mercy on us! Spare this one You've given me. Grant rest to Powell's soul ... healing to my wounded ... wisdom to your servant. In Jesus' name, Amen.'

Then, prayer without words, opening my spirit to God, was the most important thing I could do. My vigil relaxed into slumber.

Torquil

I roused in a daze and heard groans. How to help? ... till I realized I was hearing myself. I clamped my mouth hard shut. My back felt like fire was eating it away. Shuddering breaths, like I'd run too fast, too far.

Whipped—horrible shame that made me worse than nothing among men, a pariah. Worse than my worst imagining. I'd prayed for grace to thank God for the due process of his law. I tried to do the penance of gratitude.

'Dear God ...'

'Dear God, I couldn't even thank You for the day. I'm ruined. I can't do it.'

Force of will: 'Dear God, thank You for making me your son through Jesus the Christ . . .'

Words wouldn't flow; I made myself express the form of submission.

'And for ... did I deserve that! Thank You for chastising me, not casting me away. In the Christ's name, Amen.'

Breathing in short gasps, every muscle tense, at last I prayed from my heart in honest communion with my Lord. Broken-hearted tears sealed my surrender and spoke despair and pain my Lord already knew.

'Dear God, I never knew I could hurt this bad. Please, why?'

Into my mind came understanding that justice was accomplished, greater and far beyond anything I knew. Into my spirit flowed God's sweet grace.

To my astonishment, I was satisfied, better comforted than if all the kinds of pain had ceased. My lifelong ideal was alive, after all. I could hope.

'Thank You, dear God!' I prayed, with relief and heart's true gratitude.

Clenching my fists till I could feel the tendons' pull all the way to my elbows, I opened my eyes. MacLeod was looking at me with grave concern.

"It's ... that bad?"

"Yes. I'll see if Surgeon Barnes can give you something for the pain." He started to rise.

I held up my hand. "Food? ... empty."

"Haven't they been feeding you?" His smile was kind. He looked surprised to receive a serious answer.

"Bunkie tried ... Iago caught him."

A frown. "You'll tell me about all this later, my lad." He gripped my hand briefly.

Dr. Barnes

His pulse was firm but occasionally quick. No fever. I gave him plenty of water. Through a tiny incision, I injected morphia beneath the skin of his shoulder. Relieved to see him able to feed himself cold chicken and bread, I stayed to observe morphia's effect.

"You don't feel much like eating, do you."

"No, sir."

I checked his pulse again. It had slowed. The morphia was taking hold.

MacLeod

My lad was too weak to question at length, but I got a laconic report. His voice trailed off, his breathing slowed, his eyelids drooped. I settled him prone and drew up the blanket.

"Good night. I'll pray for your recovery."

"Good ... night."

Heels hitting hard, I stalked across the parade. If I don't cashier that reptile, it's only because I shot him first!

Torquil

I wept inside for my lost honor till I fell asleep. Woke before dawn … sick and hazy-witted … hurting in body and soul. But not in spirit, with work to do. I raised myself on my elbows and bowed my head.

'Dear God, I have to thank You for keeping me alive … that's what You want! … but I still have to forgive him … again!'

Terror and bitterness. A lifetime of death by torture at intervals sank my heart.

'Dear God, will he do this all my life? I thought You'd forgiven me. …'

Into mind and spirit, with such comforting love that even in pain and despair I couldn't mistake it, came Truth: "Whom the Lord loveth, he chasteneth … every son whom he receiveth."

I bowed my head lower in submission.

'Yes, Lord. I was wrong to doubt You. So … dear God, I will to forgive him. I offer forgiveness as a sacrifice on your altar … to You, in the Christ's name … and on his behalf.'

The gift I hadn't prayed for was granted. My spirit overleaped the raging opposition within, carried on the wings of grace to true and unconditional forgiveness that left me clean … free of bitterness … with fresh courage. In holy elation and the shining Light of eternal truth, I pitied my enemy.

'If You can save him, please do it. In the Christ's name, Amen.'

Then I fretted. I'd been content with the look of my body and my battle scars, but now I was branded with dishonor, shamed and disfigured … for life. I couldn't bear it. The sweet dream of reunion with Da and Douglas fled. I'd be ashamed to face them.

Dr. Barnes

Forty-eight hours after contamination, the wound was inflamed. Drummond began to run a fever and was sicker than before. I injected morphia again. The opiate is most needed during the irritative stage when the body reacts to the wound, pain is worst, and fever runs high.

Torquil

I felt sweet languor stealing over me. The pain went away. Then I followed it into blessed oblivion.

* * *

MacLeod

"Private Drummond, this is an official inquiry into the events of last Friday and Saturday."

I had him sit up, and scrutinized him without appearing to do so. Fever spots on his cheekbones, bright eyes dulled, mouth taut. I trusted the chill formality of my words would warn him to guard his.

"I shall ask questions, which Corporal Johnston will put in writing. He will then write your answers. These will serve as a deposition before a court martial. Answer only what I ask. If you wish to make a statement, you may do so afterward. The entire document will then be read to you, and you will swear to the truth of your statements and sign it. Corporal Johnston will witness your signature. Do you understand the process?"

"Yes, sir."

"Very well. You were accused of insubordination ... did you refuse to obey?"

"Yes, sir."

"Why?"

"I had reason to believe he intended to kill me."

"What was the reason?"

"He had sworn to do so, sir."

"When was that?"

I looked directly into his eyes.

"When last he spoke to me."

I breathed a mental sigh of relief while I kept my expression stern. I suppressed the wrath foreknowledge roused and kept voice, expression and questions judicial. He swallowed hard—tried to do it undetected—then kept answering. I had to question for one fact at a time.

Tremor in his voice as I forced him to recount his experience, short answers all he could give. I hated to distress him, but the record must contain every detail, to make my case against Yohanson watertight. Johnston kept his eyes on his page while the harrowing question and answer dragged on.

"Very well, Private Drummond. Do you wish to make a statement?"

"No, sir."

His voice was almost inaudible. He clenched his fists to help him endure the document read back to him. Neither he nor Johnston looked at anyone; I fixed my eyes on the opposite wall. But I was satisfied. Johnston would spread the tale, turning nominal guilt into good repute. Past history remained private.

Next task: deal with a madman.

Dr. Barnes

Death is my personal opponent. I fight the last enemy in single combat, on behalf of every patient.

Drummond couldn't always sustain consciousness. He wakened screaming. Suppuration from his wound, instead of passing into healing, gave way to a thin, serous secretion in one night.

Taking half measures would be to trifle with his life. Had the gangrene occurred in a limb, I would have amputated. I put him under anesthesia, excised the necrotic tissue, and treated the entire surface with strong nitric acid. The pain is beyond endurance: I injected morphia to annihilate it.

Death had thrown down the gauntlet. I took it up.

* * *

"Why is he shivering?"

Walker, my hospital steward, wiped sweat from his brow. He held Drummond's body in position while I washed putrid fluids out of the wounds.

I answered with only a curt, warning shake of the head. I had him warm a stone, put it at the boy's feet, and cover him with extra blankets. Later, elsewhere, I explained, "A man in that stage of decline isn't able to respond, but he can hear all you say. It registers at some level of his mind. I don't want to discourage him. He shivered because the body's economy is so depleted, the next stage will be death."

It taxed my clinical detachment to break the news to MacLeod.

"I won't concede that I'm losing him, but I've done everything I know. His fever's so high, the poor little chap's delirious. Calls for his father and Douglas as if his heart would break. A hard life he's had, for one so young."

In my profession, one must develop his powers of observation to a minute degree. MacLeod tried to cover deep concern by speaking matter-of-factly.

"Surgeons are privileged to discern such things. How else does he indicate it?"

"He raves about battle. He cries, 'No!' once in a while, and asks for an Uncle James."

His carotid artery pulsed very strongly.

"I wish I could give you better tidings."

Macleod

In my quarters, I knelt before God and confessed my failure to protect Torquil, and begged forgiveness, before I wrestled in prayer for my lad's life. I didn't rise till I received assurance of both.

Dr. Barnes

I'd retired for the night when I recalled an old-fashioned treatment. The bark of spruce-fir roots, first to wash the wound with its juice and then to apply as a poultice, was said to be very painful, but to destroy proud flesh in a few days.

I performed the procedure and gave him morphia. In the morning, I repeated it. He hadn't strength to stifle his groans. I changed the poultice three times a day. Several days later, the wound had only clean, sound tissue. Fever abated. Granulation tissue began to form in the natural way. I put my patient to sleep. A constitution so excessively awake as his benefits especially from relief from the fretting and the muscular tension caused by pain.

MacLeod

I rejoiced and gave thanks to God as fervently as I'd besought His healing. I stopped at the hospital each evening, hoping Torquil would be awake. By now, he was the only patient. I laid down the book I'd brought and sat by the bed, not reluctant to pray but wishing there were something tangible I could do. His expression was troubled even in repose. I laid a hand on his head and silently beseeched God for blessing upon his life.

An all-encompassing prayer! I petitioned God to supply the specifics. I yearned to provide trustworthy ground for the son of my heart to stand upon.

Had God removed his shield of protection from over one of his own, to let unrestrained evil teach him a lesson? Or was it the result of rousing a madman's fury?

"Whom the Lord loveth, He chasteneth ..." came to mind. Was the severity in direct ratio to my lad's potential for good or evil? Was it in proportion to the sin which made it necessary? Was it measured by the hardness or openness of his heart? He didn't resist God, but defended his Maker's decrees! Yet for a year vengeance had consumed him.

Was it a murder attempt by the enemy of souls, because his satanic realm would be threatened by the good my lad would accomplish in the future? Not a theologian, I left the questions to be answered when further understanding was granted me. I affirmed faith and comforted myself by recalling a verse from Lamentations: "The Lord doth not afflict willingly."

My hand of blessing still rested on his head when his eyelids twitched. He looked bewildered.

"Uncle James. How can you be here ... Yankees got you." He seemed to work through the question in his mind, which at last must have registered my blue uniform. "Oh. You *are* a Yankee, that's right."

His expression darkened. His gaze dropped from my face.

"How did I get captured? I shot you ... but if I'm dead too, where are Da and Douglas?" He raised his head, shaking off my hand, looking around in agitated confusion. "They ought to be here!"

I cupped his head with my hand, its warmth on the nerve center at the back of the neck.

"Hush, Torquil Dhu. You're alive on earth, and so am I."

He still looked puzzled.

"Iago's dead. He can't hurt you again."

As though he recognized the metaphor, he subsided.

"You're getting well. That's all you need to do now."

Torquil

Itching. Bright sunlight. Itching! No mental haze. *Itching!* I opened one eye, saw I was in the hospital, and shut it before they could discover I was awake, to steal time to reason it out.

Rousing and sleeping, treatments, drinks that tasted like food, bitter draughts, pain—I felt my face turning red—indignities. I'd reveal I was awake if I scratched my itching back. … Whipped! Shame seared my soul. My insides curled up. Would it happen again? No. MacLeod told me Iago's dead. Had I dreamed that?

'Thank you, dear God, there's no pain, and for this day.' I opened my eyes.

Grey lay in the next bed, left shoulder bandaged, staring at the ceiling with eyes half-shut. Experimenting, I turned on my side. Still nothing hurt, but I felt stiff. I scratched my back with both hands. Ah!

"Sssst! Grey!"

"Reb! Back to us, are you?"

"I reckon. What happened to you?"

"Sioux're better shots than I took them for."

"What's been afoot?"

"Indian fights. We've lost three since you entered your eternal sleep, and there's a half dozen wounded. The captain and lieutenant are out chasing the guilty ones every day. Hard to make headway, there's so many attacks."

"Which lieutenant?"

"DuChemin.

"After you passed out, Yohanson went raving mad. They had to tie him up and drag him to the guardhouse, and then he tried to tear the cell to pieces barehanded. He tried to strangle Graham when we were bringing water, and I couldn't club him off, so Smith had to shoot him.

"What'd you do to light his fuse?"

"Insubordination." I wouldn't be drawn farther. "How long have I been here?"

"About two months."

I rolled over on my back and was delighted it only itched and prickled. It felt like lying on sole leather. I stretched every muscle, reveling in the motion, and sat up. The room spun. I put my feet on the floor, but when I tried to stand, my knees buckled and I went sprawling.

Between guffaws, Grey sputtered, "Newborn calves do better than that!"

"Whisht!" My face felt red, but then, sheer relief: Iago can't kill me anymore! I leaned against the edge of the bed, threw back my head, and laughed like I'd stored it up forever.

"Stop yer din, ya howlin' hyenas!" came from a farther bed in the row.

* * *

The spirit of a man will sustain his infirmity; but a wounded spirit who can bear?
—Proverbs 18:14

I was pretty sure since Yohanson was dead, torment was over, but, forbidden by the *Regulations* to defend myself, I saw God's power over circumstances. I was afraid of the Arbiter of my fortunes. Was there worse to come? I wished I could discuss it with Dominie Gilchrist or, better yet, if miracles could be granted, with Da. I was still alone before God.

Dishonor crushed me. The felon's brand would bar me from the officer corps. Only in the ranks could I obey God's calling to protect, so I couldn't marry a lady, and I'd never have children, and I'd be kinless, isolated, vulnerable, and an object of scorn the rest of my life. But—I'd be faithful and do my duty. I couldn't live with myself if I didn't.

> For thus saith the Lord, Thy bruise is incurable, and thy wound is grievous. There is none to plead thy cause, that thou mayest be bound up: thou hast no healing medicines. ... for I have wounded thee with the wound of an enemy, with the chastisement of a cruel one, for the multitude of thine iniquity; because thy sins were increased. Why criest thou for thine affliction?
> —Jeremiah 30: 12-15

CHAPTER 15

PRECEPTOR

1. Revelations

MacLeod

The day my lad was released for light duty, I sent the scouting detachment with Sergeant Rector—DuChemin was unfit for duty *again*—and put him to work on returns and reports pushed aside in the urgency of campaigning. I still felt guilty because I hadn't protected him. Now I had to help heal his body, soul, and spirit.

He'd never looked so thin and pale. He was neat and clean; his hair was freshly trimmed; but his fitted uniform looked too big for him, especially around the neck. He held himself straight but gave attention with an air of weary endurance.

"They're months in arrears." I set a sheaf of papers on the table in the adjutant's room, motioning him to a chair. "You'll be enrolled as a clerk for the time being, which pays thirty-five cents a day extra, and disenrolled when you go back to regular duty."

I laid three fair copies on his edge of the table. The extra pay, which almost doubles his wages, didn't seem to interest him.

"Use these as a guide for form. I'll find Kautz's manual so you can refer to it." I explained the tasks, but his attention still seemed clouded.

"Have you heard a word I've said!" I snapped.

"Compose the report, submit it for your signature, send a copy each to the Department of Missouri at St. Louis, the District of Nebraska at Omaha City, and the War Department at Washington City. Keep one copy here." He gazed fixedly at the report in his hand.

I shut the heavy door and sat down at the other side of the table.

"What troubles you most?"

"My honor is laid in the dust." He couldn't hide despair.

I reserved the bracing rejoinder that leaped to mind. He'd sacrificed boyhood to protect those he loved and suffered brutal treatment to keep his enlistment oath. My ire rose again. I was ready to rail against God for allowing it. My reverent, honest questions were still unanswered. I set the emotion aside to be resolved later.

"You gave your word to obey when you enlisted. Other than by breaking it, you couldn't have got out of that scrape, could you?"

"Only by murder—it would've been bairn's play to kill him!— or desertion. A lawful order wouldn't have sent me in such sneaking style."

"Its unlawfulness was one charge against him, besides the unlawfulness of the punishment."

His mouth twisted with disdain. "Well understated!"

"You may write a letter of complaint to Colonel Hale about your maltreatment."

"Useless gesture. Dominie Gilchrist said evil would overtake me. I'm doomed for life."

"You risked a great deal to save your life. You must've been bluffing when you told me you didn't care if you died."

"I wasn't. You said Southern people coming west need protection. God showed me, protecting them's the duty He's called me to—my life's vocation, if you will. He forbade death by my own hand.

"So when I saw what Yohanson was trying to do, I couldn't walk into it. I still don't care, but I don't have a choice any more. I decided to make the best of it and become an officer. But now I can't. I'm disgraced forever. I'll bear the mark of a felon all my life! Without my good name—my honor—I don't live but half a life."

"I didn't leave you to Iago! I ordered him out on scout while I was at the court, but he feigned sickness and Mr. DuChemin went instead."

Torquil

Forsaken. My lifelong Light had turned away. God refused my plea when I was in Yohanson's power ... put me where by law I couldn't defend myself ... foiled MacLeod's attempt to protect me. I knew, more than ever, I deserved chastisement, but I dreaded God's future intentions. Fear choked me.

"The result remains." It was work to keep my voice.

"The scars don't prove you're a felon. You may truthfully state they're enemy vengeance. As to your honor, no one can lay it down but yourself."

What!

"Men can attack it, lie about it, deny its existence—and so loudly the world will believe them—but the only one who can build or destroy it is you."

Da said the same thing, the night before he died! He never lied to me.

"What counts eternally is the truth, though known only to God and yourself. You refrained from murder for murder. You made a dangerous choice to save your life. In both, you chose to obey God rather than man. It's always costly."

"Then a commission is still possible?"

"Yes."

"There's bound to be more food."

"You're hungry, with breakfast just over?"

"Like a wolf."

"You've got weeks of broth to make up for. I'll give you some stew."

My stomach growled. I blushed for embarrassment.

MacLeod

I brought a large tin cup full of stew and set it on the little stove.

"Not as good as Mrs. Greig's, but it'll be warm in a few minutes." I leaned back in my chair and folded my arms, with what my brother calls a wicked grin, at the sometimes-frustrating aspects of the work I was about to give my lad. "You can consider yourself acting assistant adjutant, since you disposed of half my lieutenants!"

"Noblesse oblige. You don't have to thank me." His mouth turned down at the corners.

"These are the accounts and this is the way you set up the page." I laid down ledger books. "Crossfoot your sums at the bottom and carry them forward. You see how I've done it."

Brows drawn together, he studied the sample, then nodded understanding.

"I don't need to tell you, do I, that none of this information leaves this room."

"No, sir."

Turning away to prevent the stew from scorching, I quirked an eyebrow in comment to myself. Did his first non-public use of "sir" indicate respect, or a retreat into formality, from the unspoken bond we forged in the cave? My curiosity wasn't satisfied when I set the cup in front of him. "Thank you, Uncle James!" was accompanied by a mocking, wolfish grin. I fell back on a riposte I'd used when the Rangers teased me.

"Plague take your impudence, nephew!"

He looked wistful, then puzzled. His words were hesitant.

"I think I meant it, sir. Uncle James?" Slowly, he offered his right hand across the table.

I grasped it, barely able to say, "Nephew Torquil." A silent prayer of thanks was cut short by greater fulfillment of my hopes.

"The papers ... don't have to be a formality?"

"No. Are you sure you don't you want them to be?"

"Yes, sir."

"Don't be too certain till you hear what's included!"

"I can trust you—Uncle James."

Torquil

I liked the reassuring title of relationship. Much more, I liked being able to trust.

"Nevertheless, nephew, know that I'll take a strong hand in whatever concerns you. No more laissez-faire. I'll hold you accountable to a stricter standard than mere military discipline."

"I can meet it."

"You can and you will. No more escapades such as the cannon-turned-mortar!"

"How do you know about that!"

"When you yourself attain to the dubious glory of post commandant, you'll find you have to be omniscient, and you'll create the means just as I have."

"Why didn't you do anything?"

"Lack of evidence. Otherwise, I'd have had you before a court so fast you wouldn't have known what struck you! Under my personal authority, you'd have been punished, with knowledge substituted for evidence. If you ever put on such an exhibition again, I'll give you a caning that will have you taking your meals off the mantelpiece for a week!"

"Assuming I survived." I mocked a grin.

He sobered more.

"I've beheld too many children's bodies torn and broken! I don't want to see another—for no good cause, that is—especially yours. The question is whether, knowing what I promise, you're willing to submit to my personal authority. It's all of it or none. I won't have you walking into it blind and then kicking over the traces and saying you didn't understand."

"It's *in loco patris.*"[17]

"Exactly. I don't presume to replace your father, but I will guard his son to manhood."

I felt my color rise. "I've been glad of it before. You were present when I was … torn … or at the end of all I could do … or bear."

"I was also present when you succeeded, as at Granite Bend. I don't intend to sound like all grief and punishment. I hope, once the uprising is quelled, we can go hunting. You may as well know now, God sent me to you in Virginia, and you here to me, for reasons of His own."

I looked far away, through the wall behind him.

"That must be why I didn't send you to the army the time you tried to capture me. I kept you with us because you were good for

---

17 Latin: "in a father's place."

my men—and to have you where I could watch you! The army couldn't have kept as close watch as I did. I cursed myself for a fool later."

"And tried to shoot me."

"Of course. It was you or Abercairn."

"As you thought at the time."

"How is it so?"

"You heard my warning. I knew you'd heed it, whatever you believed of me, and move your base. I sent them to the old one. Spectacular, wasn't it?"

"It rang the kirk bell. But I did my part to keep them fooled. Did you ever try to shoot an exploding shell with a catapult?"

"Not even in my schooldays! They thought it a real defense. Until you struck in the winter, they thought they'd killed all of you.

"You did well by Abercairn. They have enough to get by till harvest is in. You'll have to forgive me for not giving your neighbors credit. I led the Bureau to assume they didn't support your efforts."

"Are you still connected with it?"

"Very little now. Why do you ask?"

"You know so much about Abercairn."

"I have a correspondent who keeps me informed."

"I wish I had! I miss them, but if I wrote to anyone, they'd jail him. Is the hunt still up?"

"No active pursuers, but a detachment at the Court House is on the lookout. If you want to write letters, I can get them delivered."

I gave half a smile and devoured stew.

"It will cost you some off-duty time at night, because this work needs to be accomplished speedily, but now I'm going to keep my earlier promise to tell you why I'm keeping you here."

He omitted neither his reasoning nor his doubts nor his faith.

"Eventually I understood that rather than trying to harm you, I was to protect you."

"I didn't need protection."

"You didn't know all that was arrayed against you. I did. Hence my warnings.

"Beyond all likelihood, God sent you to me, the one man who would save your life, not sell it. Keeping you here, only a name in the ranks, is the best means at my disposal."

MacLeod

That night I wrote:

> The day is come. He has yielded to my authority. If I trembled at the gravity of my responsibility before, I now do so doubly. A son! The gift of a son! Yet only lent, as I have learned through loss that all children are only lent to us. I am resolved to "improve the time." I am thinking about plans for his education. I must think up a scheme to take him hunting without it appearing to be favoritism. My thoughts boil over, my words run away. You must think me delirious! Perhaps I am! I have hoped so long for this blessing. I thank God with "all that is within me," and beseech Him that I shall be worthy of it.

Torquil

I could write to my friends and have home ties again. The prayer that was only a wish was answered: in Uncle James I found the preceptor I longed for. He'd met all my suspicions with truth. The honor that drew forth my trust in the beginning was still there. I wasn't alone.

* * *

"You're in better spirits today." Uncle James shut the door to the adjutant's room and gave me a handful of his scribblings for more reports, out of a bushel basket full of them!

"You'd never seen me without a sentence hanging over my head, but, by the mercy of God, it's been carried out now."

"It didn't seem especially merciful to me."

He sat down to listen and motioned me to the other chair. I told him how it was, till the terror returned and my voice shook so bad it stopped.

MacLeod

"Admitting he's wrong is one of the hardest things a man can do. You submitted to God's judgment. It's the severest test of your faith, to thank Him for something bitter and painful—and it's the truest demonstration of your trust.

"Sin brings punishment, but when it's over, it's done. God doesn't torment you endlessly. Such incessant torments come from the eternal enemy of our souls. Men like Yohanson are his slaves. You could have sunk to that, had you not repented.

"You weren't fighting against flesh and blood, but against 'principalities and powers, and spiritual wickedness in high places.' You felt the power of the eternal enemy and learned the depths of the evil you gave yourself to."

The words were not my own.

Torquil froze. His face was white beneath its remnant of tan. Fear shook his voice.

"I came closer to spiritual death … than bodily death."

Evidently, the fact became real to him for the first time. I gave him time to absorb it.

"God preserved you from both."

"I didn't know it. I had to try three times to thank Him!"

"When was this?"

"When I came to ... before you knew I was awake. I had to go to God first. But I broke, it hurt so bad. I couldn't keep faith. I asked him why."

"Did He tell you?"

"Do you remember when I thought justice was dead? Somehow He made me know, all through me, justice was done, more so than I could know, and I was happy, though I never hurt so bad in my life!"

"What's your definition of justice?"

"A man gets what he deserves, good or ill, and somehow it puts things right. It's like having solid ground to walk on."

"God's justice has that same intent, to a higher standard than we can know, because it's based on his eternal, perfect character. What He ordains, therefore, is always right, no matter what we, in our imperfect knowledge, may think of it. We may be part of a plan of His that's too great for us to know.

"His justice is also holy, because He is holy. He goes beyond reward and punishment, to offer mercy and redemption. Then it's up to us to accept and receive them."

I concentrated on the revelations God was giving me. My nephew's questions as well as my own were answered.

2. In Quest of Man's Estate

MacLeod

A week later at Reveille, I glanced out my front window when I heard a mule braying on the parade. Picketed to a pin in the ground, it wore DuChemin's French kepi tied to its headstall. A piece of blackened rope attached to the noseband mocked the foppish moustache. The men lined up for roll call laughing, hooting, and braying. One of my incorrigibles saluted the mule!

I'd sent my orderly and trumpeter to look for evidence when Torquil approached Headquarters with cap perched at a rakish angle, expression saucy. He was strutting.

"What do you know about the mule on the parade?"

"He's the nigh wheeler for the Number One howitzer, sir."

"Do you know how he got there?"

"At the Walk."

I quit sparring. "Was anyone in it with you?"

"No, sir." The corners of his mouth began to twitch.

"Did you leave any evidence?"

"No, sir." The wolf grin.

Any boy with a spark of spirit will make trial of authority sooner or later. I'd have preferred it be personal rather than public! I picked up the cedar switch used for dusting clothes, motioned him into the adjutant's room, and shut the door.

"Grasp the seat of that chair with both hands! I'll keep my promise now. You won't be able to appreciate it later."

"What are you going to do to me?"

"Company punishment."

"Two punishments?"

"This is my duty to Torquil Dhu, to assure you, for the good of your soul, I mean what I say! The other's my duty in regard to Private Drummond, for the good of the service."

"I'd be willing to spare you the trouble of one or the other." His eyes glinted.

When I pointed to the chair, and he grasped the seat, I knew I'd established my necessary rule. The caning I gave was more symbolic than punishing. But when he stood up, red-faced and round-eyed, he didn't stop his impudence.

"I reckon I have to thank you instead of God, since you stand *in loco patris*. It's a lot easier when you chastise me." He pursed his mouth to mimic prim hypocrisy. "I'm sure I'll be the better for it."

I twitched the cedar. "Would you care to be better still?"

"No, sir!"

"Return to your duties."

Torquil

My backside burnt like a furnace! Uncle James had a heavier hand with a switch than Da did, and a heavier switch, too. I set my work on top of the box where the post records are stored, so I could stand. I worried about which punishment he'd order. Not a one but it hurt or made a fool of a man.

He fined me to pay for DuChemin's ruined hat and made me sit on a high stool in the middle of the parade for four hours, from half after Dinner Call till Stable Call.

MacLeod

"Report to Sergeant Flagler. Dismissed!" I handed Torquil the order.

"Yes, sir." He saluted and turned to leave.

"Wait." I fished a small tin out of my pocket and tossed it to him. "You were chewed alive last time. It will keep the gnats off. Compliments of Mrs. Greig."

I savoured his incredulous expression. He rubbed ointment on and handed back the tin.

"Blessed are the merciful."

All impudence was gone. He looked crestfallen, so I stiffened him to endure the afternoon by administering a harsher mercy.

"Then bless me by showing you still have the sense you were born with! Dismissed!"

Torquil

I had to sit like I was at attention, eyes front, with my hands folded—like what they do to schoolboys! I was so mortified, it felt like even my ears turned red. Gnats keened around my ears, but none lit. The laundresses' brats jeered, threw dust, and shied stones at me. DuChemin, with gloating and malicious glares in my direction, instructed drill all around me. By the time that was over, my back ached from holding it stiff—and it was still an hour till Stable Call.

Would Uncle James hold my joke against me and stand cold and remote behind the iron line? At least he hadn't deprived me of dinner. I didn't remember, then, that Da offered reconciliation only after he was sure we'd learned the lesson. Honesty finally brought me to admit I deserved what I'd got. I berated myself for thinking the mule was such a good joke. Sore and sorry, I tried to work out the stiffness when Stable Call sounded at last.

A bad night. Graham gave me jesse so's I wanted to crawl in a hole. Sore places ached. I could only lie on my belly. I prayed in silence.

'Dear God, I'm sorry I acted so bad. I don't know what's the matter. I don't want to be like this! Dear God, help me keep my honor and … and … do what's right! I don't want to be away from You. And if there's any way I can earn Uncle James's good opinion … I want to!'

No matter how tired I am, wariness inside keeps me from falling full asleep. I knew I needn't fear a surprise attack here in the fort, but knowing didn't go deep enough to release me from watching for one. It's been part of my soul since Da and Douglas were murdered. I tried to reason it out.

Why do I feel like I'm in deadly danger all the time? Do I still think justice is dead? At her death, the earth had opened beneath my feet and dropped me into an abyss of chaos. Do I have some false fear of death—false because my temporal death is the gateway to eternal life. Any road, it's false because I've never faltered at facing death, except by torture. Am I afraid unending, unbearable torment is lurking in the darkness to seize me if I sleep?

Myth and madness! I shook my head to clear it. What allowed me to believe Uncle James for safety that first night and sleep well for the only time in years? The shining thing was, I did believe. In spite of the breach I feared—and had to admit, caused—could I trust again?

The answer was, for that one night, my soul—thought and will and feelings—surrendered to my spirit. In my spirit, the Holy Spirit of God dwells. He joined Truth to truth—the truth that I wasn't under attack—and freed me from vigilance.

My spirit led me to trust Uncle James when I was so far gone I couldn't help it. Even by keeping his promise to punish misconduct, even by revealing the post at Raven Crags, he'd never failed me nor veered a hair's breadth from his word. In trust, I accepted him as guardian and uncle. Now I could honestly extend my trust, to believe his word in this, too, and know God's justice was over me.

'Thank You, dear God! Into thine hand I commit my spirit.'

"Hurry up!"

Grey nudged me out of a sound sleep. I was mighty sore, and stiff as wood from neck to tailbone, but moving worked it out some.

> As an ear-ring of gold, and an ornament of fine gold,
> so is a wise reprover upon an obedient ear.
> —Proverbs 25:12

In the adjutant's room, my guardian sat at the table, behind a complicated structure built of matchsticks. He motioned me to close the door.

"How are you this morning, nephew?"

"I'm all right, sir." I was so relieved not to be cast away, I almost said so.

He quirked an eyebrow. "Requisite tale having been told?"

"I've been worse, Uncle James."

"Sit down and study this."

I examined the matchstick structure from several angles.

MacLeod

"What do you see?"

"The number of pieces in each level progresses from most at the bottom to only one at the top. All the pieces support each other, by notches, or forks, or leaning."

"What does it represent?"

"An engineering exhibition?"

I shook my head. It'd taken plenty of engineering knowledge, plenty of time, and a steady hand to construct—and reconstruct!—it last night.

"What organization has most of its members at the base and only one on top?"

"The Army? With a lot of soldiers, a few officers, and only one General-in-Chief?"

"Yes. Each level is built on—and supported by—the one below. But those above also give strength to the lower levels, like the top chord of a bridge."

"Soldiers lean—that is to say, *depend*—on each other in garrison as well as in battle. They depend on their officers to command and train them, and provide them with food, medical care and so on. Officers depend upon soldiers to obey, so in battle, we can win, with the fewest casualties. Each holds the other's life in his hands."

"It was like that in my company."

"All the parts of this structure likewise support each other. Watch it carefully."

I bumped the edge of the table with the heel of my hand.

"That represents an outside threat, such as enemy attack. Every stick quivered, but, holding together, each one and the whole structure held firm.

"Now, tap that one." I pointed with a pen staff.

"Won't that weaken it?"

"Tap it!"

Every stick from top to bottom fell in a jumbled heap. He looked at it in dismay.

"That's what you did yesterday." I gave my sternest expression. "You denied an officer's authority, by disrespect in the form of public ridicule."

"I don't respect him!"

"You need not respect his character, but you can and you will respect his office! Remember your Latin: *officium* ... 'duty.' Inferring that an officer is a jackass can bring men to the false conclusion that they needn't obey him. If they act upon that conclusion in the field, they'll be slaughtered piecemeal. Do you understand what I'm saying?"

"The bond of the whole is broken, and that makes it ineffective, and dangerous to its members."

"Well summarized. Do you see now what I meant by 'the good of the service'?"

"Yes, sir."

"What did I mean?"

"The threat to the whole company had to be promptly and publicly punished, to show it wouldn't be tolerated, or the threat was annulled. And show them they were still safe ... make it whole again ... show it can't be broken."

"I doubt they understood all that, but I'm glad you do. It'll stand you in good stead when you're commissioned yourself. Keep it as a goal for your own duty.

"On the character side of this business. Were you seeking vengeance on the lieutenant?"

"No. I forgave him a long time ago. I thought the mule would be comical, and the more I thought, the more comical it was. I couldn't laugh out loud, or I'd wake everyone, so I started thinking how it could be done ... and did it."

It was clear he'd had no malicious intent.

"It's cost you some, to learn this lesson, so I'm not going to berate you, but you must hear a few things. You were brought up to be a Christian gentleman. You must apologize and ask forgiveness. You know now what an attack it was, to say nothing of the insult."

"Hasn't he had his satisfaction!" He scowled.

"I'm not talking about the *Code Duello*! God's Word requires you to do it."

"But he'll only sneer and gloat."

I kept voice and gaze dead level.

"Are you going to allow the quality of his conduct to dictate the quality of yours?"

"You sound just like Da!"

"That's the highest compliment you could give me."

His expression turned thoughtful.

"You're right. I have to do it. May I write it so I don't have to watch him sneer?"

"That would be best in any case."

"I'll do it today."

"One thing more. You've brought trouble on yourself by not testing your ideas in the light of good judgment. You'll get better results if you do."

"I always used to. A few months ago I was in command of a company and protecting a whole county the best I could, and now I'm doing so bad everyone wants to beat me! Why? What's happened?

"I'm not who I am any more!"

"I'll have to think about an answer for you. To be going on with: before you act, ask yourself—be rigorous about it!—if it would make your father proud of you."

That night I wrote:

> … so I hope 'to lure this tassel-gentle back again' to the paths of righteousness (more mixed metaphors and sources!) so he won't be his own worst enemy in years to come.

> I am vexed beyond expression at such retrograde behaviour!

* * *

"You asked me why you're doing badly," I began next morning. "A couple of reasons have come to mind. Neither excuses your conduct.

"You've been under a number of strict constraints. What does your horse do when you turn him loose after a day's work?"

He looked puzzled. "Runs around and kicks up his heels, then lies down and rolls."

"Do you see any comparison?"

"Am I acting like being turned loose?"

"That's one conclusion you could draw. Another is that some boys find it hard to situate themselves in life and therefore think they have a bone to pick with the settled order of things. They do so by flouting it."

"I'm called to protect, in the army. I can't disobey what God told me to do. I've no complaints, if I'm commissioned. But I'm seeing chances to 'kick up my heels' and I've been taking them, harmless jokes like I let my men play. It was an antidote to the work of war. Uncle James, even my bones are tired!"

"How have you been sleeping lately?"

He pretended to consider the question carefully.

"Almost always ... horizontally."

I grinned. He explained. Grateful for such complete trust, I prayed to be worthy of it.

"Some of your lack of self-control is the result of too little sleep. You'll find it easier to make right decisions when you're better rested."

"I admit the mule wasn't right. But I get hurt no matter if I do right or wrong! I always get punished double! I reckon I can do anything I'm willing to pay for."

He set his mouth so defiantly, I wanted to shake him. I refrained from rising to the bait.

"Virtue is its own reward. Do you know what the full price is?"

"Punishment or retaliation."

"Don't you see it goes farther?"

"No."

"What about your reputation? If you're thought a troublemaker, you'll be treated as one. What will be written on your descriptive roll concerning your character and military history? That will follow you all through the service. It will affect decisions about your duties and where you'll serve."

"Are you going to record everything I do wrong?"

"Only if you persist in wrongdoing. For the good of the service, remember?"

He scowled. "Yes, sir."

"Need we go over it again?"

"No, sir."

"Then I expect to see you come up to the mark."

Torquil

I tried. I did my duty the best I could. I playacted the required courtesies to DuChemin. I ate every bite the mess hall provided and all I could afford to buy. I slept like making up for lost time.

MacLeod

I observed a peace in my lad's demeanor that I'd never seen before. I wrote,

> It looks as if our tassel-gentle has settled to the glove,
> with self-control it rejoices my heart to see.

Reading it over, I thought "our" might be too presumptuous. If I struck it out, I'd only call attention to it, but I didn't have time to rewrite the sheet before the mail was dispatched. I let it stand. I know my heart. How would she respond? Would she deign to do so at all? To venture yet more boldly, I closed the letter: "With affection."

Torquil

Though my body was healed, my soul was not. Only by trust can I hold on to God's presence within, trust born of belief in His righteous character. My trust was shattered. I repeated the truth to myself and held to it with all my strength of mind and will, but my heart still questioned. My best logic couldn't make right of wrong. I couldn't justify the loss of my family. All I could do was swallow the grief and keep trying to do right.

Uncle James could manage the post with only the help of his sergeants, so he took official notice of all DuChemin's derelictions of duty. DuChemin abused his officer's privilege of ordering liquor from the sutler to develop a following among the habitual drinkers. All of us in barracks knew it. Facing subversion, Uncle James forced him to resign.

* * *

"This arrived Thursday." On the eighth of October, he smiled and handed me a thick-packed envelope. "I waited till today to give you happy birthday, nephew."

"Thank you!"

At this moment, I loved my uncle, but I shied off from saying so. After duty, I took out the letters. On top was an envelope with my name in his unadorned, well-known hand.

My dear Nephew,

Today you reach another milestone on the road to manhood, toward which cherished goal I am happy to see you advancing. I am pleased that you are setting aside "childish things" and returning to duty, the fruits of which will establish the honour you prize. In the eyes of God and man, duty faithfully performed is beyond valuation.

God bless you, my lad.

Your servant and Uncle,

James MacLeod

Enclosure is for your wants or wishes.

* * *

I put the five dollars in my pocket and read my letters as soon as I had free time.

My Dear Lad,

How it gladdens all our hearts to know you are alive and in health! Many the joyful tear hath flowed, not least mine own, at these best of news! My wife and children send their affection and blessings. The laddie would have us set forth to find you. The wee lassie wishes to know your wants so we can send a box. My wife and I keep a son's place for you at our fireside until you can return to take it up.

These are hard days for all, but the land is good. We begin anew as our forefathers began. God giveth the increase. Though the corbies aye croak, I am grateful for the bountiful harvest. Most think first how to help each other, as aye they have. The

Northmen send sharp dealers among us, mayhap thinking to take advantage of our lowered condition, but we join in putting forward my co-trustee to do business with them. We jest he was born a diplomat out of place, so well doth he foil them.

In hope this finds you well, as we are, I remain, proud still to be your neighbor,

aff'ly, yr obt svt

Dear Beau,

They said not to use names, so you'll have to guess who I'm talking about! It cheered us all up no end to hear you stopped short of China. Glad you didn't stop any arrows or bullets. The newspapers say the redskins are on the warpath so I suppose you're in the right middle of it. Hold onto your hair!

My sweet wife is very busy these days taking care of our baby boy. We called him after me and our late captain. I've been working with Father on our place however I can. It doesn't hurt a bit to drop a hammer on your wooden foot! That was when we were fixing the roof. Your place is being well looked after by the Older and Younger Ladies of the House and the usual ones outdoors.

The Bluebirds have come to roost. Their head rooster took rooms at the inn. He was going to use the Chief's house but decided against it, after they searched the whole place again. Special orders from some General, I've heard.

The first batch that came here strutted around insulting us and flaunting their power, but they were relieved by some of our friends from Granite Bend. They don't cause much stir. They had to call on us to clean out the Beechams and Fromers and their like. Some of those may be coming your way.

Half the twins is at the V.M.I. and Blackeyes and the jokester of the med. corps are going next year. Everybody else is working on their farms. That's all the news I can think of, and I'm out of paper. Present my regards to Uncle James. God bless you. I remain ever Your Friend, Sir Goodheart.

I read what wasn't written and knew why the occupation troops were causing so little trouble. I figured out the other writers from their styles and handwriting.

Nannie confessed she feared God had turned his back on Virginia when our country was defeated. But the very next Sabbath, Dominie Gilchrist urged them to trust God in this calamity. Though his purpose was mysterious, He would not forsake them. Then he reminded them of Jesus' command to love their enemies, pointing out how much it cost Jesus to love his! He ended by challenging them to "be strong, acquit ye like men" in the battle to recover from destruction. She said the new purpose encouraged her. I took heart from her bright spirit.

MacCammond was outraged by the wrong of defeat. The whole war, he said, was like when one person deliberately wrongs another, gets mad when the other reproaches him, and blames the injured party for it all. He was ready to try again to drive them out, or else go out to the Territories.

Loudoun calculated Abercairn's losses at ten per cent. of its men and another fifteen per cent. disabled or weakened, and the Confederate dollar at fifty-three to one Federal greenback. Everyone including himself was working hard on their farms. They were up before cockcrow and fell into bed, exhausted, at night.

Menteith gave news of the Court House, where his father, the Commonwealth Attorney, had to work under the Yankee provost marshal, who had the final say in everything.

"We preserve all we can for ye, lad, though the battle hath scathed us sore. God keep ye weel," Mrs. Grieg closed her letter.

For all that, families were happy to have those who survived gather around the hearth again. The four Grieg sons had all returned.

I studied Mr. Ogilvie's report, to learn to manage Glenlochie, in case my turn ever came. What I was learning from Uncle James's work would be useful. Mr. Ogilvie wrote of current uses and future plans for the land, acquisition of more teams, and lending Glenlochie currency. He lamented the shortage of labor and mentioned a temporary partnership with Mr. Mitchell's store. He gave relief to the neighbors and reserved funds for my education. The mill on Willow Run was burnt down, some livestock presumed stolen. Everything needed repair.

I had much to give thanks for, and much to pray about. Matters at home were better than I'd expected. It wasn't safe to return, but I'd send some money home. I bowed my head, tears of joy starting, at being restored to those I love, and prayed God's blessing and continued care over them all.

MacLeod

I laid aside a letter from my sister to take up another, postmarked Washington, D.C. It looked like an official envelope.

Dear,

I am so happy he has shown his trust by accepting you <u>in loco patris</u>! No, you aren't delirious, only overflowing with the joy of Proverbs 13:12.

It is vital for him to have a father at this time of his life. We have observed that if a boy loses his father, when he still needs a father's presence and example to achieve manhood, it somehow bars him from advancing, in his soul, beyond the time when the tragedy overtook him. Torquil will always have some of the sweet grace of boyhood—and probably some of its waywardness! You call it "retrograde behavior," but remember, he gave up boyhood for the duties of war.

It shouldn't surprise you if he takes some of it back! Conversely, he will always be a father, protecting those under his care. He gives what he is most in need of.

The letter ended, "I remain, affectionately, faithful." I gave God thanks: my cup was refilled to overflowing.

I kept Torquil detailed to headquarters. I had no better assistant, and I could continue my cherished work *in loco patris.* His general health benefitted from the physical rest. By mid-November, he weighed but little less than he should and had grown an inch taller.

Torquil

The down on my face was beginning to curl. In the washroom, I soaped my face and experimented with how to hold the razor. When I got done, I looked in the glass. I didn't look any different.

3. The Awkward Squad

MacLeod

My new lieutenants reported within a few days of each other. First Lieutenant Porter had won promotion from the volunteers. Red-haired, jolly Rush was a July graduate of West Point. Blessed to have subalterns I could trust, I didn't waste either's talents on basic chores. My sergeants were fully occupied, so I appointed Torquil lance sergeant to train the new recruits.

Torquil

When supply wagons and the new recruits arrived, I waited till everyone else went bustling about known business, wagons and all, leaving ten men standing perplexed in front of headquarters. I strode unhurriedly up to them.

"I am Sergeant Drummond. Come with me."

I took them to a corner of the parade. One can learn something even from enemies. Yohanson had disconcerted me by walking behind me, so I called each to stand while I circled and observed him

Duval. Vibrating with energy though standing still. Not tall, barrel-chested and broad-shouldered, looking content with himself. Curly black hair and black eyes that confidently met my scrutiny.

Hoffmann. A fair German, tall, broad shoulders, long legs, and the body of a warrior out of legend. His voice was guttural, his mouth hard, and he stared fixedly over my shoulder.

Jeffries. Bowlegged, long, bronzed face, brown hair, piercing blue eyes under drooping brows. Mouth a disapproving line, he matched me stare for stare. Where had he served before? He looked like he could master Diablo, our fastest, wildest horse.

Mueller. Another type of German, short, square, and dark, with a roll of flesh above the collar of his fatigue blouse and a business-like expression on his face.

Murphy. Even in the prescribed response, his voice sang. He trod with a springing step. Medium height and build, wavy brown hair, laughter lines around his mouth, green eyes that glinted his invitation to share the joke.

"Perkins."

"Here, Ser'nt!" An English accent had Perkins, a slight body of medium height, the dreamy blue eyes of a poet, and a pink-and-white complexion badly sun-scorched. Would he survive? The recruits were all dishevelled from their journey, but this one looked like a rag-picker.

Trelawney. Dark eyes, turned-up nose, boy's mouth. Short and slight and wiry, he stood like he'd be first off the mark in a race.

The others were Callahan, Copeland, and O'Reilly.

Sergeant O'Shea

I had me doubts, if the Rebel boy could be breakin' a bunch of John Raws, more when he said he'd be "honored" to learn what I could be teachin' him. Was I iver that young!

"Are ye forgettin' the word I told ye to learn?"

"Respect?"

"Respect. Ye respect and obey iveryone from the Blessed Savior to your nearest senior in grade. Ye respect your equals. An' ye respect your men, but ye do not do it in words."

He looked at his feet.

Seein' what he had to work with, I couldn't keep meself from a word or two.

"If ye must put one down, give him both fists, full power on the breastbone—knock out his wind. Ye're a lightweight, ye need to be quick. Then ye can be doin' wid him what ye will."

"I'll remember. But I hope not to waste any time. We need them now, and I've got to make them ready! If the Sioux cut them up, their blood will be on my head, and so will everybody else's!"

That gentry way he talks! Now, glarin' at the wall, his brows was all tangled. Into the pool of silence, past the eaglet glare, soft, soft, I dropped me question.

"Was ye ever thinkin' yer duty was less?"

He talked from depths I wasn't thinkin' he had.

"No, sir. My duty is always to protect, but up to now, I've done it with the sword."

"Ye can be savin' yer 'sir' for the shoulder straps!"

Sober as an owl, face turnin' red, "In Virginia, that's how we address men we respect."

He tried his gent's way, an' I'm admittin' he got 'em ridin' an' made 'em mind him, but not so fast as he wanted to. Till the day two of his old squad was killed.

Torquil

"Attention!" I faced the recruits. "Uncover!"

Cap over my heart, I about-faced to honor the little cavalcade. Lieutenant Porter had taken fourth barracks in the field today. Woods and Anderson had stuck together to the end of life.

That night, I found Smith in the storehouse, where he'd lit a candle and set it at the head of the rough table where his cousins' bodies lay. He'd closed their eyelids with coins and stood, head bowed and hands crossed. I stood next to him.

"Cain't tell 'em apart now. They was defendin' each t'other. Always did. Ah had ta take a al-mighty lickin' from the two on 'em afore Ah learnt it. Then they was the three on us agin ever-body.

"That's how we got he-ah. All-fired big fight an' then we got to sippin' Pa's whi-skey. We was lookin' for more fight. The recrui-tin' of-ficer was in town. In the mornin' when we woke up, we was so-jers."

"They brought honor to their blood. All your people can be proud of them."

The funeral was held after Guard Mount next day. Losing Woods and Anderson showed me the time for patience was past. I harried the recruits into basic competence.

MacLeod

One of my scouting detachments discovered the Indians on the other side of the Laramie Mountains and returned amid the first blizzard of the season. When the skies cleared, Dr. Barnes read the thermometer at thirty or more degrees below zero for three nights. I sent another party, wrapped in furs, to keep the Indians under observation.

CHAPTER 16

WINTER WARFARE

1. Combat

MacLeod

Late in November, the Indians brought matters to a decision by launching a series of attacks along a hundred-mile stretch of the Overland dispatch route. I met some of my brother officers for the first time when five companies of the 16th Cavalry, Colonel Hale commanding, marched with artillery, supply and ammunition wagons, and ambulances in the column, on a morning as bitterly cold as it was bright. We rubbed gunpowder on our faces to prevent snow-blindness. Through deep snow in many places, first one company, then another, was sent forward to break trail. Colonel Hale accepted my proposal to place Torquil as the foremost lookout because of his peculiar attributes and experience. He rode with two citizen guides and was excused from guard duty at night. On campaign, procedure was adapted to meet the necessities of strategy. Uniform clothing was sacrificed to the demands of weather.

Torquil

The Indians' backtrail was muddy slush that had thawed and refrozen twice since it was originally churned up.

"When did your scouts sight 'em last?" asked grizzled old Crowley.

"Morning, three days ago. The whole camp was here then."

"Two days' start, with wimmen, babes, old ones, lodges an' all." Blake shook his head.

The motion on the distant, next hillside was so slight I wasn't sure I'd seen seen it at all. Mottled tan and pink, it was oval when contracted and about two feet long when extended. Scanning with my field glasses, I saw another irregularity, a good-sized, motionless, mud-colored bundle near the edge of the Indians' trail. The scouts went to investigate while I rode back to report to Colonel Hale.

Colonel Hale

Headquarters, Department of the Missouri
St. Louis, Missouri

Maj. Genl. George M. Dodge, U. S. Vols.

In the field near LaBonte Creek
November 26, 1865

Sir:

I have the honour to report that when informed of the hostiles' direction, I sent couriers to telegraph orders to the stations along the Platte to watch where they might try to cross the river, and intercept them if possible. I sent Captain Johann Ostwalt's Company K, with the guides, on forced march to find the enemy, and took the rest of the column at best speed, beside the trail where footing was easier for the horses.

The guide Blake dashed into the midst of my head-quarters party and thrust a white baby found in the hostiles' trail into the hands of my chief surgeon, saying its mother was dead.

We struck a diagonal to the hostiles' track and advanced faster than they till we began to follow down the West Fork of LaBonte Creek. At 4 ½ o'clock the guides spotted our quarry a few miles ahead. We halted before we could be detected. …

Torquil

We got no rest in the fireless bivouac. Colonel Hale disposed us for battle and ordered breastworks constructed of deadfall and boulders. We could see by starlight, and the work kept us from freezing in the icy wind.

At dawn the Sioux came whooping and shooting. We stayed behind our works and volleyed shots into them. They galloped their ponies back and forth, downstream of our defenses. Some plunged forward, then retired, to dash forward again from another spot, trying to draw us out to chase them. Bullets whizzed and arrows whistled around us. Sioux war cries quavered loud in the bitter air.

Full daylight showed our losses. Some of the wounded could still return fire. Others writhed and died in their own blood. Indian dead and wounded were only a small percentage of the hostiles. So intent on our defense were we that I only noticed the artillery at its opening salvo—all eight guns. From a flanking position on the gradual slope to the south, shells exploded among the Indians and over their heads. Ponies leaped and bucked and squealed and bolted, but most of their riders stayed mounted.

Shells thrown with perfect accuracy wreaked havoc. Through my field glasses, I saw, with no surprise, Uncle James directing the guns as coolly as a practice exercise. When the Sioux charged him, he replied with double-shotted canister that sent them reeling back with heavy casualties. I watched with admiration till a bullet carried away part of my collar and recalled me to my work.

The Sioux finally gathered their dead and wounded, bunched up, and headed north toward the North Platte. M and L Companies were ordered to pursue. I gathered my fur cap and collar close about my head and narrowed my eyes at sun glare on vast expanses of snow. The footing on the Indians' back trail wasn't too bad for the horses, but we couldn't match their unencumbered speed.

When the sun westered, the wind felt arctic. The Indian ponies' lesser vigor nullified their head start and lighter burdens. Our strong, well-fed horses overtook them in late afternoon.

Colonel Hale

> ... I planned an encirclement if the hostiles didn't retreat, M and L companies under Major George Jennings to fight dismounted from the sparse timber on K company's left, and H company to support the artillery, while I kept Company I in reserve. From my position uphill and upstream from the battle, I sent couriers to deliver revised orders as the fight developed. To begin a flanking movement on the Indians' right, I ordered M and L companies to defile left oblique forward, staying in the trees. I ordered Captain James MacLeod to direct his guns at the Sioux rear as well as their left, to bring them under fire on all sides.
>
> Though suffering large numbers of casualties, the hostiles didn't break off the fight as they usually do when resistance proves costly. In the case of this punitive expedition, however, because of the death, mutilation, and destruction they have wrought, if they were determined to stay and die, I'd oblige them. It is hoped they will be discouraged from further attacks.

They picked up their dead and wounded, and re-treated. Facing and returning fire on all sides, they massed and broke out toward the north. M and L Companies poured concentrated volleys into their flank as they passed. Captain MacLeod, elevating his guns to the fullest effective angle, pursued them with exploding shells. I ordered M and L companies, under Major Jennings, to pursue, trusting that the alerted stations along the North Platte would be ready to attack them in their front while my force took them in rear. I sent the artillery north, along with the supply wagons, blacksmiths, and three ambulances. K company was badly diminished, so I left them as rear guard with the wounded and one ambulance. Ordering them all to overtake the northbound force as soon as they could, I led H and I Companies, with two wagons and one ambulance, to follow the trail of the village.

It traveled slowly. I sent the guides ahead to learn if it was escorted by warriors. They reported it was not, and had not moved far since last night's camp. My column caught up around midafternoon.

My orders were:

(1) No killing except in self-defense, should there be deadly resistance.

(2) No injury be done to the women, children, and old men.

(3) Look for any white captives. (These we kept with us and will attempt to restore to their relatives. Their reports may lead us to others who need rescue.)

(4) Company I to defile left oblique, H Company, right oblique, to surround them.

While we advanced, the scout Crowley delivered my demand for surrender to save their lives. We surrounded them and received their surrender without a shot being fired.

Several captive white women and children told me about various attacks. (See list and descriptions enclosed.) I settled all these victims into the ambulance for rest and shelter from the wind. Crowley translating, I explained to the old men what they had to do, and the whole village with its military guards proceeded toward Fort Liberty.

Matthew Hale
Colonel, U.S A., Commanding
Battalion of 16th Cavalry

MacLeod

Major Jennings set the battle in array in flatter, more open country where the ground dropped gradually toward the frozen Platte, L company the right wing and M the left. I marched the artillery in rear of the center. The Platte was a blinding swath of frozen gold in the low rays of the sun. The Sioux were within three miles of it. My binoculars showed their ponies laboring with heavy breath through the snowdrifts.

I halted and unlimbered my guns. The Sioux turned to dash furiously upon us. They met M and L with crash of gunfire and roar of drumming hooves. I sent exploding shells over the army's heads into the hostile onslaught, placing my shots with deadly effect. A couple of my drivers and three from the gun crews fell dead or severely wounded, but the slightly wounded begged to serve their guns.

Torquil

Astride Severa, I plunged into the midst of the fray. In the white-hot blaze of combat, my body was aware of her moving at my slightest touch, precisely when and how and where I needed her to go, like she was part of myself, but the fluid action touched my mind not at all: she was the platform I fought from. I accounted for six of the hostiles with my revolver. My strength was boundless, my senses accurate, tuned to inform and instruct a flawless performance. The daemon worked me to the peak of my energies.

I brought up my carbine and paid shot for shot till Recall sounded and recalled me, one nerve at a time, to my ordinary senses. Still dazed, I saw a diminished band of Indians escaping toward the river, and my comrades, on horses as exhausted as my own, scattered about in ones and twos. They looked like so many Esquimaux in their furs. Why were Esquimaux here? Was this the Arctic?

Only Uncle James and the guns seemed familiar. Distinctions of rank hadn't returned to my mind. I circled Severa behind the firing line to savor his expertise.

2. Pursuit and Rescue

MacLeod

I was fighting my guns with mind ticking over like a well-oiled watch while I orchestrated sighting, elevation, choice of shot, size of the charge, and order of firing. Startled to find Torquil next to me, I scowled at him—he interrupted my concentration.

The source of a high, inhuman shriek was well-nigh obscured by powder smoke and twilight. We each seized field glasses and saw a soldier dragged along by a stick through his shoulder. The wordless outcry of pain and terror and despair screamed on.

"Can you?"

Torquil

I rallied my depleted energies and braced myself to go on without the collapse my brain and body cried for. Words tripped over racing thoughts.

"I'll need a fresh horse and two half shelters and—"

"Number One! Fire! Number Four! Fire!" He called over his shoulder, "Use my name for what you need and be gone!"

* * *

An hour later, I was still undetected, riding a strong, fresh gray horse, its shod hooves and jingling harness wrapped with white canvas. I'd buttoned two half shelters together and cloaked myself in them. The wind made them ripple. In the dim starlight, the horse and I were ghosts.

We'd crossed the Platte half an hour ago. The night was still but for sweep of the wind and whisper of blowing snow granules. Even the prairie wolves must have sought their dens. The captured soldier had been silent for some time. I hadn't seen his body, nor as much blood as if the axial artery had been severed. He might still be alive. Slight changes of direction kept me downwind. The hostiles were plodding. Would they camp or push forward? Ahead, low bluffs broke the force of the wind. They'd camp there.

They built fires and let their ponies go to find what meager graze they could. I passed through a ravine out of the firelight to the top of the bluff, crept to the crest, and looked over.

The Indians pulled the stick out of the soldier's shoulder. He screamed in bleeding agony. They were drawing knives when I back-crawled down the slope. Holding an exploding shell with fuse cut to five-second length, I rode silently near the lip of the bluff where I wouldn't be silhouetted against the stars. I lit the fuse, counted four seconds, and lobbed it over the edge.

The shell exploded just over the hostiles' heads, raining fragments of itself and of the bluff upon them. While their eyes were blinded by the explosion and their ears deaf from the blast, I hastened down behind the bluff to the spot closest the soldier.

Dodged Indian ponies fleeing in all directions ... tethered the horse in a shadowed gully ... covered myself with the half shelters and snaked forward on belly and elbows, a second shell in one hand.

In the undulating motion of blowing snow, under cover of the wind and the agitated voices of the Indians, I closed in. They were disabled by wounds or milling in confusion. I lit the second fuse, counted three seconds, and threw the shell at the campfire ... scrambled to the wounded soldier, twitched the half shelters to cover him, clamped my hand over his mouth.

"Sixteenth Cavalry. Be silent or I'll gag you! We're leaving now."

The second shell exploded in the Indians' midst, wounding more and throwing the others into greater confusion. The terrified ponies kept running.

I pulled the soldier into the shadows, helped him mount, and swung up behind him, draping the half shelters over us while I spurred the gray into a trot down the hidden, gradual ravine. The drumming of ponies' hooves covered what little sound the gray made. I spurred it to a canter as soon as terrain allowed.

"Put your arm into the front of your coat. Where else are you hurt?"

"Leg. Stabbed." A sharp intake of breath between clenched teeth.

I kept the horse at the best speed the ground and a double load permitted, by instinct. We were soon mincing across the ice-bound Platte.

He waked as he had waked more than once on that uncanny ride, with a feeling that the next step would carry his horse over an awful precipice. He had been broken down from loss of sleep at the start, and the ride had almost finished him. All the phantasms and vagaries imaginable attended it. Men cantering along-

side and in front of him were ghosts to the touch; river and forest and mountains blended confusedly, but the powerful will controlled the body and it acted mechanically.
—Written about Private Thomas D. Ranson, Confederate States Army

Hooves on the ice were distant artillery fire. Sioux surrounded me. One in front was heading my horse over a cliff.

"Halt! Who comes there?"

"Friend!"

"Advance and give the countersign!"

"I don't have it!"

"Hands up!" Biggs rode forward and scrutinized our faces. "They're lookin' fer ya. Both of ya." He lowered his carbine and waved us on.

Perkins

M company were encamped in a "wash" where the wind was less severe. Our mess had erected shelters and were feeding sticks to the campfire when Drummond returned, carrying his saddle.

"Here's your burnt offerings." Grey handed him a tinware cup.

"Jeffries would be a fine cook if he could determine when to stop!" I said.

"I don't like my meat live and kickin' like you do!"

"It's superiah to charcoal!"

"Bet yew two bits he's asleep afore he's done et," Smith hissed. He's a stellar specimen of the frontier American I'd heard so much about.

"Done!"

"Well? What happened?" demanded Grey.

"Crept up on them, pulled Marbury out, came back."

"And the explosions happened all by themselves!" Trelawney scoffed. "Here's your mule!"

"I used some shells for a diversion." He yawned.

"Were ye accountin' for many?" Murphy asked.

"I didn't wait to see how many got up again." His eyelids were drooping.

Smith tapped me in the ribs. 'Watch!' he mouthed.

I blared, "Capital work! How did you employ the shells?"

"Over the edge of the bluff, then into a campfire."

"How badly was the chap injuhed?"

"Bad stab wounds in the leg. If he keeps his arm, the surgeons are magicians." He yawned again, but spooned more bits from the cup.

"How was he called, again?"

"Marbury." He set the cup down, stretched out, and laid his head on his saddle.

"Did you go berserk?" Grey always makes the most awkward queries.

"Not then." His eyes were half-closed.

"In the other fight?"

"Yes." He pulled his cap down and shut his eyes.

"What's it like?"

His body relaxed, a long breath escaped. Slow, regular breathing began.

"Any-thing left?" Smith asked Grey.

"Not much. You still hungry?"

"Yew can have it."

I made a wry mouth and dropped a quarter dollar into Smith's open palm.

New orders arrived during the night and sent us all back to our respective posts. We heard the Indians had joined others farther north and were sojourning in those villages for the winter.

Torquil

"Ahe we being presented to the Queen?" moaned Perkins.

"If you'd polish your 'coutrements the way you do your jokes, you'd pass!" Grey had no sympathy. "Extra duty—much thanks!"

"Get on with those tables!" rumbled Graham, now sergeant over fourth barracks. Disgusted at our poor showing, he was trying to "cipher out" how to bring Perkins "up to snuff."

I could have told him it was next to impossible! Perkins rode with better style than the rest of the squad and joked like an educated man, but he seemed to know only a dictionary definition of the word *clean*.

We were sentenced to scrub down the mess hall and all its furniture. We had to melt snow for scrub water and endure Sergeant Jacquard's black looks and blacker imprecations when we got in his way and disturbed the perfection of his kitchen. Perkins was in bad odor with us all.

CHAPTER 17

PARTINGS, PLANS, AND PROMOTIONS

MacLeod

Soon after New Year's, I composed a Valentine verse and dispatched it in hopes it would reach Virginia by February 14. By the same post, I ordered confectionery sent from New York.

Torquil

On March 30, there was a total eclipse of the moon. In April, Uncle James sent for me.

"There's no indication of the Ironclad Oath falling into disuse, but I'm going to prepare you as well as I can to pass the officers' examination. You must serve for two years as a non-commissioned officer. Colonel Hale has approved your appointment as corporal.

"He'll approve a sergeancy, to reward your service during the last campaign. When I believe you ready, and one opens, you shall have it. I'm requiring you to wait so you can learn while performing similar duties under an experienced sergeant."

"But, sir, I commanded a whole company."

"The Regulars aren't the boys you grew up with! To draw out the best that's in them, you have to know them. Your—so to speak—apprenticeship will give you that opportunity.

"Officers aren't supposed to notice that sergeants keep their stripes by physical force. I won't have the disorder that will result from putting you in that situation. Nor have you a man's strength, so you'll have to learn the necessary diplomacy.

"I intend to keep you from further injury. You've recovered your health only because of the bodily renewal and recuperative powers of youth. Severe injuries exact heavy toll from the health you'll need to perform your duty well over the course of a long career. Field service is hazard enough.

"Seniority needn't be considered when appointing sergeants from among the corporals. I expect you to use your time in that grade to show you've earned the promotion."

* * *

If my squad mates thought I deserved promotion, they took care not to say so.

"Yew'll catch it! He won't let yew off of anything!" Smith elbowed his bunkie. They were a strange combination, unlike as could be in speech, in background, in amusements—in everything except an aversion to military standards of cleanliness.

"I'll put on such style, he won't need to," sniffed Perkins.

"If you're the height of style, they'll make you orderly and you'll have to look trim all day for the captain," said Grey. "You couldn't stand up to it!"

We all laughed. We'd threatened to name Perkins "Rags."

"Yew'll have to wake up, Reb, or those boys'll hawg-tie yew for tar-get practice!"

Does Smith think I sleep my way through life!

* * *

Due to rearrangements among the barracks, I ended up in second under Sergeant O'Shea. I came down hard when Westhill was insolent. Behind my back, a retort just loud enough to show I was meant to hear it: "Too much wind for such a little horn!"

Former corporals among the Old Issues knew the responsibilities and preferred to avoid them. They tolerated and obeyed the one they thought was fool enough to accept the duty. By example, hard work, and instruction, I brought the details assigned to me up to the mark I set. I raised the standard gradually and was prompt with rebuke or the slow nod of approval they came to know me for.

The other corporal was Steptoe. He was thick in the body as I was thin and stood but a couple inches shorter. With eyes glittering under jutting brows, his derisive laugh could laud or lower a soldier in a second. By sarcasm he coerced consensus and sycophants. Sidestepping regulations, he was careless about keeping arms and accoutrements clean and in good repair. The men in his details knew it and were also slack. O'Shea had to prod them.

Colonel Hale

I came with Inspector General Hazen for the general inspection in late May, to review my far-flung regiment. If Jennings can't keep Fort Liberty fit for inspection, I'll find out why! The night after the inspection and due commendation published in orders, I invited MacLeod to ride a circuit of the nearby terrain. After a short distance, I cleared my throat.

"Hem! I've seen all there was to see, and believe me, if you'd been hiding anything, or glossing it over, I'd have spotted it. Hem! Too many of the slack or inexperienced think they can fool me, but I'm not in my dotage yet!"

"No, Colonel."

"What I see here is solid, well in hand. Your men's morale is outstanding. You're developing your lieutenants well."

"They're good men for the work."

"You'd have to appreciate them compared to the two you had! Why'd it take so long to get rid of them? Even the shavetails at Liberty knew them for worthless."

"I made sure to build a watertight case, first, sir. They'd have been worse millstones around my neck if tried and acquitted."

"Enough damage as it was! Did you know DuChemin's running a gambling tent at the Union Pacific end-of-track? I had it from Parnell. His company's the construction guard."

"The Sixteenth will soon have a company in every Territory."

I wasn't to be diverted. "What of the boy Yohanson nearly killed? I should've received a letter of complaint from him."

"The regiment is redressing the grievance, sir. He's Drummond, the one you intend to appoint sergeant."

"The one who rescued L Company's man from the Sioux? Medical skill, too, I recall."

"Yes. The Army's his vocation. He wants to be commissioned. I'm bringing him along as quickly as is good for him—and for the company."

"Has he ... hem! ... the background?"

"Born and bred a gentleman."

"I'll keep him under my eye."

MacLeod

1866 brought a quiet summer to our part of the Department of the Platte. General Sherman's policy was to maintain peace in the West during Army reorganization after the war. At the Fort Laramie peace conference, the Indians were requested to allow passage of gold seekers and emigrants over the Bozeman Trail. Sent to build forts along the trail, Colonel Carrington and his

18th Infantry unfortunately arrived while the conference was in session. The Indians saw that the new route would be established under military guard whether or not they consented. Some signed the treaty anyway. The others, Sioux and Cheyenne under Red Cloud, returned in disgust to the Powder River country. The volunteer regiments were discharged that summer, their three-year enlistments completed. I was losing all my good Widefield County men.

Torquil

Most of my old squad were itching to get home again. Smith wasn't going with them.

"Ah'm aimin' to be a guide. The redskins won't give up their huntin' grounds without a fight, and Ah aim to be in it." He set a quart bottle of his whiskey in a cleverly constructed, concealed niche. "Ah'm leavin' yew this, agin the bad day."

"Thank you. One's bound to come. I reckon I'll see you now and again."

"On cam-paign."

In late summer, Lieutenant Porter pushed hard in pursuit of hostiles who'd come south of the Platte and attacked ranches along Lame Horse Creek. Some were mounted and some had dismounted to kill and pillage. Some were alert, others engrossed with their victims. We struck like a thunderbolt.

Half a dozen galloped away, lashing their ponies furiously. O'Shea, Steptoe, Trelawney, Jeffries on Diablo, and I raced in pursuit. Infuriated by seeing savage butchery, we spurred hard. The horses caught our fury, putting heart and lungs, muscle and sinew into the chase. As we closed, Steptoe aimed at an Indian who had a soldier in his sights. His carbine missed fire, missed fire again. Little Trelawney fell from his saddle, wounded in the chest by the Indian Steptoe failed to shoot. We left not a Sioux to carry away a dead or wounded tribesman. I dismounted to bind up Trelawney's wound.

O'Shea demanded Steptoe's Spencer. It'd missed fire because the lock was clogged with dirt and congealed grease.

"Ye lazy scut! I told ye to be cleanin' it!"

"The dirt got in during the march!"

"Arrah!"

At the ruined homestead, a burial detail was doing its grisly work. Dr. Barnes found that the rifle ball had deflected off Trelawney's rib, torn its way out below his shoulder blade, and lodged in his blouse. Nightmares seized me that night. The carnage I'd seen brought back contorted corpses on many battlefields.

> A consciousness of their superiority ... constitutes one of the strongest factors of *esprit de corps* in a military body.
> —Jennings Cropper Wise, *The Military History of the Virginia Military Institute from 1839 to 1865*

In early autumn, I was appointed sergeant. Uncle James transferred O'Shea back to fourth barracks to break in some more recruits. I moved into the sergeant's room in second barracks and took my seat at the sergeants' table in the mess hall.

"Whose coat's that you're wearing?" joked Matthews, the near-sighted Quartermaster Sergeant.

"Memory like yours ought to be in the Soldiers Home!"

"Naw, let him be," intoned Fisher, the brawny Pennsylvanian who kept the incorrigibles in first barracks under his iron hand. "Them boys'll have it off'n him if 'twas a mistake."

"The Captain's not afther makin' mistakes," O'Shea said in my favor.

"Them Raws you're inheritin' is a handful—an' no mistake!" grinned Rector, duty sergeant of third barracks.

"He'll chew them up for breakfast." I returned the compliment.

"You'd know!" Rector rejoined. "What's that smudge under your nose?"

"My razor wore out."

"Any Americans among them Raws?" inquired Fisher.

"Half are tellin' me words to the other half. Did that Hoffmann of yours ever quit talkin' Dutch?"

"When he has to. Mostly he and Mueller talk like the Rhineland."

"I hear Mueller's finding favor with the shoulder straps." Rector dangled the rumor.

"He don't leave no loose ends in his splice," said Fisher. "He could be useful."

Sergeant Jacquard stalked up to the table. One of the kitchen detail followed, bearing a plate of food. He set it before Jacquard and retired in haste.

"Put zee salt pork in water to freshen!" Jacquard barked at his back. "Zey need told what ees a kettle! Zey know not zee worcestershire from zee garlic!"

"Do they know a sow from a boar?" asked Fisher.

"No need. I do not let zem butcher."

"When will we be tastin' some o' them hogs ye're raisin'?"

"Too soon, eef zey break zee fence again. Zee Capitaine, he warns me zee peegs will be shot eef zey run loose!"

* * *

My moustache grew in thick and silky. Before there was enough of it to force a decision how to arrange it, I received Mueller as corporal. Knowing the stout German's precise ways, I put him in charge of the squad's equipment and record keeping. I assigned Steptoe to maintain arms and accoutrements, and oversee the cleanliness of them, the men, and the barracks. I inspected his work and condemned its quality so often, he got sick of hearing, "Do it right or do it twice!"

I didn't let up. Cleanliness and order were vital for health and discipline's sake, which improved our chances for survival. I'd suffer rebuke and derision and loss of reputation if my barracks fell short of Uncle James's strict requirements. Steptoe hadn't learned the lessons Trelawney's unnecessary wound should have taught him. I caught him leaving breechblocks uncleansed and ungreased—again!—though the surface of the weapons was clean and bright.

"Who else do you want to get shot! Do it again. If you do it right, you don't have to do it twice!"

"If Yer Majesty don't like the way I do it, let him lick it clean hisself!" Steptoe puffed himself up and shoved me.

I kept gloating out of voice and expression. I already knew who I'd ask for in his stead.

"Behind the stables, after Tattoo." A cold, deliberate order.

Second barracks all came to see the contest for command. They posted lookouts against official intervention and made bets in hoarse whispers. I stood with arms folded, like I already knew the outcome and only had to go through the motions.

Steptoe took off his jacket and advanced, chest out, fists clenched, till he was nose to nose. "You're not big enough to be sergeant, little horn!"

"Might you be?" I purred.

"Take off them stripes and I'll prove it!"

"Are you fighting the stripes or the man?"

"The boy!"

I looked like bored hauteur. Shucked my coat and flung it aside without moving my feet an inch ... looked hard into his eyes ... allowed my mouth the least twitch of contempt.

He aimed a right at my head. Following O'Shea's advice, I drove my whole weight, behind both fists, into his sternum before he regained balance. He fell on his back, grunting and gasping for breath.

I felt my daemon rising, up the back of my neck and into my brain. My muscles thrilled with it. My blood ran hot, pouring extra life and strength all through me. My vision focused sharper, and my lungs expanded till I could feel air and energy pumped clear to my fingertips. I'd meant to use every savage bit of fighting I knew, not only to win but to show the squad I could and would, but the daemon could do it better. I grinned like a wolf.

He did me some damage, but every time I beat him down, he was slower to get up. The last time, I ground a knee into his chest. I smashed his jaw.

A slow, cold, hollow growl: "I'm giving you a whipping." I hit him harder.

"You're a menace to the company." I pounded his right eye.

"You don't make men ready"—I hammered on the left cheekbone—"to defend themselves." I beat his nose.

"They can't defend themselves … or each other. You let them go to war with weapons that *don't fire*."

I smashed him on the jaw again. He went limp. His head lolled back.

My barracks knew the accusation was true. My case was established. I rose easily to my feet … waited till he moaned … clenched my fists and stood over him.

The deadly growl: "You put our lives in *needless* danger! Confess it!"

"Aaah … c'fess."

"To whom?" I snapped.

"You."

"Who am I!"

"Sarssh-nt."

The squad edged closer. I acted like I noticed them for the first time.

"You all know where you bunk."

I pivoted smartly and stalked away, picking up my jacket with a fluid swoop. If Steptoe's cronies wanted to aid him, they could. If they wanted to punish the one who jeopardized their survival, I'd refuse to know about it. I sat on my bed to let the daemon's thrumming fade. The men returned. As Taps sounded, Steptoe staggered in, alone. I collapsed into darkness.

* * *

"He's discredited with the squad, First Sergeant, so he won't command the respect necessary to accomplish the duties of the grade." I felt my bruises today—a lot.

"I'm supposin' ye'd know how it happened."

"Yes."

"Are ye thinkin' more ... umm ... discreditin' ... is wantin'?"

"Only to reduce him."

"Hev ye a replacement in mind?"

"Perkins."

"The nastiest scut in the squad! Ye're jokin', me bhoy!"

"Responsibility will bring him up to the mark. He has it in him to discharge it well."

"An' a winnin' way wid him, ye'll be tellin' me, in spite of the dirt in the ears! Faith, what's it comin' to, when a Sassenach can pull the wool over the eyes of a Gael!" Dunahan looked amused. "I'll send it up to the Captain. A joke will be doin' him good!"

That night at parade the order was read. Perkins came to my room in dismay. I motioned him to close the door.

"What have you done to me, Ser'nt!" With grand theatrical gesture, he flung up an arm, covering his eyes in mock despair.

"You once mentioned putting on some style." My mouth twitched in amusement beneath the moustache that now over-hung it—I must've looked like a walrus before I figured out what to do with it. "Show me!"

Perkins pantomimed deep dejection as he left, leaving the door open as my gesture bid, but he went immediately to work. He beat dust out of his clothing till Smith complained about the cloud. He re-blacked his shoes and belts, then polished all his buttons and accoutrements. He routed out the barber and the tailor.

Next morning, he was perfect: freshly shaven, clothing trim, accoutrements gleaming, new chevrons bright. The squad jeered good-naturedly. His clowning and elegant riding had won him a place in spite of his slovenly habits. I approved with silence and the slow nod. I gave him the duty Steptoe had failed in, the bar-racks' overall cleanliness. The squad jeered uproariously.

In the days that followed, as I tried new arrangements of my moustache, I supervised him without seeming to. He went to work cheerfully, putting his theatrical ability to such good use that he gained the squad's cooperation and inspired good humor. He caricatured himself and me and *Army Regulations* freely. I heard a frequent exhortation.

"Oh, come, come, chaps, this will nevah do!" as if taking their agreement for granted.

Another, all in conspiratorial tones, was, "You know Eagle Eye is watching! You suahly don't want *his* style of rebuke! You must do bettah!"

I smothered amusement and was satisfied with the reputation ascribed. I lived it.

Perkins did have a winning way about him. Using himself as an example of what could be achieved by the slackest, he teased and joked and chivvied his squad mates into accepting and main-taining the standards I upheld. Second barracks began to take a new kind of pride in themselves. To their rough self-portrait as seasoned fighters, lording it over the recruits, they added a smartness and swagger that raised them in their own opinion and that of the officers. I drilled them to a high degree of precision. Mueller made sure they were turned out for all duties on time and with all the necessary equipment. Perkins composed a new reproach.

"Do you want to sink to the *othah* barracks' level!"

* * *

"You makin' dandies out o' them boys?" teased Rector.

"It won't hurt them. It gives them something to do besides lounge around and growl."

"You gonna do anything with 'em besides shine 'em up and parade 'em?" jibed Fisher. It was impossible to make his incorrigibles accomplish the minimum.

"Hope for a chance to fight them. It's a right quiet summer."

"They're havin' hot work, up along the Powder and Big Horn," O'Shea reminded us.

"D'you suppose we'll get sent to reinforce them?" Matthews no doubt thought of the massive effort of transport and supply.

"The shoulder straps only know!" Rector shrugged.

* * *

The boy's heart was pure, his life had been clean, and his ideals of womanhood were all derived from the virtuous and unselfish guardians of his own childhood.
—John S. Wise, *The Lion's Skin*

I was absorbed in my new duties, but not so much that I didn't notice the looks some of the women gave me. I was polite but didn't respond to the blatant overtures. My sights were set on a commission and a lady wife.

CHAPTER 18

FORT BANKS

MacLeod

Shortly after the year turned, we heard about the massacre of Captain Fetterman and eighty men, almost within sight of Fort Philip Kearny on the Bozeman Trail. Surgeon Horton's report stated that only six of the men had died of bullet wounds. The others had been "mutilated and attacked with clubs after being wounded." There'd been few alarms in my jurisdiction for the past year, but much fighting to the north, so I prepared the company for a change of station.

The Indians took the warpath throughout the department as soon as the grass was sufficient. They attacked stagecoaches, railroad construction and surveyors, and a twenty-mile stretch of the Union Pacific. They attacked isolated ranches and the town of Julesburg, stole horses and mules, and killed citizens. Camp Sherman was ordered abandoned. When I built the post, I knew I'd one day be ordered elsewhere. Yet it saddened me to leave what I'd created, to scavengers and wild animals. I was losing independent command, too.

Torquil

I hadn't needed to resort to Smith's whiskey, but it was valuable medicine for wounds and pain. I took the risk of carrying contraband.

MacLeod

Our first stop en route to Fort Banks on the Bozeman Trail was Fort Liberty.

"Find everything you need, MacLeod?" Colonel Hale motioned me to a chair. "Jennings was glad to hear you're joining him. We've too many political appointees, but experienced officers are at a premium. Hem! How's that boy sergeant shaping?"

"Very well, sir. Did you notice the polish of my second squad? They're his."

"Saw 'em." He nodded. "When do we need to send him up for the examination?"

"He has to serve as a non-commissioned officer till his enlistment's up next May, to complete the two years *Regulations* requires. After that, he needs instruction."

"Hem! Send him to a crammer, I suppose."

"His trustees have written to me about his schooling. His father's will requires him to complete his education before he inherits, and his father meant college graduation."

"All the better for a commission, but how long will that keep him from service here?"

"Four years."

"He'll want his inheritance, on a lieutenant's pay. Hem! Do you know anyone who can get him sent to the Sixteenth?"

"There are some I shall approach. Your request, too, would carry weight."

"I'll make it when the time comes."

Torquil

M company were enjoying the opportunities of a regimental post. Encamped in tents upstream from the cluster of buildings around the parade, we had liberty to enter it when our days' duties were over.

The well-stocked sutler's store drew those who still had any pay in their pockets. We were all eager to hear the news we'd missed in isolation at Camp Sherman. Fort Liberty was a "wet" post, so those inclined to whiskey found no shortage. Uncle James couldn't countermand the general orders of the post, but he tightened restrictions on our freedom. After the first day, we all had to return to camp at Recall. Enforcement fell on the lieutenants' and sergeants' shoulders.

Not assigned to the guard one night, I got a pass and went looking for Smith. He was at the sutler's, carving a bounding rabbit out of a piece of gnarled cedar while he listened to other men talk about the gold mines in Montana. His back was turned. I picked up a wood chip, stopped a short distance away, and flicked it onto his hand.

His knife stopped in mid-cut, but that was his only sign of surprise. Moving nothing but his eyes, he looked around, grinned and stood up.

"Yew young hound!" He clapped me on the shoulder

"Been a wolf, I'd have bit you, buckskin!" I motioned him along to the counter.

"So them boys didn't tar-get practice on yew—not 'nough target, Ah rec-kon."

"I keep them too busy!"

I bought a pie. Outside, we sat leaning against the building, spearing pieces of fruit and piecrust with our knives.

"Ah see yew sprouted an-other stripe."

"Better than another nose. I reckon scouting keeps you busy."

"We been on the hunt. It' right good, gettin' paid to do what we been taught." He nodded to acknowledge my skills. "It's sure the beat o' drill and Re-veille."

"The Army'd be all right if we had more fights. I'm full alive only when I'm in one, it lifts me up so high." I flamed with anticipation.

"Nothin' like it ... seems like a man cain't miss."

"Nor tire ... nor hurt."

"An' see ever hair on man or horse, through the back of my haid, almost."

"The fire inside ... and the power ... and it's all going like a rocket."

"An' so's your own self."

"And if I win, I'll get to go Home."

"What's at home?"

"Da and Douglas."

"Yew ought to wait till there's some pret-ty lit-tle wo-man there, too, 'fore yew go a-tryin' to catch a fur-lough wound."

"I meant my long home."

"Yew ain't makin' no more sense than yew ev-ah did."

"It's the only good place. The rest is a desert."

"Yew ain't hardly star-ted livin'. There's more than yew know."

"Perhaps."

"Ah'll show yew. There's some now."

Two women came out of the sutler's store, good-looking in a vulgar way, but they weren't ladies. Starting across the parade, one caught sight of Smith. Inviting him, she waved a hand and rolled her shoulder suggestively. Smith unfolded himself to rise.

I stood and tipped my hat. They were females, after all. The women slowed their steps.

"Come on."

"No." I looked away as from a rejected horse and hardened my voice to warn Smith I meant what I said. "I'll wait for my own."

Smith

I waved "Later!" to the gals and sat down again. Ever' time I think I know him, the Reb turns out different. 'Twasn't for his nerve, Ah'd be done with him.

"Well, there's others if those ain't to your likin'."

"I'll know her if I ever meet her."

"Yew ain't a-goin' to meet no one if yew don't look fer poss-ibles."

He stayed shut as a door.

"Ah reckon yew're wonderin' where yew'll find the redskins. It's more … they'll find yew."

MacLeod

The Indians were never out of sight for long. We corralled the wagons, picketed the horses, and set a double guard every night. We bivouacked at Forts Reno and Phil Kearny en route. After thirteen days on the trail, we rounded a point, and every bit of Fort Banks was visible. On a steep bluff above the river, it faced east and was flanked by a deep ravine to the north, broken country to the northwest, and the river valley to the south. It was stockaded, and so was the quartermaster's corral. We forded the river, angled up the bluff, and passed through the gates.

* * *

"That ravine to the north is one of the hostiles' trails. There's no telling when they'll haunt it." Major Jennings was a bluff veteran dragoon with the aura of Churobusco and Cerro Gordo still about him. He continued about the strategic situation.

"They killed and scalped a man in full view of the post last December. About a third of the command came down with scurvy, and it got worse till the middle of March when Story's train finally got through with vegetables and molasses. Then in April, they got Van Valzah, the mail carrier. We've had to triple the escort on all the trains."

He detained me after Officers' Call next morning.

"What reinforcements have you brought me? I'm not going to waste any of them."

"You know we brought your supplies from Fort Liberty, Major." I recounted artillery, ordnance, commissary and quartermaster's stores, company records, Dr. Barnes, Walker, and the hospital, the men, horses and mules, Torquil as a scout, artisans and mechanics for the construction going on, and Jacquard as a chef fit for Delmonico's, "besides being enterprising about raising meat." I smiled. "We might have run the fat off his pigs on the way up the Trail, though."

"Drummond. He's the boy that rescued L company's man two winters ago?"

"Yes, sir."

"I'll look at the descriptive rolls."

Major Jennings

I aimed to put all resources to the best use. I squinted at the captain in the prime of life and remembered a young lieutenant with a survey party twenty years ago.

"I recall from Texas, you're an engineer."

"Yes, sir."

"Construction's been slowed by the scurvy, but most of the men are recovered now." I handed him my sheets of plans. "You'll have enough to get the work done in good time."

The hostile threat was so severe that I ordered all soldiers to sleep within the stockade and kept the gates locked from Recall to Reveille. I put Lieutenant Porter in command of the chain of outposts and assigned the vedettes to Sergeant Drummond. I sent him and his squad on scout with old Crowley, to learn the lay of the land, but I gave him his orders myself.

"Mind you, Sergeant, I want a full report of your observations! After the sun dance, they're taking the warpath. It's not whether they'll strike us, it's *when* and *where*. You're responsible to warn the pickets and the post in time."

> [The fort] once stood an assault against a force of Indians twenty times the strength of the garrison.
> —Major E. R. P. Shurley, Second Cavalry Regiment, United States Army

We beat them off. The friendly Crow Indians returned briefly, en route to their winter grounds. They reported the Sioux making no plans for another mass attack. I withdrew the large force from my perimeter and assigned Drummond and his squad permanently to escort duty.

CHAPTER 19

THE BOZEMAN TRAIL

Men who fight wars, especially when they lose those
wars, are older than their years.
—Daniel E. Sutherland, *Seasons of War*

They hold a man in great esteem who in action sets
them an example of contempt for danger.
—Lt. Col. Arthur J. L. Fremantle, Coldstream Guards,
British Army

Every atom of authority has to be purchased with a
drop of your blood.
—George St. Leger Grenfell, Inspector General of
Cavalry, Confederate States Army, June 2, 1863

Torquil

The mails sometimes came only at intervals of months.
Mr. Ogilvie's second- and third-quarter reports, written three
months apart, arrived together. The farm made steady progress
toward its former thriving condition. MacCammond, working
as a teamster for passage to the Montana gold fields, stopped to

refit at the fort. He told me the infuriating conditions created by Yankee rule, and news of my friends and the county. I listened to it all through all the off-duty time I had, but it seemed like a far country and a time long since vanished. My connections to Abercairn were fading.

Perkins

We'd established the point some time or the other: Drummond's a gentleman and so am I. Even as enlisted men, we kept the standard insofar as we could. His advocacy of me came at quite the right time, when I'd sunk to—no, below—the level around me. Between us, we raised it, and brought the squad up with us. Polished in appearance, quality of quarters, drill, marksmanship, horsemanship, and combat, their swagger in garrison increased to a veritable *strut*.

They'd come to admire and trust him. They forgot his youth because of his invincible demeanor. Unyielding, he demanded their best. But he gave them his best, and they knew it. We could do little to distinguish our uniforms, but we all bought blue bandana handkerchiefs and wore them as a badge to set ourselves apart. They wore theirs as neckerchiefs, but I folded mine into a cravat. We presented one to him. He did the same.

I must say, his courage was quite too far on the reckless side, but it drew forth theirs, and they prided themselves on it. He never went to his rest in camp till they were taken care of. He carried a medical kit and treated their wounds. In battle fury, he seemed beyond human. Afterward, however, he blew up at the least provocation. But they expected scorching invective from sergeants. They bragged about their "Old Flint."

MacLeod

Repeated hostilities as the year drew in kept the Sioux threat uppermost in everyone's minds. Scarce a single train escaped attack.

I seldom saw Torquil, but I heard stories. "Old Flint" pitched right into the middle of them. "Old Flint" rescued his wounded from under their very noses. "Old Flint" killed two Indians single-handed. Taken together, the accounts made evidence that he was succumbing to the daemon's power against his soul. But I had promised to guard a pure heart and turn him back from a course deadly to himself and others.

My sergeants attended tactical recitations at my office on Wednesday nights, so my immediate plan for his welfare was based on his being seldom in garrison. To give him instruction he'd missed, I said, I told First Sergeant Dunahan to have Torquil report to me every night he was at the post.

For the future, I planned to bring my lad under the severe, unrelenting, day-in, day-out discipline that would teach him command of himself, and, I hoped, enable him to defeat the daemon, by sheer consistency of enforcement. I wrote:

> ... so I urge you to secure him an appointment there. He is called of God to protect, as a soldier, he believes, so instruction by the Chair of Military Strategy will be of immense practical value. The courses in scientific agriculture will enrich his understanding of the management of his inheritance.
>
> As to the cost, I shall defray it. I must entreat you to indulge my indulgence. He is to me, my only son. ...

Torquil

I wore my men's tribute with satisfaction but found the lack of lifelong ties to them a help. In the balance between their welfare and tactical success, I'd had to weigh my Rangers' lives heaviest. Now I could risk men without a qualm. I risked myself most of all. They never knew I did it because my life felt like a curse—but what I really wanted was to live the pure heart I hoped I still had.

What character I could still claim was undermined by my crude life. On the Trail nearly every day, in subzero blizzards or hundred-degree heat, we were often attacked. I'd seen carnage during the War, but much was unpremeditated—where a shell chanced to burst or an unaimed bullet hit home. The atrocities I saw aggravated my nightmares. Harshness obliterated any mercy I formerly used. I didn't read God's Word, nor did I pray. I didn't heed Da's word that enemies were souls for whom Jesus gave his life, because I judged intentional butchery of living men, the work of devils. The burden of life and duty felt too heavy to bear. Mr. Ogilvie's next report came from a world that had no meaning. I was too exhausted to read it.

I didn't know, then, that past horror set off an explosion of destruction against present menace—and made it seem the right thing to do. During the War, I didn't know what the daemon made of me, but now I learned. It goaded me to charge headlong into annihilation, to escape the life I hated—and undergo the ultimate purification at last.

I had to refuse it at the onset or be consumed. I forced myself to delay the collapse, like I did when I went after Marbury, till I'd brought my men off the field and completed after-battle duties. Whether I succumbed or overcame, it wore me down, barring me from the virtue and righteousness I longed for. I didn't know how much its daily assault on body, soul and spirit, had stolen from me till one winter day on the Trail.

We started during a thaw, encouraged by sunshine, springlike temperatures and warm chinook winds, to escort a contractor's train of twenty wagons to fill with provisions at Fort Phil Kearny. Every day, small bands of Indians appeared. Many of their ponies stumbled from weakness. Better mounted warriors dashed upon the train, but our accurate fire drove them off.

Though we had to fight mud every afternoon ... use ropes to line the wagons down the high, steep, slippery bank of Mallard Creek ... double or triple the teams—even with empty wagons—to get them up the other side ... once had to corral the train to fight off an attack ... we arrived safe and enjoyed a short rest while the wagons were refurbished and loaded. I was given charge of a mountain howitzer, its limber and teams, and a wagonload of ammunition, but no gunners. I called the men from their rest to instruct them in firing the gun. I had to discuss it with the wagon master, who had full charge of wagons, teams, and drivers, but I made sure the gun was next after the ammunition wagon, in the middle of the train. We left the fort under clear skies.

The fourth day out, the vast dome of the sky was dimmed with thin clouds from horizon to horizon. Temperatures were colder. By night, the cloud layer was thick. When we left camp next day, hard rain made a tumbling turmoil all through the air, and roiled along the ground. It turned to snow while we climbed the divide between Black Cliff River and Mallard Creek. The January thaw was done. We put on our winter furs.

At the top, ice granules scoured our faces. The wind boomed. All across the broad plateau, the mules had to be forced into it. Only hard spurring kept the horses moving forward. Knifing blasts from the north scored us till they brought the snow in a driving blizzard so thick and steady that the trail and all landmarks disappeared behind a whirling white wall. Day was darkened to twilight by the shadow of countless snowflakes. No shelter, nothing to break the wind. The eerie light gave more deception than guidance.

The temperature plummeted far below zero. Men cried that their hands and faces and feet were freezing. Teamsters became numb and clutched their lines with hands like frozen claws. A few men slid from their saddles and had to be lifted back on and made to travel. Others begged to be left in the snow and allowed to die. Some wandered away in confusion and were forced to return by stout Mueller, lively Perkins, or myself.

I gave the order to march on foot. Though the snow was half-thigh deep, it was warmer than the Arctic gale enveloping us, and the exercise increased blood circulation. I paired my steadiest, strongest men each with a weaker one and marched the most promising gunners next to the howitzer.

If we stopped, we would die.

The wagon master and I agreed our objective must be the valley of Mallard Creek, where we'd have a windbreak and fuel for fires. We'd never survive the night in the open. Leading Severa, I used my feet to find the miniature cliffs denoting the ruts of the road. I squinted into the white gloom, but the sagebrush was invisible. Its absence would have told me where the trail lay.

Mallard creekbank was a chute of glare ice. The waggoners chained the rear wheels of their wagons together for maximum drag. Ten men handled each braking rope to keep the loaded wagons from crashing to the bottom. The wagon master directed this cordelling, while I took Knowlton and our horses and slid down the bank. I ordered him to start a fire, and the wagons to be corralled, with the howitzer aimed outward, on a large hummock which rose above the ice. I went up and down the long chute to lend a hand here or shout a warning there till the wagons were down, the last one in pitch-black night. Snow sifted down into the ravine, but the worst of the storm raged horizontal above. Men and animals alike huddled around the fires. I treated frostbite and injuries sustained in the day's march and issued half a gill of whiskey to each of my men.

The blizzard howled four more days. During the last guard relief before dawn of the fifth day, I spied the Pole Star.

Soldiers, horses, and waggoners toiled well past Meridian to get the wagons out of the creek bed. I took the howitzer first, limber chest filled, and emplaced it to command the ravine and the terrain above. After drilling the crew one more time and leaving the piece loaded, I ordered Mueller to fire it if he saw Indians. On Severa, I fought through drifts to the summit of the nearest rise to survey the country. Even with field glasses, I discerned no trace of Indians.

The weather moderated. Twenty degrees above zero felt like a summer's day. We shed our furs and completed a third of the distance to the fort. The next day was likewise moderate.

The Sioux took advantage of it. Corn, foodstuffs, ammunition, and a chance to fight were prizes not to be ignored. They must have moved behind the bluffs, and in gullies and ravines, where neither they nor their tracks could be seen from the Trail, before they massed in a ravine. Whooping and yelling, a couple of dozen decoys brandished their weapons and plunged out of it.

"Corral the train!"

"Front into line! Forward!"

The sudden alarm roused my nerves and senses, blood and muscle, to flash point.

"Draw ... Revolvers! At the Gallop ... Charge!"

Intending to make a feint, I spurred Severa to speed. The men followed. Some of their horses floundered in drifts while others dashed over bare spots to close with the enemy.

"Fire!"

I shot the warrior in my front. Pierced by the daemon's spear! Overcome! I rushed Severa at the retiring hostiles with no thought, only blind thirst to destroy them all. My men raced forward in my wake.

As if through the wrong end of a telescope, I saw only a broad, gradual, white ascent to the heavens, peppered with tiny, gesticulating horsemen I could annihilate as I swept upon them.

"Fire!"

I brought down one of the tiny figures and spurred again. Severa laboring heavily to give the speed I demanded, we broke through drifts and crusted snow toward a glowing white high road of release from earthly burdens. Severa lost her footing on a patch of ice and went down so fast I couldn't jump clear. My head thumped on the frozen ground. My brain cleared in a shining white flash of light while I leaped to my feet. Beyond the retreating warriors were a hundred more! My men charged past me to the death I'd led them into.

"TO ME!"

I bellowed so loud it tore my throat and pierced my skull with a headache, but I was obeyed. In such a swoop that the enemy were taken by surprise and slow to follow, the squad returned. Severa was uninjured. I mounted again. Turning at intervals to face the hostiles' full force and fire a few more volleys, we withdrew. Murphy was hit and spun from his horse. I doubled back to pick him up and took a bullet in the leg. I threw him over Severa's saddle, vaulted on my good leg, up behind him, and raced back to the line and handed him over to Duval. I could hardly shift him. Then Knowlton slumped in his saddle, but he was close. The lurch to grab his rein made me dizzy. The squad passed into the corral.

I rode around the enclosure, dismounted my men, and posted them to reinforce the teamsters. My boot was full of blood. The ammunition wagon was within the corral and the howitzer aimed outside it. But its barrel drooped. The whole scene wavered.

"Mueller! Assemble the crew ... open fire! Canister ... till they run ... then ... elevate ... exploding shells ... right on top of them." I could hardly hear myself.

Mueller closed in to catch the words.

Falling ...

* * *

Sharp gouges hurt my leg.

"What in blazes are you doing!" I could only whisper.

"Mining for lead! Go back to sleep now, theah's a good chap." Perkins held hard pressure on a blood vessel while Jeffries dug for the bullet.

"No! Wash it with whiskey and bind it up, before you cut me into dog meat!"

"It iss pleeting too much," Hoffman objected. A red pool seeped into the snow.

"Get my kit!"

With help to sit up and to find the severed ends of the vessel, fighting faintness threatening my brain, I managed to tie the ligatures that saved me from bleeding to death.

* * *

Silence. Darkness … faint, warm-colored glow. Heaviness over me, too much trouble to shift. Warm, inviting languor. Drifting into its cocoon. Shrill creaking. Hard weight shifting against my body. Jolting back and forth like a wave. Darkness. Gloaming. Perkins's features on a head upside down. Tenor hum … no meaning. Twilight. Darkness.

Broad daylight. Terrible thirst. Blankets and fur clothing over and under me, hundred-pound sacks of corn around. My left leg was elevated. It hurt when I moved. But I could move. I pushed the coverings aside. Cold air chilled me. I hauled myself over sacks to the front of the jolting, creaking wagon and looked out.

Heavy snow fell straight from sky to earth, but landmarks showed we were approaching the fort. No wind. Perkins was closest.

"My horse!" I croaked. "Water!"

I rode the rest of the way, fighting weakness and a slide back into night. My mind accused me. My soul was in anguish. Enmeshed in the daemon's toils, I'd given a fatal order.

At the post, I sent about half the squad to the hospital and received orders from Dunahan to report to MacLeod. I didn't hear I was to do it later.

MacLeod

My lad's face was reddened from cold and weather, and smeared with gunpowder. His eyelids drooped over dulled eyes. His hair was matted down, his moustache white with frost, and melting snow dripped from his greatcoat. His trousers and left boot were blood stained. He stood with all his weight on his right leg. His voice was a rasping whisper.

"Sir, you must reduce me."

"We shall discuss it another time! O'Hanrahan!"

Torquil

The trumpeter helped me to the hospital. I could stand no longer: I lay on the floor to wait my turn, and dreamed of the beautiful white high road to holy purification. Being carried to the Farther Shore possessed me as it had upon my return from Gettysburg. The loveliness of my real Home brought a wistful smile.

* * *

Consciousness returned by stages. I lapsed into the pleasant vision of going Home. What I'd have to endure to get there was my nightmare. Waking before any tinge of dawn lightened the windows, I saw again my men rushing toward slaughter. I almost groaned aloud for shame and guilt. My leg hurt.

My demand to Uncle James was right. I wasn't fit to command men when I couldn't command whatever beset myself. I had willed to do better—but at the time it compelled me.

I didn't know, then, what trauma did to me, what foundational change it had wrought in my righteousness, my innocence, my understanding. I didn't know it intermitted my ability to rule myself, to make right decisions and act upon them. I only knew something was there, something more than the sinful nature of all mankind, something that made me do wrong, made me act completely opposite even to common sense, let alone righteousness and Christian virtue. I didn't know I was in the merciless hands of a destroyer trying to join me to itself. My sense of truth told me the wrong came from outside, but I condemned myself as demoralized—sunken far below the right standard of character, unfit for my office.

> If we confess ours sins, He is faithful and just to forgive us our sins, and to cleanse us from all unrighteousness.
> —I John 1:9

> Blessed is he whose transgression is forgiven, whose sin is covered. Blessed is the man unto whom the Lord imputeth not iniquity, and in whose spirit there is no guile.
> —Psalm 32:1–2

In the long hours before Reveille, the Holy Spirit within bade me seek my heavenly Father's face for pardon. In bitter remorse before my Lord, I confessed neglect of Him, contempt for souls the Christ of God gave His life for, pride, lack of self-control and judgment, and showing no mercy. I mourned my sinfulness. It is sin, to know to do right and do it not: I was guilty. I was afraid because I also knew, knowing right and intending to do it, something outside me, and stronger than I am, barred me from it.

I laid the sin and fear and mystery before my Lord. I humbly and desperately begged forgiveness—and was flooded with a glory of it! It embraced me and was through and through me in an instant! God must have had it long in store, awaiting my repentance and petition. I marveled. I'd known in my mind I was forgiven when I sinned in the past, because God, who is faithful, promises forgiveness when sin is confessed. But now I felt forgiven in my heart. It was alive, as real as blood and breath. God had blotted out all my past sins as well as the latest ones. My spirit overflowed with relief and joy. Being human, I would sin. I realized how dependent I am upon God's mercy.

I prayed for the accompanying promise of being cleansed from all unrighteousness. For years, I'd longed for heavenly purification to make me whole again, but now I received with open, hungry heart its earthly prelude. I lay breathing as deep as if I'd run a race. If I didn't move my leg, it only ached.

I prayed for strength not to commit the same sins again, and for God's help to vanquish whatever made me commit them. Refreshed and chastened in spirit, I thanked and praised my Savior, whose infinite grace is greater than the power of sin. I lifted both hands in worship and quoted from the One Hundred and Third Psalm.

> Bless the Lord, O my soul, and forget not all his benefits: who forgiveth all thine iniquities; who healeth all thy diseases; who redeemeth thy life from destruction; who crowneth thee with loving-kindness and tender mercies.

Repentance was accomplished. My battle to live it and mend my soul had only begun. I had to repair my character one hard-fought decision at a time. I trusted my Lord to direct the quest.

Reading my Bible again, I found Him there, in His Word. I spent time in communion with my lifelong Light. For many days, I also slept till I could sleep no more, while my body restored itself from the wound, blood loss, and work I'd never admit was too hard for it.

Uncle James requested Dr. Barnes to send me for tactical recitations as soon as he thought it wise. I was relieved that I hadn't yet been reduced to the ranks. But the consequences of my homicidal action were still to be faced. The session I attended, on crutches, a few weeks later, was a short one.

"Sergeant Drummond, you will remain to receive instruction you have missed."

The others left.

"Sit down, Torquil Dhu. It's come to my ears you've been berserking. Out with it!"

I held nothing back. I blamed myself. I told of my repentance and tried to express the glory I'd experienced, but I couldn't find words magnificent enough. Uncle James was silent so long I feared I'd not merely be reduced to the ranks but drummed out of the service. At last, he froze me with that sad, stern look he has, the one I'd crawl over hot coals not to deserve.

"The purification you hunger for is a Christian's most treasured goal. But that ultimate blessing is reserved until the end of his physical life, so he can be presented faultless before the throne of God. Be grateful you've seen it clearly. It's a vision of what you're striving for.

"You will never attain full purity and guiltlessness on this earth. The enemy of our souls, Adam's original sin, and man's resulting sinful nature prevent it, for even the purest hearts. We must live out the years God allots us, fighting to overcome sin.

"It's not a sin for a soldier to meet deadly force with deadly force, at the behest of his country and for the protection of her citizens, including his fellow soldiers. But when killing, itself, becomes his primary objective, he has crossed the boundary into wickedness.

"Neither do you promote your soldiers' welfare by setting a reckless example! Your usefulness to the service requires discretion in addition to prowess in battle.

"I'm pleased that God convicted you of your sin. I'm pleased that you repented and are now resisting it."

His sad expression hadn't changed. I waited for what was sure to come.

"If, however, you are guilty of such sabotage again, I shall reduce you to the ranks."

I winced inside. I'd deposed Steptoe for destructive leadership. Uncle James should have reduced me. The undeserved mercy chastised my soul more effectively than punishment. It put me under powerful obligation to live my repentance.

"You once asked me why you weren't yourself any more. Berserking—going the way of the daemon—is a mortal enemy to you. If you don't vanquish it, it will subvert your soul, and you will despise yourself.

"I shall pray that you conquer, my lad. My heart's desire is that all be well with you, in body, soul, and spirit."

How could he still care? I'd disobeyed the principles he cherished and lived by—and received mercy and renewed trust. But I had to be sure.

"Sir, I once refused to recommend a man as a scout because I couldn't trust the lives of my squad to his skill. Can you trust their lives to me—now?"

"I shall trust them to you, but not to you alone. Do you not see how, long before you called upon him, our Lord's hand over you kept you and your men from destruction? Men may call it chance, but the combination of objects and events that brought you to your right mind in time was His provision—His gift."

I was humbled, awed afresh at my Lord's aggressive, out-reaching goodness. I'd been wrapped in it when I was least deserving, so my men's lives were saved. My heart was so full I couldn't speak.

MacLeod

I dismissed him with all my usual cautions. I hadn't known till now how close it had been. I bowed my head in thanksgiving and worship. I'd received the same enormous blessing of forgiveness after I killed my countrymen. It was like the story of the prodigal son in Saint Luke's gospel, whose father had also been waiting to receive and forgive and bless him. I was twice his age when I learned the spiritual truths my lad was experiencing now. Does God intend him for something other than a soldier?

* * *

When the catalogue arrived from the school I'd chosen, I read the superintendent's philosophy of education. It's exactly right for the behavior that must be instilled in Torquil.

> There is no part of the duty of the Superintendent which weighs so heavily on his mind and heart as that connected with the control and government of the moral conduct of those committed to his charge.

> We see but too often the early beauty of the character sadly marred ... its tenderness hardened. Innocence is grievously polluted. To the knowledge of good and evil are we born, and it must come upon us sooner or later.

> *The victory of fallen man is to be sought for, not in innocence but in tried virtue.* After this, there comes, as it were, a second beginning of life. ... Resting on faith and conscious principle, and not on mere passive innocence, stands sure for the middle and the end.

I am thoroughly persuaded that the system of government of a Military Institution, when combined with
careful, systematic Bible instruction, furnishes the
best possible instrumentality for the awakening and
development of religious character. ... The vices, the
irregularities, the follies, and the errors of the young
are brought to light ... in the forming period of their
lives, by the regulations to which they are subjected,
when opportunities and means may be availed of to
correct them ... to discipline such before it is too late.
—From *Register of Officers and Cadets of the Virginia
Military Institute*[18]

Torquil

I led my men down the Trail with all the care I'd led my Rangers
to war. God helping me, restraining me, I refused the daemon's
deadly allure before I was ensnared, and was strengthened to resist its next onslaught. I didn't turn skirmishes with the Indians
into killing for killing's sake, and found that we could stand our
ground and suffer fewer losses—a successful battle plan.

My own battle was desperate. I'd done the daemon's bidding
so long, I had to call to mind the stark revelation of my sin and
renew my determination to put it under, every day. Sometimes
every minute. And turn to God for strength to do it. I heard my
men.

"Old Flint ain't strikin' so many sparks no more."

"I guess he's losin' his dash."

I had to put hurt pride under, too. But I consoled myself it
was for their good as well as mine. I was their sergeant, not their
boon companion. I was responsible for them.

---

18 *Register of Officers and Cadets of the Virginia Military Institute,* Lexington,
Virginia: 1867, pp. 5 ff., italics original. VMI Archives.

MacLeod

When I sent for my lad late in April, he was still favoring his wounded leg.

"Your enlistment will be up on May twenty-ninth, but you won't re-enlist.

"Your trustees and I agree it's time you complete your education, according to your father's wishes. Since you hope to be commissioned, you need preparation for the office and the examination. We have therefore secured you an appointment to the Virginia Military Institute. You'll report by June twentieth."

Torquil

My world turned about-face! Virginia—home!—instead of the frontier! Another chance to become who I am, to regain my true character.

"It's still impossible to get you appointed to the Military Academy, but General Smith, the superintendent, was graduated from it and has modeled the school closely after it. You'll find similar discipline and instruction to prepare you for whatever God ordains for your life.

"College will improve you in the moral principles of society, and its manners. It will do you good to be with people of your own class again. You must regain your former polish to be respected among the men who will be your brother officers."

* * *

Tattoo is the longest and loveliest call in the trumpeters' repertoire. I stood beside my squad in our last roll call together, then passed down the line to shake their hands and bid farewell. Uncle James had said he was giving detailed instructions and would keep me tonight.

MacLeod

Sad to be parting with the son of my heart, it's my duty not to let him go without sound advice. Rather than assault him with it—surely he feels the parting, too—I set a pitcher of milk and a pie I'd bought from the post baker on the table and served generous wedges.

"What concerns do you have about your new venture?"

"If anyone sees my back, he'll think I'm a felon!"

"You need only say it was enemy vengeance."

"Would any man believe me?"

"He will accept your word, based upon your good character."

"I hope so. Honor's what I've always trusted in you. You're like my father."

My heart was touched. My joy was full. All at once.

"You are a son to me."

True sentiments expressed struck us both silent. I found the opening I wanted.

"You're about to embark on the most important four years of your life. The V.M.I. is similar to West Point. I learned some things that will help you succeed. In your academic duty, it's vital to do each day's work and learn each day's lesson *on that day*. If one doesn't, the result is confusion and failure."

He settled himself to listen.

"You're starting life all over. Your accomplishments, and the character you demonstrate, are all that matter. Everything you do is marked either for or against you. Your superiors will observe you more closely and know you better than you can imagine, inside and out. College is also a tribunal where the elders of your society will observe you and judge your ability to contribute.

"First year cadets—the fourth class—are called plebes. You'll appear as raw and awkward to the upperclassmen as the recruits you trained appeared to you. The first year is the hardest. You will be 'tried, as silver is tried,' and your mettle tested in every conceivable way.

"You'll be under discipline, surveillance, and scheduling that makes the Regulars look slack! You'll be forced to establish habits of obedience and self-control. In that the latter is an uphill fight for you, it will do you good.

"The fourth class is disciplined by the three upper classes, and they'll show you the severest face you'll ever see, day in and day out. Sparta and the Hessians were nothing to it, believe me!"

His mouth made a wry twist. "I feel oppressed already!"

"You'll feel it more. They do all they can to keep you from finding your feet, in order to make you receptive to discipline."

"I know who I am, and they shan't make me less!"

"Humble yourself to receive instruction, and you will become more!"

"Yes, Uncle Polonius, sir!"

"Polonius?"

"This reminds me of his speech of advice in *Hamlet*, before Laertes left for France."

"It's prompted by no lesser concern for a young cub's welfare!"

"I know. I'm sorry I was rude, sir."

I nodded, accepting the apology. "Are you ready for the peroration?

"The burden of the discipline you will bear is hard, and it's also effective, because it addresses your whole being by regulating it all, all at once.

"There's one more thing. You'll have jokes played on you—the fate of newcomers to most things. One night when I was a yearling, we stole the plebes' clothing while they were asleep and piled it in the Area. They had to report to Reveille in nothing but their shirts!

"Then there was Heth and Burnside's court—"

"*Gerneral* Heth? *General* Burnside?"

"The same. They accused a green new fellow of monstrous crimes and convinced him he was guilty. They sentenced him to be shot at sunrise, then 'relented' and ordered him to stand all night with his head in a mortar. He did it, too."

"I'll look out. But I'm resolved to learn all I can. I'll get through the rest all right."

"I'll look forward to hearing you have!" I couldn't help the wicked grin.

My son spoke somberly.

"Rather than before the garrison tomorrow, I'll make my farewells now. Words can't say how grateful I am to you, nor express how deeply I honor you. You preserved my life. As long as I live, I'm dedicated to serve you, sir." He held out his hand.

I grasped it. Then I let my affection show. I embraced him.

Torquil

As the vanguard of the escort passed headquarters, Uncle James came out and shook my hand.

"Goodbye, sir."

"Only *au revoir*, in heaven or earth. Godspeed … my son."

I gave my best half-smile and trotted Severa to my place in the column. During every scout, I look back often, to observe everything. Today I looked back oftener, till I couldn't see him. Then, full of hope and determination, I looked forward.

Going home.

MacLeod

I climbed to the firing platform and inspected one of the guns in perfectionistic detail while I watched the train and its escort—and my son—out of sight.

That night I wrote:

My lad left this morning for Abercairn, hoping to have some time to visit before he must report to the V.M.I. It will do him good to rejoin the society he was born to, since he's become a "Regular" and rough in his ways. These mask a heart vulnerable and naive. Evil wounds and bewilders him. He cannot penetrate its face to grapple with its heart. Despite his war experiences, he is too young for any world he lives in, save one, and that is perished. I hope to protect him four years more.

Abercairn C.H., Va.

May 30, 1868

Dear One,

I had the pleasure and pain of receiving your letter in the fewest number of days it has ever taken one to reach me. Though I am well—I may say <u>blooming</u>, as only a well-loved woman can—my heart throbs with yours at the parting you have suffered. You are right, he is too young for any world but the one he lost. He is an orphan at heart, still stunned by being left solitary, seldom able to move past where his soul lived before the blow. You have seen that in times of crisis, he and his reasoned initiative come into their own. A just cause in which to fight is his natural dwelling place. We can only be patient and encourage him as he learns the ways of peace.

BOOK III
THE VIRGINIA MILITARY INSTITUTE

CHAPTER 20

HOME IS THE SOLDIER, HOME FROM THE WARS

When the righteous are in authority, the people rejoice: but when the wicked beareth rule, the people mourn.
—Proverbs 29:2

Torquil

The Baltimore and Ohio Railroad brought me across the Potomac into Virginia. Just outside Washington City, I made connection with the Orange, Alexandria and Manassas Gap to carry me to Culpeper through country I'd fought to defend. My devastated State was rebuilding, but sadly slow. I'd been reading Mr. Ogilvie's reports at last, longing to know Glenlochie again. I didn't know I yearned for a home that no longer existed nor ever would, imagining instead that I'd feel the old familiar house enfolding me again.

Would my friends know me? I thought of them as when we were boys and soldiers together, but three years, and the command distance I had to keep in the Shield, might have broken the bonds forever.

In the army, I was a nomad, belonging nowhere, but now I'm a gentleman traveling, not a soldier on the march: I tried to tidy myself before the cars reached Culpeper. Stuttering on sanded tracks, the great drive wheels slowed and finally stopped. Grieg advanced from the cluster of people around the depot.

"Och, Lieutenant, 'tis weel to see ye!"

"I'm glad to see you, too. I trust you're well."

"Aye. Come, we'll find your baggage."

"Where's the carriage?"

"Worn oot by use as an ambulance. Mind ye no' the braw soldiers we carried during the war? The family has no ladies noo, so it has no' been replaced."

I said little and learned the news of the farm during the long drive till Grieg drew rein in the stable yard.

"Mrs. Grieg weel have supper ready."

"I'll see the horses afterward."

I slung my saddle pockets over my left shoulder and swung down the wagon wheel. As I strode toward the gate, a hasty rustle in the haystack startled me. By instinct I stepped silently to it and grasped a small foot which I spotted only while I pounced. I hauled a plump wee child out of the hay by the hem of its frock and held it up to view.

Unafraid, it regarded me with round blue eyes.

"Aw you Wieutent Dwummond?"

My half-smile quickened all by itself. "I am. Who might you be?"

"Wobbet Ewen Kendwick!"

"Would you like a ride to the house?"

"Yes, siw."

I swung "Wobbet" up to sit on my shoulder. The stepping-stone path seemed too short. The kitchen garden gave off the rich odor of moist earth and tender new shoots. As I reached the porch, out came Mrs. Grieg and Robbie's wife, who plucked her son from his perch, brushing hay from his hair and clothing. Mrs. Grieg embraced me and motioned me inside.

"Your chamber is ready, or here's refreshment."

Hot bread, butter and strawberry preserves, a pitcher of milk. Supper keeping warm on the big black stove. The familiar kitchen looked strange. Robbie's wife looked lovelier than she had as a bride.

"It's a pleasure to see you looking so well."

"We're all pleased you've arrived safely. I trust you had a good journey."

"A swift one, nearly all on the cars." I felt alien among feminine company and took refuge in facts. "The Union Pacific has passed Cheyenne now. I suppose your good man will soon be home."

"I'm surprised Grandfather kept him this long. He's reading law in his chambers."

"Maybe he's looking ahead to public office."

"You'll have to ask him. Until we get a constitution approved, a citizen can't hold office."

"Except by Yankee appointment!"

Robbie stumped into the kitchen, using a cane. I shook his hand heartily, feeling like reinforcements had arrived. He was thinner than I'd ever seen him, and his face looked strained. I questioned with brows and a twist of the mouth, but he warned me off with a tiny headshake.

* * *

After dinner, promising the Kendricks a visit later, through the kitchen to compliment Mrs. Grieg's dinner, I went to meet Grieg in the stable.

"This must be the colt you wrote me about."

I let myself into the loose box where a sturdy black colt eyed me curiously. Fondling the face of Flora, his dam, I murmured to her and let him sniff and nuzzle me.

"Aye. Nightfire gangs weel aboot his siring yet, but this laddie may gang e'en better."

"Sooooo, then, laddie." I smoothed a hand over the colt's body, and drew breath long and softly before I stroked the little head and scratched between the ears. The colt leaned into my touch.

"The very spit o' his first sire, think ye no'?"

"Neicht Dhu?"

"Aye."

"Neicht Dhu was legend before I was born. You could say better than I."

"I say it, then. See here … and here."

Running gentle fingers along the lines of leg and breast, he pointed out the infant beginning of bones created to carry a titan's load of muscle. "He'll ne'er want for wind, nor limb 'neath load."

The colt seemed to know he was being shown off and posed like a champion. He cavorted around Flora and tossed his head at us as if in challenge. I wanted to smile, but half a smile is all I have.

"Ye ken we're training and selling some few for draught, the noo."

"Mr. Ogilvie wrote me."

"The war took toll o' beasts as well as men. Not a neighbor but has need o' a guid team, and not all have them."

Followed by soft nickers, we ambled down the passage and came out to Nightfire's pen. I stepped up the fence and offered him my hand. He sniffed it before he nudged my chest. I sat on his back, stroking his powerful neck. I clucked; he walked round the pen and broke eagerly into trot and canter when bidden.

"He's all I remember, and more."

"Aye, in his prime, noo."

Greig never allows a horse off the property looking less than its best. I went for a halter while he brought Nightfire to a polish. The blue lights of his black coat reflected the evening light.

Walking him into the familiar lane to Murrays', through the home farm, I observed how the outbuildings had been repaired. I nudged him into an easy trot, remembering how Ewen, Douglas, and I had gone this way and made each other's homes our own. My soul turned harsh, trying to throw off the pangs of memory. I slackened the reins. Nightfire leaped out fast to challenge me. I'd brought Severa to her best, but no other horse could match this one. Like running before the wind, we raced up to Murrays'.

> We are not just now in a condition to sacrifice much to fancy or ornament. We must address ourselves to the useful and substantial. Every mother, wife, and daughter must now … excel in neatness, industry, usefulness and economy. A crisis is upon us which demands the development of the will and energy of the Southern character. As woman has … performed so gracefully the duties of the mistress of the establishment, so she will, with a lovelier grace, perform whatever labor duty demands.
> —E. W. Warren, "Introduction," *Mrs. Hill's Southern Cook Book*

Captain Murray

I stepped oot frae the barn and shaded my eyes. Nightfire, by gait and conformation, but wha's the lad astride? In a minute, a stamping halt, the lad's boots barely touching the ground, I clasped him in a bear hug. He clung to the welcome.

"It doth my heart guid to behaud ye, lad!"

Torquil

My heart was so full I nearly choked.

Arm over my shoulders, kilt swinging with every long stride, he steered me toward the house. He pointed out new-planted apple trees and twin calves thriving in spite of small birth weight.

William ran to meet us. He stopped short and held out his hand. I shook it with corresponding dignity. A boy of eleven should be encouraged in good manners. Eleven! I remembered William as only recently breeched! Time in Abercairn had stood still only in my memory.

"Did Papa show you my calves?"

"In passing. Will you tell me their points later?"

Budding husbandmen also deserve encouragement.

Mrs. Murray and Miss Mary greeted me in the porch. Miss Mary, a demure little girl wearing short skirts and long hair, had the same sweet grace of movement as her mother. I bowed over the hand she extended.

"Forgive me if I don't stand on ceremony, Torquil Dhu!" Mrs. Murray embraced me like I was her own. "Let's go in. We've a fire on the hearth. The nights are chill for this time of year."

Treated like a son and brother, I felt less constrained with the Murrays than in my own house, but steered the conversation away from myself with brief responses. Though they'd escaped plundering by Yankees, and by marauders loyal to none but themselves, they'd lost not only their firstborn son, but much of their substance. Captain Murray was optimistic about recovering prosperity, but some of their land still lay fallow and overgrown. They'd been blessed to hire one of the Griegs' grown sons. Mr. Kendrick, driven by the Yankees from his office as county surveyor, which included supervision of roadbuilding crews, now worked as foreman of farm labor. It was still impossible to do all that needed doing, nor yet reclaim the fallow land.

William had his father's heart for the land but not his father's brawn to work it. By grazing as many animals as the overgrown acreage would sustain, he contributed to the family income, while Captain Murray cultivated small grains for the profitable market. Mrs. Murray and Miss Mary raised chickens and did the dairying. They sold milk, butter, and eggs, cheeses, and live and dressed fowls at market on Court days.

* * *

Though called by God to the army, I felt guilty to leave the work of Glenlochie in other than family hands, I mused as I rode away. It startled me again to realize that I, alone, was left. I hadn't stayed long enough in my chamber to miss Douglas, but, moving through passages and rooms, I'd half expected to greet him and Da.

It's better the house is lived in, but I felt like a guest instead of son and heir. I atone for amputating Robbie's leg, and the Kendricks have no other home of their own; but instinct said only Drummonds really belong here. I fought it down. What I call home is only lodging! I'll be away again before a fortnight passes. Four long years of education before I can claim my own, and then, duty will keep me distant. My heart hungered for my homeplace. I feared it could never be satisfied.

No sound, but I knew it and was already dismounting when Keir appeared through the gloaming. We shook hands and paced silent along the lane. His taciturn presence quietened my soul as all conversation had not. Angling off into the woods in the perfection of our silent step, all was still. Traversing a slope, he led deep among the trees to the secret glen where the does bear their young. Birthing was accomplished, but we sat back on our heels while the doe nudged her fawn to stand on its sinewy legs and suckle. Time dissolved. I was surprised to see Orion barely arrived at the southwest when we reached the lane again.

"The morrow?"

"Twa morrows, ere t' dawnin.'"

"Aye weel."

Greig's lantern was garish in the luminous darkness. I took it and let him go back to his wife in their snug home above the carriage house. I rubbed down Nightfire, postponing the visit with Robbie, fearing bad news about his health.

In the library, he was composing a brief amid law books, notes, and documents scattered over the desk, and he rose as I entered. It was deference, when we're equals; it was the host's welcome, when the house is mine. Both disturbed me. I fought it down.

"Time to rest from your labors?"

"Not till the wee hours, if I'm to pass the bar next Court day."

"It's law rather than Shakespeare, then."

I motioned him to the comfortable sofa and turned the wing chair to face him.

"It's what I can do. No college or academy would have a professor as little educated as I am, and the University is beyond my means. This way, I can earn a few coppers, clerking, while I learn a profession. Emily's grandfather thinks he can send some clients my way."

"When you win their suits, you'll attract more. You have a gift for speaking."

"More than for legal language, but too much depends on cunning.

"The law should manifest the virtue of the country, to protect, and rectify, and help society. It should embody our moral sense! But too much of it doesn't, it's like a game where business interests compete for advantage. It's been right in Abercairn till the Yankees replaced our own civil officials. Now I can't act as guardian of what's right for us."

"You're too honest not to!"

"And too impatient to be bored with conveyances. But I have a family depending on me." He smiled at the thought of them.

"You're blessed with a fine, brave son. When I pulled him out of the hay stack, he didn't cry. He asked if I were Lieutenant Drummond, calm as could be."

"He's a little scapegrace sometimes, but we think he'll do. MacHugh writes that you're going to join him at the V.M.I."

"I have to report by the twentieth. I'll go sooner, to reconnoiter. Da's will requires me to complete my education before I inherit, and Uncle James says it's next best to West Point to prepare for the officers' examination."

"It's good your education's provided for."

"I sent some from my pay, too. The Army pays hard money if not much else."

"You sound like you don't like it."

His astuteness, speaking the thought I try to bury, set me aback. It makes him a good attorney, but I was nettled that he took the initiative I'd meant to. My reflections gave me time to build an answer.

"I'm surfeited with drill and Indians, but it's God's calling on my life. I have to obey."

"That's why you enlisted, wasn't it. Will you again, if you don't pass the examination?"

"I might have to, because of the Ironclad Oath."

"It must've been hard lines, with all the Yankees. What are they like?"

"Not like us. The Regulars are the hardest cases I've ever known. What were they like here?"

> When a man's ways please the Lord, he maketh even
> his enemies to be at peace with him.
> —Proverbs 16:7

"The first batch were scum. The second batch knew us from Granite Bend—and elsewhere! They were right formal, till they needed help cleaning out the marauders. Their strength was too few, and they didn't know the country. They called a meeting at the Court House and asked us if we'd ride. We did, and Abercairn's been tolerably quiet ever since.

"They didn't pester us much, compared to some places, but that was only the beginning. Now we're under the heel of the Radicals, and they're grinding it in our faces! Civil government's by Yankee appointees. They had to scour to find men who could claim—or lied to claim!—they never supported the Confederacy. Some at the Court House now don't know *habeas corpus* from a quitclaim deed!"

"I was surprised they didn't confiscate Glenlochie out of sheer spite."

"They made themselves a nuisance for a while."

"You said they knew us from Granite Bend! Reckon it was you they remembered!"

"Oh, pshaw!"

"Justice must be balked entirely."

"Not quite. The Judge and Sheriff MacKeith receive a lot of 'social' callers, and any signature of Mr. Menteith's is honored whether it's stamped and sealed or not. MacHugh's father keeps a record, but it's taken page by page to a safe place. Honorable men's words are still their bonds. It's round-about now, and done without the blue Hessians knowing. We had a close call when the scalawags took it in their heads to search MacHughs' house, but Nannie kept them occupied till Mr. MacHugh could put the evidence in a birdhouse."

"What about the Freedmen's Bureau? They've been raising a dust in a lot of places."

"The agent hasn't found anything to complain about. When he talked dissatisfaction to Dick Murchison, Dick sent him off with a flea in his ear! Said he didn't want his trade disrupted by the likes of him hanging around to drive off custom! But MacHugh says the agents in Lexington are tyrants, even to little children."

"I'll find out when I get there, I reckon." I took over the initiative. "You look like it's going hard with you these days. How's the leg?"

"Better than I ever hoped. Virginia's providing replacements for us, and they did a good job of mine. The other's only till I pass the bar. After that, I won't work so long at night."

"Judge Carmichael must be driving you fast."

"No. I'm doing it. I want to get established as soon as I can."

"I hope you'll live here. I don't expect to be home often, and it's not far to the Court House."

"We already owe you too much."

"I don't see it so. I owe possession of Glenlochie to you! You're doing me a kindness."

Emily Kendrick

I paused in the hall, uncertain whether to interrupt. I felt like my future was being decided. Then, as Judge Carmichael's granddaughter, I chose to have my say.

Torquil

"I've been trying to convince your husband to continue his favor to me."

I hoped that acting the supplicant would ease my old friend's pride. "Perhaps a word from you would soften his heart."

Robbie laughed. "Trying to come under my guard!"

"Robert's judgment has always proven wise." Emily sat next to him and tucked her hand into his. "What's the question?"

"Whether we should stay on here."

"I contend that your keeping my house from ruin constitutes a favor. Wouldn't you agree?"

"If I thought it were true. We've imposed upon your generosity a long time."

It was becoming a debate. I hoped to win the point that would overcome my instincts and establish wise reality. I feigned surprise and disbelief.

"I hope you've found nothing wanting for your comfort!"

"Quite the contrary!"

"You don't find the Griegs too overbearing … or too slack? Does Mr. Ogilvie interfere?" None of those would be true.

"Oh, no!"

"Then how have we failed you, that you wish to leave?"

Emily looked to Robbie.

"I am the one to provide my family a home." Firmness but no unkindness.

"You will. But duty prevents me from being here myself. It disburdens my mind, when I'm gone, to have friends here. I can't think of anyone who reassures me better than you." I looked square at him. "Could I impose this one more task upon you?"

Pretending the matter was settled, I changed the subject.

"I know you all never surrendered, but where's our flag?"

He accepted the truce.

"We gave it to Murrays, in Ewen's honor. They bring it out on Decoration Day, when we honor all our dead, at the kirkyard."

"We don't forget them," said Emily.

"No more do I. What became of the wolves we caught?"

"The officer over this district upheld the sentences Grandfather imposed. Little Andrew recovered, and I think our not having hanged anyone helped them see the justice of the rest. They went over all the evidence and consulted their regulations and orders before they agreed, though."

Robbie cast a brief glance toward the desk. I'd kept him from his work long enough and talked far beyond my usual capacity.

"I hope you all will excuse me. I'll take a stroll before I go upstairs."

* * *

I spread my bear skin next to the panther skin on the library floor. Roving Glenlochie's woods with Keir showed how well the ghillie had performed his trust. Dead trees harvested for firewood, and repair of buildings and implements, left room and light for younger trees to flourish. Game animals abounded, and the little brook was home to fish and muskrats. Birds sang in the branches. The war had proven Keir's wisdom in advising against broad ways through his domain, but old narrow, winding paths were preserved. My soul was refreshed.

Mr. Ogilvie's office is a room of his cottage, across the side garden from the house. I sat where I could observe all approaches while he told me the present business of the farm. I'd learned to prize his fiscal agility in the demands and chaos of war and defeat. He recognized the realities and jettisoned old practices which no longer served, to adapt to present necessities. Since Glenlochie produced both animals and crops, the farm met market demands and took advantage of high prices for one or the other. Plenty of pasture allowed retaining animals, and sufficient storage protected grain, until the market changed. The mill on Willow Run was rebuilt and operating, and the merchant ship sailed. Glenlochie continued its banking service. Though some grasping Yankees had visited after the war, they'd found no weaknesses to exploit in Abercairn's economy, nor in the characters of most of her citizens.

Riding Nightfire, with Mr. Ogilvie on his sedate old dun, over the eight thousand acres, I renewed my connection with the land. My homeplace drew my heart to it again. Mr. Ogilvie pointed out the progress of ongoing plans and resources for future prospects. I met the tenants of the four farms we rented out. Mr. Ogilvie agreed to build a new room on Iain Grieg's house, to shelter his increasing family, and promised another man to pasture sheep on fields that needed manuring.

He promised to serve till he was no longer capable, and to train his successor. One of his grandsons had a bent toward organization and an increasing knowledge of farming. He spent summers with the Ogilvies and hired out to help with the farm work.

My trustees said that though funds were sufficient, I had to wait till my furlough to purchase a rifle. I accepted their decision with the best grace I could, but I'd be a petitioner four years, and I didn't like it.

Mrs. Grieg corralled me next. I'd sent her my measurements and the V.M.I. list, and she had all my new fittings ready, socks to hairbrush. One pair of the Monroe shoes fit me. She'd also had a fine gray linen frock coat, vest, and trousers tailored.

"I'll wear these tomorrow to kirk."

"Ye'll find the sarks and collars in yon kist."

She'd embroidered the Drummond clan crest and our sept's motto, *Fidelis*, on the quilted comfort. Her motherly care touched my heart. I didn't know what to say, but I had to try.

"They'll know me asleep or awake! Thank you for such a lot of work."

"'Tis little enough we can do for ye, noo. Ye maun make us proud wi' your learning."

* * *

Faces once filled with joy and proud resolve and valour, which made them hope for the impossible;

now pinched with suffering ... prematurely aged ...
from staring death and ruin in the face.
—John S. Wise, *The Lion's Skin*

Before kirk, I joined the men awaiting the service. Nearly
every man in Abercairn who could carry a gun had done so.
Though among them were borne some empty sleeves and trousers legs, and David Carmichael and Andre DeVique would be
among the worshippers no more, and Mr. Stafford walked with
a limp, and my friends' fathers looked careworn, yet their spirits
were good. I responded to welcomes with the warmest courtesy I
could summon and said little of myself in order to learn of their
welfare. God had brought them through catastrophe alive, and
they were confident He'd enable them to rebuild their lives and
provide for their families. Abercairn worked together to lift one
another out of trouble.

They speculated whether Virginia's proposed constitution
would be accepted by the Yankee government. Delegates to the
convention hadn't truly represented the citizens, since former
Confederate Army and civil officers were barred. Would the
new constitution gain our readmission to the Union, since the
Radical Republicans, who hated the South and viciously sought
to hurt her, held so much unjustified power in Congress?

After kirk, Nannie took my arm and drew me into the group
of young people, but I was still attuned to deadly battles fought
only two weeks ago. They were talking the trivialities of peace.
I'd been gone more than three years, too long to watch the girls
grow up, so I recognized some only by family resemblance. A soldier's prowess gave me a place among men, and the laundresses'
daughters at Fort Banks had considered me a "good catch," but,
at age twenty, with real ladies at last, I was so aware of my weath-
er-beaten face and frontier manners that they were formidable!

All my battle senses roused—and that seemed to interest them! But it put the young men on their guard. I had no fund of polite conversation, nor did I want to tell of what would be alien and barbaric to them all. I listened but scarcely spoke, except to regret that I'd be away again before I could enter a horse race next Saturday.

We Drummonds hallow the Sabbath by giving all in our employ that day off, to rest. I could raid the cuddy when I chose. I postponed invitations to dinner, pleading a previous promise, and postponed keeping that, too. I rode at a walk, though Nightfire wanted to run. I tethered him to the iron fence of the family cemetery, to confront the evidence that I'd never see my best-beloved again on earth.

Among the moss-grown, weather-worn tombstones of my forebears, my family lay in a row, the infant Robert Bruce by our mother, Da beside her, then Douglas. I took off my hat and knelt where I'd sworn my oath five years ago. The last sight of their faces filled my mind. I bowed my head, closed my eyes. Mind and spirit choked up.

'Dear God … I don't know what to pray … I long for them only less than I long for You … could You … of your mercy … tell them for me … I love them and miss them with all my heart!'

Did they know I thought of them? Did they know I was hardened and rough, no longer the tender-hearted boy of our last night together, when we sang to God? But before the next nightfall, my soul was overpowered, crippled from that day to this. I'd repented, tried again to live honorably, suffered my punishment, learned from it. I'd done my duty.

But it was a façade propped up to hide a void. Or like going through the motions of a play, myself disappearing into nothingness when the lights were doused, only, when they were relit, to reappear and have to go through the motions again. And again, until the tender hand of death released me. Da and Douglas were the blessed ones. I wept for loss of them, and for loss of who I was before they died.

Angered by the breach in my armor, I dashed tears away and left the cemetery, my face again my mask. Naught on earth could bring them back, nor restore me to my old life and peace.

Nightfire took no single step where two or three were possible, dancing to release his strength in speed. At the high road, I slackened the reins. He burst from walk to his fastest run, a pace he could sustain for four miles. We both exulted fiercely in his power and speed. If we broke our necks, I didn't care! If we flew till we exploded into oblivion and the starry sky of night, it would be a fitting end.

* * *

I brought cheese and milk from the spring-house, got bread in the kitchen, prayed thanks, and filled my hollow stomach. I wandered alone in the empty house. Da's possessions stood in all their old places. Though spotless, his room had the barren cold of disuse. It felt like everyone was dead but me, and the house an echoing desolation.

I scowled and shook off the morbid fancy. Truly, I was grateful my inheritance was so well cared for, and for everyone's loyalty and kindness to me. Robbie was going to stay till I finished school. I thought I should give more of myself to all who gave so much to me, but I don't know how. I might once have known. I had an affectionate heart then. All that was gone now. I resolved to go through the motions the best I could.

* * *

A few nights later, I lay awake, severing ties to my homeplace. I was only a visitor here, and that wouldn't change till the army was through with me. The V.M.I. regulations forbid cadets to keep a horse, dog, or waiter, so I was going to have one last ride on Nightfire—not in the wagon with Grieg and my trunk—all the way to meet the stagecoach at New Market.

"He who lives by the sword shall die by the sword," I misquoted in cynical resignation. I'd taken up the sword in agony and fury at losing the family who were more important than the whole world, and the sword would never let me go.

I swallowed my pain and tried to think into my future. Though I'd taken a man's part for seven years, society considered me a boy till I finished my education, was pursuing my calling, and was married, with a home and family of my own.

Doing well at the V.M.I. was the means to that end. The first families and other gentry send their sons there. We'd know each other. The school's stamp would confirm my standing, its polish give me advantage, in any society. I'd concentrate on the goal—graduation, with all my course material mastered—rather than pleasure along the way. A gamble, as far as the army was concerned: the Yankees might all go to the grave enforcing the Ironclad Oath! But I'd receive my inheritance if I stayed the course. The austerity suited me.

Mrs. Grieg

I bided till he waved his hat and was awa' round the bend. Then to the pantry, shut the door. I grieted like a lorn lass, for parting wi' my littlest lad.

CHAPTER 21

JOURNAL OF
THE RAT YEAR

MacLeod

I leafed through my mail and found two pieces postmarked Lexington, Virginia.

June 19, 1868

Dear Uncle James,

I hope this letter finds you well, as it leaves me. Please excuse my haste. It's only a few minutes till Tattoo. Beau arrived safe today but has become the object of an insulting rumor, viz., that he was whipped for committing a felony. He won't tell his friends what happened. If you can shed light on this matter, so I can publish the truth and thus remove the slander against him, I should be very grateful.

Respectfully, Your Obedient Servant,
Aidan MacHugh

I'd walked into the drama in the midst of the second act! I opened Torquil's letter.

June 24, 1868

Dear Uncle James,

Did you know you were sending me to a <u>boys</u>' school!

I'm now enrolled, initiated, and among old friends. I'm going to clean out some enemies, and have some fun out of the halfwit old cadets who think they're going to best me!

I arrived at 3 AM the 19th inst. and walked up to the post …

Torquil

I disembarked at the National Hotel too late for sleep. A cynical whim decided me to walk up to the Institute and surprise Aidan Beag, Airlie, and Loudoun when they woke. I'd scout before I submitted myself to the authorities who'd rule my life there. With turrets on corners and south façade, Barracks was silhouetted against starlight. Vision adjusting, I followed the pike back toward North River and stopped at the bridge leading over a creek to the canal basin. Barracks lay southwest, atop a bluff. Gliding through the underbrush along the right bank of the creek till I was beyond it, climbing the bluff through trees and underbrush, my energy seemed unbounded, and I wasn't winded when I gained the top. But I was taut inside, and my heart beat so fast, its pulse almost choked me.

I drew a deep breath and let it out long and slow, gaining control before I walked silently to the woodshore. To my right, a line of elegant houses fronted the parade ground. Barracks dominated a line of brick cabins and another small building to the east. Beyond, something massive was being built.

In my heart, I renewed my determination to do well. I've always been hungry to learn. I'd reconnoitre and enter quietly, keeping my dignity, do as a plebe should, and meet my own criteria of discipline and studiousness. I didn't know I was bringing the hurricane within to meet the one that waited to remake me. I took a deep breath and stepped out.

Behind Barracks, I was awed: I'd never been on foot so close under such a huge structure. A short, small sentinel in front of the east wing came to the end of his beat, turned about-face, marched back. I let him get well away before I entered the U-shaped fortress, making for the stairs opposite.

> When we arrived at Lexington, as a matter of course we became legitimate prey for the old cadets; many of whom imagining that a residence of twelve months at the Virginia Military Institute supplied all deficiencies of mother wit, would, upon the … arrival of a new cadet, immediately proceed to … amuse themselves with his greenness.
> —*Boy Soldiers of the Confederacy*, p. 294

Swift, stealthy footfalls. Before I could pivot, the stars disappeared into heavy folds of stinking wool thrown over my head. Hands grabbed my arms while others bound them to my body, tied my wrists behind me, and strapped my ankles together, all with stout leather straps.

"What in blazes—"

"Shut up!"

"Not only the traitor but a mink, too! Won't Stone be surprised!"

"He'll revel!" The voice choked off a laugh.

"You let a mink onto the post!" somebody roared low.

"I never saw him!" squeaked a boy's voice.

Sounds of a scuffle, squawks, squeaks, gasps: "Corp—!"

"Gag 'em both, before we have the subs out!" Laughter bubbled in the voice.

I tried to bite when they forced my mouth open, but my teeth clamped on a stick they tied tight between my jaws. Dumb, blind, nearly breathless, I kicked when they hauled me like a bag of meal to I-knew-not-where, and dropped me on my tailbone. A frisson like pain combined with electricity shot up my backbone till I sat up and flexed my arms and legs.

I was so mad I could chew nails! Real authorities would've turned me over to the guard, so my captors were having fun at my expense. They wouldn't have much! I began working the strap around my wrists free of the buckle.

Too soon, hasty footsteps. I was picked up, carried—not far—dropped. They removed gag, blanket, and straps, but left my wrists bound. The little sentry struggled in the grip of two larger cadets dragging him out of the room.

"Let him go! He couldn't have seen or heard me!" I commanded. Shoulder forward, I lunged, but the guards held me back.

The sentry sank to his knees, imploring the "court."

"Oh, please, sirs, please don't shoot me! I'm not prepared to die in all my sins! Give me time to repent! My mother will grieve! Let me see her one more time!"

"He may have ten minutes to write to her and prepare his soul!" the "judge" decreed.

The warders dragged him out.

A mock trial: four cadets at a table, trying to look stern. Too young to be convincing. A single candle to shadow their features, blankets over door and window to keep the light inside.

"Bring the prisoner before the bar." The lean, white-haired "judge" used a sepulchral voice.

The guards pushed me forward. I studied the "court" while they studied me. I worked on the buckled strap, pretending to flex my hands. How to escape while bound, stared at, and outnumbered!

"Does the prisoner swear to tell the truth? How do you plead?"

"I don't plead! Release me from this farce at once!"

"Prisoner, state your full name."

"Torquil David Drummond." I bought time to work on the strap.

"Where were you born?"

"Abercairn."

"What is your father's occupation?"

"Deceased."

"Decedence is not an occupation! What was he?"

"A planter."

"Do you have a guardian?"

That would lead to matters better not reveaed! I counter-attacked.

"This nonsense wouldn't fool a suckling bairn!"

"Guards, see what the prisoner carries."

What gall! Personal questions! Searching my pockets! They handed him my letter of appointment. He recognized it in triumph.

"The prisoner is *ordered* to answer the question. Have you a guardian?"

I realized too late, I'd be required to obey their orders, but I aimed to elude whatever deviltry they planned. I worked on the strap, kept the coil concealed.

"My uncle."

"Who is he?"

"James MacLeod."

"What is his occupation?"

"Army officer."

"What army?"

"United States."

"Rank and regiment?"

"Captain, 16th Cavalry."

Strap through half the buckle ... make them pry out every bit of information! Signs of nervous impatience ... must be almost

Reveille … they'd have to answer it. Spurious formality unraveled into fast-fire questions.

"Were you a soldier?"

"Yes."

"What regiment?"

"First Virginia Cavalry."

"Was that all?"

"No."

"What else?"

"Sixteenth U.S. Cavalry."

"What rank?"

"Sergeant."

"Who was your father?"

Prong freed from eyelet … guards would try to club me when I overset them to get out....

"Robert Bruce Drummond."

"Who is your mother?"

"Deceased."

"Who was your mother?"

"Mary Elizabeth MacKintyre."

I tore the strap loose and charged the guards. They wrestled me off and held me.

"I demand to present myself to proper authority!"

"No turncoat may address gentlemen! Execute the sentence!"

Turncoat!

They looked at me with contempt. It was no longer a farce. Black cold climbed up the back of my neck into my brain. My chasm exploded wide open. One of the guards picked up a stoneware crock. They all came at me at once. I couldn't fight free. They wrestled me down, stripped off my clothing.

"What in hades!"

"A felon!"

Heart felt like it stopped, but I answered dead level, "It was done by the enemy."

"What enemy? The penal system?"

"No."

Drums and fife somewhere close by.

"Hurry! We'll find out later."

"They'll throw him anyway!"

They poured molasses all over me, bundled me into a big sack of straw, and shook it. They carried all to the front of Barracks, dropped me, and ran. I scrabbled out just in time to hear my name called.

"Drummond!"

I had the habit of duty. Cold with rage and humiliation, I stalked to the end of the line of new cadets and stood at attention.

"Here!"

Cadet Sergeant Thibault was so startled he couldn't call the next name on the roll for a long second. Plebes turned in the ranks to stare.

"*Eyes forward!* Ettinger!"

"Here!"

I retreated deep within myself and made dignity deny that barefoot, bareheaded, and near naked, dripping with molasses and bristling with straw from hair to toes was anything amiss. Expression wooden, eyes front, I didn't know I'd passed my first test.

After roll call, cadets slowed to stare. Laughter, then hisses behind me: they saw the felon's brand.

Cadet Sergeant Thibault

The name had appeared on my roll. Beyond that, I knew nothing—except my duty.

"Mister Drummond! Have you registered yet?"

"No, sir."

"Where is your clothing!"

He gestured toward Barracks. "Somewhere in there."

"Go to the Nile and wash yourself!" I gave directions to Woods Creek and stalked off to reprimand "Rats' Funeral Arrangements"—again.

Torquil

It was the creek I'd followed earlier. Emotion had vanished and left me cold and empty. I'd waded in when another plebe arrived.

"Here's your clothes and some soap."

"Drop them and lob it," I growled.

He shrugged and climbed back up the bluff. I sat in the cold water, ducked my head, and scrubbed. I didn't want to inflict myself on my friends. It might make them outcasts, too.

> Let another man praise thee, and not thine own mouth.
> —Proverbs 27:2

How to clear my name? I'd spoken the truth and wouldn't stoop to prove the facts that would vindicate my honor. It can't be done that way. It didn't matter that my great-great-grandfather founded Abercairn, it didn't matter that I'd helped save it from devastation, it didn't matter that my military record was honorable. I had to make a new start—from lower than zero! I had to earn honor, just like Da said, and I would! Rumors be cursed!

* * *

His house, the post headquarters, looked like a miniature castle, and General Francis Henney Smith, the superintendent, a lean man with gray hair and beard, who wore gold-rimmed spectacles, looked as distinguished as Judge Carmichael, though he sat with one leg crossed over the other. His keen blue eyes seemed to study my very soul. I respected him instantly and hoped never to displease him, but I feared he'd soon believe my name disgraced. A small but civil conversation revealed that he knew both my father and me. He asked a few incisive questions before assigning me to the fourth class.

His clerk, in an adjacent office, administered the matriculation promise.

> I hereby engage to serve as a Cadet in the Virginia Military Institute for the term for which I have entered, and I promise on honor, while I continue a member thereof, to obey all legal orders of the constituted authorities of the Institute, and to discharge all my duties as Cadet with regularity and fidelity.

I signed the matriculation book and was sent to the treasurer. Captain Campbell required me to deposit all funds in my possession and said I had permission to draw pocket money—next month! Stranded without money in a hostile place!

Colonel Ship, Commandant of Cadets, had pale eyes, close-trimmed black hair and moustache, and a little goatee. Innate and vested power, and its deep voice, were so formidable I was afraid of him already—not without cause, as I found out later. He assigned me to Company A, room No. 68 upon my friends' request, and warned me I'd be reassigned if I caused any trouble.

"Go to the hospital to be inspected for bodily condition and disease. Then report to Mr. MacHugh, your First Sergeant. Dismissed."

* * *

At the hospital, east and downhill from Barracks, I heard drums beating again and assumed they were the post signals, but I didn't know what each signified. I was conducted to a room and ordered to strip to the skin. I was measured, weighed, and thumped to determine chest capacity. Every crevice of my body and all its surface area were examined. Dr. Barton tested every sense and muscle and vital organ, sought and evaluated all evidence of present or past disease and injury, and finally passed me.

*   *   *

I have been initiated & it went pretty hard with me. They whipped me with a bayonet scabbard & they spelt my name, county & state, the Virginia Military Institute & what class I was going to enter. You know what they mean by spelling you is they tie your hands together put them over your legs and knees & then run a stick between your legs, turn you over & then whip you with a bayonet scabbard. They call it bucking you. They give you a lick for every letter in your name, county, state, Va Mil Institute & what class you enter. I do tell it hurts awful bad. They twist your arms nearly off, & I don't know what they don't do. But I can tell this much there is not a Cadet in the Corps but what has been done the same way
—A. C. L. Gatewood, V.M.I. cadet[19]

"Could you direct me to No. 68, sir?" Speaking to the first cadet I met in the Quadrangle, I stood like the patrician I am, to defy earlier humiliation.

He ushered me into a room. The "court" followed! They pounced. I exploded, but hit only the one who'd lured me into this ambush, before they wrestled me down.

---

19 A. C. L. Gatewood, VMI cadet, letters August 4 and 25, 1860. VMI Archives.

"You'll be Cyclops tomorrow!" a bulky redhead jeered at him.

They tied my wrists, forced my arms down over my bent knees, slid a stick under knees and over arms, hoisted me onto a table, and rolled me on my side. I couldn't see above their midsections—I'd look like begging mercy if I looked up.

"What's your name?"

"We use 'Constantinople' for missing names, a lick for every letter."

"Cyclops" took the first turn, laying on furious blows. The stick could be slipped out, so I pretended to be thrust toward the side of the table, until it was past the edge. I widened the space between knees and elbows, and recoiled to shake it free.

I sprang off the table and drove both fists into the nearest one's face and knocked him down. One caught my neck from behind. Others grabbed my feet, slammed me on the floor, and pinned me before I could blink. They bent me over the table, held my shoulders down, and took turns plying the limber bayonet scabbard. My dignity was in ruins. The whipping was bad.

"Tell whoever asks, you're Mister DeLigny's Rat. Get out!"

The "Court": ToombsStoneGraves, Jenner, and Deligny

"I thought we'd never get his case attended to!"

"The look he gave us!"

"He must think a Rat can get away with it!"

"Think he'll call us out?"

Torquil

A turncoat's punishment? I was burning mad. My modest plans for entering the Institute were upended. I felt like I was, too. I'd lost command of my situation.

In No. 68, walls of ashlar masonry, nine-light window in the upper half of the door. Large wardrobe, musket rack opposite, where hung the odious bayonet scabbards on white belts. Blacking stand, row of shoes arrow-straight against the wall. In corners, a bookcase, rolled mattresses bound with too-familiar leather straps. A tall window pierced the wall opposite the door; by it stood a washstand with looking glass above. A large oak table in the center held a coal oil lamp and was surrounded by chairs.

Where were my friends?

Aidan Beag

Airlie and I tossed our caps on the table. "Beau! We looked all over!"

"Where were you?"

"Set upon by a pack of roughs, strapped fast, and whipped!"

Airlie winked at me. I returned the slightest nod.

"You've a heap more to come!" Airlie feigned woe.

"What kind of school is this!"

"The best!"

"Whose Rat are you?" I asked.

"DeLigny's, *he* says."

"You're doomed! He beats his Rats daily before breakfast."

I shook my head. "I wouldn't be in your place for anything. You'll be sore all term."

"If he tries, I'll beat the waddin' out of him!"

"Was anyone else there?"

We sat down while he described them.

"ToombsStoneGraves ... Rats' Funeral Arrangements!" Airlie stifled a snicker.

"Comical!"

"They think so. They're more comical than wicked, taken by themselves, but with DeLigny in it, you're up the spout! He's the lowest minded, meanest man in his class!"

"I hit two of them, and I'll call out the others!"

"No, you won't," I said.

"The devil I won't!"

"Mind your language!"

"Nobody insults me like that without a reckoning!"

"They do here. As a new cadet, you have to take it without fighting back." Airlie looked as sympathetic and sincere as anyone could while gulping down a guffaw.

"Why? It's nothing to do with getting our education!" Beau sat backward, very carefully, on the other chair.

"It shows you you're under subjection." I sounded as serious as my rank requires. "The fourth class has to be silent, humble and obedient, or their backsides get blistered."

"Or there's twisting your arms, pulling your ears … but if it doesn't draw blood it doesn't count." Airlie contrived to keep a straight face.

We built the tale taller. "A good warming's a good warning!"

"Whisht!" Beau's face was red as a beet root.

"Remember: keep your head cool so your tail stays the same!" I raised an admonitory finger.

"*Whisht!*"

We couldn't not laugh! Beau scowled like thunder!

"Carry me back to Mister Stafford! It's a *little* boys' school!"

"Fear not, little Rat! You'll like it better when you're older!" I patted him on the head.

He batted my arm away. "I'm not a rat!"

"You *are* a Rat, and you will be till they play 'Auld Lang Syne' when the first class is relieved—next year! All new cadets are Rats."

"Charming! Is all this in the regulations?"

"Of course not!" Airlie scoffed. "Old Specs and Old Billy and the subs enforce those—and watch out for Old Billy!—but we have our own rules. Those who don't heed, don't stay."

"I fought the Yankees four years and the Indians three, and I'll be blamed if I'm going to be treated like I was still in short breeches! I'll get my deposit back and go re-enlist!"

"No, you won't! It won't hurt for long. If you behave and keep your tongue between your teeth, you won't get whipped again," I counselled. "Bucking's your initiation. Every new cadet gets served the same way."

"As soon as we can catch you." Airlie went on, "And it's not a joke about DeLigny."

"It's not a joke about how you have to behave, either," I warned. "You come under absolute discipline here. Obey every order, official or not, immediately."

"And don't argue or laugh or show any disrespect," Airlie added. "It's impudence, and you never get away with it. Officially, there's a demerit system. You get reported for everything you do wrong, on purpose or by accident. You're responsible for perfect conduct, and if you don't give it, it's counted your fault. If you get too many demerits, you're dismissed—flat!"

"During the War, they hung a Rat till there was no life in him—" I began.

"We stuff the tenderfeet with stories like that on the frontier, too!"

"It's true. He joined Otey's Battery after a year or two. They revived him, of course."

"Rats are lower than weasels, all term." Airlie summed it.

"What happened this morning?" I asked.

"We've been hearing ugly stories."

"It was my own fault. I decided to reconnoiter and then come up here and surprise you." He told us the events, and ended, "... and they all looked at me like I wasn't fit to black their boots!"

"One rumor says you're a felon who was whipped in prison."
I looked square at him.

"The other says you deserted to the Yankees."

Beau set his mouth in that stubborn line he always does. "I've
done nothing dishonorable, and they can believe me or not!"

"What happened? We can—"

"Let it alone! Why were they all out on the sentry line?"

"It was a trap for Hazelwood. He's a little gamecock."

"Don't they honor sentries!"

"The ones who weren't in the War never saw a man die," I told
him, "so they don't understand that guard's a sacred duty. Now,
though, the only threat would be a mink."

"What's a mink?"

"Washington College student." Airlie grinned. "We skirmish
with one occasionally. Their campus borders the post. General
Lee is the college president."

"Tormenting the Rat sentries is routine, and they're getting in
the last licks they can before Graduating Day."

The drum began. We jumped up and took our caps.

"DeLigny was running it on you," I explained. "You're my
Rat, 'cause I'm your First Sergeant. He can't claim any, he's only
a private.

"Report to the parade ground for drill! West of Barracks."

Torquil

I left the Quadrangle past the tower and turret on the end of
the ruined west wing. Squads of new cadets in citizens' clothing
were being drilled by old cadets in uniform, in tones from treble
to *basso profundo*, a lot louder than I'd ever found necessary.

"Mister Rat! Form up on the end of the line!"

Lance Corporal Todd glared at me. A slim, ivory-headed cane
was his baton of office.

"Stand at attention!" he bellowed at the squad. "Palms of the hands forward! Don't lock your knees! Draw in your chins! You look like a gaggle of geese hissing at the clouds! Eyes forward!"

I made minute corrections.

"Mister Hatch! Straighten your arms, sir! Mister Wilkins! You stand like a cow, sir! Set your feet at a sixty-degree angle from each other. Mister Althouse! Stand up straight! This is a drill ground, not a parlor, sir! Mister Ettinger! Hold your head up, sir!"

With my stance, he could find no fault.

"Mister Drummond! You smell like taffy, sir! Are you concealing food? Turn out your pockets!"

"Yes, sir."

"Be still, sir! Speak only if questioned!"

I began to turn out my pockets.

"No soldier stands with hands in pockets! Stand at attention, sir! You were not ordered to stand at 'Rest'! Draw your elbows back! Little fingers on the seam of your trousers! Palms forward! Chin down, sir, or I'll report you for disrespect! Remove your hat!"

I tried to obey conflicting, rapid-fire orders. Todd exploded like a burst boiler.

"You were not ordered to salute! You are forbidden to appear with your hat off! I shall report you for that, sir! I shall report you for pilfering food! The odor is stronger now! Carrying food on the person is forbidden! Where are you concealing it! Put your hat on, sir! You were just told not to appear with it off!"

I stood like a monument, holding stoic dispassion for all I was worth.

"What do I smell on you, sir!"

My mouth tightened and the corners turned down with disgust.

"You rage at your superiors! I'll report you for that, too!"

He sniffed. Then he inhaled deeply.

"Molasses! Did you bathe in it? Use it for scent? Or"—he feigned an expression of returning memory—"could it be you were this morning's raree show?"

Wilkins, at the other end of the line, giggled, tried to choke it back, and snorted instead. Todd turned on him. Drill lasted till a drum began to sound triple beats, with a pause between each.

"Squad ... Halt! Stand at attention! Dress left!" Todd's voice was growing hoarse, but he rasped an explanation before he marched us to the Quadrangle and dismissed us.

Aidan Beag and the other First Sergeants commanded, "Fall in!" The old cadets formed ranks, but the new ones milled about. Another lance corporal, handsome as Hoffmann of M Company, gave me a ferocious glare.

"You're late, Mister Rat! Right end of this rank, sir, and be quick!"

The new cadets wore every variety of clothing, from city fashion to coarse homespun. The old cadets were marched out first, the rest of us straggling along behind. I listened to the commands and obeyed them, but I was one of few who knew how. Sergeant Thibault, the corporals and lance corporals on the flanks of the wobbling little column shouted orders at us by name. Corporal Jamieson bayed vituperation like a deep-voiced sheep dog. I kept my eyes on the collar of the boy in front as instructed, but the boy behind took too long a step and stumbled into me, while the one in front kept losing the step and pausing to correct himself. I marked time in place to avoid walking on that one's heels, and the one behind trod on mine, nearly tripping me.

"Halt!" bellowed Thibault. The flock floundered to a stop.

The magnificent lance corporal yelled at the top of his voice. "Mister Drummond! How you can disrupt the step of three men at once is beyond comprehension! You will be severely punished, sir!"

I felt my face grow red. What a pack of incompetents! The drillmasters got the column moving again. At the parade ground, drums and fife played and the officer in charge put the battalion through its drill. They marched with spirit and precision, in such perfect time that every step resounded. It would have drawn even a flighty antelope into step.

The day's orders were read, including the examination schedule, urging the cadets to behave and study well. They had five minutes after parade to change clothes for supper. Having none to change, I stood in the Quadrangle by the sentry box, studying the arrangement of Barracks.

The main pile was four stories high, its turrets loftier. From inside, it looked like rows of doors and railings. Cadets entered and left four tiers of rooms in the east wing, and three on either side of the massive arch on the south. The corner rooms fronted aslant between the wings; the stairways were placed outside them. The west wing was still a ruin from Yankee General Hunter's arson in 1864. Tiers of tower rooms flanked the great arch. I expected to learn what they were all used for.

At the mess room, I was assigned to a table full of strangers. The meal was bread, cornbread, and butter, and milk, coffee, or tea. I tucked in with a will to my first food in twenty-four hours. The corporal at the head scorned and corrected some of the Rats' table manners. I swiftly dispatched every bite that came to me, then sat quiet, studying all that went on, hoping for more.

"Mister Drummond! Consumption of food is not a race, sir!"

My face got hot.

"Conversation at table is also held to be a civilized attainment, however golden your silence may be elsewhere!"

My face got hotter. Every thought leading to speech vanished.

The waiter unloaded a tray for the corporal to serve out. I received a second helping, but, chasm gaping, couldn't think of a word to say till I noticed the Rat I'd offended, two places away. I spoke under cover of the others' talk.

"I was unjustly rude to you this morning, and I'm sorry for it. Will you forgive me?"

Long pause, accusing look. I felt repaid for my discourtesy. "Yes."

I held out my hand. He spurned it.

"Not with a felon."

Supposing they all condemned me, I sat in miserable silence.

"Mister Drummond! Were you not ordered to make conversation!"

"Consider the source." Low, suave words at my left: Althouse from squad drill. "Just answer. Who do you think will take the elections this fall?"

"The Republicans."

"They've been sweeping all before them, haven't they. I've heard, though, that the Democrats and some conservative old-line Whigs are trying to combine against them."

"They'll have to sink a lot of differences!"

"There's more similarity of purpose than one might imagine. A lot of Whigs are thinking twice about having made common cause with the Republicans, especially since the Radicals are so vicious about revenge on the South."

An elbow jostled me from the right.

"*Verzeihung!*" A friendly voice. "You must today herein have come?"

I faced a short, well-muscled boy with a shock of wavy blond hair, blue eyes, and a cheerful expression. "Yes. My name is Drummond."

"Vogelsang, vom Tenth Legion."

I grasped his extended hand.

"A well-named place, considering all the fighting you must have seen."

"We were marching down, or they up. Our place off vom Pike is, so some I missed."

"I hope you escaped The Burning."

"All but the ground and our teams, we lost."

"I'm sorry to hear it."

"Ach, the family all unharmed are, and we since, one good crop and a pair lesser ones have made. Then der Grandvater got me appointed cadet."

"They must find it hard to get along without you on the farm."

He grinned. "I'm the baby. You should my brothers see! They say I have *'mehr Sind als Starke'*—more mind than might. You sound like you know the Valley, but you don't look like you live here."

"My home is Abercairn."

"You were *mit der* Shield?"

"I was."

"You must be Black Drummond they yammered about. We of you heard, along end of the war, when Yankees after you were chasing."

"You must have been in the reserves, too."

"I to join ran away, but der Vater caught me—*donner und blitzen* because I the last gun im house took! I've got it here, now he can spare it."

"Can I see it?"

"Yes! After the eating, kommen."

When the First Captain marched us out, I was surprised: Vogelsang had the longest arms and legs I ever saw and stood several inches taller than me. We'd just broken ranks when gangs of old cadets, intent on deviltry, bore down on us.

"Follow me, do what I do, and we can leave the Hessians to themselves!"

We went nonchalantly around a little knot of Rats who stood like mesmerized rabbits, awaiting their persecutors, and reached Vogelsang's room on the fourth stoop.

"Few do that so well."

"I was he who with the horses hid. I could not let the Yankees hear."

He went to get his gun. A sharp rap at the door could only mean an officer, so I stood at attention. Corporal Jamieson ushered in two more new cadets.

"How thoughtful of the State to provide a servant, since we weren't permitted to bring any," remarked one as he slouched into the room.

My face got hot with indignation. Jamieson blared orders to the others about placing their belongings before he left.

"I'm not your servant!"

"Not even my 'very obedient,' should you ever write to me?" responded the slouch, smiling. Plump, medium height, blond hair long as a poet's, round blue eyes. His moustache owed more to barbering than whisker. "Who are you, then?"

"Drummond, new cadet."

"Harry Carter, the same." He extended a pudgy white hand.

"Of Shirley, no doubt." I gripped it firmly.

"Of Richmond. Only a poor relation—though genteel, mind you! My uncle of the wealthier branch decided to see to my education by getting me appointed as a charity cadet."

My chasm's bridged by the overtures of others, but I wasn't about to reveal my finances!

The other newcomer was taller, lean and lithe. Light brown hair and full beard, gray eyes. Coat dating back to the Revolution, homespun woolen trousers. But even in rough boots, he prowled around the room with noiseless tread, observing. He broke the deadlock.

"Andrew Jackson Bouleau, from Buchanan." He extended his hand.

"Such strength. Hardy sons of toil, I'm sure," Carter combined insult with compliment. Seeming to abhor silence, he chatted on, looking out the window.

"Not much of a view in the foreground, is there. It's a wonder the State leaves so much bare ground to be mud or dust, instead of seeding it. Some border plantings would show to good advantage. Perhaps some ground cover."

"D'ye do much plantin'?" Bouleau talked like someone should say something.

"I'm an aesthete, rather than the actual tiller of the soil. May I?" He sat on the only chair and slouched against the table.

"Where're yew from, Drummond?" Bouleau tried again.

"Abercairn."

"I shudder to think of the journey," said Carter. "How long does it take to get to civilization from the remote mountains?"

Corporal Jamieson barged in. "Redd out that mess!" He marched out.

"Do they always *bawl*?" sniffed Carter.

"I'd better go see what's keeping Vogelsang. He's your roommate. I live on the second stoop. Pleased to know you both."

"Equally, I'm sure." Carter sounded like he meant it.

"*Au 'voir.*"

When I reached the first stoop, a door flew open. A crowd of old cadets emerged and encircled me like a solid wall.

"Mister Drummond, we're having entertainment in Mister Gunn's room. Come along."

They were all past boyhood. The look about their eyes showed them seasoned by war. I respected them as equals but suspected I'd be the entertainment. Keeping me penned, they climbed to the second stoop. They disposed themselves comfortably on chairs, rolled-up mattresses, and the table.

"A song, Rat, and be quick about it!" snapped Ashland.

"O, Shenandoah, I long to—"

"I said 'quick'!"

I started "Keep Your Powder Dry." Before I sang two lines, Martin: "A love song, Mister Rat!"

A year of it yet to come, but I was sore all over and mad at being made sport of. I turned it back on them, pretending to woo each in turn: red-haired Boatwright, calm-faced Sergeant Major Gunn.

"Believe me if all those endearing young charms,
    That I gaze on so fondly today—"

Ashland: "A different one, Rat!"

"Like the blackbird in the spring—"

Respite after supper was brief. Martin cut me off. "Give us a parody instead!"

The opposite to the dainty blackbird is an ungainly buzzard; the opposite of spring is fall, but I had no idea how the ditty would continue.

"As a buzzard in the fall,
    Awkward on the ground,
Hopped and walked, I heard him squall,
    'Where can meat be found?'
Buzzard meat, buzzard meat,
    Lying all around:
Confederate brave or Yankee foul,
    Carcasses abound!"

"Assail our ears no longer!" Ashland ordered. "Present your history—*in tableaux vivants!*"[20]

---

20 French: living scenes; pantomime.

I prepared my escape. Placing a chair in front of the door, I sat on it, pantomiming schoolwork. Stood on it, waving an imaginary newspaper and declaiming silently. I sounded a nonexistent trumpet and followed it to war, straddling the chair and pretending to do battle, hat on my head. I spurred my phantom steed, looked back over my shoulder to enact the flight west. Raising a hand for patience, I opened the door and placed the chair outside on the stoop ... closed the door, knocked, opened it to stand before the imaginary Uncle James ... stepped through, shut the door, and jammed the chair under the doorknob.

I'd disappeared when I heard them break out and give chase, shouting, "Catch that Rat!"

They passed me at a lope. I made a great clatter along the second stoop. When they sighted me, I gave a sardonic wolf grin, swept them a bow, and disappeared again.

Boatwright

"We'll have a job of work with that one," Gunn predicted as we all sauntered back.

"We'll have our comedy, too." I grinned.

"He'll be shipped for deficient moral character," growled Ashland. "He's a felon! Did you see his back?"

"No. Thibault sent him away before I heard about it," said Gunn.

"He wouldn't be enrolled if he were a felon," Martin demurred. "Why do you think so?"

"He's been whipped."

"Are you sure?"

"Nothing else leaves scars like that."

"Let's not judge yet," counseled Gunn. "First, find out the truth. I'll do it. Meanwhile, he's in A, so we've got to train him up for 'one of ours.'"

"First we have to put him under," Ashland grumbled. "We can have him in for private instruction—every night, till he's broke to discipline!"

"He'll give us thunder before that!" I said. "He doesn't scare and he isn't fooled."

"He's seen the elephant—all competence and dominion." Martin picked up the splintered chair and brought it in.

"The hospital in Abercairn—that's where I saw him!" I remembered. "A standing skeleton with a hole in him the size of a goose egg. The matron wouldn't let him in till the old Scot cleaned him up. Joss and I had to help hold him while the surgeon burnt it clean. Never saw him after that, had to go back to the lines. But they said he'd brush-crawled all the way from Gettysburg!"

"MacIntyre ... MacIntyre ... didn't some of them live next upriver from Linden Hall?" Martin wasn't really asking us. "And one of their girls married into Abercairn."

* * *

> He that refuseth instruction despiseth his own soul:
> but he that heareth reproof getteth understanding.
> —Proverbs 15:32

Torquil

I was reading my Bible when my roommates entered and started in on me.

"You're right cool after starting such a row!" scolded Loudoun.

"I saved my distance."

"It won't save you a reckoning," Airlie predicted. "Anyone could have caught you."

"But they didn't."

"Wait till tomorrow and see what happens!" Aidan warned.

"Tomorrow I'll be the perfect humble Rat."

"It's too late. You're already a target." Airlie shook his head.

"All I have to do is whisht or 'Yes, sir' … and try not to laugh! This is ridiculous, after war."

"You don't understand! The idea is discipline into the corps," insisted Aidan. "You have to give yourself to it. It's like what we had in the Shield."

"I've been under discipline, and I've enforced it. I can be my own discipline and satisfy the standard anywhere."

Aidan shook his head. "Wait and see. You have to bend, or they'll break you."

"Let him dream!" fussed Loudoun. To me: "Put your possessions in place! And go over to Mr. Vanderslice the minute you can tomorrow! The longer you wait, the more will be ahead of you."

"For what?"

"To have your uniforms made. He's the tailor."

"I'll do it first chance I get. When will it be?"

"After dinner. He's on the fourth stoop. If your deposit's sufficient, you can order dress as well as fatigue clothes—if Old Specs could get the cloth—but you have to get permission from him. You also need to get your mattress and chair from the Quartermaster store."

Tattoo at 9:30 was another roll call. I could feel them all staring and suspecting me. I spread down my bedding afterward feeling besieged, knocked off balance, and subject to tyranny. I hadn't had a minute all day to get my bearings in this confounding new situation. I started to thank God anyway, but I fell asleep.

A peremptory din roused me to battle in an instant. In dim light I jumped up, but soreness ripped through my body and stopped me at all-fours. My tailbone must be connected to every nerve and sinew in my back!

"Don't fash yourself, it'll be worse tomorrow!"

I scowled at Airlie. The racket outside got worse: banging drums and screeching fife, till we were all formed up and shivering in the pre-dawn chill. Roll call, then ranks broken and back to quarters.

"Inspection in half an hour," Aidan said.

"Roll up your bed and put it away!" Loudoun ordered.

I jumped to attention and saluted. "Yes, sir!"

"Go to the barber today and get your hair cropped!" he went on. "That length is against regulations. Shave off the moustache now. It's not allowed."

"Yes, sir." I stood at attention again.

"What are you doing!"

"Practicing Perfect Plebedom, sir." I primmed my mouth. Lord it over me, will he! "I shall reek of rectitude … be saturated with subordination … trample on the temptation to transgress! May I have the honor of answering any other questions for you, sir?"

Aidan and Airlie laughed. Loudoun scowled.

"Quit smirking and dust the furniture! The brush is in the wardrobe."

After inspection, my roommates studied. I was turned out for drill. I missed the familiar caress of my moustache. Carter strolled, I marched, Bouleau stalked, and long-legged Vogelsang took one step to our two. Lance Corporal Bergennacht, too, carried an ivory-headed cane. When he took the same squad for more drill after breakfast, it appeared the arrangement was permanent. After dinner, the main meal of the day, I ordered uniform clothing, and the barber cut my hair so short my hat felt loose. I charged my mattress and chair to my cadet account, took them back to No. 68, and met my roommates.

"Let's talk on the way." Aidan stood up. "On Saturdays, we have permission to go out of limits, and all evening free till Dress

Parade. We'll show you the post and the town and how we do things."

"First, every old cadet has the right to exact service from you," Loudoun began. "If you keep your temper, they'll get their fun out of someone else, but you have to obey all old cadets as if they were officers."

"Including you all?"

"Only *ex muris,*"[21] Aidan assured me. "Out of public, we're Abercairn just like before.

"The code is truth and honor. Your word is your bond, like always. *We* judge. Some things can be set right, but anyone who lies is cut dead. If anyone infers you're not a gentleman, or calls you a coward or a liar, you have to resent it."

"Two yesterday called me a felon! I'll find them!"

"The sooner the better," Airlie advised. "Some of the subs turn a blind eye and let us settle our own quarrels."

"What's a sub?"

"Assistant, or sub-professor, of tactics—military subjects. They live in Barracks to keep discipline and make inspections."

Aidan pointed out the buildings under construction, south of the hospital. "The new mess hall should be finished soon. The houses are for Dr. Madison and Colonel Morrison."

We ambled west along the road in front of the faculty residences. "General Smith's house is the only one Hunter didn't burn, because the general's daughter was too sick to be moved," Airlie explained. "So he forced himself on them and used it as his headquarters."

"It was awful, what little was left of Barracks. We were quartered in town first, and then in those brick cabins," said Aidan,

---

21 Latin: "outside the walls"; by context: "in public."

"and they made some of us move into Barracks two years ago December."

"'Made' you?"

"The cabins have coal fireplaces. They're heaps warmer than Barracks. You'll see. The winter we moved in, the steam heat was out of order. Then we had such a severe cold spell all but necessary duty was suspended. We stayed in bed!"

"We've had some good partridge hunting back there." Airlie pointed into the woods behind the houses. "The Yankees don't seem to care about our sporting guns. Did you bring your shotgun?"

"Yes."

"Speaking of Yankees, how does Uncle James?" Aidan asked.

"The same."

"How did he convince you to enlist!" Loudoun demanded.

"He pointed out I should still fight to protect Southern people by protecting those who had to go West. Or I could be sent to Virginia and hanged. I didn't care. I didn't hear about the surrender till he told me, and it felt like there was nothing to live for."

"We were on scout with Keir," said Aidan, "We didn't find out till a week afterward, not for sure. We all felt like the world ended."

"Then God called me to be a protector, even if I have to be in the ranks all my life. I can't take the Ironclad Oath, so I can't be an officer."

"Not yet, anyway," said Aidan. "This tyranny has to end someday." He pointed toward the town of Lexington. We all pivoted. "The Yankees are still raising hob!"

"That's the Presbyterian Church." Loudoun pointed ahead. "We don't have a minister on post, so we march to town to worship. General Smith holds Bible class every Sunday, too, and we're all required to recite, but evening prayer meeting is voluntary."

"None of the ministers are as deep as Dominie Gilchrist," judged Aidan, "but the girls in the congregations ... some are friendly and some are pretty, and some are both."

"He speaks from experience." Airlie grinned.

Aidan retorted, "You could, too, if you wouldn't stammer!"

"I'm only the shadow of the Count of Abercairn, here."

"I'll look on. I can't marry if I'm an enlisted man." I cocked my hat at a rakish angle. "But I'll stay in practice!"

"Polish your manners, or they'll think you're a bear from the Territories!" Loudoun was "Overseer" worse than when we were boys!

"Speaking of your Countess ..."

Two young ladies, accompanied by an older one, passed on the opposite sidewalk. Aidan blushed and smiled fondly. We tipped our hats and would have crossed the street, but the lady hurried the girls along. One with brown hair and eyes looked back, giving a sweet smile. Her looks weren't anything special, but Aidan stood stock still and looked after her till we nudged him forward.

We feasted on cakes at Barclay and Kerr, and I saw the ivory-headed canes, an item of fashion, on display at Compton's, gentlemen's clothier. I wanted the one carved into a horse's head.

* * *

Loudoun stabbed at the list of misconduct reports. "Late to Reveille, improperly clothed at same, absence from morning drill, late to afternoon drill, disrespect of a superior, disrupting parade! It doesn't look like your discipline agrees with the Institute's!"

How did I do all that! How much demerit would I get! What would they do to me!

A Rat came up and relayed orders to report to Mister Gunn's room. Expecting retaliation for escaping last night, I knocked on the door and was bidden to enter.

"Stand at attention." Gunn's voice was quiet and even. He was alone in the room, sitting beside the table. Blue eyes, gaze calm but determined.

"Mister Drummond, are you a felon?"

"No, sir!" I gave him my command stare.

"Have you been whipped?"

"Yes, sir."

"Why?"

"Respectfully, sir, I decline to answer."

His voice and inflexion didn't change. "Mister Drummond, why were you whipped?"

"Respectfully, sir, I decline to answer."

"Dismissed."

* * *

I finished my letter to Uncle James.

> It's like you said it would be. We're drilled to death and dinned to deafness and prey to the whims of the old cadets. It hasn't been bad so far, I've only been beaten once. They call it bucking, and all new cadets are served the same way as their initiation. The old cadets say they "discipline" for "impudence," but it all looks right foolish to me, so I ignore it the best I can and try to learn how to do my duty. But I have to call out a couple who called me a felon. The fare's all right, but I'd like more.

> I've gotten a lot of demerits the past few days, but I'm learning how to do better, and I will. I want to justify your confidence in me, and show my gratitude for this opportunity.

You know all my roommates, Airlie, Loudoun, and MacHugh. They all send their best regards. Carter, Bouleau, and Fokelzank are good fellows, in my squad at drill. I've gotten to know only a few others yet, they keep us so busy.

I miss you. God bless and guard you.

Believe me your obedient servant and respectful Nephew,

Torquil Drummond.

P. S. Give my good wishes to all inquiring friends.

* * *

The cadet is hedged in by a code of regulations more rigorous than those of Deuteronomy.
—John C. Tidball, United States Military Academy, class of 1848

Every day was drill—infantry drill, more intricate than cavalry's dismounted drill. Bergennacht was furious and insulting. I presented the outward demeanor required, kept my thoughts to myself, and dismissed his incompetence with occupational disdain.

Every day was Sergeant Major Gunn.

He'd send a plebe to find me wherever I was—I hated being spied on!—with orders to report to his room. He was always alone, sitting beside the table. His voice was always quiet and even, his gaze always calm but determined, his question always the same. Always.

He only asked why I'd been whipped. I returned a look as determined as his. Didn't he know he had the only answer he'd ever get! How dare he pry into what was none of his affair! It was ill-bred. It accused me of not being a gentleman. I needed to call him out!

Gunn

Drummond couldn't mask his anger. I'd pierced the mask and could probe into him. I thumped on the floor to signal my roommates they could return.

Torquil

Almost time for drill after breakfast, but Gunn sent for me again! I took the steps two at a time and knocked sharply on the door. He kept me standing there, when seconds counted, then looked at me with the same relentless gaze. I returned it.

"Mister Drummond, why were you whipped?"

"Respectfully, sir, I decline to answer."

He drove the question at me over and over, till it almost sounded like a fact.

I hated the shaming words themselves. Did he believe I committed some base deed that deserves whipping? Spirits lowered, I couldn't utter the rebuke I planned.

The drum began for drill.

"Mister Drummond, why were you whipped?"

He drew the words out long and slow. I began to worry.

"Respectfully, sir, I decline to answer," I snapped.

A long pause. "Dismissed."

I wouldn't give him the satisfaction of hearing me run! The drum beat on, and I did run when I reached the Quadrangle. I rushed into position by the third-to-last beat.

"Mister Drummond, you are LATE!" Bergennacht roared. "Are you deaf to drums! Need you a formal invitation, maybe? *Stand at attention when I speak to you!*"

I snapped to attention. My face turned hot.

"Mister Drummond is *cordially* requested to bestow the favor of his company upon his *humble* drillmaster and squad of *unspeakable* Rats, whenever his lordship's pleasure permits.

"Form up! Dress left! Squad ... Forward ... March!"

After a few steps at the Common time, Bergennacht increased the tempo to the Double Quick. Disturbed already, I grew more so under his rapid orders and scalding scolds. I lost step so many times I thought I'd forgotten everything I knew.

He drove us back and forth across the parade ground. He didn't try to keep the pace himself, but shouted orders from a distance. Every time I passed him, he bellowed, "LATE!" We were exhausted and straining for breath before he called a halt. I felt like a beast to have brought punishment on the others. Nor was it over.

> The "goose step" ... the object of which was to teach the principles of marching ... consisted of standing, like a goose, on one foot while the other was flung alternately to the front and rear at the commands "Front, Rear" and after awhile "Ground." This "Ground" represented a step, and it was succeeded by the other foot. ... Let anyone who is skeptical try this for a quarter of an hour at a stretch, and he will be convinced that the tortures of the Inquisition were a failure without it.
> —John C. Tidball, United States Military Academy, class of 1848

"Form up! Dress right! Open Files! Balance Step! Left ... back ... forward ... back ... forward. Ground!"

He kept us at it till it hurt. At dinner, I was too ashamed to say anything. Afterward, I apologized to my squad mates.

"What I'm a-thinkin' we oughten to do," said Bouleau, "is one of us be late ever time. Then he'll have an apoplexy fit and git sent home."

Carter had suffered the most and still didn't look recovered, but he nodded.

I was grateful for their forgiveness. Then a Rat none of us knew brought orders to report to Gunn's room.

Angry at yet more theft of my scant freedom, I repressed a scowl and knocked.

Gunn

In placid tones, I ordered him in, and focused a piercing look into his eyes.

"Stand at attention."

He eyed me just as hard.

"Mister Drummond, why were you whipped?"

"Respectfully, sir, I decline to answer."

He was smoldering. He started to speak. I cut it off. I forced the pace and made him follow it.

"Mister Drummond, why were you whipped?"

"Respectfully, sir, I decline to answer."

"Mister Drummond, why were you whipped?"

Pausing less than a second between repetitions, I asked and was answered. Drummond's anger burned till he was hard pressed to contain it, but he kept his tone of voice dead level. I dismissed him only when the drum began.

Torquil

"Whipped … whipped … whipped" beat a tempo in my mind while I fled to drill, more determined than ever to call Gunn to account.

That evening, I was surprised to be reported for disobedience of orders. Would this be the final demerit before the Institute dismissed me? I was much relieved when Aidan told me if I wasn't guilty, I could write an excuse and give it to Colonel Ship. If "Old Billy" accepted it, the report would be taken off my record.

Supper was barely over when I was again summoned to Gunn's room. At the door, I gave the Officers' Rap.

Gunn

I couldn't mistake that signal! Drummond was taut with belligerence. I kept my even demeanor and tone of voice.

"Stand at attention. Mister Drummond, why were you whipped?"

"Respectfully, Mister Gunn, if you continue this importunity, I shall be obliged to resent it!" His voice snapped with command.

"You have not the standing."

"Are you saying I am not a gentleman, sir !" His face flushed. He glared like a startled eagle.

"I am saying you are a plebe. No further definition is needed." I gave him no respite. "Mister Drummond, why were you whipped?"

"Respectfully, sir, I decline to answer." His color stayed high.

I repeated the question over and over till his wrath was exhausted and he replied only by rote, then intensified my voice till I forced him to focus on me and return his mind to the question.

"Mister Drummond, why were you whipped?"

I kept him till Call to Quarters. He marched out, heels hitting hard. I thumped on the floor, and Boatwright returned.

"Any success yet?"

"I took some of the nonsense out of him. He's 'to the manner born.'"

"And meanwhile?"

"Progress."

Torquil

Still smarting from defeat at Gunn's hands, I lay awake after inspection was over. A Rat having "no standing" confirmed my friends' warning that I ranked below the bottom of the corps hierarchy.

The next night, Gunn looked and talked the same as always, but he somehow conveyed he not only had the right to ask, but the right to know. I was seized by a sudden, compelling urge to answer. Thunderstruck, I put it away. If I told him, I'd sound like a braggart.

I ran down the stairs afterwards, astonished by whatever in me wanted to sabotage my purpose. Too preoccupied to be wary, I strode into the Quadrangle.

"Stand at attention!" bellowed Toombs.

"Look, here's the sergeant!" Graves called to his friends.

I was surrounded instantly. Recognizing the "court," my mind took hold again.

"Let's learn how to hold a court, since he knows all about it!" Toombs jeered.

"Quote the procedure, *Sergeant*! What comes first?" Stone prodded.

"First, sir, catch your prisoner."

I drove hard between two of them, dodged, and disappeared behind a crowd intent on tormenting another Rat. No trouble staying out of their sight. They'd try to make me pay for it, but I wasn't sorry I mocked them.

I found a secluded clearing among the brush and leaned against a tree to reason it out. Why did I feel coerced, when Gunn's manner was so temperate? Something in him demanded my obedience. My heart wanted to answer—but my will defined the question as slander against a gentleman's truthfulness. I'd never surrendered my will to another man's, even under torture. If I answer, I won't have only lost a contest of wills, but some wellspring of my life will be altered in its course. If I yield to Gunn, he'll be my master. I won't have it!

But the idea that I ought to answer preyed on my mind.

* * *

I handed in my excuse and stood at attention before the Commandant. I wasn't guilty. Colonel Ship would see the justice of it. I stood confident—till the thunder pealed about my ears, and the sky fell on my head!

"Disrespect of superiors. You have broken a fundamental law of military duty." "Old Billy"'s voice was deep as the foundation of earth and rumbling as thunder above it.

My face felt hot, and then like all the blood left it. My confidence dissolved.

"There is no excuse for disrespect! The report stands."

I shook inside. Would he dismiss me from the institute here and now? He let his words echo. Was I guilty of worse offenses?

"Disobedience!"

He hurled his lightning-bolt above the open Delinquency Book. He didn't need to raise his voice to give it the ring of dominion. He paralyzed me with a look like the Day of Judgment, and continued in a lower, ominous tone.

"You have seven years' military experience. You know obedience is indispensable to discipline. Disobedience is inexcusable." He scanned the book.

"Disobedience … disrespect … habitual tardiness … other breaches of discipline are recorded here against you. Have you begun as you intend to go on?"

"No, sir." I choked it out. This man held my future in his hands!

"You will walk post on the parade ground for an hour tomorrow, starting at 2:00 p.m. From 3:00 p.m. until evening parade, you are confined to your room. You will read the *Regulations* for this post, consider your misconduct, and resolve upon means of correcting it.

"That will do, sir!"

I'd never been so roughly censured, by such a powerful superior, in all my life. And it was mean of Bergennacht to report me late to drill when I wasn't, but I was forbidden to speak first and tell him so. I went away disheartened.

* * *

I walked post for an hour, ashamed to be seen undergoing punishment. Then I went to No. 68.

I'd been here only nine days, up to my ears in trouble. My scarred back and Yankee service were extorted by the "court." Some cadets cut me dead rather than order me to join the other Rats they were hectoring. They must all condemn me. I was afraid of Colonel Ship's hard judgment. I'd failed at every turn and was a disgrace to my name, to Abercairn, to Uncle James. And a liability to my friends.

Disrespectful? Absolutely! Old-cadet standing and artificial distinction—it wasn't Army rank!—weren't going to make me respect them. They were only pretending to be soldiers!

Regulations said the corps of cadets was a Virginia military body guarding the Institute and the Arsenal, which erased my sneer. The course of instruction, demerit and punishment systems, and rules for discipline were spelled out: confinement to quarters was only a step away from being dismissed! Would I be cast out?

But I'd fought a war and fought the Indians and survived much. I won't be defeated now! I laid my head on my folded arms and prayed that my career at the V.M.I. hadn't already ended.

I didn't wait to be summoned, but went to Gunn's room after supper to have done with the pest. The calm voice bade me enter. I stood at attention and looked him straight in the eyes.

"I didn't send for you. Dismissed."

Boatwright

Gunn thumped on the floor. I returned.

"Any success?"

"Yes. He's begun to retreat."

Torquil

I felt worse than rebuffed, yet it was just. Rats had no right to go to an old cadet's room without orders, and I'd assumed I was required to be there every day.

That night, I lay watching the stars through the window. Institute regulations and the cadets' unwritten code were adamant. I hadn't intended to test either. I wasn't rebellious. I embraced willingly the duty I'd promised.

I longed for home—but I'd had no home since I went to war, and less than none after Da and Douglas were murdered. Glenlochie hardly belonged to me now, nor I to it. Uncle James was my only "home," and he was half a continent away. Someday, perhaps, I'd establish a home of my own. But marriage was out of the question for at least four years. Then I'd have to convince a lady to love me, and—what might she find in me to love!

I felt daunted, trying to make new friends. I can't trust. It's hard to open my heart to anyone, and it isn't my nature to be outgoing, so men think me haughty.

I shifted position and turned my pillow over. No matter what friendships I had, I was still alone, with my own life to shape. I laid down my head, gazing at the stars, and prayed again to succeed here. The pangs of loneliness pierced my heart.

* * *

A few days passed without a summons from Gunn. Was I cast away as reprobate and unworthy of discipline? I was relieved to keep my past to myself, but the whole matter felt like unfinished business. I couldn't shake it out of my mind, I felt compelled to complete it. I wanted to be vindicated, not condemned out of hand! At least Gunn wasn't going to vex me anymore.

I'd mistaken my man.

When he summoned me, all was the same, including his determined, piercing gaze.

"Stand at attention."

I obeyed, looking him hard in the eyes.

"Mister Drummond, why were you whipped?"

I wanted to answer, merely because I hadn't been cast away. I hesitated, gathering determination in a tight grip that almost failed to serve my will.

"Respectfully, sir, I decline to answer."

"Dismissed."

"Yes, sir."

I turned about-face and left. My breath came fast as if I'd been running.

Gunn

I was satisfied. He'd dropped that glare for a split second—the first crack in his shield. I thumped for Boatwright.

"Did he answer?"

"Not yet, but he's losing ground. It won't take much more to rout him."

"Do you really think he's going to tell you? This has been going on a long time."

"It's the only way."

"You could order him to answer."

"No. That would invoke general authority. The only way to bring him under subordination is to break his will to mine. When I have, I'll know the truth of the felon story and what to do."

Torquil

Next day, taking my account book, I went to the tailor for my uniforms. Charged against my deposit, they cost over a hundred dollars! Was there still enough for pocket money? I had to save hard money to buy the ivory-headed cane. The shopkeepers don't let us run up bills.

Aidan Beag

I collected my mail from the Quartermaster and read her dainty note first. Her parents had accepted the invitation to visit Cousin Eleanor on Saturday and would bring her with them! I tucked the precious message under my coat next to my heart and opened Uncle James's.

> Fort Banks
> Dakota Territory
> June 25, 1868

Dear Aidan,

Please excuse this hasty scrawl. I am keeping the mail waiting.

Thank you for your concern for Torquil's good name. I am not surprised he doesn't want to talk about what happened to him, nor, I am sure, will you be.

When I was sent West in 1864, Mssrs. Yohanson and DuChemin were assigned to my company as lieutenants. (You recall they were the two that tortured him during the War, and, when he escaped, Yohanson swore to kill him.) In July, 1865, I was summoned to sit on a court martial fifty-some miles distant. I ordered Yohanson out on scout for the duration of my absence and left Torquil's squad at the post. Yohanson disobeyed the order, and DuChemin went in his stead. Yohanson tried to kill Torquil by starving him and putting him at hard labor, beating, spread-eagling, and whipping him. He went insane before he accomplished it and was arrested and confined.

I leave it to your good judgment, how you will overcome the slander with the truth. Please accept my heart-felt thanks for your desire and effort to do so.

Give my greetings and warm good wishes to all from Abercairn. I am honored to be,

> Your obedient servant,
> Uncle James

I was stricken. I hunted up Airlie and Loudoun and took them to No. 68.

"Read this."

When they looked up, they looked shocked.

"It was because of us. He wouldn't betray us."

"None of us would have," snapped Airlie, more moved than he wanted to show.

"Who can say he wouldn't break under torture?" I shuddered inside.

"Why wouldn't he want the reasons known?" Loudoun asked. "The scars are common knowledge, given the worst interpretation. But it was a nine days' wonder. I don't hear it now."

"No one's going to say it to our faces!" Airlie exclaimed. "We have to talk to the liars."

"We shall, starting with Stone and his friends," I decreed.

Torquil

Ordered to report to Gunn's room, I was determined not to be mastered.

"Stand at attention."

I matched gaze for gaze.

"Mister Drummond, why were you whipped?"

I am *not* going to answer.

"The Yankees captured me. They wanted me to betray—"

Gunn took command. "Go on."

"I refused. Two ... questioned me."

Gunn used his power. "By what means?"

Terror ... black evil. Hot all over, then ice cold. Trembling inside ... heartbeat raced till it stopped altogether. Couldn't speak above a whisper.

"Torture."

"Go on."

"I escaped."

Hard to breathe. Couldn't see Gunn.

"One of them swore to kill me. The ... was part of it."

"What was the rest? Answer precisely!"

I choked out the few words and gave myself up to judgment.

"Dismissed."

Unseeing, I stumbled down the stairway. I escaped to my haven in the brush and dropped in a heap, shaking inside and out.

The Yankee tent: solid evil ... beaten ...knifed. The fort: starving, helpless ... overpowered, beaten. Whip tearing my back. Terror ... agony ... drowned in shame. Forsaken.

I bowed my face onto my folded arms and wept—and prayed no one would see me.

Horror overset me ... hadn't expected, hadn't thought of it. It was *buried*. All my mind was on fighting Gunn.

I felt wholly subjugated for the first time in my life. My will had failed to save me. My soul was eviscerated, my inmost haven desecrated and destroyed.

Gunn

I thumped on the floor. Boatwright returned.

"Well?"

"He's no felon. He's worth knowing. I'm going to see MacHugh."

A few strides along the second stoop brought me to No. 68.

"MacHugh, will you come with me?" We went through the great arch and along the road toward the limit gates. "I finally learned the truth about Mister Drummond's injury. Did you know it?"

"Only today. I wrote to his uncle to find out. His roommates and I will tell it in the quarters where it needs to be heard."

"I'm no less interested in scotching the rumors. How much should the corps know?"

"Enough to base their opinion on facts. I knew only what happened here. After he lured the Yankees away from Abercairn, news was scant. He was on the frontier three years. Besides, no one's going to write a home letter about being whipped!"

"I understand it was revenge for escaping questioning during the War."

"He didn't escape till they'd tortured him most of the night."

"That's hard to believe even of Yankees!"

"He preached from the day the command was formed, how important it was to protect each other. That brought it home, just like the other time."

"What was that?"

"We were pressed too hard, and he ordered us all away and surrendered himself. He was the chief, the one they wanted. They'd published, they'd hang any guerrillas they caught. We weren't, but that's how they painted us."

"What happened?"

"We captured a Yankee detachment and used their uniforms and horses. Uncle James impersonated a brigadier, and we marched into their camp in broad daylight and brought him off. Afterward, he gave us all jesse for risking ourselves!"

"If Mister Stone and his friends hadn't made a show of him, he'd have made his way on his true merit."

"Which is considerable, and of course you'll never hear it from him. He's always been quiet, and he went silent after his father and brother were murdered. When he was commanding, we hardly saw him except in the field.

"He's ... a hardened soldier, but ... an innocent somehow."

"I'd have tried to learn the truth some other way if I'd known what happened. I've been questioning him for a couple of weeks, and tonight he answered. He broke. Now I see why."

"I didn't know. He never mentioned it."

"His friends and I will say we have a witness that the felon story is false, and see whether they dare accuse us of lying. They may think us biased, but they ought to believe it from you."

"I'll publish the truth in the form you suggest, and tell Mister Jenner and the Rat Whitesmith to apologize."

Torquil

After Taps, I lay exhausted but too troubled to sleep, trying to reason out what Gunn did to me. Forcibly reminded that emotion could sink me, I'd reach conclusions by cold logic! I put on dispassion like armor. I wanted to keep my chasm as a moat in defense of the citadel that is my soul.

But the chasm was already transgressed, the citadel breached. My will was overpowered for the first time in my life, I didn't know how. I'd never been conquered. What power Gunn used, I couldn't understand. My will—my wellspring—was all that saved my life before. I wouldn't survive without it. I was subjugated and free, sorrowful and joyful, all at once. Why?

Feelings drove thoughts into confusion. Exhaustion dragged me into sleep racked with nightmares. Helpless before the murderer, the torturer, black evil suffocated me. I wakened gasping, "No!" My roommates didn't rouse: I thought they were dead till I realized the cry sounded only in my mind. Shaking, sweating from terror, telling myself the horrors were past—but they'd never be over! I fought them till Reveille called me to Graduating Day.

The corps formed on the parade ground to hear the orders and promotion list. Loudoun stood at the head of the third class. Aidan was promoted to Captain of Company A. Thibault was named Adjutant, Gunn became First Captain of the corps, at the head of the new Company D, and Bergennacht *wasn't* named corporal. Back on post after the commencement exercises, the fifes and drum played "Auld Lang Syne," and each class moved up a grade. I shook my roommates' hands and spoke real pleasure in their success.

Later, both cadets who'd called me a felon apologized and sincerely asked forgiveness! I meant to fight my horrors alone in the woods, but I met my squad mates and went exploring with them. I needed to make a good reconnaissance, any road.

* * *

Fort Banks, D. T.
July 11, 1868

My dear Nephew,

Your intention to do well makes good hearing. You'll succeed as soon as you get your feet under you. I look forward to seeing the evidence when I receive your quarterly reports. It's regrettable that you have to fight so soon, but one must, in such cases. I hope your enemies will apologize for their insults, for, in a close community such as the Institute, it is vital to maintain cordial relations with one's fellows. I trust you will 'as much as lieth in you, live peaceably with all men.' It's better to reap the rewards of friendship than to drink the bitter cup of enmity.

Uncle Polonius's advice: don't try to have fun out of the old cadets, or you will pay dearly, with attention from them that you will find very unacceptable. Plebes weren't customarily beaten at West Point, but they were made to feel their inferior position in many other humbling ways. Your reception was more humiliating and public than usual, I suspect, but you acted with proper dignity, which will have been noted. With that, I hope, the worst is over. They'll run you ragged, and there will be more trials, but don't be disheartened. Bear it patiently, and it will soon be over.

M Company are well, though our detachments and other parties along the Trail are frequently attacked. The Indians sometimes change their decoy-and-ambush tactics, to stand-and-resist. They come much closer to the post, attempting to run off horses and mules, and drive in the infantry. This unusual aggressiveness may be caused by knowledge of the order from General Grant that all the Bozeman Trail posts, and the Trail itself, are to be abandoned! It was part of the treaty signed at Fort Laramie April 29 and is being implemented now. Men arrived at the end of May to bid on the public property we cannot transport, and two companies of infantry have been transferred to Fort Phil Kearny. We are to receive 25 wagons from P.K. to bring down the other three companies. I don't know where I shall finally be posted. Continue to direct your letters here until I inform you otherwise.

When you left here, I committed you to the keeping of God. Nor day nor night do I neglect to pray his blessing and protection upon you, to guard you from all evil and harm.

Your affectionate Uncle,
James MacLeod

MacLeod

Virginia Military Institute
Lexington, Virginia
July 5, 1868

Dear Uncle James,
I have met the young lady I want to marry.

I put a hand to my eyes and drew it down over my face till it rested on my chin. Already calling upon God for skill to thread the narrow channel between the Scylla of first romance and the Charybdis of common sense, I read on.

She is a cousin of MacHugh's sweetheart, and of Carter, my squad mate. I met her and danced with her at the Graduating Ball and spent the evening with her yesterday. She is Miss Julia Woodhurst, of Lynchburg. She is very pretty, with curly blonde hair and blue eyes. She is small, only stands about to the middle of my chest, and she has a sweet voice and a lively disposition, and she likes me.

I think if I were to transfer to the University, it might be all right if a student is married. If not, there must be other colleges where it is. Or I could simply marry her and bring her to Glenlochie and work out the matter of the inheritance some way. But I must do it now, lest another win her away from me, and 'it is better to marry than to burn.' I can't sleep at night, I burn so much with desire.

He extolled the real and imagined perfections of the girl and sketched scheme after scheme for immediate marriage. West

Point, I reflected, prohibited plebes from going to dances. They attended lessons to learn the steps and were saved from daydreams by the class being all male. This superior plan prevented premature attachments like the one now distracting my lad.

He noted that the slanders against him had been disproven and criticized the abandonment of the Bozeman Trail. He wrote a prayer for God's protection on me in the field and hoped my new posting would please me before he returned to his heart's desire.

> I know if you could meet her, you would like Miss Woodhurst as much as I do. Please write soon and tell me your ideas how we might soon be married.
>
> Your obedient servant and respectful Nephew,
> Torquil Drummond.
>
> P. S. To your "run ragged" nephew, you sound like one of <u>them</u>.

CHAPTER 22

CORPS ENCOUNTERS

Cadets will hold themselves in readiness to commence
regular recitations next Monday.
Strict attention to all academic duties will be required
of all cadets present for duty, & this order will be enforced by appropriate penalties.
—V.M.I. Order Book, July 9 and 11, 1868. VMI
Archives.

Torquil

Summer was given to military instruction and recitations
in French and Mathematics. After the struggle to stay on my
feet, I was true to my duty and lived up to my own code: hon-
or and *Fidelis*. I was diligent in my studies. Measuring success
by my comprehension, I knew I was succeeding. I followed the
Regulations as the law governing my life. I obeyed the old cadets'
orders without complaint, but obedience as perfect as I could
make it brought nothing but furious tirades. It was a solid wall of
blame whichever way I turned. But no misconduct reports for a
couple of weeks!

Rats hadn't a minute to draw breath outside of duty, Call to Quarters, and meals. The yearlings took turns ordering us to their rooms for "extra drill" or "special instruction" at the Double Quick. We had to do police duty while they exulted in not cleaning anything. They demanded servants' work, such as carrying their clothes bags to and from the laundry cart or fetching water from the hydrant to their rooms. Or one on the first stoop would order me to run up to the fourth stoop with a message for another. That one ordered me to run back down with the reply, and they kept me running up and down till the available time was spent. I put up with the nonsense, with a sneer in my heart and a wooden mask on my face.

Aidan Beag

The Rats, once his true character was known, respected and admired Beau for standing against oppressors whether old cadets or Yankees, without bending under their punishment. But they did it from a distance. His demeanor put off easy approach, nor did they want the notoriety he acquired among the yearlings, who had face-to-face responsibility for new cadets' training, discipline, and drill. These liked to goad Beau because they saw some fight in him, and it was fun to watch him struggle to keep it in check. They didn't find him saucy or boastful, but they sensed that his subordination was in form only. His manliness made some of them look bad in their own eyes, and they hated it. They were determined to humble him.

He slept every time and place he could, head on folded arms after studying or stretched out on the floor, Sunday evenings after dinner. He maintained our close friendship but never spoke of the maltreatment he received, nor of Rat subjection. He performed his duty to the letter and kept a wooden expression. He was primed to explode.

Torquil

President Johnson proclaimed amnesty on July 4. He pardoned all former Confederates except those under indictment for treason or other felonies. I'd qualified among those he pardoned last September, and now it looked like another barrier to a Regular Army commission was down.

Then I raged inside at Yankee arrogance and hypocrisy. Fighting for Southern independence—government by consent of the governed, a principle as old as Creation!—and to defend my home and neighbors, I'd done nothing I was ashamed of, nothing wrong, and certainly nothing I needed pardon for! It was all a lie! The Yankees were using military victory to cover their own crimes and try to justify vilifying, hating, and looting the Southern States. In Virginia we were under humiliating, grinding military occupation, and political and personal liberty were obliterated. I longed to strike back!

ToombsStoneGraves and Company sank to mean ugliness far below the level of ordinary harassment. I was running some other yearlings' farce of an errand when they caught me in a corner of the Quadrangle and penned me among them—right under the subs' noses—by acting like a friendly stroll together, all the while hissing their threats.

"Mister Rat, you're habitually impudent, and we're going to whip it out of you!"

I almost fought them right there: a man doesn't let himself be whipped like a schoolboy! My squad would've hooted me to scorn and deposed me! I couldn't have shown my face! But I already had so much demerit that I'd be dismissed—disgrace myself and Uncle James and Abercairn and ... never be commissioned! Honor and instinct warred with wisdom: a proud fight or the far-off prize? I'd try for both: attack when we got out of the subs' sight, in the room they were herding me to.

But they know me. Two grabbed me on the threshold. The only question was how much they could do to me before the drum. They all took turns. The brass ferule of the bayonet scabbard raised blisters till Call to Quarters began to beat.

"Now, Mister Rat, will there be any more of your impudence!" Stone gloated.

I didn't answer, refusing to allow their claim to power over me. They could beat me, but they couldn't break me any more than Yohanson could.

"Make sure there isn't, sir! Dismissed!" His injunction was lame, and we all knew it.

I was sore for a week, and they crowed over it in public!

"What happens to an impudent Rat, Mister Rat?" jeered DeLigny.

"He's whipped, sir."

"Too crude, sir," drawled Graves. "Refine your terms."

"He receives punishment, sir."

"Not fine enough," judged Stone. "Be gracious, Mister Rat!"

"He is disciplined, sir."

"Still too rough, Mister Rat," Jenner sneered. "Try again."

"Surely, Mister Rat," purred Toombs, "a sergeant of Yankees has not fallen so far that he cannot express his thoughts after the manner of a better station in life?"

I stared into nothing, past their heads.

"Cat got your tongue, Mister Rat?" jibed Stone.

Again I chose the wiser course, but I vowed to myself they'd pay for it!

"He is taught the error of his ways, sir."

"How is he taught, Mister Rat?" growled DeLigny. "Name the first step!"

"His error is told him, sir."

"How?" Stone asked.

"He is described as impudent, sir."

"What constitutes impudence, Mister Rat?" demanded Graves.

"Retorts, blows, laughter, or threats, sir, or any other disrespect, by a new cadet towards an old one."

"Only towards an old cadet?" Graves challenged.

"Towards any superior, sir."

"What is the next step in the Rat's lesson?" Toombs's voice was silky.

"Chastisement for his error, sir."

"Chastisement in what form?" DeLigny smirked.

"Whatever his superiors deem best, sir."

"In what spirit should he receive it?" Graves goaded me.

"A humble spirit, sir." If he were spineless!

"And he should be grateful for correction, Mister Rat! If he isn't, he's rebellious and must receive further correction, until rebellion is eradicated."

I didn't answer the threat. Aidan Beag was right. There couldn't be more absolute subjection than being forced to contribute to my own humiliation.

"Are you grateful, Mister Rat?"

If I spoke the truth, they'd whip and shame me again. I racked my brain for an acceptable answer.

"On that point, sir, I must let my future conduct speak for me." I already knew how it would!

I was thankful the right words had come from somewhere. In creating a diplomatic answer, I'd found a new weapon. I'd been their prey, and delivered myself.

Airlie had told me how cadets settle matters among ourselves. A few days' observation showed me where and when to stop the persecution. I chose DeLigny, the biggest, heaviest one, caught him alone, and gave him a beating about half as bad as I gave Steptoe.

"Tell your friends they'll get the same if they pester me!"

They evidently chose not to.

Aidan Beag

We sauntered toward Lexington Saturday evening after dinner.

"I see someone finally gave DeLigny his comeuppance." Boatwright twirled his cane through all his fingers till it rested at a smart angle in the crook of his arm.

"It's long overdue." Thibault looked satisfied. "After he mauled 'Kitten,' I was itching to do it myself."

"Wonderful what a fresh breeze from the west can clean out," I said.

Torquil

At the end of July, Uncle James's letter arrived.

Fort Banks, D.T.
July 16, 1868

My dear Nephew,

It was a rare surprise to hear you have met a young lady so pleasing. By now you will have reflected that your sacrifice in waiting to marry will be the best gift, after your love and protection, that you can offer her. Your education will enrich your life together by giving you both much more to enjoy in activity and conversation, than you would have if you had cut it off now. Besides that, of course, preparation to be commissioned, and fulfilling the requirements under which you will inherit, will go far toward providing security against the possible storms of life, from which I know you want to shield her.

I am left in command of the only company remaining, and thus of the post, until we withdraw. Dr. Barnes is with us, and I kept Sgt. Jacquard, so we fare well. The hostiles hover, and would pick off any soldier who strays, if I allowed any to do so. We double-guard the livestock, maintain post routine, load wagons, and send the auctioned goods off (mostly toward the Gallatin Valley) with their purchasers.

M is to be stationed next at Fort Liberty. Between the teamsters and the company, our party should be strong enough to resist or discourage attack on the way down. Wyoming is about to be established as a territory, so the proper direction will be Ft. L., Wyoming Terr.

I am well pleased that your reputation is now grounded in truth. Your merit will be known long before it is acknowledged by anyone except your class-mates.

Please give my congratulations to Aidan and Donald, along with my hearty good wishes for success in their new honors.

And for you, my lad, my prayers ascend to His throne day and night, for His mercy upon you and His protection over you, and His guidance for your every step. Try to be sensible of His presence with you, for it is very reassuring.

I remain your affectionate Uncle,
James MacLeod

P. S. If I sound like 'one of <u>them</u>' ... I am! Don't forget I both survived and administered much the same treatment before you were born! You will, too.

The best antidotes for untimely desire are restraining your imagination, and cold water applied liberally to the affected parts.

Virginia Military Institute
Lexington, Virginia

August 2, 1868

Dear Uncle James,

Your wise counsel is noted and obeyed. There is no longer any danger I shall throw up my education to rush into marriage. She refuses to correspond and her father will have the law on me if I try. <u>Finis. Sic fugit gloria amoris.</u>[22]

MacHugh is doing well as Captain of A company, he's so busy I see him only at nights. Loudoun and Airlie must be having a first-rate time at home, we never hear from them. Bouleau found the best fishing hole in the Nile (Woods Creek), so we have a fish fry sometimes. Carter tells us all the *on dits* from Richmond, and Fokelzank brings friends upon both flanks and the center, too.

I am run as ragged as you said I'd be. You said they'd light down hard if I crossed them, and they do. If I do wrong, I'm wrong, if I do right, I'm wrong, so I'm not going to depend on their opinion. They act like they're the Almighty!

The only sceptre that rules me is kindness. To those who use me so, I am a willing servant. To the others, I am a resentful slave. Kindness is exceeding scarce here, so I am resolved to rule myself. I'm beaten for it betimes, but I gang my ain gait.

I hope you like your new post and fellow officers. I hope your new quarters are comfortable. Barracks is luxurious compared to the frontier. I'm reading Frederick the Great's instructions to his generals. What others do you suggest?

I pray God will bless you and protect you.

---

22 Latin: "It is concluded. Thus flees the glory of love."

Your ragged but respectful Nephew,
Torquil Drummond

I bowed my head onto folded hands and prayed for Uncle James's safety and good health. I thanked God for him and for the opportunity of being a cadet. I worshipped God in my heart. Communion with my Lord calmed my spirit. In that haven of rest, I began to think.

Events and duties had come at me so fast that I'd pushed aside Gunn's inquisition, but now it returned to prey on my soul. Agony, terror, and shame were not memories. They blotted out the present, and I lived them again. They gouged my mind and drove my nightmares. Gunn's conquest had to be reasoned out.

He neither threatened nor cajoled, but only asked his question and somehow bent my will to do his. I'd been mastered. *Nolens volens*[23], I was Gunn's man. My feelings were still contradictory: subjugated and free, sorrowful and joyful, all at once. I couldn't understand any of it.

Subjugation. Freeze like a whipped dog and say, "Yes, sir," act oblivious to humiliation, obey ridiculous or unjust orders—any halfwit could do it. If he didn't, there was punishment. We lived under punishment for everything from a missing button to mutiny. The standard's nothing less than perfection. No excuses accepted if I fell short, by myself least of all.

Sorrow. It's part of my soul. I'll sorrow for my family till I'm dead myself, and for loss of who I was before they were murdered. I miss Uncle James, tenant of Da's place in my heart. Loneliness pierced my heart the night after confinement to quarters. And I mourned whatever within me was destroyed by defeat in the contest with Gunn.

* * *

---

23 Latin: unwilling or willing.

Spending Saturday evenings with my squad mates helped me keep feelings and horrors buried.

Carter was gamely trying to learn the military milieu. He had pleasant address when he chose to use it, and a fund of drawing-room conversation and social knowledge none of the rest of us did. He raised his genteel complaints to the level of a literary form and put up a good-humored front. The yearlings named him "Sunshine."

"I would him to sweep the floor with have used, if he to me that had said!" Vogelsang's English syntax deserted him.

"One learns much by being a poor relation. Never tell men they have bad manners, or any other fault. Make them show it in the presence of others. One does not reply in kind, but awaits a chance to lead them—in all seeming innocence—to discredit themselves."

"A verbal ambush?" I didn't have the guile to premeditate such a stratagem.

They called Bouleau "Dan'l," for Daniel Boone, because of his clothing. Besides the handsomest face among us, he had an earthy sense of humor that pained Carter. Like him, he was a state cadet whose board and tuition were provided by the State of Virginia in return for teaching in a Virginia school for two years after he was graduated. He knew "mountain" as a description meant "backward and inferior." Every veiled or blatant slur found its mark, so, while honoring kinship, he intended to overcome its limitations.

Vogelsang's background was similar to mine, a close-knit society and language, among Germans who emigrated to the Shenandoah Valley about two decades before my sept arrived in Abercairn. He was eager and friendly as a Newfoundland puppy, at seventeen still trying to coordinate his long arms and legs. He liked other people and took it for granted they'd like him. Inevitably, since he was German, he was called "Dutch."

They called me "Sergeant."

CHAPTER 23

A WORD FITLY SPOKEN

Honor traditionally was attached to blood … its shedding assumed a consecrated character. … it also became the warrior's mark of inextinguishable glory.
—Bertram Wyatt-Brown, *The Shaping of Southern Culture*

Torquil

The younger yearlings, fifteen or sixteen years old, campaigned to lower me. Some envied my war record or said I put on airs because of military experience. On guard on the second stoop one night, lugging the heavy old Belgian musket, I stopped, alerted and silent, in the shadow between doors, and saw three of them cross the stoop and tiptoe down the stairs.

"Sirs! Return to your rooms."

"How would you stop us, Rat?" one demanded.

"With the least force needed, sir." I kept my voice soft. "Return to your rooms at once, before I am obliged to report you."

Knowing I was giving them a second chance, because I could have reported them for being out at all, they went.

My beat during my next relief was the first stoop. Taps had called the cadets to slumber half the night ago, but I didn't relax. Escapades occurred at all times of night. Approaching the north end of the stoop, I heard the softened footsteps of three cadets cross the second stoop and descend the stairs. The sound cut off when they went around the corner of the great arch.

I paced to the south end but saw no sign of them. Reversing north, I wondered if they'd pounce from a hiding place or set a trap farther away. Or had they mischief somewhere else? Near the corner, I smelled them. Loud, insistent rustling in the brush to the north showed where they hoped to lure me.

I stopped short of the corner and marched in place. The ruse bore fruit when a head, silhouetted against the night sky, edged around the corner.

When two leaped at me, my daemon rose up for battle. I put it under. Reversing my musket—I know how to kill or avoid killing—I pushed the first one in the midsection with the musket butt only hard enough to set him down. I swung the musket to bar the other's advance before he could develop his attack.

"Corporal of the Guard! Post Number Two!"

Leaving them for the corporal to take care of, I advanced.

"Come out of there, Mister!"

He stepped into the starlight and raised his hands.

"Oh, don't ... please don't club me, Mister Sergeant Rat!" he mocked.

Next day after dinner, they retaliated. All Barracks gathered. A Rat can't be allowed success in defending his post.

"Stand at attention, Rat!" ordered Croft.

"Did you think the Yankees were fixing to burn Barracks again last night?" Tanner wasn't laughing.

"Was it Indians!" Helms accused me.

"No, sir."

"Then why did you proceed like it was?"

"The honor of a sentry's duty must be upheld, sir."

"Thus speaks the real soldier!" jeered Tanner.

"Are you a *real* soldier ... 'Sergeant'?" smirked Croft.

"Of course he's a real soldier!" Helms exclaimed. "Didn't he make an heroic defense of Barracks? Didn't he withstand foes who outnumbered him three to one?" He struck the pose of a dramatic orator. "Single handed, armed with only an outmoded, unloaded weapon, he swept all before him ... three unarmed men!

"The hero! The scarred veteran of many hard-won victories—"

The jibe was also at beloved ones who'd died. In dead cold level voice, I misquoted.

"He jests at scars ... who never felt a wound!"

I stepped hard at him.

"We defended your home and your weak, miserable life."

Another step. My command glare and menace kept him rooted in his tracks. If he hit me, he'd get demerit—and my fists. If he ran, he'd be a laughingstock.

"Some of us fell, some were wounded—for what? So a baby can play nonsense and mock at soldiers? No"—I looked him up and down with contempt and sneered as an afterthought—"sir."

"That's sufficient, Mister Drummond. Come with me."

Did Gunn ever raise his voice?

Gunn

I hadn't fought the Yankees down the Valley and back up again to have my service mocked, either. A Rat being right was never to be acknowledged, but Helms ridiculed the sacrifices made by Virginia's defenders, including the V.M.I. cadets who died in battle.

> A word fitly spoken is like apples of gold in pictures of silver.
> —Proverbs 25:11

Torquil

What punishment this time? Gunn didn't sit down nor call me to attention.

"There's a fine balance to be struck between merit recognized at the V.M.I. and elsewhere. When I started, the old cadets were veterans. I received much the same treatment as you, but at the hands of those who fought for Virginia.

"Boys are now enrolled who haven't been to war. Their souls have not been tried. You must not only tolerate your lot as a Rat, but also forbear their ignorance and callowness. Next year, your distinctions will exceed theirs, and you will be their superior.

"I won't be here a year from now. Lieutenant, I'm proud to know you."

He held out his hand. Mute with astonishment, I grasped it.

"Call upon me if I may serve you in any way."

I'm sure he knew I'd never admit the need, but his offer was genuine.

"You have my service, sir."

* * *

It was good. It was inexpressibly good. The only approbation I'd received from a superior sent me back to duty vindicated. Gunn upheld the requirements, but he'd acknowledged our soldiers' brotherhood. I understood now: his interrogation was meant to clear my name. Jenner and Whitesmith wouldn't have apologized without knowing the truth.

A barrier I still didn't understand was removed. I was free to pursue the course of obedience and duty I'd intended from the first. Without sacrificing honor, I could embrace regulations and custom rather than have to defy them to keep my self-respect.

Freedom and joy returned in a warm wave to refresh my soul.

Freedom was more than mere relief that Gunn's inquisition was resolved. He'd conquered me, and I'd yielded, but he hadn't humiliated me. Neither had he degraded me, nor assailed my self-respect. Instead, worth, respect and dignity were now affirmed.

In war, I'd trusted my superiors to make decisions that might cost my life. Uncle James's matchsticks and his maxim that all members of the army depend upon one another showed also that all the members of the corps were to do the same. In subordination, I had freedom to depend upon my superiors. I resolved they could depend upon me. I could use and test this paradoxical new freedom, and use my will after all, for the good of the corps and the men in it. With freedom came responsibility to act for the welfare of both.

When Gunn conquered me in the contest of wills, I thought I'd lost what my life depended on. Now I understood what I'd gained. By yielding, I'd given myself to something that transcends me. Except in obeying the laws governing kirk, public, and military life, I'd never submitted myself to others outside my family. I'd walked alone since they were murdered. But now I was catapulted into a crucible where I was being founded in a new mold with other men. That explained the joy.

It lay in belonging—the antidote for loneliness. I and the other cadets were members of a single larger unity. The new creature had the traits of no single one of its elements, but a nature of its own that overarched them all. Its ideals of honor and truth were like my boyhood home. I hadn't till now made the connection between my longing and this present means of fulfillment. I hoped I'd have permanent bonds, intimate bonds, dearer bonds to treasure in the future, but, for now, through giving myself to the corps, my longing was eased.

I thanked God. My heart was changed. From now on, Gunn was not only my master, but my model. He'd invited me into the corps so I could give it my best, with will and heart together.

I drew upon the inner sufficiency gained during my first months at Camp Sherman, and responded with the respect O'Shea preached. An identical training ordeal had helped make Uncle James the man I honored. I hoped it would do the same for me. I yearned to become again who I was before Sharpsburg.

MacLeod

Fort Liberty
Wyoming Territory
August 19, 1868

My Dear Nephew,

We are mostly settled. I have two generously sized rooms in the bachelor officers' quarters, with kitchen across the passage. Porter and his family are in married quarters northwest of the parade, the men in barracks along another side. Rush has joined the young blades who share the rooms below mine. They're a jolly set, if noise signifies it.

My duties include the artillery again (we have eight guns) and oversight of M and K companies while Major Jennings is on leave of absence. No more rank, no more pay, only more work; but the post is short of officers. One is on recruiting duty, another on sick leave, others on detached duty, &c., so we who are present must get the work done and satisfy Division, Department, &c.

Nevertheless, Dr. Barnes and I have made a few excursions as naturalists, studying the flora, geology, and fauna of our surroundings. We intend to submit a descriptive report to the American Association for the Advancement of Science soon. I shall in a later essay ascend to interpret the factors of elevation, ground water, prevailing winds, soils, and how all was created. It is a pleasure thus to be engaged in science again. Previous explorations, mapmaking, and interpreting the findings have kept my appetite whetted for such things.

I'm pleased that you've been avoiding demerit so well. I trust you have by now reversed yourself in the matter of 'ganging your ain gait.' In a military milieu, that usually means, 'out of step.' As far as you are concerned, the yearlings are almighty. They are your superiors, worthy or not.

Men respond or react to authority, I've found, in one of four ways. Some obey it, others rebel against it, some avoid it by removing themselves from its jurisdiction, while others become it. When one becomes authority, comes the greatest duty: giving up of self to serve others.

The discipline of the corps is one of unyielding rigor. They're testing your strength and ability to endure. They assay your metal, my lad, to see what dross must be burnt away and what gold must be polished. Bear it patiently, for the good it will do you. By both processes, you will be refined.

My prayers for you have not ceased, nor will they. I pray God to protect you from all harm, and guide you, and solace your heart in this lengthy testing.

> I remain your affectionate Uncle,
> James MacLeod

P.S. After Frederick the Great, try von Clausewitz, <u>On War</u>. Your French won't yet be up to his, but you can puzzle it out. Then see what Napoleon himself can tell you.

* * *

Fort Liberty
Wyoming Territory
August 25, 1868

Dearest Elizabeth,

Now that my son seems to be making his way well enough at the V.M.I., I feel at liberty to pursue a matter even closer to the core of my heart. I hope you have noticed that my affection for you has increased and continues to grow. You speak (write!) my thoughts sometimes before I know them myself. You share intuitions suited more perfectly to the purpose at hand than I, though I labored long, could have generated.

Your steadfast trust in our Lord reinforces mine and prevents me from asking Him how some matters could possibly be part of His will. He continues to exercise me in Proverbs 3, verses 6 and 7: "Trust in the Lord with all thine heart; and lean not unto thine own understanding. In all thy ways acknowledge Him, and He shall direct thy paths."

But has He directed our paths so far apart forever? I long to have your lovely presence in <u>my</u> presence!

Yes, I am asking you to marry me! I love you as I never dreamed I could love a woman. Your spirit and image ever rise before me, and I think how much more blessed I would be if you were with me.

But would you be likewise blessed? Could you--would you--consider it? I mean exactly what I say here: consider. Consider leaving your family and home to be with me alone. Consider the distance--about 1,600 miles--that would lie between you and the many friends you love. Consider the hardships of frontier life, especially in such a severe climate as this, when you are accustomed to the gentler airs and temperatures of Virginia. Consider the difficulty of material supply: weeks or months pass between ordering and receiving goods, and then they may be lost or damaged en route. Consider the strictures of garrison life, where travel and outings may be forbidden because of hostile threat, and ladies' rank among themselves follows strictly the comparative rank of their husbands. Consider that I might fall in battle and leave you widowed at any time--not only widowed but homeless, since *Regulations* requires the dead officer's quarters to be vacated very shortly. Least of all do I mean to discourage you, but these are the genuine conditions of the life I offer you. Consider whether being with me is what is best for you. Consider whether gratifying the desire of my heart is too great a sacrifice for you to make.

I offer these points in my favor: my heart is single and steadfast toward you. I have sufficient financial resources beyond my Army pay to provide for all our wants and many of our wishes, with some to establish in life the children I hope God will give us. I am in the best of health and strength to protect you, and come of a family blessed with long life. I have prayed long and earnestly before proposing marriage and trust that it falls within the will of God.

I do not expect, nor desire, an immediate decision. Such a revolution in your life must call for continued prayer and thought.

Whatever your decision, know that I will always love you. With prayers for God's blessing and best provision for your welfare, I remain,

Your faithful and obedient servant,
James MacLeod

He that is slow to anger is better than the mighty; and
he that ruleth his spirit than he that taketh a city.
—Proverbs 16:32

Torquil

I took fresh heart from Uncle James's counsel. I was beginning
to understand how his self-control was built. It isn't the taciturn
withdrawal I practice myself. Rather, it's full reception and eval-
uation of the matter at hand and making disciplined, judicious
response to it. Stoic.

My cynical humor returned: the yearlings were like children playing. I rated their harshest rants as less disturbing than
O'Shea at his mildest and felt amused while keeping my face a
blank. But, joined with the corps now, it was my duty to support them, and help make them into the worthy leaders Virginia
needs. They're as responsible for their subordinates' performance
of duty as I'd been. Superior in age and experience, I could be
generous enough to save their pride. They weren't willing to
learn military discipline from me, but I could exemplify it and
let them observe.

Like when I took command of the Rangers, I stepped as from
one room into another. I could not only use my will, but take the
initiative. I could save myself the confusion of having to respond
before I was ready, and have advantage in competition among
men. I didn't know I'd need more diplomacy than I yet possessed.

As August waned, we all hoped to be transferred from squad
to company drill, but Vogelsang was too stiff, Carter too languid
in marching. Near the end of drill one evening, Corporal Saxton's
temper was unraveling. He called us to attention.

"Mister Carter, you not only look like a baby, sir, you march
like its rag doll! Put some vigor in your motion!"

I lifted my knee and scratched it.

"Show you're a soldier, Mister Drummond! We've heard so much about it!"

I gave him an insolent stare and slowly raised an eyebrow. He stamped up to me. Nose to nose, he lost his temper completely.

"You disobeyed the first thing you ever learned, sir! You act like a buckskin scratching fleas! You haven't the smallest idea of your duty, sir!"

The drum began for evening parade. I spoke so softly that only he could hear me.

"Iron sharpens iron, Mister Saxton."

* * *

"This is not the way I expected to prepare for service to Virginia!" Carter's face crumpled with discouragement as we broke ranks.

"Aaah, 'Sunshine', yew're cloudin' over!" Bouleau nudged him with his elbow.

"I am *not*!"

"Ach, der Corporal expects perfection angels could not make!"

I stalked along silently. I didn't regret drawing Saxton's tirade away from Carter, but I shouldn't have admonished a superior. I deserve whatever report he writes. We gathered in my room.

"What does he mean, marching like a rag doll?" Carter slumped into a chair.

"Movements not energetic enough," I summed it.

"A gentleman does not move *abruptly*, but smoothly."

"He kin do both," said Bouleau. "Before the end o' one step, yew start coiling fer the next 'un."

"Ach, if so I do, I hit some body, *als*—thus—I draw back."

"Use your joints for springs," I said.

Vogelsang and Carter looked at us like a blank.

"We'll show yew," Bouleau promised.

We started that night.

* * *

Determined to locate food to forage, I spoke of reconnaissance after dinner on Saturday.

"It don't hurt to know the ground." Bouleau turned with me toward the woods. Carter and Vogelsang, Althouse and Whitesmith came along.

"At home, police duty would be servants' work," Althouse grumbled.

"Not only such menial tasks, but they want us to amuse them," fussed Carter.

"They demand of me animal noises," Vogelsang related. "A glad audience they were till I made the voice of the slaughtered swine!"

"McIlwaine shouted right in my face, 'Mister Rat, are you listening?'" I picked up a stick and practiced sabre drill with it. "I said 'Yes, sir,' and he asked what he just said. So I looked sober and quoted his exact words but made it sound like he meant himself: 'You said, sir, you march with all the agility of a hippopotamus!'"

"It's a wonder you didn't burst right then," said Whitesmith.

"I'm not such a fool, but they think I'm a buckskin."

"No …" Carter delivered his judgment like it was tentative. "A Scots Othello, perhaps … 'little blessed with the soft phrase of peace.'"

"There's no use for it."

"There will be. A … protector … must not seem forthright, but keep power *sheathed* under suave discourse, for better advantage over adversaries when occasion arises. Though one's thoughts be of the most *sanguinary*, one's words remain bland."

"It's different in the army."

440

"Only in the ranks. You hope to be an officer, I presume. They're *polished*."

"I reckon I have a lot to learn."

Carter took it as permission to instruct.

"The customs of social intercourse among gentlemen are universal. One does not go about seeking … *combat* … but rather, with the intent to please others in company, and the hope of being pleased."

I hadn't realized till he spoke it plainly, my entire stance and outlook were antagonistic. The idea of pleasing others rather than expecting them to attack me hadn't occurred.

"When will the hickory nuts be ready?" I asked Whitesmith.

"Middle of October or a little later."

"I want to collect a store of them if no one beats us to it."

"It's not allowed," said Althouse. "But it can be done. I heard some of them talking about hiding things in clothes bags."

Where I'd cached my medical kit and whiskey, I didn't have to disappear far to retrieve them.

"Air we huntin' food?" asked Bouleau.

"Yes!"

"We can pick fruit at my uncle's," Whitesmith offered.

"Iffen we kin git meat, too, we kin make a mess o' pemmican."

"*Why*?" Carter's lip curled with distaste.

"It keeps yew warm in the winter."

"MacHugh says, in Barracks we'll need to. It's sort of like mincemeat," I told Carter.

"Yew kin keep the fire goin'," Bouleau told him.

"Why?"

"No time to dry the meat, no other road."

* * *

MacLeod

Virginia Military Institute
Lexington, Virginia
September 10, 1868

Dear Uncle James,

I hope this letter finds you well, as it leaves me. I feel very healthy, though I've never been sole-ly on foot for so many days in a row in my life. Regular recitations began yesterday. The fourth class has Mathematics, English Language, Latin, French, and Drawing. Drill at four and a half, then Parade, supper, and Study Hours till Tattoo.

Airlie was made Orderly Sergeant. He & Loudoun are back, gullet-full of news and brought letters for us all. Most of the crops are made now, and it looks like everyone will have enough till next year. Kendricks are well. K. passed the Bar last Court Day and has had one conveyance and one case to plead in Court, and Mrs. K. is with child. Airlie thinks Miss Gilchrist has a beau, though no one has ever seen him. Loudoun demands his evidence, and Airlie can only say she looks too happy.

I smiled to myself. Does she favor my proposal of marriage? I returned my attention to my son's letter, to assess his progress and identify what counsel he may need.

Mrs. Grieg sent a box of good things to eat, so we had a feast. I don't mind being a boy sometimes if that's the result! But that's how I'm treated here, and it's very strange. In fact, everything seems strange. Home isn't home any more. It's military here, but not real military—no fighting to do.

My heart has changed regarding corps discipline. I'm not fighting them anymore. But I spoke out of turn to our drillmaster. I deserved a worse report than he wrote, but I feel bad for doing it and wonder if I <u>can</u> do things right. I really want to, but something about me won't let me. And I'm still not who I am, or who I once was. All I know is that's who I want to be, like you and Da.

My smile faded. I thought he'd conquered his contrary behavior.

If you don't count the yearlings, most of the old cadets are gentlemen just like in Abercairn. Some of them drink and swear, and one was dismissed yesterday for "grossly improper conduct," but mostly their conduct and character are as good as at home. The professors and officers all are, of course.

Some of my courses will be hard, and I've forgot a lot of my Latin. I'm going to keep up with the work every day, as you told me.

I pray God will keep you safe and lead you to honor in the field.

Your obedient servant and respectful Nephew,
Torquil Drummond

Wyoming Territory
September 21, 1868

My Dear Nephew,

Thank you for your prayers. I'm sure God hears them, for He has kept me from harm through a series of fights with the hostiles. They're attacking the railroad and near-by region. We're establishing Forts Fetterman and Sanders, west of here, to protect the line and its construction. Captain Parnell's company at the head of construction has suffered most.

I trust you have an idea of your class standings, by what sections you are in. I look forward to hearing you stand well, in spite of the gap in your schooling. It pleases me that your stance toward your superiors has improved. You will be known by the opinions they are forming now.

Feeling that much is strange in your situation and in your own being is the natural effect of many causes. First, your particular situation is intentionally made difficult to enter, as a test of character, which I believe you have passed. You are not the same boy you were, nor need you expect to be. You have gained understanding through grief and pain and hardship. Your Christian faith has been tried by fire, and brought to a higher level. You have experience of war, command, and earning your own living. You will combine all of these elements in the man you are becoming. He will not be the boy you were. Innocence must be replaced by tried virtue as we mature.

You are building the foundation now, upon which your future is based.

That it may be solid, and of lifetime service to you, is the prayer of

> Your obedient servant and Uncle,
> James Macleod

> Lexington, Virginia
> October 4, 1868

Dear Uncle James,

At last the corps have muskets! I don't know how General Smith arranged it with the Yankees. They are Austrian muskets and some heavier than the Spencers and Henrys. They make us leave our own guns with the Ordnance Sergeant except for Saturday evenings. My friends and I have shot enough partridge and squirrel to make several messes of pemmican. We made a burying hole in the woods (within limits) where it looks like everything is keeping all right. We want to have enough to eat to keep us warm in the winter.

General Smith remitted all the reports against us from July through Sept. 10, so all the trouble I got into before I learned how to act here isn't going to mar my record.

I'm doing all right in recitations, but I feel ignorant as a Hottentot. There's so much to know! How to learn is like a subject in itself. It's like another war. It seems strange to be fighting without weapons except my mind. I'm in the second section in everything, but in Latin I stand first, so I have to be section marcher and responsible for all disorder while marching and in the recitation room, and report misconduct.

Last Sunday General Smith resumed Bible recitations. The 4th class recite to Col. Preston at 8 ½ A.M. We start with a hymn, then he prays and reads a portion of Scripture and talks about how to apply it, and closes with a benediction. Later we march to town, alternating churches by company once a month.

In four days I shall be twenty-one. I have been pondering it. Under ordinary circumstances, I'd be old enough to vote and conduct my own affairs. As it is, I'm disenfranchised even if I'd been here for the registration last year. The proposed Radical constitution allows the freedmen to vote, but not the citizens who defended our State. It was scheduled for a vote in June, ultimo, but Genl. Schofield cancelled the election, and no one knows when it will take place. Since then, Gov. Wells (a military appointee) vacated all the State, county, & municipal offices & replaced the officials with carpetbaggers & scalawags. They try to extort money and property from the citizens, under threat of confiscation of all our property if we don't bow down to them. Mister Ogilvie and Captain Murray and Judge C. and the real county leaders plan ways to circumvent all this robbery and injustice, and so far everyone has survived with holdings intact. The strategy is, not getting indebted to any of them, and putting up with their arrogance and demands with the best courtesy possible. Land isn't worth much now, and taxes are ruinous.

So I can't vote and I don't control my own. It's like I've taken a step backwards in life. I'd try to set some marks to aim at, but I'm called to protect, as a soldier, that's all I know.

> Your obedient servant and Nephew,
> Torquil Drummond

> Fort Liberty, W. T.
> October 18, 1868

My Dear Nephew,

I am much gratified by your quarterly report dated October 1st, which describes your general merit, habits, conduct, and health as 'good.' That you stand in the top quarter of your class in all your courses pleases me greatly. I was glad to be able to quote the report to Col. Hale when he inquired about your progress.

Fighting a "war" with no weapons except one's mind is mostly what officers have to do. You refer to a soldier's life being ordained as though your calling leaves you no choices. Trusting you will one day be commissioned, the question is: what kind of soldier will you be? Too cautious or too rash, a martinet or too slack, erratic or too predictable, or maintain a balance between these extremes? Will your outlook and understanding be broad or narrow?

Do you think you are concentrating too narrowly on military topics, to the exclusion of the broader range of knowledge there available to you? In the past you benefitted by reading a range of topics. Does time permit, to interest yourself in other disciplines? I think especially of history and philosophy, music, the fine arts, and literature, which enrich the content of your mind, and, especially if you are stationed on the frontier, provide a source of pleasure for off-duty hours and matter for conversation and discussion with your associates.

With prayer for your well being and God's wisdom for your decisions, I remain,

> Your obedient servant and Uncle,
> James MacLeod

> Lexington, Virginia
> October 25, 1868

Dear Uncle James,

It's beginning to be cold in Barracks. My roommates say it will get a lot worse. We're not allowed to wear our overcoats in our rooms, and they were allowed outdoors only as of the first inst. I don't want to waste money on a studying coat. I'm saving up to buy a cane with an ivory head, it's taking a long time. General Smith published orders last week that were a lecture on practicing economy. He said it's not only a virtue but a duty. I reckon in these times, he's right. He doesn't let us have but a little bit for pocket money, that's why it's taking so long for the cane.

Loudoun's staying at the head of his class. MacHugh is courting Miss MacPherson, but he keeps the rest of his mind on his captaincy and does it well. Airlie thinks he'll become a doctor because he already has a start, so he's most interested in Chemistry and Physiology. He knows more about how the parts of the body work than I knew there were parts. We didn't learn half what

Dr. Gask could have taught us. Some of the cadets must not study, by how they do in recitations. One was severely denounced in Orders for using a book during recitation to gain unfair advantage, violating honor as well as the Regulations & what's right.

In Drawing we're doing topography with colored inks. I like it, and it's useful for the Army. I'm sinking into sloth about command because my superiors take the responsibility while I only follow. I miss leading my squad. But I like learning, there's so much to know. English Language demands a standard I haven't had to meet for a long time. Our professor says, choosing precise words sharpens thinking as much as the logic that calls for their use.

We have excellent professors. Col. Brooke who invented the Brooke gun, for Physics, Col. Williamson was Chief Engineer for the Army of Northern Virginia, Col. Maury who mapped the oceans and was decorated by the crowned heads of Europe, and Genl Custis Lee (General Robert E. Lee's son) for Engineering and Mechanics.

I've got to study now. I have to work hard to keep a leg up on French.

> Your servant and respectful nephew,
> Torquil Drummond

> Fort Liberty, W.T.
> November 18, 1868

My Dear Nephew,

"Sinking into sloth," compared to the responsibilities of command, and having "taken a step backward in life" may be considered an interval during which you can consolidate your strength. Your boyhood was given to war, when, from necessity, you performed a man's duties. Your present situation could be seen as an opportunity to apprehend what you then missed of freedom from care. Subordination is indeed galling, but it is also a shield behind which you are not required to carry the full burden of manhood's obligations. They will come to you soon enough. You are now being prepared to undertake them. ...

Virginia Military Institute
December 5, 1868

Dear Uncle James,

I hope and pray you're in health at home and victorious in the field. I am well and have fattened about seven pounds since I came here. The steam heating system in Barracks doesn't do much. We all wrote home for extra blankets, which we keep folded out of sight in our bedding, and at night we make a sort of tent and huddle together in it. The pemmican we made helps more. We take turns going to the burying hole and bringing some back for us all every night. I warm my share over the lamp, and Loudoun fusses about the mess and makes dire predictions what will happen if I get caught with food.

He sometimes has to explain the Math to me. He says he does it so I won't shame Abercairn. He's so smart he and his friends trade Math problems, like a debate with numbers instead of words. He sent the enclosed problem for your amusement. I'm sending a drawing that <u>wasn't</u> made in the Drawing Academy. I'm in the first section in Drawing, Latin, & Eng. Lge and second in Math and French.

I grinned at the cartoon of my son juggling artillery shells with fuses burning, each bearing the name of a course or duty, including one labeled "French" about to fall on his head.

The new Virginia constitution must be harsh enough to satisfy the Radicals and their war on us, because so far there's been no howl against it in the House of Representatives. Old hateful Stevens died last August, and I hope some of the hate died with him. Perhaps his gang in Congress will back down some without him to spur them. There's still no telling when Virginia will be a State (other than in her sons' hearts) again.

Rumor says the mess hall will be done by Christmas, and we'll get a special dinner that day. I hope so! The pemmican is lasting well, but it tastes the same and the same and the same. It helps keep us warm. General Smith allowed us to have winter vests made, at last, and that helps, too. I didn't know there'd be ice skating, but I wrote asking Mrs. Greig to send my skates. She did, with a box of food and woolen shirts & drawers. They all take good care of me, at home. The farm did well this year.

I pray every time I think of you, and that's often. God bless and guard you, and keep you in good health. Write soon, I miss you.

>With a son's gratitude and affection,
>Torquil Drummond

P. S. I hope you have a happy Christmas.

I had the happiest Christmas since before the War. I don't know if, or how, she calculated the time, but her answer arrived on Christmas Eve. She'd never questioned my love or sincerity, but, over time, only inquired about pertinent aspects of the life she might lead as my wife. I couldn't always give her comfortable answers.

Abercairn Court House, Virginia

December 10, 1868

Darling James,

Without further ado: Yes!

I also long to share all the days of life, together rather than separated. I have considered at greater length, perhaps, than your endearing ardor would have desired, and make no excuse. One does not enter such a sacred covenant lightly.

I do think, having come to the decision, that we should not wait too long to become one in God's sight. Desiring a family of our own as much as you do is the reason, since women's reproductive years are limited. Though I hope to bring up all our children to maturity, they are so vulnerable in infancy and childhood that we must make allowance for possible tragic loss.

I couldn't read another word! But even while jumping up and dancing a delirious jig for sheer happiness, I hoped the bachelors in the quarters below would think I was chasing a rodent!

Torquil

Virginia Military Institute
January 14, 1869

Dear Uncle James,

Examinations are over and we have suspension till the second half of the term begins. We don't have to be back to Barracks till Tattoo. I feel a lot better now than I did this time yesterday, waiting to be examined. I went in to Math so scared I wasn't worth shooting, because of all the dire warnings Airlie stuffed me with, and there were all the professors and subs sitting in a row, with Old Spex in the middle. He's imposing enough when he's being friendly like he was when I reported, but when I knew he was my judge, looking right into my soul with eyes like ice, all the starch went out of me and I don't know what all along with it, besides my mind. But I plucked up after a while and hope I didn't disgrace you. All the questions seemed easy.

This evening some of us went skating on North River. We played 'tag' and had races. Upstream didn't seem like uphill, I wonder why because water flows downhill. A lot of citizens come out to skate, ladies among them. My friends introduced me to some, and one of the families invited us to supper. It was lots better than the suppers they give us here. We've been drawing heavy on our pemmican, but I think there's enough to get us through the worst of the cold. It's my turn to go fetch it tonight.

Pres. Johnson issued another amnesty proclamation on Christmas, that includes General Lee and leaves only a few still condemned. Maybe I'll be able to vote after all, if they ever allow us to hold an election. I wonder if it allows me to hold a commission?

Continued January 15. Loudoun's uncle's family have company for the season from Old Christmas, including Loudoun's family and two young ladies from Abercairn. He and MacHugh, with their fine records here, can get permission for visiting in private families, and they somehow get it for the rest of us.

The two Mr. Loudouns got up a sleighing party. It snowed all the time, so we were busy keeping the girls from getting wet and taking a chill. There were Misses Nannie MacHugh and Kate Airlie, Loudoun's sisters Lydia and Elspeth, and his cousin Ellie. I only saw the Abercairn girls once at kirk since before the war, and they are much improved. Miss Ellie didn't seem to mind when I wrapped a buffalo robe close around us to keep off the snow and cold. The girls were all talking like it was a race to say everything. There will be a great removal around the County soon, if all the marriages they predict really occur. The Murrays are all well and their farm doing better. The dinner was the best I've had since I got here, and there was dancing afterward.

Recitations begin again tomorrow. I am studying all the same subjects, except Geography instead of English, and Trigonometry and Descriptive Geometry in Math. They have given out the assignments, so I expect I ought to study.

I pray God to bless you and protect you. With filial affection, I remain,

Your obedient servant and respectful Nephew,
Torquil Drummond

Probationary status became full cadetship when I passed my examinations. I stayed in the second section of all my classes—first sometimes in Geography—and Loudoun scolded like he always does when I fell to third section in Trigonometry. I was scrambling to memorize theorems, so when he wound down, I asked him to explain it. It was like opening floodgates, but days later, when I finally understood, I liked working out the solutions, and thought how useful Trig would be for gunnery.

Most Saturday evenings, I went a-visiting. With introductions, my acquaintance broadened, but the chasm between me and others made society difficult. Only Miss Ellie bothered to draw me out: I made more conversation than I was used to, and built a stock of responses I could draw upon in company.

I told my room-mates I was only reconnoitering, since I couldn't dream of marrying till I was commissioned. They hooted, it was just an excuse for flirting. They were right! Dancing at some of the houses was for the families' enjoyment, like it was at home. The young ladies taught me new steps and dances. Wild surprise! They were soft! Knowing before, only my own taut body, solid horseflesh, and men's hard handclasps or combat, brought sensual explosions, close to them in the waltz! I burned with desire! Now I knew what Smith was talking about. But I'm too good a hunter to rush my fences—let alone frighten the quarry.

MacLeod

Fort Liberty
Wyoming Territory
April 7, 1869

Dearest Elizabeth,

I write sadly of another necessity to wait upon the Lord, until we can delight in the culmination of our desires. Due to increased hostile activity and threat of more in the region, my request for leave has been denied. We are too short of officers present for duty, for any more to be absent, and the summer campaign season is close upon us.

I long more than ever to be joined with you. My trust in God's timing is being severely tried. ...

Abercairn Court House
Virginia
April 19, 1869

Darling James,

My poor dearest one! In such severe conditions, doing such hard duty—and never shirking it!—with so little relief, and now denied the solace of your heart we both desire so much! Do you think perhaps by autumn you might be free to journey to claim your bride?

Torquil

We looked ahead to the festivities of Graduating Day and hoped for promotion. I invited Miss Ellie to the Graduating Ball because she's the prettiest. She's a dark beauty, with delicate features and the same black hair and deep brown eyes as the other Loudouns, set off by the fairest skin. She accepted.

Aidan's family were coming to his graduation and bringing Miss Mary Murray and Miss Mairi Dunnachie, the piper's daughter. We had the privilege of selecting the girls' escorts. Airlie blushed scarlet and claimed Mairi for himself. We chose Loudoun's scholarly rival, Lanier, to match minds with Aidan's studious sister, Miss Amelia.

Nannie's the feminine image of her twin. She's too tall for a girl, as freckled as Aidan, and has the same red hair and rich blue eyes. Lively and confident rather than gentle and self-effacing, heart made happiest by others' happiness—there's no one like her. We chose sensible, unassuming Thibault. I asserted my right to choose Miss Mary's escort. The little girl I'd seen last was much too young to attend a ball! No one could give her the brotherly protection I would, but cheerful, friendly Vogelsang would take good care of her. I asked him immediately. He agreed.

* * *

The examinations being so near at hand, the Superintendent hopes that the cadets will see at once their duty, as well as his own in restraining at this time absences from the Institute for the purpose of visiting their friends. Let the intervening time be earnestly spent in preparation for the Examination, that the Superintendent may be enabled to give to the Board of Visitors and to the distinguished gentlemen invited by them to attend the examination as flattering an exhibition of their proficiency as possible.

He feels sure that the soldierly bearing and general tone of gentlemanly conduct which have so justly merited the encomium of all will be no less conspicuous at this time than at the last examination.

—VMI Order Book, June 12, 1869. VMI Archives

"He said the same last year," Loudoun remembered.

"And the year before," said Aidan Beag, "in the same words. It's as good as a calendar!"

"Now I think of it, we know it's spring when he publishes the one about not bathing in view of the public roads." Airlie grinned.

When the new Rats began to arrive, I was one of the first turned out as lance corporal to drill them. None of my four had a beard yet. Two were scuffling with each other, and one blew his nose. I raised my voice only enough to give it authority.

"Form in line facing me! Answer, 'Here, sir!' when your name is called!"

They made a straggling line. I shook my head in disbelief. They goggled at me. The fourth hurried up and stood.

"Eyes front! That is, look forward and fix your gaze upon the ground fifteen paces in front of you."

They looked in whatever direction they happened to be facing. One grinned, made sure I saw him, and lifted his eyes toward the sky.

"Mister Rat! Kneel and bury your nose in the grass!"

He obeyed, but he took a mouthful of grass and mooed. I ignored him. His squad mates named him "Bossie" then and there, and everyone took it up.

"When your name is called, answer, 'Here, sir!' I marked each with my command gaze.

"Callend! Helms, G.! Kilgore! Springer!"

"Here, sir!" was muffled by grass.

"Take the Position of a Soldier at attention!"

Springer jumped up.

"Mister Springer, I did not order you to rise! Resume your previous position!" My voice was cold and low.

Springer looked surprised, but he obeyed. I described Attention and enacted each part of it. Springer tried to watch out of the corner of his eye.

Using my ivory headed cane as a baton of office, I kept a stern expression and military demeanor that overawed the youngsters. I explained in level, matter-of-fact tones till they all understood and could begin to perform. They'd learn subordination and respect because of me, not in spite of me! Only kindness rules me, but it could come later, as I learned what treatment each would need. Helms, G. looked sulky and Springer amused, Callend affronted, and little Kilgore looked plain frightened.

* * *

"Whose case do we still have to take care of?" Carter asked after dinner. "What about the one who got here late this morning?"

"Kilgore. Vogelsang and I attended to him. Brave little lad. He was so scared he almost cried, but he wouldn't take any shortening of his name. Did you see him strut when he came to dinner!" I half-smiled. "He'll do all right."

"That's more than can be said for some of them. I heard one telling his friends that if anyone was rude to him—rude!—he'll get his father to interfere and make it hot for him."

"Whoever bucked him will be 'in danger of the judgment,' I expect!"

Mrs. Aidan Mor MacHugh

Aidan Mor and I reserved a parlor at the hotel and ordered a supper. Besides honoring Aidan Beag's graduation, I intend the Abercairn girls to meet their escorts less formally, and under my eye. I'd invited the other boys and girls, and the MacPhersons, of course. Smiling to myself as I set the place cards, I kept the girls apart from their escorts. Not only would they make new acquaintances, but, after supper was cleared away, I'd have the fun of seeing who gravitated toward whom. With ideas for the future and anticipation of their surprise—both have grown so much!—I placed Mary and Torquil side by side.

Miss Mary

Mr. Vogelsang clicked his heels as he bowed in German style over my hand. With the grace Mama taught me, I returned his greeting, and gave like courtesy to all. I was bemused by the sway of ladies' skirts eddying about the columnar full dress of gentlemen, like wavelets rippling among bridge piers.

The pattern parted. I was face-to-face with Torquil Dhu! Broad shouldered and straight, with a new scar on his face, but less sun-scorched than a year ago, he was handsomer in his dress uniform than I'd ever seen him. His eyes glowed when he looked at me.

Torquil

I was dumbstruck! Ewen's sister, my little neighbor, out of short skirts and wearing a long dress! Her hair was up except for one sweet curl that lay along her white neck. Slender as her mother's, her form had blossomed into a young woman's.

"Miss Mary."

My voice felt thick. My heart beat faster. Never taking my eyes off hers, I took her hand and bowed over it, just brushing it with my lips.

"I'm happy to see you." She smiled.

I laid her hand tenderly in the crook of my arm like it belonged to me. She didn't question my guardianship. She looked up into my face.

"I hope Uncle James is well."

It's like her to be concerned about others. Endearing and familiar, it eased my disquiet.

Mrs. MacHugh

It's droll to see who has to make eyes at whom from a distance! Torquil had recovered his voice and was talking with Mary as if they had everything on earth to tell each other. David, teasing my Amelia, never missed a glance from Mairi. Mr. Vogelsang and my Nannie shared quiet laughter and lively conversation. For the engagement they'd announce, I'd placed Miss MacPherson next to Aidan Beag. Their adjoining hands disappeared beneath the damask tablecloth.

Torquil

Miss Mary's prettiness and daintiness bemused me. She smelled sweeter than the flowers pinned to her gown. It revealed less of her shoulders than the older girls' did, but I was seized with urgent desire to shield her from every man's gaze but mine. This new-fledged young lady wasn't the little girl I'd always known, and yet, I felt like I'd talked with her only yesterday instead of a year ago. Affection welled up. It's *brotherly*.

Miss Ellie Loudoun

I've no especial *tendresse* for Mr. Drummond, but I take a woman's pride in having brought him from awkwardness to at least minimal competence in society. I was smiling at the impression he was making on his little friend when I was interrupted by a voice at my side.

"Ma'am? Could you tell me your name again, please?"

I looked up into the earnest gaze of the big, solid, gray-eyed cadet. I appreciated his humble honesty but was miffed that he hadn't remembered. I'll make sure he doesn't forget again! I'm not vain, but neither do I ignore the evidence of my looking-glass! I kept my little smile and turned a deep gaze upon him, but showed my displeasure with a long pause before I spoke.

"I'm Miss Loudoun, Donald's cousin, Mr. Thibault. I hear you will be graduated tomorrow."

"Yes, ma'am."

He should have responded … more! After a few seconds, I bridged the hiatus.

"I suppose you'll have some time with your family before you take up your occupation."

"Yes, ma'am."

I forbore a sigh and forged ahead. It must be my fate to enliven the silent ones! I stretched etiquette to ask a direct question.

"Where do they live?"

"Rockingham." His expression brightened. "Our farm's almost under the Massanutten."

"I hope you escaped The Burning."

"Oh, ma'am, I wish you could see how well it's all coming back in heart!"

Listening to his eloquence about the land his family cultivated, I thought I knew where his heart was set. He spoke as if it must hold equal fascination for me. Books and music are my pleasures, but I suppose a civilized farm could be pleasant. I showed polite interest and thought his education had done little to broaden his outlook.

CHAPTER 24

EAGLET IN FLIGHT

Torquil

Graduating Day orders promoted me to second corporal. I stood fourteenth among the seventy-nine in my class who finished the term. Which would make Uncle James prouder? Of the second class, Loudoun stood first, and Airlie was named second lieutenant of Company A. Aidan was sixth in a class of twenty-three. My squad mates were corporals, too. Other appointments confirmed gentility and would make corp relations pleasanter. My mind shadowed a little because I was still at odds with "Rats' Funeral Arrangements."

The drums and fife played "Auld Lang Syne." My Rat days were done forever! I'd completed a fourth of my education. I was a third classman. I was second corporal ... and Miss Mary saw me receive promotion!

"Am I not a true prophet, Lieutenant?" Gunn, first to meet me, wrung my hand. A smile lit his face. "Your distinctions exceed those of your detractors."

I couldn't speak, only look my gratification.

"Give your hand to some more of your friends!"

"I knew you had the right makings!" Boatwright grabbed my hand.

"We had to winnow out the rest so there'd be room for it!" Ashland clapped me on the shoulder.

I felt my face color, and gave a hesitant half-smile. My heart responded for me. "I learnt a lot from you all."

"And we're taking it with us, to astonish the capital!" Ashland laughed.

"The Balance Step in Richmond will get you astonished into the lunatic asylum!" teased Martin. "I thought you were bound for France."

"The exiles are coming home, now we're almost a State again, to start fighting to win it back from the carpetbaggers and scalawags. I'll be the colonel's aide in Richmond now, instead of Paris."

"MacHugh says you plan to work on the Orange, Alexandria and Manassas Gap," I said to Gunn.

"I start surveying for bridges a week from Monday."

* * *

"You won't be too hard with us, will you, *Corr-pril*?" drawled Stone.

The three came up from behind my left. I tensed inside till I remembered they were no longer my superiors. Are they ever separated? shot through my mind just as I recalled that none of them had won any distinctions. Our ranks were now reversed. Caught without a plan for dealing with them, my mind scrambled for a correct response. At last I used Carter's "soft phrase of peace"—I wasn't inclined to love them—in a proper corporal's reply.

"No harder than I have to be. It's up to you."

"You hit hard." Graves reminded me.

"Would you say we all might be even now?" suggested Toombs.

"Yes."

"Let bygones be bygones?" He tried to get it confirmed.

"Is enmity really gone?"

"On our part, it is," declared Stone, and the others nodded.

"I won't hold any against you."

It was a patched-up armistice. None of us wanted to shake hands, but conciliation wouldn't be sealed without it. Conscious of my new position, I extended my hand to set the example. One by one, the "Funerary Establishment" shook it.

* * *

With Miss Ellie in her hooded wrap, I arrived at the mess hall for the Graduating Ball just as MacHughs' carriage drove up, Aidan Mor and Aidan Beag on horseback alongside. He'd soon be on his way to Fredericksburg, the tidal end of the river corridor that had long connected Abercairn with the commerce of the wider world, where he was taking a position with a firm of civil engineers. Father and son handed the ladies out. I couldn't imagine how all the hoopskirts fit in the carriage.

* * *

Miss Ellie returned from leaving her wrap. She'd taught me a little of the language of flowers, so the yellow rosebuds in her hair showed she considered me only a friend. We received our dance cards and strolled aside to plan the evening. We'd have the grand march and the first dance together, and I was to have the supper dance.

"Your other friends will want the favor of a dance," I suggested.

"I'd like to congratulate Mr. MacHugh on his graduation."

Whitesmith approached and asked her for the Lancers. I bespoke a waltz for Aidan. Airlie wanted the galop.

"It's 'Storm Galop!' We'll carpet the ballroom when your flowers shake loose!"

She granted him the galop with a look of indulgent tolerance.

As I sought Aidan, Carter approached, carrying dance cards.

"May I enlist you for a dance with Miss Woodhurst?"

The name showered my mind with fragments of all the hurt and juvenile lust I'd put behind me. Carter observed the effect of his bombshell. When I could form a coherent answer, my voice was hard.

"She wants nothing to do with me, and her father forbade any messages between us."

"They've both thought better of it."

"May I have some indication from them directly, lest I offend."

"They're here." He nodded toward the lookers-on. "He brought her to Lexington."

"Perhaps you'd introduce us."

"With pleasure." His voice never sounded so silky.

Across the room, Miss Woodhurst was holding court among the cadets she'd met last year, and others were being introduced. Foremost was Bouleau. She didn't look our way. We approached a gentleman standing near.

"Mr. Drummond, may I introduce Mr. Woodhurst to you."

I didn't miss the significance of Carter's introducing the other man to me, instead of the younger to the elder. The back of my mind registered that my social position was higher. Mr. Woodhurst would have shaken hands, but I made only the curt bow of acknowledgement. Carter smoothed the awkwardness.

"Mr. Drummond hesitates to incur your further displeasure, sir."

"Highly commendable, highly commendable. My original response was too hasty, Mr. Drummond, too hasty—not considered with the care which the merits of the case should have called forth. I hope you will accept my apologies, sir. I hope the matter can be rectified."

I was too wary to yield. I retreated into formal courtesy.

"I trust it will be, sir."

"I retract my prohibition of communication between you. My daughter fears she might have hurt your feelings."

I didn't know what to say. Carter stepped into the breach again.

"Shall we go and see what she says?"

"It's a pleasure to meet you, Mr. Drummond."

"Pleased-to-meet-you-sir." I kept my voice cold.

Miss Woodhurst looked up as we joined the outer circle of her admirers. She gave me a longing smile that made me wonder if she wanted me in spite of all. She and Carter reserved a waltz for me, and I went my way troubled at the Woodhursts' sudden reversal. And why was Carter escorting her, his cousin, when he'd been calling regularly on Miss Hamilton?

I hastened to Miss Mary before Vogelsang could fill her dance card and exclude me. Her promise of a waltz and the last dance assured me of two delights for the evening. I invited Abercairn girls and Lexington girls to dance and was amazed that none declined. Friends asked me to partner their girls. I secured Aidan for a waltz with Miss Ellie and returned to her.

Miss Ellie

I was chatting with Mr. Thibault and Miss MacHugh when Mr. Drummond returned and gave me his half a smile.

"I doubt you need me to find you more partners."

"I should like to fill this line." I pointed to the last dance with my pencil.

"May I have the pleasure?"

I froze when Mr. Mills appeared.

"We were introduced at my aunt's reception."

I tried to dissuade him. "That was so very long ago."

"But surely you remember," he pressed. "I'm Mr. Turner's cousin, Mr. Mills."

Mr. Thibault rescued me. "I don't wish to sound reproachful, but I think you must have forgotten to write my name in that blank."

"Pre-empted, I see." Mr. Mills looked sulky. He stalked away.

I let my breath out softly, looked my thanks to Mr. Thibault, and wrote his name in the blank. Miss MacHugh proclaimed him a quick thinker. The idea surprised me. Could it be true?

Torquil

The band struck up for the Grand March. I treated Miss Ellie with respectful courtliness but found it hard not to march in step with her. At the same time, I enjoyed all the girls looking their prettiest and speculated which ones were fond of their escorts and which were not.

"I see you were promoted."

"I hope to prove worthy of it."

"From what our friends say of your skill in the military line, I'm sure you will."

We joined a set for a Scottish reel. We lifted hands to reel with the lead couple coming down the set, turned Donald and Miss Maury on their way and met Carter and Miss Woodhurst.

She, instead of holding my hand, caressed my palm with her fingers. I didn't miss a dance step nor allow my face to show shock. I think she was pouting as she danced away.

No time for reflection, Miss Ellie and I were at the top of the set. I led her down with the ease of having danced it since boyhood and had her smiling before we reached the bottom.

The evening floated on waves of melody. Lifted above my usual soberness by the gladsome music, the exhilaration of dancing, and, especially, the evident approval of young ladies, I made a celebration of the polka with Miss Amelia and geometric figures of all five sets of the Lancers with Miss Maury. I trotted through the galop with Nannie and pretended reluctance in the contra dance with Miss Mairi, who gave it back in kind, laughing to see Torquil-the-Owl getting above himself.

I enjoyed my partners so much that each held my undivided attention. By words I didn't know I'd ever thought, and by manner at once respectful and appreciative, I made my pleasure known. I was happily surprised to find it reciprocated—and not from mere courtesy.

I was operating at the same high pitch I did in battle, all senses heightened and body concentrated like a coiled spring. In the instinctive part of my mind, I registered every touch and sound, every sight and smell, interpreting them to know completely all that was around me. It was no longer a conscious process, but I could bring any part or all of it into mind at will.

From the advantage of my height, I missed not a step nor a gesture Miss Mary made, without missing a word or a glance from my dancing partner. I didn't know that if I'd detected any impropriety toward my little dear, I'd have thrashed the man who committed it.

I only knew I felt invincible.

The first waltz with Miss Mary brought me on wings to the reality where I was still bemused by the sweetness of her, still full of brotherly affection, still determined to be her protector. Her gown was some light bluish-greenish color, which set off her blonde hair and brown eyes in perfect harmony. Her hair, entwined with the daisies signifying innocence, was in a crown around her dainty head. She looked like a princess from a mythic realm. As one paying homage, I led her into the graceful figures of the dance. Let it be a long one!

"I hope you're enjoying the ball."

"Oh, yes! But I've never met so many new people in such a short time."

It made me want to take her home and shelter her and admit a stranger only once a year.

"But think what a pleasure it is for them to meet you."

"That would be terribly proud!"

"Not since it's true."

"Oh, please, don't flatter! It's not worthy of you."

Her care for my character touched the depths of my heart. I felt at one with her, at peace in the center of joy. I wanted to clasp her to my heart to express pure delight, but I feared she'd think my feelings toward her—weren't pure. That she knew them without my speaking, I had no doubt. Then I feared she disliked what I felt; she changed the subject.

"Thank you for choosing Mister Vogelsang for me. He's very kind and lively."

"He's a close friend. We trained in the same squad, and we hunt together. I wonder what you think of the others."

"Mister Carter is so polished and knowledgeable. He was telling me about society in Richmond."

"That must have seemed a world of wonders."

"It sounded like such a flurry, it would be hard to keep up."

I was relieved.

"Mister Bouleau is very handsome."

I was instantly on the *qui vive.*

"The Abercairn boys are the same as always, only grown up.

"I like all the ladies. Miss Loudoun is very accomplished, and Miss MacPherson is sweet. I'm glad Aidan's marrying her. Miss Maury speaks well on any subject and makes them all interesting."

"Her father's professor of Physics here. He's going to make a physical survey of the State."

"I wonder what he'll make of Abercairn. We have such a variety of soils and stone. Papa says we could find the perfect place to grow almost anything on our farm alone."

It all led to home. I resonated with happiness. I looked long into her eyes and pressed her hand before I relinquished her to Vogelsang.

When I gave Miss Ellie my arm for the supper dance, her beauty delighted me again.

"I've been looking forward to this dance with you."

"I'm afraid I must deprive you of part of it." She gestured toward a torn, trailing flounce at the bottom of her gown. "If I don't get it pinned, I might trip on it and embarrass you."

"I wouldn't let you fall or be hurt."

I escorted her to the ladies' dressing room and stood with my back to the entrance, a discreet distance away. Thibault brought Nannie for similar repairs and likewise turned his back. We discussed the new promotions.

Miss Ellie, flounce secure again, emerged a few minutes later. Rudely close to the dressing room door, and between her and me, loomed Mr. Mills. He thrust a hand against the wall to bar her progress.

"Why won't you dance with me?"

He leaned toward her. She drew back.

"What's the matter, looking for a richer match?"

Miss Ellie retreated a step, head high and nostrils flaring with pique.

Thibault

I caught Mr. Mills with a hold that looks friendly to the casual observer but inflicts intense pain on the offender and turned him round to face me.

"The lady doesn't care for your attentions, sir."

"Mister Drummond, Mister Whitesmith, will you see Mr. Mills to his friends and send him home?"

Still accustomed to my right to command, they forgot I was now relieved from duty. They each took an arm and, feigning good fellowship, walked him to the exit. I turned to Miss Loudoun.

"I hope he didn't harm you."

"No."

A polka redowa began for the supper dance. I offered my arm.

"I'll see you to your partner."

"You just sent him away."

"So I did." No sign of Drummond's return. I wasn't sorry one bit! "May I offer myself as a substitute, so you won't miss the pleasure of the dance?"

Miss Ellie

Though Mister Thibault might dance other figures passably, I thought the polka redowa would be too intricate for him. It might cost me another torn flounce, but of course I want to show gratitude for his second timely intervention. I gave him my hand.

He stepped with ease into the middle of a measure and led me through it. How could such a big, solid man be so graceful! He led with strength and assurance.

"This is my favorite redowa of all Waldheim composed. He used deeper-toned harmonies—hear how the violincello is actually carrying the melody? The others are almost shrill in comparison."

"You must have studied them."

"My cousin sent them from Berlin after the war. He took pity on my being without new music while the blockade was on."

"I suppose you've played all your life."

"Mother taught us the pianoforte when we were little, but my best instrument is the flute. I carried it with me on campaign and practiced when duty allowed time."

I had to revise my opinion. Mr.-Thibault-the-Farmer is a man of accomplishment! He must be able to perform long passages on his flute. His chest is deep and broad enough to contain much breath. I softened my stiff carriage and flowed into the dance. How many more pleasant surprises will he give me?

Nannie

I was displeased that it took so long to repair my gown and less pleased with Mr. Whitesmith, whose clumsy foot did the damage. I hated to keep Mr. Thibault waiting, let alone miss the redowa. If I do judge it myself, I dance it well, so it's my favorite. I composed my expression and sailed out. Everyone was dancing, and Mr. Thibault wasn't to be seen. My sense of romance overcame the irritation threatening my composure when I saw my partner dancing with Torquil's. The expressions on their faces made me laugh; intuition was confirmed! With delight no less than Mother's, I'd watched Mr. Thibault transfixed by Ellie's beauty last night.

Torquil

I arrived where I'd left my partner and found Nannie instead. Grinning, she looked more like Aidan than ever.

"Quick! Let's not miss the rest of it! I'll explain!"

I led her into the dance and gave her a quizzical look. She almost giggled—about what?

"We are the victims of bad manners … and neglect …and it's the best thing that could happen!"

"Make sense, Nannie!"

She told me how the wind blew and asked for my indulgence. I frowned.

"Won't she think I'm discourteous?"

"She won't think of you at all. Now do help me! We've got to make sure he takes her in to supper, too."

"That would leave me with the wittiest girl instead of the prettiest," I teased.

"Torquil *Dhu*!"

"Do you know how to be invisible?"

"If I did, I shouldn't choose to be!"

"That's the only way to make your plan succeed."

"What shall we do? Quick! Those are the closing measures!"

I located the entranced couple and noted their direction. I'd reconnoitered all the ways in and out of the mess hall the first time I set foot in it.

"I'll lead us to a covert where they won't see us. Prepare to quickstep!"

I changed our direction, avoiding collisions by inches. Nannie poised herself for any vector and followed. I whirled her through west door on the last note of the redowa and stood close to the wall of the portico, putting her behind me.

"I expect you've thought how we'll excuse ourselves for deserting them," I whispered.

"We shall take a high hand and say they deserted us."

"*Whisssht!* Your voice carries. Stand quite still."

I watched the ballroom as sharply as I'd ever observed an enemy. Every time Nannie drew breath to speak, I waved her to silence. I stifled laughter, watching Thibault and Miss Ellie looking about in bewilderment. At last they descended together to the supper room. I gave Nannie my arm.

"Besides," she continued, "they deserted us first. All we did was make the best of it! And if anyone reproaches us, I felt faint and you took me outdoors for fresh air."

"Yes, Lady Ann! What are the rest of my orders?"

"We'll sit as far away from them as we can, so they won't feel obliged to press through the crowd and speak to us. That will give them more time together. Oh, this is fun!"

The situation was too complicated. If everyone had followed the regulations, it wouldn't have happened. Nannie hadn't used to be such a plotter, not when she was little and she and Aidan Beag were with us everywhere. Hoping she felt assured of a better outcome than I did, I found seats that put much of the company between us and our proper partners, and didn't face them.

"I suppose you have a fine appetite for food as well as plotting."

"Yes! Aidan says they make good coconut pie. I'd like some."

"I'll get you a big piece. I reckon you don't want anything else."

"Torquil *Dhu*!"

I gave her my wolf grin, ascertained Thibault's location, and approached the serving table. I loaded her plate and mine and escaped Thibault's and Miss Ellie's notice.

After supper, I went to waltz with Miss Woodhurst. Remembering last year's misplaced lust and callow infatuation and humiliation, I felt repulsion. Strict courtesy would have to sustain me.

She showed the same lively appreciation of me she'd shown before, like she'd never rejected me. She smiled invitingly as I led her onto the floor. I wanted to know why she gave me the mitten, but I had no words.

But when I put my hand on her waist, passion devoured me! My blood raced. My body burned and gave other signs. My face got hot. Hardly knowing what I did, I clenched the hand I held and tightened my mouth to make myself dance the steps of the waltz. I forgot to control my expression.

Then I was disgusted with myself. I set my will. A year's participation in good society, her previous rejection, other young ladies who found my attentions pleasing, all combined to drive out the untimely desire. I regained command of myself and set my face wooden. I hoped the cadet button she wore as a brooch wasn't the one I gave her! Now that she wasn't my entire experience of young ladies, I knew she wasn't one I'd want. Miss Mary had set my new standard: I'd never feel happy at home with Carter's cousin.

Miss Woodhurst

I saw him blush and noted other sure signs of my effect, and was gratified. With that particular kind of attraction, it'll be easy to win him back. Then I saw—and felt—him change. It was time to act. I answered the question he wouldn't ask.

"I didn't really know my feelings then." I put on a look that pleaded for understanding. "You were so … impassioned. I was … a little timid."

Torquil

An hour ago I'd have had easy words to answer her, but humiliating memories and my embarrassing physical reaction had doused my spirits. I used rote courtesy.

"You need not worry about it again."

I returned Miss Woodhurst to Carter, escaped, and collected Nannie for a quadrille. I tried to shake off my upset and be good company.

"Whatever is the matter?"

"Nothing."

"Something is! You're an owl again!"

"I'm always an owl."

We performed a figure and took place again.

"Torquil Dhu, I don't know what to make of you! You were so happy earlier." She kept her voice low, and looked concerned.

"It's all right, Nannie. I'll get past it."

"I do hope so!" she murmured. "She's only here to find a rich husband."

I looked at her in consternation. How Nannie reached her conclusions, and how she was so sure of them, was past understanding. She pulled trifles out of thin air, embellished and interwove them, and presented them as facts. Could she be right again? She whispered her evidence so softly, I had to incline my head to hear her.

"She gave herself away when we were all putting off our shawls. She pretended to be trying to learn where all you boys are from—to be able to respond properly, she said—and the look on her face when the place was the name of anyone's seat ... well! It was a first-rate giveaway."

"It's lowering to have been so mistaken about someone."

Nannie

I'd heard the story of his first romance, third hand, in Abercairn. Now I knew whether he was still wearing the willow for her. He was not. His voice betrayed no longing but only self-reproach. I squeezed his hand.

"Cheer up. We're all mistaken, sometimes."

I got him to grin.

"Even you, Miss Wisdom?"

"If you say I am, I'll say you're telling tales!"

I did my best to restore his good spirits. By the time he escorted me back to Mister Thibault, I thought he looked less grim. He whispered in my ear.

"Be sure I have a ticket of admission when you thicken the next plot!"

I giggled.

Torquil

The finale, my waltz with Miss Mary, was slow, with no intricate steps, to allow lovers to concentrate wholly upon each other. I concentrated. It wasn't love talk. This girl was more important to me than all the others. I didn't want to say anything wrong, and the constraint kept me from saying much. I'm not good at casual talk, in spite of Miss Ellie's tutoring.

"I hope you'll be staying in Lexington a while."

"Oh, no. Aidan's all packed to go home. He has to be in Fredericksburg as soon as he can, to take up his new position."

"I wish you could stay longer."

"So do I, but it's too much work for Mama, without me. I hope she's not worn out in just these few days. Bossie's about to come fresh, too, and you know how much fuss that can be."

"As mis-chancey as foaling. It's not her first, is it?"

"Third, but Papa and William had to help her before."

"I hope it will go easier this time. Bossie's the Jersey, isn't she?"

Miss Mary

I looked up into his face and saw his care for what concerns me. I felt selfish. His is such a stern life, with so few comforts, and I can do so little to make it less so. I wished I could stay longer and do much.

Torquil

What had I said to bring forth her sober expression?

"What is it, little dear?"

"I was wishing I could stay."

"I don't like to part with you, either, but we both have our duties."

"Yours is so hard."

"I'm used to it."

"I wish I could make it easier for you."

"You do. Wherever you are, you make me feel like I'm home."

"What does that mean?"

"Something in me wants home before anything else. You make me feel like ... home."

"Oh."

She didn't understand. How could she? Home wasn't lost to her.

"May I write to you?"

"You always write to us."

"I mean ... to you."

"If Papa allows. I think he will."

Half a smile is all I have, but I gave it to her tenderly.

* * *

I exulted with all Virginia! All in the month of July, the State's new constitution was approved, the Conservatives won the election, and the State Legislature was to meet in spite of General Canby's repeated efforts to block it. Confederates regained our right to vote and hold office. The Yankees would have to leave! Abercairn was free to govern itself!

I didn't know how heavy a burden the Rat year was till it was lifted. Buoyed up by my achievements and the good reputation I'd built, and by being acceptable company to young ladies, I felt I could overcome everything that stood between me and my inheritance ... and a commission ... and marriage to a lady. Much of life had come at me too fast, before I could reason out what to do, but now I faced a familiar duty: training.

My Rats made me feel paternal, but I couldn't be too easy. I had to eradicate slack habits of mind and behavior. Though I'd been merciless in time past, I had since received mercy. I had to be guide and example as well as disciplinarian. I had to teach them to trust and love me as I'd come to trust and love my preceptors.

Da's and Uncle James's kindness, Mr. Stafford's sharp-witted understanding of boys, Gunn's unrelenting demand that cleared my name of slander, and his gift of encouragement at the most effective time—none had compromised on standards to meet, and none had degraded or humiliated me. Nor, because they were fair and just, had they roused my enmity. I remembered O'Shea's creed: "Ye respect your men, but ye do not do it in words."

I enforced the highest standards without resorting to insult or shame. I showed no favoritism, but never hesitated to write a report if it were justified. I wrote many on Callend, but some of my classmates thought me too lenient.

Helms, J., who'd scorned my military service last summer, now thought I was taking revenge on him through his younger brother.

"You single him out for ridicule! You never let him take a step without a scold! He says you're always picking at him."

"He often needs correction. You know, yourself, we can't set a foot down carelessly and be in step, or sling our arms. He doesn't."

"You won't let up on him?"

"Not till he learns. As for ridicule, that's not how I train."

"He said you called him a goose."

"I demonstrated errors I observed among them all and likened them to the gaits of animals. Perhaps he recognized his. I showed how to correct the errors. I hope he noticed that. He has fair command of his motion, and I'm sure he's capable of improving."

Helms scowled. "It takes practice. Don't be too hard on him!"

"No harder than I have to be."

* * *

Miss Mary wrote,

> I had such a happy time in Lexington, thanks to
> you. Your friend Mr. Vogelsang was particularly kind
> to me. The fireworks were spectacular compared to
> our little crackers at Christmas, and the Ball was en-
> chanting. What beauty and music, and dancing with
> you, and seeing you honored. ... Bossie's calf is a heifer
> and they're both healthy now.

News of our friends and our farms, and, as an afterthought:

> P. S. Papa is well pleased for us to write to each other.

Dear and sweet as her letter was, it made me sad to remember
what she'd said at the Ball.

Her pure-hearted estimate of my character made me feel
like an imposter. I still longed to regain my original self, the untarnished soul I'd possessed before the vengeance. Who had I
become!

I didn't know, then, how much the wounds inflicted by evil
power had scarred and crippled my soul. I knew its deadly viru-
lence, but I didn't know that my trusting soul, in boyhood, hadn't
had strength to withstand it. Everything is either right or not,
and I'd sinned. I feared I'd gone too far beyond the bounds of
righteousness, ever to win my way back. But I tried. Uncle James
had told me my character was still being formed. I supposed I
had a chance to regain the boyhood grace and virtue I thirsted
for.

Military and academic successes lulled me. They were accomplished by acts of my will. I didn't know I couldn't repair the
damage to my soul. I'd learned to bridge my chasm when I chose,
but I also chose to appear grave and hesitant, to give myself time
to create responses. I didn't know social experience and military

and intellectual discipline had merely trained me to perfect the playacting I'd despaired of. I thought I'd buried my grievance about the murder of my family. I didn't know I'd only buried the pain of loss, of terror, of agony—not resolved it.

I felt free to allow myself pleasure for the first time in years. The curse seemed gone. Life was good. I neglected my spiritual nature. I forgot my yearning for purification. By and by, I thought I'd won back my former virtue. I mistook my new façade for my real self.

Miss Mary

The more often worldly ideas and viewpoints appeared in his letters, the more I feared for the pure heart I treasured. I prayed it was not sullied.

* * *

> I escaped all demerits and I did it by intense obedience to the rules. I felt I was at school to learn; to learn its discipline; and from being a wild, harum-scarum, frolicsome boy, I became at once a disciplined soldier. This was enough to arouse the prejudice of my fellow-cadets and, with the half dozen others in the corps who made it a point thus to be punctilious in the discharge of military duties, I became unpopular.
> —Randolph Barton, VMI class of 1861

Torquil

I maintained my position in the first or second section in all my coursework, and performed my corporal's duties to my own and my superiors' satisfaction. My Rats each needed different treatment. No trouble with Kilgore. He'll end up First Captain if he stays so diligent and respectful. But Callend cost me an inquisition by Colonel Ship!

"Mister Drummond, the Superintendent has received a letter of complaint from the father of one of the cadets in your squad! I have summoned you to ascertain whether it has a basis in fact.

"In sum, he complains that you have been persecuting Cadet Callend. In detail, that you have used offensive language, have rebuked him unjustly and too severely, and have written an excessive number of misconduct reports against him.

"Do you confirm or deny these complaints?"

"I deny them, sir."

"What is your stance towards Cadet Callend?"

"The same as toward his squad mates, sir, strict, demanding proper conduct, repeating drill exercises till they can perform them. I confine my rebukes to their performance of duty, use reasonable language, and write reports only as necessary."

"Such have been my observations and those of the sub-professors. Your statement confirms them. That will do, sir."

* * *

"I knew Callend in Richmond." Carter was visiting in No. 68 after dinner. "His mother makes him think the world was created for his very own pleasure."

"I wonder who's going to break the news that his complaints are unfounded?" queried Loudoun.

"Old Spex, I suppose."

Bouleau, making one of his frequent deposits at the treasurer's office, overheard most of it. Mr. Callend laid the matter before General Smith, who, patient and courteous, explained his policy of firm, consistent discipline and added that the complaint had been investigated and was groundless. Mr. Callend recognized the truth and requested a meeting with his son. Callend the elder had admonished Callend the younger to stop whining and obey the rules, and left his spoiled son to his fate.

The account lost nothing in the retelling. Callend was named "Sukey." I was relieved that the matter was resolved and annoyed that it had been taken out of my hands. But with opportunity to speak a word in season, I asked my roommates for privacy and sent for Callend. Like Gunn, I sat relaxed in my chair and spoke calmly.

"Mister Callend, stand at attention!"

He obeyed. He looked miserable.

I let silence lengthen. He fidgeted. I kept my voice soft.

"Mister Callend, you will succeed here ... as soon as you set your mind to it. Dismissed!"

He looked like he'd expected to hear anything but what he did hear, and like hope was dawning.

Springer was a leader most beguiling, whose chief aim was frivolity. At Troop, I found my Rats all lounging on the ground. They smirked and looked sidelong at each other between sly glances at me.

"Boys, take your ease. Men, stand at attention!"

They all jumped up. I rattled off the roll and taught them the Balance Step. I made them practice it for ten minutes before I put them through the rest of the drill at the Double-Quick. They marched to recitations panting and perspiring.

The nonsense had to be Springer's doing. I sent for him after dinner and ordered him to come to attention.

"Mister Springer, have you noticed that your squad mates suffer for your foolishness?"

"No, sir! They all think it's fun!"

"Continue to observe, sir! Dismissed!"

The next morning, knowing the squad would have sore muscles from the Balance Step, I ordered Springer forward. He bounced two steps to the front.

"Conduct drill identical to yesterday's."

Bossie's buoyancy sank. He looked at me in dismay. I stepped back a few paces and stood at Rest, holding my ivory-headed cane, face expressionless while he botched the orders.

"Attention! Uh … stand in line! Look right! Make the line straight!"

"SQUAD! THE BALANCE STEP! LEFT … ONE, TWO, THREE, FOUR! RIGHT … ONE, TWO, THREE, FOUR!"

He bellowed himself red in the face till his voice was hoarse. The squad strained to follow the too-fast count. Kilgore's lips were set in a firm line. Helms scowled. Callend gasped.

"… FIFTEEN … SIXTEEN! HALT!"

Bossie croaked, "Is that enough, sir?"

I said nothing. Springer chose marching. Back and forth from my position to the edge of the parade ground, he ran his squad mates at the Double-Quick. What form would their retribution take?

After supper, I sent for Springer again. He looked as lost and scared as Callend had.

"What is your squad mates' opinion of fun today, sir?"

"Against it, sir."

I drew silence taut before I delivered judgment and encouragement as one.

"Mister Springer, you have an inclination for laughter. You must decide whether to use it to injure your squad mates … or to cheer their hearts.

"Dismissed!"

Action was required when some of my classmates tormented Helms, G. beyond what the mildest human nature could forbear. He'd turn and rend them if jabbed with the goad again. None of them bore distinctions, and I'm his drillmaster. I used my office to intervene.

"Mister Helms! Come with me, sir!"

My voice rapped like gravel on iron through my sternest expression. Balked of their prey, the others growled. I led Helms out of their hearing.

"Stand at attention!" I kept my voice harsh.

He obeyed, still furious.

I rapped out, "Mister Helms, what you encounter this year requires self-control beyond human ability! Continue to exercise it!

"Dismissed!"

Later, the classmates I'd frustrated accosted me.

"What did you mean, taking him off just when we were about to teach him a lesson!" demanded Selkirk.

"He'd have blown up in another second, and learned what he's spoiling to have pounded into him!" Fouts added.

"He's my Rat. I'll teach him."

"Not a cent's worth, you won't! You're too soft on all of them!" Fouts accused.

"I don't need to give them thunder to make them do their duty."

"Fine work you're making of that sniveling Sukey!" jeered Selkirk, "Or Stumbles Helms!"

"They started a few lengths behind the line."

"And you're going to make racers of them! Here's your mule!"

"They'll stay the course." I reverted to corporality before I provoked them to say or do anything I had to report. "If you all will excuse me, I have some work to do before Guard."

My strictness stemmed from my war days and prevented acquaintances from teasing me not to write the reports they earned. Most of my friends now were officers who'd report me, too, when I deserved it. The others knew to keep me ignorant of any misconduct they contemplated. My stance caused resentment, but I kept to duty.

My Rats came to know I was for them, not against them. At the end of the summer, I had the satisfaction of seeing them all join company drill. When recitations resumed, I was section marcher for Latin, but I had to lean on Loudoun's expertise in Mathematics.

I went hunting with my friends most Saturdays. When General Smith published the order prohibiting trespass in neighboring orchards, we laughed. Whitesmith's uncle was still generous. We made more pemmican than we did last year and dug a new burying hole at the far edge of limits.

All the other Saturdays, I visited young ladies. At church socials and impromptu entertainments, escorting them on walks or rides, or sitting in parlors if the weather was forbidding, I teased … paid court … enjoyed every minute of it … considered close ties with one or two.

On Sundays, I wrote to young ladies farther away. Miss Mary's letters were sweet and warm and full of news of our own corner of the county that satisfied my heart and mind. David Carmichael's widow opened a classical school, she wrote, taking up where her husband had left off. Her parents said she could study the Latin language and classical literature, so she and Nannie, her best friend, went together. She wrote of her social activities guilelessly, seeming to have no idea of the significant attention she received. I hoped Captain Murray kept her always under his eye, guarding her for me. I tried merely to suggest it, but I must've been as subtle as a round of canister!

Nannie wrote about Abercairn social life. I teased that she wrote about all the romances except hers. She wasn't encouraging the attentions of any special man, she said, which allowed her to enjoy the company of them all. Remembering how deftly she'd enlisted me to keep Thibault and Miss Ellie together at the Ball, I joked that she was too smart for me, or I'd marry her myself.

She retorted, she wouldn't be guilty of the death from heartbreak which that event would cause *another*.

I gave my social life, long delayed for want of acceptable opportunity, all the time I could spare from duty. I stopped attending prayer meetings, prayed seldom, and read my Bible not at all. The spontaneous, powerful revival of Christianity among the cadets that year brought many to salvation, including, to my stupefaction, Toombs, Stone, and Graves! Showing a godliness I'd never imagined them capable of, they came to me desiring a true reconciliation. I accepted it as my due and didn't notice I was neglecting the Wellspring of my own eternal life.

MacLeod

Hanover Court House
Virginia
November 15, 1869

Darling James,

You are no doubt surprised by the direction above. Leaving my brother in the kindly care of the congregation, I have come here to nurse Mother. She suffered a bad fall two weeks ago, and sister Louisa has her hands too full with her little ones, to give her the continuous care she must have. Mother was so frail to begin with, and now can do very little for herself. With her sweet spirit, she laments the burden she fears she must be. I assure her that my care is much less than her due, since she not only gave me life, but so tenderly and lovingly nurtured me, so many years.

Oh, James, it seems we suffer one delay after another before we can become one! I am so sorry for the disappointment this must cause you. But I know God has us in his hands and watches over us. He must have good reason to require us to wait. ...

M Company had just returned from quelling the latest hostile attack. I'd thought I might get leave to travel to her and our marriage during the winter, when the Indians hole up in their villages. Despite the weather, the Union Pacific ran most of the time, and I could make my way to Cheyenne somehow.

I was disheartened, but I knelt to pray God's healing for Mrs. Gilchrist and strength of body and soul for my Elizabeth. When I rose, I wrote to my sister Joan in New York, enclosing a bank draft and asking her to select and express dainties to tempt the invalid's appetite and to cheer and strengthen my love and the household. I didn't know, then, how long Mrs. Gilchrist would survive to inspire her family, nor how many times my petitions for leave would be denied.

* * *

Torquil

Mr. Loudoun kept open house for the Christmas season. Miss Mary was here from Abercairn! Airlie paid half jesting, half serious court to Mairi. I wasn't surprised to see Thibault with Miss Ellie—he's a sub-professor now. But Vogelsang? He paid marked attention to Nannie.

"You're a sly-boots! You never told me!" I teased her.

"Gerhardt didn't either, did he!" She grinned.

"*Gerhardt*? You must be getting mighty close!"

But she danced and chatted as much with Loudoun as with "Dutch."

Sitting with me in a window seat between dances, Miss Mary was as sweet of person as she was last July … prettier, if that were possible. Her thoughts meshed with mine so well, she made me feel almost home. My senses burned when she put tender fingers to my lips to stop my teasing. Whatever was left of my purity of heart was touched when she spoke well of my character. I courted her with hesitant expression … couldn't reason out what to say.

Miss Mary

If I felt hesitant, it was only because every time I saw him, he looked … how did he look? He could never be called handsome, but his face was so dear … steel-blue eyes … firm yet tender mouth. He seemed … how did he seem? The feeling I felt that he felt, wrapped me in happiness and made my heart beat faster.

Two and a half years before he'd be graduated. Hurry would only lead to impatience. But the War taught me how suddenly a life can be swept away. The thought of what happened to Ewen, happening to him, brought hot tears beneath my eyelids. Overcoming them turned my lips downward. I felt a tiny crease form between my brows.

"What is it, little dear?"

"Oh, don't die!"

Torquil

Instinct: hold her close to comfort her. Stunned she'd think of such things when all was light and love. Love? I'd learned no correct response to this! While my mind scrambled for words, my rough soldier's heart replied.

"I won't. I'm hard to kill."

Disconcerted, I dabbed at her tears with my handkerchief before I handed it to her. I felt like my face mirrored hers of a moment ago. She dried the droplets and tried to smile. I knew her heart then. I was as dear to her as she to me. We gave and received a gift beyond price.

* * *

Trapped! Returning from a late trip to our cache one night in April, carrying contraband—we aren't allowed food in our rooms except by special permission, the one regulation I ignore. Trapped by Captains Peake and Fairfax, tactics instructors. I melted into hiding behind a tree. They sat on a fallen log. I froze, afraid to breathe.

"I had a letter from MacLeod today, first since the War."

"Pole?"

"Was that his name? He was graduating when I reported for plebe year, so I didn't know him well till the survey in Texas."

"He had to stand twice to cast a shadow in those days! We were classmates. He was in the 'Royals,' so he went directly into the Army List and then to the topographical engineers."

"I'm glad he survived. It wrenched all our hearts when we had to part company to fight for our convictions. I suppose he's still in the Army."

"Company officer out in Wyoming Territory. It's a pity. He was destined for greater things, but he joined a company of our partisans, I'm told."

"Pole! Coming over to us! We can't be talking about the same man."

"Sharpe picked him for a spy because he was a map maker— probably had somewhat against him from their courtship days, too, when Pole won the fair Eleanor!—any road, he sent him to the Blue Ridge to ferret out some partisans who captured a shipment of Henry rifles, and map the area for operations against them."

"He didn't do it?"

"Sharpe ordered him to capture the leader and come back and make the map, and then the troops could move on the others. He stayed with the partisans. Sharpe had to capture him! Huntingdon actually saw him wearing gray and riding with the boy company out of Abercairn who came to the Valley in 'sixty-four.

"According to Perrette—you know he stayed with the Yankees—they accused him of treason. Why they didn't hang him, or cashier him, I don't know, but they dropped him from the Engineers and sent him west with a line company. Exile, like they did Pope. Discredited. He must have some powerful voices in high places, still to be alive and in the service at all."

The drum beat Call to Quarters. The subs ambled back to Barracks. I stayed frozen.

I reported to Colonel Ship, confessed my breaches of regulations, and offered no excuse. He looked at me so long, I fidgeted inside. Then the thunder!

"You have not only disobeyed regulations, but have betrayed the trust the Institute reposed in you by making you an officer!"

I blushed for shame. The denunciation was just.

"Your conduct was thought exemplary, which makes it all the worse that you acted in such a secretive, self-serving manner."

Cadets broke the rules about food whenever they could! The post baker, Old Judge, was famous for his generosity when they sneaked out of limits to ask for some of his bread. But a mild offense among the general run of cadets was a serious one for an officer, whose duty was to maintain discipline.

"Since your demerit has been insignificant, and you have volunteered an honest and open confession of your offenses, I shall recommend to the Superintendent that you be suspended from your office for a month, rather than reduced to the ranks. Dismissed!"

* * *

I'd failed Uncle James. I knew now, what he never said, how much he'd sacrificed. His career was all to smash and his chances for promotion reduced to the minimum, for my sake, who now deserved it less than ever. I felt so guilty and ashamed, I couldn't write him. No words could be great enough to thank him.

I was also angry. If the Institute wouldn't provide enough food and heat, I wasn't to blame for supplying the deficiency! I'd chosen to obey, but I was still proud I could set the authorities at naught if I chose. It made me feel unconquered.

I didn't know, then, my inmost soul believed if I made complete submission, I'd be erased from existence. I didn't know I was driven to defiance by the wound that wouldn't heal. I only knew something from outside prevented me from doing right.

When I was reinstated, furlough was only two months away. I was to spend two weeks at Glenlochie and the rest with Uncle James. I invited Miss Mary to the Graduating Ball, but she wouldn't ask her parents to bear the expense of the journey, when reestablishing their farm was so crucial to the family's future. She's such a generous, dutiful little person that I knew she'd sacrifice pleasure for family welfare and expect me to agree. Her thinking reiterated her good opinion of me. I fell far short of it.

I was sure she returned my affection: her tears at the mere thought of my death, and our letters since. Her heart had opened to my heart, where she had a home before I knew she lived there. I wished I could ask Captain Murray's blessing, speak my heart to her, and put substance in my dreams. But if I could obey God's calling only in the ranks, I'd have to relinquish her. It would only be just to tell her while I was home.

CHAPTER 25

FURLOUGH

1. In Extremis

Come, and let us return unto the Lord: for he hath
torn, and he will heal us: he hath smitten, and he will
bind us up.
—Hosea 6:1

Torquil

They all kept me busy. Robbie explained how the General
Assembly's Enabling Bill had removed the Yankee appointees
and returned our own men to their former positions. With dearest hopes hanging in the balance, I gave close attention to Mr.
Ogilvie's report. I received permission to buy a rifle. I put off telling Miss Mary how uncertain our situation is, till my last night
at home.

Miss Mary

"I have to talk to you about the future. I can't say what I want
to say."

"Did Papa refuse?"

"No."

I thirsted for an explanation, but I let him lead. I waited for him to find his words.

"I refused, and do refuse, to offer you a society where you would be disdained—considered a member of the lower orders and treated as such."

He explained. I wanted comfort—and to comfort him.

"Are you not dreading a future that may never come to pass?"

"I'm considering all the possibilities. The Yankees rule all public business, so, in order to obey God's calling, I'll likely have to enlist. I'm sorry, little dear, more than I can say."

Torquil

"So am I." Her lips quivered, but she controlled her voice and lifted tear-bright eyes to mine. "But hope and prayer remain, until you know for sure."

I loved her more than ever for her faith. How little the facts could justify it!

"They do remain, but you can't let hope obscure reality! It would be best … for your true future happiness … to go on like they didn't. You know my heart: you live in it. I can't encourage you in false hope."

"My hope is no more false … than you are!" Her slender fingers clenched on my arm as she overcame a sob. "Let us wait and see."

"Gladly, if that's your desire. But there are fine men here in Abercairn who—"

She put her fingers to my lips. "Who are not you."

I kissed the fingers warmly before she could retract them, and said no more.

* * *

Riding the railways westward, I daydreamed about my little dear for a hundred miles. At last I thought to pray. I didn't consider how seldom I'd so much as thought about my Creator the last year and a half, but prayed to Him as the One who had the power to grant my heart's desire.

Called to be a soldier ... but educated for refined, cultured life. I wished God had ordained some other occupation. I'd warred for seven years and lived with horrors enough. Da and Douglas stark and cold ... stench of corpses ... screams of agony ... hideous mutilations—a cheerful friend reduced to pulp by a bursting shell or carved to dogmeat by a savage—still gave me nightmares. Starvation not only for food but for rest, driven to such exhaustion that I'd nearly perished—and still the blessing of the Farther Shore was denied me.

Future: more of the same!

Commissioned, I'd lose my home. Enlisted, nothing left of the life and love I longed for. Yankees owned the Army, so I'd be punished for defending my home and constitutional beliefs. Yet more pain as reward for doing right!

In St. Louis, I bought a Winchester Model 1866, loaded it and kept it close. It loaded through a gate in the side of the frame, fifteen rounds. The magazine was sealed to keep out dirt, and covered by the forestock so it wouldn't dent, a big improvement over the older Henry I carried as a Ranger. Apprehension about being among Yankees again, added to resentment against God's calling, made me burn for the release I found in a hard fight. The frontier was the place to find one!

MacLeod

"This is how they keep the treaty!"

Changing into my old field uniform while Torquil dug campaign boots and clothing out of his trunk, we'd been at the post only a day when the third squadron were ordered out against some Sioux. Reports of murder, theft, and mutilation incensed officers and men alike.

"Didn't you write me there were some who wouldn't sign?"

"Our consulate at Winnipeg sent word at the end of May, they were moving south. War parties crossed the Union Pacific at the last of June and attacked the wood train at Fort Fetterman and killed a man, the first of this month."

Major Jennings, commanding, remembered Torquil from Fort Banks. Still wresting custom to serve expediency, he placed him with Barton, the newest lieutenant, rather than at my side.

"Stiffen up the youngster, experience next to him."

The column made a sweep west and north from the North Platte to intercept the Sioux before they could escape to a reservation, where, immune to justice, they'd boast about their kills and plunder. Returning, less than a day's march from the fort, ascending a ridge to avoid a steep canyon, we were attacked early in the morning.

Major Jennings countercharged. He dismounted the men to defensive positions among the standing rocks, close enough to support each other's positions.

Torquil

Lieutenant Barton and I were stationed with part of his company among weathered granite slabs. He being an officer, we stayed mounted. My new rifle excelled my hopes. My marksmanship was still perfect. Controlling the dancy gelding I was training for Lieutenant Porter took most of my attention. I used my ivory-headed cane for a riding crop.

After a short, sharp encounter, the Sioux broke off combat, screening each other while retrieving their wounded and dead. Unencumbered parties galloped away.

"Pity to let that war bonnet escape!" exclaimed Barton.

"Let's count coup!" Personal combat!

"With what?"

"Anything but a weapon."

"Hold the position, Sergeant!"

Grip the base of my cane ... gallop after the headpiece ... spar with Sioux. Strike! count coup! Strike! count coup! Strike! count coup! Burning white hot! Summit of all my senses ... all my powers ... weave away from their weapons. ... Strike! count coup! We snatched away the war bonnet as the warrior sped forward. Wheel, gallop back. The sergeant moved men out to give us covering fire.

Glorious! Like when my daemon took over. Release from fretting and rigid discipline. Living again on the razor's edge between life and death!

We were sent in arrest to the rear of K company. I was still on the summit of triumph. Neither Major Jennings's wrath nor Uncle James's look fazed me.

Approaching the fort, I began to sink ... went silent ... knew I'd done wrong. I thanked God for sparing my life, but didn't notice there was no connection. I thought my worst sin was against Uncle James: I'd wronged the good man who took me into his household and sacrificed his occupation to save my life. Glum and penitent, I entered his quarters. He had the sad, stern look that tears my heart to know I deserve.

"I'm sorry, Uncle James."

MacLeod

Anger and misery fought within for expression. I eyed my foster son in such gravid silence that I struck him silent also. Pain and disappointment cut too deep for wrath. When I could command words, they were cold and quiet.

"By setting an example that jeopardizes men unnecessarily, you showed yourself deficient—before the whole squadron. You descended to the mental level of the savages. You disobeyed orders."

Voice failing, I grieved, "I'm ashamed of you. I never thought I would be."

Torquil

My face went numb with shock and fear that our bond of affection was severed forever. Bringing shame upon the man who had done me only good was *unpardonable.* I could hardly look him in the face ... swallowed hard.

"I'm not worthy of your goodness."

MacLeod

I heard the contrition ... the effort it cost to keep his voice. I put my hand on his shoulder. "It's your life I care about the most."

Torquil

His sincere, humble virtue seared my heart.

"I'm not worthy ..." My voice broke. "May I walk...."

"Yes."

I escaped out the back door, down the stairs and a little decline, to the river. Heart aching because I'd treated Uncle James so despitefully, I condemned myself for losing control ... doing wickedness ... acting like a fool. My soul writhed at the depth of wrong I couldn't undo. Nothing can make amends for giving shame. I wanted punishment to expiate my guilt. His forbearance only made it worse. I was very sorrowful.

MacLeod

I tried to work off my turmoil by pacing along the river. I stalked past the infantry barracks, returning salutes absentmindedly, crossed the footbridge and turned downstream. I love my son and long to see him become the man that lies within him. I made clear long ago, wanton risk of his life and soldiers' lives is wrong! I thought he'd overcome the sin.

That he did it in such a public manner, was as if he knifed me. I allowed myself to know the pain and feel the discouragement. I paced nearly to the river's confluence with the Platte, grieving for my own hurt and my son's sabotage of his life.

In loco patris, I had to rise above my feelings and do what was right for the lad God placed in my charge: fatherhood's sacrifice. I was duty-bound to provide a penalty—a redemptive one, in view of his remorse. In affection, in pity for his besetting sin and the damage it did him, I was beginning to forgive. I'd speak it at the most effective time. I was very sorrowful.

* * *

Inner debate about what line to take—I'd found neither that nor how to correct him—frayed my temper. I prayed thanks for dinner and spoke the matters uppermost in my mind.

"You should have learned to control yourself and developed better judgment by now! You told me God forbade you to seek death. Did He leave you any exception from that?"

"No, sir."

"In our occupation, there are dangers enough without wickedly creating more! I say 'wickedly' because of Jesus' example, refusing to throw himself off the pinnacle of the temple. He called it 'tempting God.' Has it occurred to you that's what you were doing!"

"No, sir."

"Has anything whatever, in the nature of remorse, occurred to you!"

"I'm sorry I disappointed you."

"It's disappointing that you showed better discipline two years ago than you do now! What got into you—the daemon again?"

"I don't know. I just went. Nothing's more glorious than to ride the very edge between life and death!"

Appalling viewpoint! I glared ... clamped my mouth shut so I wouldn't sputter ... desperately prayed for wisdom. It came. Anger froze to ice. Before I could speak, his expression had sobered.

"And what you said about getting men killed."

My voice tolled hard as my anger. "A man ruled by a craving for mortal danger isn't fit to command! If you mean to go on as you went today, I shall prevent your being commissioned, for the good of the service! You will spend this evening in penitence!"

Torquil

My heart stopped. I faltered before the magnitude of my dread. I'd invested all my life in hope of a commission.

MacLeod

En route to Parade, I was miserable over what I might have to do. There'd always been a selfless purpose in my son's death-courting warfare in Virginia. Though he hadn't held life tightly, neither had he taken ill-reasoned gambles with others' lives. After failure during his sergeancy, he'd put heart and mind and strength into conquering the daemon. I'd given him another chance. Had I been too indulgent, too hopeful? His thirst for deadly danger made it seem he'd taken the daemon's purpose into his own soul and was trying to destroy himself. Wishing for a son to follow me in the service, had I mistaken his suitability?

'Holy God,' I prayed silently, 'forgive me for failing to correct this sin in him! Show me what you would have me do! Speak to his heart, I pray you—it's open to You and your bidding, in a rare purity. Give him strength to conquer that wicked craving! In Jesus' name, Amen.'

Dominie Gilchrist had warned me that a hand more powerful than my own might be needed to correct the evil permanently.

> God left him, to try him, that he might know all that
> was in his heart.
> —II Chronicles 32:31

Torquil

I faced the depths of what I'd done. Ashamed, I knelt beside my bed, bowed my head onto my folded hands, and closed my eyes, to begin by confession to God.

Uncle James was right about the good of the service. I thought I'd overcome it at Fort Banks, but—did the daemon drive me to-day? I'd breached discipline, I'd risked soldiers' lives.

Bringing shame upon Uncle James made me sick with remorse. No one deserved it less. Shame defaced a man's public character—his honor—and lowered him in his equals' estimation. My deepest heart and soul despised me. I'd give anything to live the day over!

Last and worst: disobedience to God. He'd forbidden me to seek death.

But something from outside myself thwarts the righteousness I desire. I didn't know yet, how much the vicious evil done to me, had stolen my ability to obey and do right.

'Dear God ...'

No one was there.

Such darkness and silence saddened and frightened me as a little boy. Now I was alone in the entire cosmos: infinitely black, arid, and cold.

MacLeod

I'd devised a correction I hoped would work for the good of my lad's soul when I returned to find as thoroughly penitent a young sinner as I could have hoped for. He was too unhappy to keep his face expressionless. Every line of it was downcast. I hardened my heart.

"You are confined to these quarters until I can make other disposition of you."

He looked forsaken. I hoped the uncertainty would move him to correct his misconduct permanently.

Torquil

Uncle James meant to cast me away as reprobate and unworthy of chastisement.

As I arrived in obedience to Colonel Hale's summons, Barton was exiting. He slashed a finger across his throat. I grimaced in reply.

Colonel Hale

"Hem! Mr. Drummond, it's impossible to see why anyone thought you could be an officer. Yesterday's episode shows your unfitness to command. What kind of officer would sacrifice his men for a fool's escapade!" My glare demanded an answer.

"I have no excuse, sir."

"Because there *is* no excuse for wanton recklessness!

"Your uncle is one of the finest commanders in the service. Has he taught you nothing!"

"Respectfully, sir"—the boy's color rose—"my uncle does all that's proper. My faults are my own, not due to him in any way!"

I scowled, wrested my reproof back on track.

"Not every man is privileged to serve his country by commanding the men who fight her battles. He earns that privilege in part by doing his duty to the men *whose lives are in his keeping*.

"Obedience is the first lesson. Any order given by rightful authority is to be obeyed, not because it's right but because the authority is right. It's how God governs the world."

The boy kept eyes forward and face expressionless. I wasn't deceived.

"A soldier's true glory is to *serve*. He sacrifices his own home … his own self-interest … his own self-direction … to—hem! yes, it's true, he *consecrates* himself—to service that could at any time require him to sacrifice his life. All this for the good of others, not himself.

"You were offered the privilege of service and haven't proven worthy. It remains only for your superintendent to dismiss you and make place for one who is.

"Since you do more harm than good in the field, you will assist the quartermaster in his inventory, beginning tomorrow. You are confined to garrison. Dismissed!"

MacLeod

Colonel Hale's informal summons brought me to his office after Recall. The staff had gone off duty.

"Have a chair.

"Hem! There's good stuff in that nephew of yours. Thought I'd sound you out so we're not working at cross purposes with him."

"I've disciplined him, sir." My mouth drew taut.

"Thought you had. At one point in a long oration, he bristled like a porcupine at the very idea you might err, said you always do what's proper. All the proper loyalty there."

I felt my expression soften. "He was brought up well. I wish I'd known his father, but he died before the boy was sent to me. What line did you take with him, sir?"

"Seeming ... hem! ... to draw the conclusion he's already forfeited his opportunity, he should be thinking his superintendent is dismissing him. Then I extolled the honor of the service so he'd know how much he was going to lose. We'll take care of matters here without bothering Superintendent Smith, but he's not to know that yet.

"I've confined him to garrison and assigned him and Barton to assist with inventories. It'll do those young bravos no harm to stew in their own juices while they wait for the axe to fall! Meanwhile, we'll bring them up to the mark before they take the field again."

I thought how similar our methods were. "We'll take our hunting trip after he's graduated, then. Last time it was put off by the Sioux!"

"He can go if he's with you, but send him to me to request permission.

"Our juniors! They want glory on the field of honor. They'll get their chance one day. By then, they'll know it for the sacrifice it really is.

"There are many worse faults an officer could have than high courage."

Torquil

Uncle James came in and asked what passed with Colonel Hale.

"I'm under garrison arrest and ordered to assist the quarter-master. Will you permit me to leave quarters to do it, sir?"

"Confinement requires performing your duties and returning immediately afterward." He looked as stony as Commandant Ship. "Did he say anything else?"

"I'm going to be dismissed."

"Did you ask for another chance?"

"No, sir. It's all decided."

"What are you going to do now?"

I'd lost his counsel forever.

"I don't know."

"You can ask God for guidance."

"No, I can't. He's finally cast me away."

"Surely not! What makes you think so?"

"I tried to pray, and He wasn't there. All day."

MacLeod

He gazed at nothing all through dinner and scarcely touched a bite. Afterward, praying silently, I pretended to read a newspaper while he stood with one forearm on the mantelpiece, staring into the black, cold, empty fireplace. I was ready when he pleaded.

"Would you pray for my soul? Maybe God will hear you. It's the only hope I have."

We knelt by his bed. I put a hand on his shoulder.

"Holy God, I come before your throne on behalf of Torquil Dhu, praying your continued mercy upon him. You have brought him through grievous dangers and cruel hardships. You have preserved his life and delivered him from much evil. He has seldom departed from You. Always, his heart returns.

"I, your servant, come before You. I offer on your altar the sacrifice of forgiving him, in Jesus' name. I leave there my sacrifice and pray that You, too, will forgive him.

"Cleanse him of this sin. Refine him with Your holy fire. Take not Yourself, his chief joy, from him, but renew a right spirit within him and restore him to full communion with You.

"I pray humbly, in Jesus' name, Amen."

I gave his shoulder an encouraging grip and rose.

"Sir ... I really am sorry for ... bringing you shame." He hung his head.

"It's the first time you have."

"It's the last time, I swear!" He looked up at me. "I despise myself for repaying so foully all you've done. I'll try to be worthy of you ... and honor you better in the future.

"I reckon I'll stay here a while and see if ... He ... answers."

"'Wait upon the Lord,'" I quoted, remembering how I'd been required to. "We'll see this through, my lad."

"Thank you, sir ... for ... everything."

Torquil

Relief that Uncle James wasn't going to cast me away went too deep for anything.

No hope of continuing at the V.M.I. paled by contrast to my eternal life hanging in the balance. Nothing indicated permission to enter God's presence. Old resentments returned. Since pain was my reward, whether I did right or wrong, I might as well do as I pleased. It didn't have the perverse satisfaction it used to. If I were going to perdition anyway, why refrain from anything that gratifies me? Even if pleasure were short-lived, or damaging. Even to others. No reason to care about them, either.

After such wicked thoughts, remorse cut deep. I remembered with longing the holy delight of God's presence. With all my heart I yearned for the Light and hungered to walk in Him again. I realized at last, the Light is my true Home. And I'm exiled.

MacLeod

Torquil's expression the next afternoon looked like he'd been struck.

"Just now I was strictly commanded, in my spirit, to look up a certain verse and obey it. Saint Mark 9:29: 'And he said unto them, This kind can come forth by nothing, but by prayer, and fasting.'"

I frowned. "An evil spirit or demon cannot dwell in a man who's filled with the Holy Spirit. He filled you when you committed your life to Christ."

"Could He have left me?"

"No. Jesus promised he'd never leave us nor forsake us, nor leave us comfortless. The Holy Spirit is the Comforter. It must be something else."

"My daemon?"

"The daemon, strictly defined, is a demon or evil spirit. Those can oppress or attack you. You can be so unwitting you don't know what's being done to you, nor make a defense against it. They can influence your thought, feelings, and behavior, but they can't enter you. The space is already full—and guarded."

"I wonder what God means, that's supposed to come forth."

"As you fast and pray, I'm sure He'll tell you."

"Fast! It's dinner time!" He looked dismayed. "But it's the only line left open. May I be excused from meals till He tells me otherwise?"

"Better yet, I'll go to the mess."

Torquil

I could think of nothing but food when I reported for duty, stomach growling—especially when we were sent to inventory commissary stores. I drank water to fill the void. It didn't help. I went straight to the sleeping chamber after duty, to pray and seek God. God sent a verse to my mind: instruction on fasting.

> When thou fastest, anoint thy head; and wash thy face;
> That thou appear not unto men to fast, but unto thy
> Father which is in secret: and thy Father which seeth
> in secret shall reward thee openly.
> —Matthew 6:17–18

It must refer to public appearances. I blessed God for the promise of reward. I hoped it meant I'd somehow be reinstated at the V.M.I. and be commissioned. It confirmed that God meant to do spiritual work in me.

I met each day looking like usual, but I grew cross and cranky. My stomach hurt, my head ached, and a strange taste in my mouth wouldn't go away. I had to hold onto my temper with both hands, but when a barrel wouldn't shift or a box fell from the stack, I sputtered.

"You're cross as two sticks!"

"Not your fault!"

"What's the matter, best girl refuse you?"

"None of your affair!"

Lieutenant Barton

I wondered who the fair rejector might be.

"Which of the girls gave Drummond the mitten?" I asked Frantz and Rush at the mess that evening. "He's riled as a bear with a sore paw."

"I didn't know he was sweet on anyone," said Frantz.

"Maybe she's someone back east," Rush guessed.

MacLeod

Barton's suggestion would explain any oddities the garrison might notice in Torquil's behavior. I couldn't have thought of a better diversion myself. Though the subalterns glanced in my direction, I held my peace and discussed the army's postwar consolidation with white-bearded Captain Parnell.

> For mine iniquities are gone over my head: as a heavy burden they are too heavy for me.
> —Psalm 38:4

Torquil

'Dear God, forgive my unrighteous anger! I know I need to wait upon You for all things. I want Your perfect work, and not to be impatient like this!'

Part of my mind really holds those ideals, but God knows my thoughts.

'But I am impatient! Whatever You want to do with me, I wish You'd do it soon! You called me to serve, but now I'm going to be dismissed instead and be in the ranks for the rest of my days. I was wrong to act like I did, and I'm truly sorry.

'I beg You, please forgive me, for sinning against You and Uncle James, and fellow soldiers. What's come of it is all my own fault. I wish You'd set things right again! I can't! And I can't control whatever makes me do that!'

My only answer was reference to Psalm 51. The verses God desired to point out seemed to leap from the page, while the rest of the print receded.

> Have mercy upon me, O God, according to thy loving kindness: according unto the multitude of thy tender mercies blot out my transgressions. Wash me thoroughly from mine iniquity, and cleanse me from my sin.

> For I acknowledge my transgressions, and my sin in ever before me … Against thee … have I sinned, and done this evil in thy sight. …
>
> Create in me a clean heart, O God; and renew a right spirit within me. Cast me not away from thy presence; and take not thy holy Spirit from me. Restore unto me the joy of thy salvation …
>
> The sacrifices of God are a broken spirit: a broken and a contrite heart, O God, thou wilt not despise.

Though I didn't know it yet, my spirit was already broken by seeing my family murdered. I'd disobeyed God's direct order and was afraid of losing the most precious Home of all. That God condescended to convict me of sin gave me hope there might still be some contact, but could it ever be the full communion that blessed me in boyhood? I'd surely gone beyond the boundary where His redemptive justice could reach me.

'O dear God, I don't know how to be sorry enough for what I've done! Please help me!'

* * *

Kneeling before my Lord's presence another day, I learned God's first priority.

> Nevertheless I have somewhat against thee, because thou hast left thy first love. Remember therefore from whence thou hast fallen, and repent, and do the first works.
> —Revelation 2:4–5

My first love! Sacred delight when I gave my life to the Christ of God and was filled with God's Holy Spirit … boyhood's innocent happiness in the presence of God … how hard I'd tried to please Him by saying only what was true and doing only what was right. It was so simple then.

It seemed simple when I led the Rangers, too. Standing alone, directly before God, I'd been single-minded in duty. I'd daily read God's Word and prayed. My Lord had sustained me at Camp Sherman, when His presence was as clear, pure light. Overcome by longing for what I'd left behind, I prostrated myself before God and let bitter tears flow, remembering from whence I'd fallen. I hungered to return to untarnished life in God's presence.

I returned to first works by making intercession for others. I was amazed He invited me to pray. I hoped that meant He'd hear my prayers. After Amen, I started reading the Psalms.

* * *

God's next lesson gave me the references with pounding swiftness. As soon as I read the last word of one, direction to the next took its place.

> For this commandment which I command thee this day, it is not hidden from thee, neither is it far off. ... But the word is very nigh unto thee, in thy mouth, and in thy heart, that thou mayest do it.
>
> Obey them that have the rule over you ...
>
> O, that thou hadst hearkened to my commandments! Then had thy peace been as a river, and thy righteousness as waves of the sea.
>
> Now the Lord hath brought it, and done according as he hath said: because ye have sinned against the Lord, and have not obeyed his voice, therefore this thing is come upon you.[24]

---

24 *Holy Bible, King Kames Version,* Deuteronomy 30: 11 and 14; Hebrews 13: 17; Isaiah 48: 18; Jeremiah 40:3, respectively..

The verses burned in my mind.

Obedience. I hadn't heeded Dominie Gilchrist's warning not to seek vengeance. I'd known God's command not to seek my own death, for years now.

Obedience. I'd thought little about obeying God. I'd given myself to pleasure and my delectable social life instead of seeking and following His direction.

Obedience. The difference between volunteers and Regulars is, in the volunteers, reasonable orders were obeyed more because they were reasonable than because they were orders. In the Regulars and at the V.M.I., orders were obeyed because they were orders, given by those who had the right to command.

Obedience. Those who obeyed orders had to trust in the rightness of the authorities who gave orders.

It struck me that instant: I might be less disobedient than unwilling to trust! It all culminated in trust in God, the supreme Authority. From His authority flows all lesser power to command.

But He is the same God who allowed Da and Douglas to be murdered! I was astonished the matter recurred. I'd *buried* it.

It couldn't be right! It still hurt so bad, I could be satisfied only if I knew the reason God, who is always right, had allowed what I believe completely wrong. They didn't deserve to be murdered! And I, who'd always loved the Light, and obeyed and tried to please Him, didn't deserve to lose the self and the world that died with them.

And yet, "This thing is come upon you ... because ye have sinned against the Lord"!

* * *

I pondered the convoluted problem, growing weaker. Stomach cramps returned. The vile taste in my mouth got worse. Thoughts swirled slowly around a center point that wouldn't stay centered, but drifted off in all directions. I did the first works. Bible reading and prayer refreshed my soul. Concentrating doggedly to keep prayers coherent brought some clarity of mind.

By strongest will, I walked erect and with purpose, but the next evening, everything went black. I fell while climbing the stairs. When I came to myself, Frantz and Captain Parnell were staring at me.

MacLeod

From exploring the west, with its dangers and some long periods of hunger, I knew the effects of starvation and saw them in my nephew. I resolved to intervene before he grew too weak to recover, if I had to force him to eat!

'How long, O Lord?'

Torquil

I wrestled in prayer about my inability to trust God. With an inward sigh, I prayed back from Psalms.

> I know, O Lord, that thy judgments are right, and that thou in faithfulness hath afflicted me. Look thou upon me, and be merciful unto me, as thou usest to do unto those that love thy name ... let not any iniquity have dominion over me.
> —Psalm 119:75, 132–133

Part of me believed what I prayed; another part scoffed. I thought I'd loved my Lord's name, in that, biblically, the name describes a being's character. I stopped just short of demanding what kind of character would have killed Da and Douglas, and instead, begged God that this mental iniquity wouldn't have dominion over me.

God spoke no personal word, but continued to direct by messages from the Bible. He was making His teachings alive. It was grace upon grace. I was experiencing miracles.

Above all, I was grateful to be allowed into His presence. I'd felt obliterated when it seemed He cast me away. For a day or two, I had no trouble going about with a cheerful countenance. That God was convicting me of sins, gave me hope that by repenting I might yet please the Holy One, and be made fit to serve Him as an officer. That the Creator of the universe condescended to tutor me filled me with humility and awe and glory all at once.

On bad days, I was sure the punishment spoken of was that I'd never be commissioned, or that God meant to starve me to death and send my soul to hell. But I kept the fast, in hope of the inferred reward.

* * *

Whether or not I trusted the Ordainer of all power, I realized obedience wasn't something I could choose to embrace or not embrace. Rather, it's the unyielding foundation upon which rests the order of the entire world, spiritual and material. In disobedience, I'd be outside that order, an outlaw barred from its society and its security. But within that order, even in doing right, I couldn't trust the ruling Power to do right by me!

It stunned me to realize I'd been holding it against Him all these years! That a Christian didn't forgive God was outrageous, when He's the Supreme Power of the Universe, the Ordainer, the model, the pattern, of all that's right and holy, He who holds my life and eternal life and everything that exists in his hands—but I was calling Him wrong in what He did! How had I dared think the One who always does right could be wrong in performing his holy decree. How dared I defile His Name—doubt the perfect holy character of God Himself!

'O dear God,' I prayed in my heart, 'It was You who called me! Make things right again, I pray You! I'm willing to bear any punishment, or make any sacrifice, only, let me be commissioned!'

For answer, I was referred to First Samuel 15:22: "Hath the Lord as great delight in burnt offerings and sacrifices, as in obeying the voice of the Lord? Behold, to obey is better than sacrifice."

I sighed. 'Dear God, I am obeying. I'm fasting and praying and doing the first works, as You ordered. Do You want me to do more? What more? Do You want sacrifice, too?'

I had to repair more than actions. I had to change my soul, and I didn't know how. I'd read through Psalms and was starting over.

> The steps of a good man are ordered by the Lord: and
> he delighteth in his way. Though he fall, he shall not
> be utterly cast down: for the Lord upholdeth him with
> his hand.
> —Psalm 37:23–24

I tried to take hold of the promise, though I'm the opposite of good.

'Dear God, thank You that you want to uphold me, but I want—' From within, from deeper desire than I consciously knew, my spirit overrode my mind and prayed desperately, *'You were my Light all my life, and I miss You!'*

Tears flowed. I mourned irrecoverable loss. Then, angry at losing control, I dashed them away. What I'd become—emotional as a woman, physically weak, losing control of body and mind—terrified me. I was riding the edge between life and death, and it wasn't glorious at all! I longed for a just peace between myself and God.

* * *

I'd been fasting fourteen days. I had to nerve myself to descend the stairs. I held the banister rail tight, trod slowly, and breathed a prayer of thanks when I reached the ground, that I was still on my feet. Then I forgot where I was and where ordered to duty, till Barton came up, looking cheerful.

"On to ordnance! Hope we don't explode any shells today."

I kept myself awake all day only by teeth-clenching assertion of my will … life-and-death matter not to mishandle munitions. I quivered with nervous tension and kept going … up the stairs and into quarters … collapsed into the east chair by the front windows, breathing hard like I'd been running. Body's reserve nearly used up … breathing and heartbeat slowed. …

"How are you?" Uncle James's entry roused me.

"I'm all right."

I hauled myself up, swayed on my feet, caught at the chair for balance. Knelt at the side of my bed, didn't know what to pray. What did God want to remove? Fell asleep again. Wakened to be told what more He wanted me to do.

> I beseech ye therefore, brethren, by the mercies of God, that ye present your bodies a living sacrifice, holy, acceptable unto God, which is your reasonable service.
> —Romans 12:1
>
> For ye are bought with a price: therefore glorify God in your body, and in your spirit, which are God's.
> —I Corinthians 6:20

My whole being was required as a sacrifice! So was all my life, now and past and future—my loss and sin and suffering, all I was, and am, and might be and do! Since I was bought at the price of Jesus' blood, the sacrifice was owed! If I acknowledged being bought, I had to admit I was owned.

I was afraid—afraid as when I surrendered myself and my weapons to the Yankees. I'd made myself defenseless, put myself at their mercy, knowing they'd have none. If I surrendered to God, I'd be at His mercy. He shouldn't have any, when I was holding things He must have ordained, against Him! My fear and doubt disregarded knowledge of mercy received: God should blot me out of existence! If He didn't, then He could make whatever He wanted of me, of my life. I deserved nothing I desired: I feared what it would be. Visions of a clerk's dull job or an enlisted man's hard life rose in my mind. And what about my past? Was the terrible injustice to remain forever unredressed? I remembered when God made me know that justice was done, after Yohanson's torture. What did it mean?

Could it mean He'd actually done right? Whatever reason God had for letting Da and Douglas die, could it be part of some plan of His so immense and mysterious that I couldn't see its righteousness, its purpose, its perfect completion—but only trust Him for it? Could the loss that broke my heart and warped my nature, and all the suffering it led to, be a sacrifice required of me, to contribute to some holy work of His? Could I ever trust Him in that?

Colonel Hale's tribute to service said the soldier consecrated himself to serve selflessly, even unto death, an ideal greater than himself. I was called upon to trust and serve God with the same devotion. I balked because one was earthly—of men's power merely—while the other was the supreme Authority I feared to trust.

I refused to obey my Lord's demand. The price I was ordered to pay was too high. Being owned would make my whole being subject to infinite, unknowable, eternal threat of suffering more, and worse. Instantly came two references.

Ye shall observe to do therefore, as the Lord your God
hath commanded you; you shall not turn aside to the
right hand, or to the left.
—Deuteronomy 5:32

And ye shall seek me, and find me, when ye shall
search for me with all your heart.
—Jeremiah 29:13

A stern command—on the very heels of the command to give
myself as a sacrifice! Obedience again, so I might find God. Yet I
balked. I could not trust.

* * *

"Twelve-pound exploding shells, mountain howitzers."

I found some loose shells, picked one up, stared at it. Its weight
in my hand took me to the bluff where the Sioux were camped. I
heard Marbury scream.

"Five second fuse…"

I cut a piece with my case-knife. Lip of the bluff … swirling
smoke set glowing by the campfire below. Fit fuse to shell …
match from pocket.

" … count four seconds …."

Barton dropped his blanks and grabbed the match.

"Are you insane! What are you doing!"

"Recapturing Marbury. You can lob them by hand, too." I saw
the shimmering heart of the Indians' campfire. …

MacLeod

My son had lost flesh to an alarming degree. His skin was dull,
stretched taut over the bones of his face. His eyes were hollow.
How long a fast would the Lord require? I almost asked, but was
warned in my spirit not to intervene:

"The battle is not yours, but God's!"

Wanting his fast be the perfect sacrifice which would be part of the perfect work God intended to do, I submitted anxious concern, by hard-held faith, to my Lord's wisdom.

'Lord, my heart is not haughty, nor mine eyes lofty; neither do I exercise myself in great matters, or in things too high for me.'

Torquil

In quarters, with strength for nothing but to be still and attend upon God, my spirit wavered. I sensed something lifting me up. It sustained me when there seemed nothing else.

I waited. The God I trusted in boyhood is unchanging. I want to trust Him still.

MacLeod

I waited. I prayed harder than ever before while my lad's life flickered away. I knelt by his bedside one noontide, silently pouring out my heart.

'Holy God, I come to You on behalf of this beloved boy You entrusted to my keeping. My care has not been perfect. ... You have made him a son to me. Now You tell me to do nothing while I watch him die! He isn't wicked. Though he sinned grievously, forgive him, I pray You. Restore him to life with You. Guide him in the course You have ordained. Preserve the purity of his heart, that he may love and serve You all his life.'

My soul wavered.

'Holy God, I beg You not to require of me both my sons, and leave me only graves!'

Strength was given my spirit.

'Yet Thou art God. Your thoughts are above our thoughts, and Your ways past finding out. If it please Thee, take him unto Thyself. I offer him up!

'In Jesus'—'

My Lord's answer interrupted. He spoke audibly, in comforting, compassionate tones.

"Be still—and know that I am God."

I was filled with the peace of God which passeth all understanding, completely satisfied.

Torquil

I saw Uncle James in prayer and felt comforted as my eyes closed. I wakened in the night as though from pleasant dreams, half my mind on God and my beloved ones in heaven, half on God and my beloved ones on earth. I paraphrased from the Book of Job.

'Though Thou slay me, yet will I trust in Thee.'

As it stood in my mind, I believed it in my heart. God's Spirit dwelling in my spirit had brought it forth.

'Dear God, I choose to trust You!' burst from heart and mind and will and spirit all together.

My spirit quickened my mind. I repented in detail.

'I offered to make any sacrifice or endure any punishment if You'd allow me to command in Your chosen vocation. I relinquish that petition and submit humbly to your will.

'You required the sacrifice of all my being, and I refused, because I demanded the reason for my pain and sorrow, and You gave it not. I held it against You. I confess these as sin. I renounce them. I repent.

'Unto Thee alone belong the issues from death!

'I offer up the suffering as a sacrifice, to Your holiness, Your plan, Your will.

'I choose You, my Light. I desire You more than anything else. I choose to trust You for the past, and now, and forever, whether I understand or not.

'So I present myself, the living sacrifice You require: my past and future, my body, soul, and spirit. I confess, You bought me at a terrible price: You own me.

'I surrender unconditionally. Do with me as You please.

'In Jesus's name, Amen.'

* * *

Next day, every time I raised my head, I began to dream, faint or be dizzy. I must be dying. I took my Bible and set the end of its spine on my chest, where I could read without bringing my head up.

The Bible lay facedown, its pages crumpled, when I woke. I left it there and prayed until consciousness left me again. I suppose, having to wait meant the sincerity of my intention was being tried. I renewed my surrender: God doesn't have to tell me why He let Da and Douglas be murdered. I roused to see Uncle James at the looking glass adjusting his cravat. I started to greet him. When I opened my eyes, he was sitting on a footstool by the bed.

"Torquil Dhu." He spoke my name affectionately. "Can I do anything for you?"

"A blanket. I'm cold."

MacLeod

The day and the room were sweltering hot. Further convinced he was dying, I spread blankets over him. The mess could do without my company tonight.

"What else?"

"Psalm 49:15. What does it say?"

I opened his Bible and read. "But God will redeem my soul from the power of the grave: for he shall receive me."

"He gave me that … I was going to read it. … I'm not … condemned … wherever my soul is going to live. And … 130. 'Out of the depths. …'"

> Out of the depths have I cried unto thee, O Lord. Lord, hear my voice: let thine ears be attentive to the voice of my supplications. If thou, Lord, shouldst mark iniquities, O Lord, who shall stand? But there is forgiveness with thee, that thou mayest be feared.
>
> I wait for the Lord, my soul doth wait, and in his word do I hope. My soul waiteth for the Lord more than they that watch for the morning.
> —Psalm 130:1–6

I prayed the words silently: I remembered the glory of God's forgiveness at Fort Banks. Truly believing in it, truly receiving it, pleading for God's answer, I gave "Amen" aloud. I shut my eyes and breathed deep before I lifted myself to lean against the headboard of the bed, panting from the effort, dizzy, but mind and vision cleared.

"Uncle James … by morning I could be in my long home."

He gave a solemn nod. "Yes."

"I'm honored more than I can say, to be *in loco filiis* to you."

"Had you been born to me, I couldn't hold you in greater affection."

We gripped each other's right hands … held tight. …

He gave me a drink of water and drew the blanket over me. I tried to smile, but my half-smile is ingrained. All my nerves jangling from the effort I'd made … almost gasping … trying to calm twitching fingers and eyelids that wouldn't stay closed.

As the dimming current carried me away, I quoted from Psalms in silent prayer.

'Cause me to hear thy lovingkindness in the morning; for in Thee do I trust; cause me to know the way wherein I should walk; for I lift up my soul unto thee.

'Into thine hand I commit my spirit.'

MacLeod

In deepening dusk, I looked out the window and saw nothing. I feared Torquil's rough breaths were his last breaths.

"O holy God ..." I poured out grief and faith and need all together: "Into thine hands I commit his spirit! A sore-tried spirit, yet, in extremity, faithful. Have mercy upon ... us ... have mercy! And still I know ... thou art God." I paraphrased from Job: "The Lord giveth and the Lord taketh away. Blessed be the name of the Lord!"

2. Redivivus

. . . by sorrow of the heart the spirit is broken. . . . so are the sons of men snared in an evil time, when it falleth suddenly upon them.

The spirit of a man will sustain his infirmity; but a wounded spirit who can bear?

Thy bruise is incurable . . . thy wound is grievous . . . thou hast no healing medicines . . . .

"I will restore health unto thee, and I will heal thee of thy wounds, saith the Lord."[25]

---

25 *Holy Bible, King James Version,* (in order), Proverbs 15: 13; Ecclesiastes 9: 12b; Proverbs 18: 14; Jeremiah 30: 12, 13b, and 17a (italics added).

MacLeod

When I returned from Sunday morning inspection, my son was dressed and sitting very still in the west chair by the front window.

"I'm still here. An anticlimax, isn't it?"

"A glad one to me. Can I do anything for you?"

"No. Thank you."

His eyes closed. I glanced outdoors.

"Look! Quickly!" I expected him merely to turn toward the window, to see the herd of antelope dashing and bounding across the parade.

Torquil

By all the strength I could summon, I raised myself to a stand. Caught myself on the back of the chair … looked outdoors.

A radiant white column of light rose around the flagpole. From the ground, it pierced beyond the firmament to a blazing white point in the center of the heavens. I gazed in wonder. Amid the most powerful assurance and love I ever experienced, I heard:

"Be not afraid, only believe!"

Jabbing of needles inside my skull … pulsing, pumping turmoil filled my chest.

MacLeod

His face went white. He dropped like a stone.

He was still breathing. I raised his limp body to a sitting position, put his head between his knees, rubbed the back of his neck. He began to stir.

A murmur: "I saw the Lord, mighty and lifted up."

Was he quoting from Isaiah? In my spirit, I was loosed from God's prohibition. I supported him into the sleeping chamber and laid him on his bed.

"Now then, my lad, it's enough. I'll take the responsibility before God, and you won't be fasting any longer!"

A gentle and genuine smile, the first I'd ever seen him give.

Torquil

Pleasant warmth and tranquil well-being all through me. Mind at peace. Body pulsed gently with life. Happiness dwelt in my soul. My spirit was full of the presence of God.

"It's all right. It's done now."

"I'm relieved to hear it! Rest, and I'll find you something to eat." I smiled more. "Yes, Uncle James, sir."

I closed my eyes and saw again the column of white fire and its radiant apex. I heard God speak a second time, and knew it was not for Jerusalem, but for me.

> Comfort ye, comfort ye my people, saith your God. Speak ye comfortably to Jerusalem, and cry unto her, that her warfare is accomplished, that her iniquity is pardoned; for she hath received of the Lord's hand double for all her sins.[26]

"My Lord, and my God," I breathed, then drifted into sweet slumber filled with the Light.

MacLeod

Finding nothing else suitable for my son's first nourishment in three weeks, I made eggnog. It would address all that ailed him. I held his head against my shoulder and put the cup to his lips. He sipped with every sign of enjoyment. It didn't nauseate him. I breathed a silent sigh of relief and thanked God.

"Thank you. Is there any more?"

---

26 Isaiah 40:1.

"Soon, once I see how that settles. I believe it counts as a meal."

I bowed my head. "Holy God, thank You for this food and for completing your holy work in my son. Grant that it fit him for his service to You. Daily direct and bless him in that service. In Jesus' name, Amen."

The eggnog settled well. At intervals, I fed him on the contents of my ice box.

"The ladies have been sending delicacies ever since you've been indoors."

He swallowed beef tea with healing herbs and tried to look grateful.

"It tastes like one of Mrs. Grieg's brews. It was kind of them all."

"Some are genuinely kind. Others act kindly to keep up their social credit. I doubt it makes a difference in the flavor of their offerings."

"Every flavor's better than the one that's been in my mouth. It tasted like corruption."

"It was. Your body had to consume itself to keep you alive."

Torquil

Frequent, plentiful nourishment brought strength. Coordination and mental ability recovered apace. Returning energy wouldn't let me sit still. I walked out, praying to my Lord the thankfulness I found in Psalms.

> The Lord upholdeth all that fall. ... He healeth the broken in heart, and bindeth up their wounds. O Lord, thou hast brought up my soul from the grave: thou hast kept me alive, that I should not go down to the pit. Blessed be God, which hath not turned away my prayer, nor his mercy from me.[27]

27 Psalm 145:14; 147:3; 30:3; 66:20.

Time spent with my Master was a pleasure now. Humbled, grateful to be forgiven and restored, I basked in the Light I'd missed so sorrowfully. God gave me the understanding withheld before. A logical progression unfolded.

Everything flowed from the first calamity. Hurt—uncomforted, unhealed, unforgiven—turned to anger which grew into rage. Rage impelled me to vow vengeance. Rage and vengeance culminated in the battle fury I named "daemon." It gave me furious delight in battle and forced me to seek it again and again. Though I'd warred against its demoralizing influence, I hadn't the power to vanquish it.

Fragments of evidence fell into place. My wounded spirit had kept me vulnerable. The wound was beyond human power to heal. It inflicted fresh injury by compelling me to bait relentless nemesis and suffer bodily wounds and soul's destruction, over and over. Only God's mercy, my conscience, and my longing to be who I'd been, had kept me from destruction in the jaws of the eternal trap. Through all the cursed years, I was a combination of pure heart and fury I couldn't conquer.

Sin had begotten sin, and I, its victim, became its agent and took all the punishment.

Now I was redeemed. Redeemed from murderous rage seething at my core. Redeemed from tense, unending watchfulness against attack. Redeemed from seeking nemesis to destroy me. Redeemed from unforgiveness of God, for allowing it. Redeemed from distrusting my Redeemer.

Sobered by real redemption from bodily and spiritual death, I recognized the vastness and the depth of my debt to the Christ of God. Upon waking each day, I renewed my vow by committing myself and what the day might bring, to His will. My faith was so quickened that in completely trusting my Master, I was content.

As I gave trust and found it answered by Truth, I received more ability to trust. Freedom: not to feel compelled to doubt! My entire life and being belong to God. What will He do with it?

I couldn't remember having such well-being since the innocent happiness of boyhood, before Da and Douglas died. Knowledge and experience were added, but my mind was no longer cynical. I kept my inborn reserve and gravity, but these were tempered with kindness of heart that, since the tragedy, I'd seldom allowed. I received anew the spirit of mercy I'd forsaken. The outward and visible sign of these inward and spiritual graces was a slow-dawning smile of such gentleness that, when I caught sight of it in the looking-glass, it softened my harsh features.

* * *

When I met Smith, he told me the Indians named me "White Coup Stick." Then he backed off a step, looking awestruck.

"There's light about yew now, not light-nin'."

Colonel Hale

I polished the last periods of my oration. My words in the ears of certain Senators, let alone the chief executive I served with when we were new graduates of West Point, would override any objections to the two-thirds vote of Congress required to remove the political disabilities from MacLeod's nephew. I also anticipate success in obtaining him a commission and having him assigned to the Sixteenth. I don't often have the opportunity to break a subaltern to my rein so long ahead of time.

"Hem! What brings you to discompose my day's work!"

"Captain MacLeod invited me to hunt with him, sir. May I have permission to go?"

"Have you learned your duty?"

"Yes, sir."

"Recite it."

"Obedience, sir."

"Pity you weren't at the Point. They'd have taught you obedience! Hem! They'd have taught you a barrel-full of things that are wanting in you, if you ... hem! ... aspire to be an officer!

"They'd have taught you to discipline your mind ... investigate thoroughly ... reason accurately. You must do these to decide how to meet all circumstances, known or unforeseen. You'd have learned complete, reasoned control of yourself—body, mind, and all.

"Only thus can you exercise wise, right judgment. Only thus, can you give orders worth obeying!

"Do you mean to rejoin the service?"

"Yes, sir."

"Why?"

"It's my calling, sir."

I summoned up a look of disbelief. "Hem! If you're determined ...

"The officer, Mr. Drummond, makes or breaks the command! Your whole duty is to the men whose *lives are in your keeping!* If you are faithful to every particular of that duty, to take good care of them, and train them till correct behavior is instinct, you will receive reward: victory! Hem! The first ten minutes of battle show whether you're faithful—or a failure!

"You must be all you require of them. You must be the prop they lean on, if necessary. Your spirit must be the wellspring from which theirs draws refreshment.

"You must be one hundred per cent. reliable ... to your men and your superiors. They must be able to trust in your truthfulness and faithfulness—your *righteousness!*—at all times, in all circumstances.

"If you *are* all these things, and *do* all these things, your voice means something, and your men will hear and obey."

The look in his eyes showed he believed himself capable of becoming the ideal I unfurled in glory. Whichever command he comes under, the service will benefit. I didn't say so.

"You might as well re-enlist now rather than waste money on a journey to Virginia."

"My father desired me to complete my education, sir. I will obey him first."

An abrupt nod covered my approval. One has to keep up the stern front. "May you find a school that'll have you! You may go hunting. Dismissed!"

Torquil

I ceased to kick against the calling of a soldier.

* * *

MacLeod

Broiling elk backstrap on a peeled stick over the coals, I sensed a separateness in my son. Our bond of affection was deeper, but his dependence was gone. He was his own man.

Torquil

Living in newly received peace, allowing my hungry soul to be filled with the Light, I hoped I was becoming like Uncle James and my kind, good father, the men of all men I'd like to emulate. Some attributes remained to be added, but now I was free to acquire them, as I hadn't been since the evil thunderbolt crippled my moral character. Nor, until my soul was healed, had I been, under God, wholly in possession of myself. Only now could I embody the pure character my pure heart longed to animate. I broiled my backstrap on the other side and told Uncle James about it.

"For years, Son, I grieved that evil wounded and beset you so sorely that you couldn't see past its face, to grapple with its heart. It's well you understand it now."

"God delivered me from it. I couldn't do it myself. It was strange: He warned me not to be afraid, but I thought I was being killed."

MacLeod

I was happy to receive confidences that did not now arise from the bondage of need, but were the freely chosen communion of an independent being. My son's character was restored. I watched the awe in his expression.

"What I wanted most—what I craved—was to be purified, free of that evil presence, and free to live to God without it preventing me.

"But I'm forgiven. God blotted out my sins. I know my Redeemer. I don't feel torn apart any more. God restored my faith in Himself—his character. Even if He ordains bachelorhood in barracks, it's all right."

He went quiet, gazing into the fire, expression pensive. It was firm when he looked up.

"I've become acquainted with some of your old friends, Captains Fairfax and Peake."

"I hope they're well. Our viewpoints may never be reconciled, but I'm gratified our old friendship has survived. Fairfax was my classmate, and I became friends with Peake in Texas."

"That's what they said."

"Did you identify yourself as my nephew?"

"No. I had to avoid them because I was carrying contraband. I couldn't get away from overhearing them."

He took a long breath. I waited. He fixed a level, direct gaze upon me.

"I heard what you did for me, and for Abercairn ... and what you had to pay."

Torquil

Uncle James was silent so long I feared he was displeased.

"A man can't anticipate all the requirements of fatherhood, my son, but, had I received foreknowledge, I'd have made the same decisions."

"You must have trusted God."

"He was teaching me to 'lean not unto mine own understanding.' My conscience and my orders were in conflict.

"I was compelled to obey Him one step at a time, including staying with you. The one thing I was sure of was protecting children. That and my responsibility for you lay behind my remonstrances about risking yourself less."

"I was the only one I could risk. And noblesse oblige, of course. I'm Drummond. The county is my duty." I frowned, struck by a disturbing contradiction. "That conflicts with duty elsewhere."

CHAPTER 26

"SET ME AS A SEAL UPON THINE HEART ... FOR LOVE IS AS STRONG AS DEATH"[28]

Torquil

Union Pacific R.R.
En route, in Nebraska
August 24, 1870

Dear Miss Mary,

I left Cheyenne, W. T., an hour ago. Uncle James was as good and kind to me as if I were born his son. He bore with my being bad company while God did a great work in my heart and mind and spirit. I hope I can repay him somehow.

But how does a man pay the debts due, for the sacrifices of others? I learned by accident what Uncle James did in Abercairn, at risk of his life. My life, and the peace of yours and all Abercairn's, were the gifts

---

28 Song of Solomon 8:6.

he bought. He cut off my thanks, saying if he'd known what he'd pay, he'd have done the same.

He inspires me the way Da did. My highest wish in life is to follow their example. Any good I've done is insignificant compared to theirs, because it's not only deeds, but the goodness flowing from their hearts that makes them act that way. I long for it to be in me.

But God has given me another chance. Since the hour Da and Douglas were murdered, I lived in a bad, dark place, and I couldn't fight or will or work myself out of it, no matter how I tried. I resolved to, and failed, time after time. Your sweet faith in me was reproof and refreshment all in one. It kept me trying to live up to what you believed I was. I hope I am that man now.

God took His presence away and required me to fast and pray. His teaching and commands were rigorous, but when He had humbled me, He rebuilt my soul and spirit. It was like being created all bran new. I have hope of pleasing Him now, because He defeated the evil presence I could not conquer alone. I know now how great is my dependence upon Him who bought and who owns me.

I have been thinking much of you. I wish I could come to see you before I have to report. I don't suppose, though, after all that passed during our last visit, I'd be as welcome company as before.

I hope you can believe me, little dear, when I say I'd rather die than hurt you. I never meant it to be as it is with us. I was going to withhold words that would affect the future, until I knew what situation I would occupy in life. But a dream of felicity began to grow in me before my future could be known, and I dread that it may cause you sorrow. Can you forgive me?

I am reconciled to whatever God's plan is for my life, unknown though it is now. If (as I dare to call them) <u>our</u> hopes are not fulfilled, it is because He, in his loving wisdom, has a better intention for us. May God bless you and keep you, with every breath you draw, now and forever. I remain always,

Your faithful and devoted servant,
Torquil Dhu

Sergeants were made before I received her answer. I was named second sergeant of Company A and Bouleau, First Sergeant. Chagrined to think the office might have been mine if I hadn't disobeyed, I took advantage of the lesson. Making right decisions was easier without having to fight the evil force for every one of them. I delighted in the freedom to do right.

Mount Murray
Abercairn, Virginia
September 2, 1870

Dear Torquil Dhu,

I am so glad. I can relate now how much I worried about you and prayed for you. Worldly ideas and judgments prompted so many of your thoughts.

I shared parts of your letter with Mama and Papa. I also told them my wishes in the matters that concern us all, and they agree we have chosen wisely, to wait upon events. Papa made it clear that he would never give his blessing to such a life as you described to him. He said it is a woe upon us all, for which none of us can be held guilty. I believe they understand our dilemma and are as discomforted by it as we are. Mama believes as you do, that God will bring all to pass for the best. I believe so, too. We shall have to wait to learn the decree of His providence.

Papa said, be sure to tell you, you are still the son
and brother who is always welcome here. You asked
forgiveness,—but there is nothing to forgive!

Speaking of Uncle James, I was, with Dominie
and Miss Gilchrist, when I took them some cheese
and butter yesterday. From what they didn't say, I
think Uncle James knew he was offering his life.

That raised my eyebrows! Does my little dear make facts out
of impressions like Nannie does?

Who could have dreamt that a Yankee would be
a hero to a Virginia county! But he is, and if he ever
visits here again, I'm sure he'll know our gratitude.
Nannie and I are working at our classical studies.
Don't you think she would be a perfect pattern for
Diana, with her strength and fearlessness?

I tried to imagine a Greek goddess with red hair and freckles, but failed. Nannie's a better pattern for Boadicea, the British
warrior queen!

She is sewing for her hope chest, but keeps it a
mystery whom she will say "Yes" to,—or <u>has</u>! Since
Donald and Mr. Vogelsang are both in Lexington,
and all the young men here admire her, no one can
guess. I'm sewing, too, and, keeping my hopes a family secret.

I read contentedly the news of friends and neighbors and
home. Robbie's acumen becoming known, he was getting
more legal work. Emily was busy with the children. Mister
Stafford's school was prospering. He'd turned over classical instruction to Mrs. David Carmichael, who was aided by Amelia
MacHugh. Grain prices had dropped, so there was less currency in Abercairn. With less demand for meat animals, William

was concentrating on dairy breeds. Dominie and Miss Gilchrist were the same as ever, and Doctor Gask planned to take David as an apprentice. Aidan, working in Fredericksburg with a firm of civil engineers, was saving to provide a home and marry Miss MacPherson.

> She loved me for the dangers I had passed / and I loved her that she did pity them.
> —William Shakespeare, *Othello*

> My dear wife explored and studied my temper, and anticipated the means of satisfying even my caprices.
> —Edmund Randolph, letter, March 25, 1810

Because my heart was fixed on Miss Mary, I spent less time visiting and wrote more to my little dear. She wanted to know the life I led as a cadet, so I promised a daily journal and asked her for the same. I opened my heart with none of my former inability.

Miss Mary

I looked forward, last thing at night, to conversation time with my dear one. The day his regular letter arrived was my happiest all week. I confided thoughts and feelings and was rewarded by his doing the same. With careful tact, avoiding direct questions, I drew from him the intimate knowledge I hungered for, of the years when war and distance separated us. He gave brief reports at first, but soon poured out his heart and experiences. I rejoiced in my heart at his successes, and praised him as confirmation of what I believe of him. I learned of painful and foolish events, too, and consoled him as best I could without having a masculine mind.

Torquil

I attended the prayer meetings after supper almost every day. They're voluntary, with an encouraging rather than reproachful character. Toombs, Stone, Graves, and others who had undergone conversion last year also attended regularly. We all grew stronger in faith and closer as brothers in Christ.

Care for their welfare brought cadets, some seemingly by chance, to my room. I gave them whatever wisdom and encouragement I could think of.

* * *

Miss Mary was coming to the Lexington Loudouns till Old Christmas! I prepared for a season of bliss. Having paid for gloves to give her, I had no pocket money. I borrowed from Stone, who, citing Christian brotherhood, wouldn't charge interest, but diffidently asked for introduction into the Abercairn circle. We took him and other friends with us to Loudouns' skating party and supper.

I fastened Miss Mary's skates to her dainty boots, buckled on my own, and assisted her onto the ice. Hands clasped and shoulders touching, we glided away.

Miss Mary

I sensed it instantly. He wasn't the boy who left for the frontier six months ago. He'd seemed grown-up then, but the man who piloted us over the ice with strength and skill was a new being. I'd always felt safe when he was near, but now I felt perfect security. I saw his gentle smile for the first time, and my heart thrilled. His eyes were full of light when he looked at me, with assurance and tenderness together. His skin in winter was fair, colored by the cold at cheekbone and jawline.

Torquil

I was entranced. My little dear in her deep green winter wraps looked as lovely as she had in summer's cool draperies. She wore a sprig of holly pinned to whatever-kind-of-hat-it-was. Her eyes shone with welcome. Her sweet smile bathed my heart in warmth. I held her close and skated in a shimmering dream.

After the supper, I settled her in the window seat and gave her the French kid gloves. She tried them on, smoothing the soft, pliant leather over her fingers and buttoning the dainty buttons. She stretched out her hand to admire the fit and the fine decorative stitching.

"Oh, thank you! They're lovely!"

"Much less so than the wearer."

"Flattery isn't worthy of you!"

"I don't indulge in it."

"How did you know the size?"

I smiled, took her left hand and laid it palm to palm against my right. "Do you remember when we measured like this, last summer?"

She smiled. "Yes. I was glad you held still so long. I was measuring, too!"

Miss Mary

He'd said his hands got cold on duty at night, so I used fine, fuzzy yarn and tiny stitches to knit close-fitting gloves he could wear under his regulation cotton ones. The fit was perfect.

Mr. Vogelsang, Mr. Stone, and Donald clustered around Nannie. The other boys attended the rest of the young ladies.

Torquil

We knew our hopes were frail against powerful opposition, but after our joyful interlude at Christmas, we ignored probability and clung to hope. We never referred to the unknown and possibly separate future, but lived in the present as though our dreams had already come true, savoring the sweetness of affection while we could still indulge it to the full. The threat of disappointment only made the present more precious.

Listening to Bouleau call the roll at Tattoo, I daydreamed, 'When I get home tonight, I'll tell her how warm her gloves keep my hands.' What! I felt married already, though I was without her and was likely always to be! The brutal contrast between reality and dream was like being thrown from a fireside into a snowbank. My face went numb. Shock stopped my heart.

Now I had to live in reality instead of the voluptuous dream of possessing her. I was disgusted that I'd been deceiving myself, and, worse, my heart's dearest. Immediately I edited my letters, writing no endearments and excising ideas suggesting a future together, with pen as sharp as a scalpel. She'd said she enjoyed learning, so I encouraged her to investigate all that interested and benefitted her. A well-trained and well-filled mind, I said, would give pleasure through all the years ahead.

Miss Mary

I read what he didn't say: during those years we would probably be apart. To please him, which I love to do because I love to see him happy, I masked my heart behind intellectual discussion. Deprived of affection, I nourished hope. I had a request of his to gratify. It was still a tie, and I'd keep it strong! I tried to be content while our letters discussed philosophy or Roman authors or spiritual matters or political events, but my heart hungered for the tender, sweet words now missing.

Torquil

I tried to draw her mind away from our hope of marriage, so she'd be better prepared to withstand the loss if our dreams were destroyed. I wrote of the accidental fire in the mess hall, fortunately discovered and extinguished before much damage was done, instead of how I burned to be joined to her.

I wrote of the cold, wet spring seeming chillier than winter. To mention how warm her gloves kept my hands might revive too much hope, but ... it was only her due to know! I told her. Then I praised her argument in the negative against mine in the positive, and increased cold formality by suggesting she learn more about the subject. But in the next sentence I invited her to visit Glenlochie and borrow from the library any books she liked or found useful.

Miss Mary

> I had rather have one letter *warm* from the heart than all the cold studied ones from the *head* you could send me.
> —Sarah Trebell Galt, letter, October 31, 1806

I tried to keep sadness to myself while the formal, intellectual letters continued. I was sure in my heart he wasn't courting another girl, but sometimes I had to fight hard against the suspicion. I accepted with hope and joy the invitation to use books from Glenlochie.

We'd played in the library-*cum*-office as children. The world globe, its colors unfaded, still stood next to the lamp on the library table. Recent books as well as old, well-read ones filled shelves that lined the inner walls, which were less subject to damp, between the passage and the kitchen doors. This had been a favorite retreat of his, and I thought tenderly about him being here as a little boy.

A new law book, and the old ones and the magistrates' manuals Mr. Drummond used when a justice, were on the shelves closest to the desk, so Robbie could reach them without taxing his bad leg. Other titles were arranged by subject. But I found Thomas Moore's poems tucked between Caesar's *Gallic Wars* and Homer and *Lorna Doone* among the works on medicine.

I smiled, idly opening a book of sermons from last century. The finely wrought script from a quill pen, and the old-fashioned looped S, made me think the Drummond who made the marginal notes must have been the first or second generation in America. Drummonds and Murrays had arrived on these shores together, and one day, our two houses would be joined!

I daydreamed about what I'd make of this house when it was mine to manage. All the furniture and appointments were old, from the early Republic if not colonial times. Such classical restraint was much out of date. The present fashion is opulent decoration. Yet my husband grew up here and might not want things changed.

Emily, entering to ask if there was anything I needed, startled me out of my reverie.

"Thank you, no." I suddenly felt weak. "I'll return this in a few days. I … need to be starting home now."

"I'll ask Jemmie to bring Prettyfoot round. I hope you're all right."

Clinging to the mundane during leave-taking, I felt like I'd been deluged with icy water! My face was numb, my steps unsteady, my heart almost stopped. We're married—but we aren't! I felt faint, but I kept tight control while Jemmie held Prettyfoot at the mounting block. I walked her along the lane. When I got out of sight, I stopped and shed the tears I don't want anyone to see.

Mrs. Murray

When I saw my precious daughter's eyes, I decided I'd suffered at second hand far too long. I brought her to my sitting room, where sympathy soon elicited her disappointments. She wept in my arms. I stroked the head pressed close into my shoulder.

"You've chosen well to love him, pet. There's no one your Papa and I would rather see you marry. It's such a pity we can't tell the future, to know whether he'll be an officer or enlisted."

"O, Mama, I wish he wasn't called to such a hard life! If he could—"

"I'm afraid the day of the gentleman private soldier ended with our hope of nationhood, dear. He can't disobey God, and you wouldn't be able to honor him if he did."

"No."

"Your studies and your sweet kindness and usefulness to us all, prepares you for whatever your future holds. All of us know Torquil Dhu wants you to be happy. Don't you see, what he's asking you to do will aid in that?"

Miss Mary

I didn't want to see. The prospect of life without my beloved was an empty, endless passage, leading nowhere and swept by bitter winds that blew through me like I didn't exist.

"He's being wise and strong for both of you, to exercise restraint until we know where God will place him. He's keeping matters from going beyond bounds and causing worse hurt."

"It couldn't hurt worse."

"Believe me, dear child, it could." A look of tender sadness shadowed her face.

It was for Ewen. I felt selfish for thinking only of my own griefs. I put my arms around her, and we mourned together.

Mama's loving counsel, and, more, her sorrow, helped me regain my sense of proportion. At first, all that made me feel better was thinking, 'At least he's not dead, too!' Next came, 'We don't know yet. There's still hope.' I tried not to dwell on hope too much, but its existence comforted me. I could bear only a little at a time, but I tried to imagine what kind of life I could live without him. No prospect pleased. All seemed hollow substitutes, ways to fill the plodding years till I could wait for him in heaven or he could welcome me there.

I hoped and kept faith. Love allowed me to do no less. His wisdom and care for my future only made me love him and long for him more.

MacLeod

> Hanover Court House
> Virginia
> March 16, 1871

Darling James,

> Mother passed peacefully into the arms of her Savior last night. My brother is hastening from Abercairn to preach the funeral service, while Louisa and I and many kind helping hands prepare Mother's body for burial and make the rest of the preparations. I only wish the season were not too early for lilacs. They were her favorite flower, and I wish I could cover her casket with them. She became ever more precious to me during the many hours and days we spent together. The year of mourning will scarcely be long enough to remember and to honor her. ...

A letter would take too long: I telegraphed my brother Andrew in New York to find lilacs at any trouble or cost and express them at speed to my love. My poor darling! Her handwriting betrayed the exhaustion from her long vigil and service. Its former graceful flow had become almost erratic, its letters sharp with strain. I telegraphed heartfelt condolences and began composing a letter to share my sorrow in her sorrow at greater length.

Torquil

I conformed to *Fidelis* in all my duty. I was sure Carter would be Adjutant when ours became the first class, and hoped I'd be promoted, too. Graduating Day wasn't the only thing to look forward to. Aidan had built a house in Fredericksburg, and Miss MacPherson had set July 5, the day following graduation, for the wedding. I invited Miss Mary to the Graduating Ball, and she was coming with the MacHughs.

After the second class was examined, I was free of all but daily duties except one day I had to help supervise the new Rats setting up tents for our first summer encampment since the War. We'd move into it immediately after Graduating Day.

When Miss Mary arrived, I received permission to visit. At the National Hotel, I sent up my card and stood in the lobby. My heart beat faster and I felt hot all through, just to think of seeing her.

I heard her light step in the passage above. I saw the instant of doubt in her expression before she changed it to a brave smile. My heart hurt because I'd caused the cloud on her happiness. I didn't notice the dress she wore, but only her dear, sweet face and feminine form.

"My heart is still the same," I whispered as I raised her hand to my lips, glove and all.

Her smile softened. Her voice was warm and gentle. "So is mine."

It was all I could do, not to embrace and kiss her for her patience, understanding and faith.

* * *

In place on the flank of A Company, I heard Toombs, Stone, Graves, and the rest of the first class receive standings for their entire four years. My own achievement was called "distinguished" because I stood in the first five, fourth among thirty-eight. Carter became Adjutant, and Bouleau and Vogelsang, lieutenants. My name was read second among the new captains. The first class was relieved, the band played "Auld Lang Syne," and my final year began. Giving and receiving congratulations, I shook hands in Christian brotherhood with Toombs, Stone, and Graves, and wished them well.

"You'll all be going home to be 'the leaven of the Kingdom,' I suppose."

"We're going as missionaries to the Indians," said Graves.

"I hope I never see your hair trimming a war shirt!"

"We hope to persuade them to become our brothers in Christ," Stone replied. "When they learn Christ loved them enough to suffer worse than they do in the Sun Dance—for them—and die, too, it's bound to reach their hearts."

"There's more than one way to pacify the tribes," added Toombs.

"I'll pray you're successful, but I can't hope for it. From all I've seen, they'll never accept a religion of peace. Their whole society is built around war. You're taking your lives in your hands! But write and let me know how you're getting on, won't you?"

* * *

"Your father would be proud today ... Captain!" Lieutenant MacHugh wrung my hand heartily. "I'm glad to see you rewarded for your work."

"Thank you, sir. I hope to deserve it."

"We don't need to measure you for a new hat, then!" Grinning, Nannie shook my hand.

"Not yet." I grinned back.

Then Stone caught her eye, approached, and bowed over her hand. I tucked Miss Mary's hand into the crook of my arm.

"I'm so proud of you," she murmured.

* * *

New insignia on my coat sleeves, I was in plenty of time to escort Miss Mary to the Institute before the ball began. Head next to hers over our dance cards, I teased, "I won't let you give a dance to anyone but me …"

"I wish I dared be so uncivil!"

"I'll have no less than four!"

"People will talk!"

"Let them! I'll be the envy of every man here!"

"Then you'd be causing your brothers to sin! I won't put that on your conscience!"

But she did. First and last dances and the supper dance were as always, and I pleaded so for a redowa in the third set that her sweet heart didn't refuse me.

We shared out the other dances. Loudoun was escorting Amelia MacHugh, and Vogelsang, Nannie. Stone appeared with Graves and Toombs and were all granted dances. Stone would have conversed long with Nannie, but Vogelsang ended it with a grin and a joke and led her away.

Miss Mary

I danced with all our friends. Torquil didn't know my pale aquamarine gown was the same I'd worn to my first Graduating Ball. It doesn't look the same after Mama and I recut it to follow the new style of skirts with less fullness in front and more in back. We've found no shade that enhances my coloring better. Supper began at one in the morning, and my dearest and I discussed moral philosophy all through it. I was gratified by his pleasure in what I'd learned.

Nannie

I danced three dances each with Donald, Mr. Stone, and Gerhardt, and felt beleaguered by intense urging from them all. When Torquil came for his dance, he teased.

"Ah, I'm grateful the belle of the ball sees fit to grant her humble servant the crumbs from her table! Just one sweet round before you're lost to me forever."

"Don't!"

"I won't. Don't what?"

"Don't propose marriage! I've had three serious offers tonight!"

"I'd only be repeating myself. I offered three years ago, and you wouldn't have me." He grinned.

"Oh, be an owl again and help me!"

"I suppose you disdained them all."

"They're not men to disdain. I pleaded for time. Now I'd like a pleasant, peaceful dance with no pressure, please!"

He let his hands and arms go limp.

"That's not what I meant!"

"I know, Nannie." His voice was gentle and reassuring. "How can I serve you?"

"Only listen."

Torquil

She was more distressed than I'd ever seen her. Always, she's been in command of herself, in every situation. I had to carry her through as she'd carried me two years ago.

"It's nothing against their characters. They're all fine Christian men a girl would be proud to call husband. They're all likeable, but in different ways."

"But you don't love any of them."

She looked down. A scarlet blush hid all her freckles. I kept on like I didn't notice.

"I assume each is able to provide for you."

"Oh, yes. It's not that."

"You really prefer one."

"Yes, but … it would be too easy … and probably a dull life."

"Which might not suit you. You've met with adventures, and conquered."

"But that's not very womanly."

"It becomes you, and makes you no less desirable."

"But I might not want adventures all my life. I want my children to be safe."

"The telling point might be the life each would offer you."

"Perhaps. But one set forth a challenge I should take up, for the good of Christ's kingdom."

"You don't mean Stone!"

"Yes. And it nags my conscience."

"It'd be wasted effort. There are better opportunities to serve Christ."

"But perhaps none so well suited to my nature. I wonder if God gave me 'pluck' instead of looks for this very purpose?"

"I don't know, but you've always looked fine to me. Your heart for others' good is more important than your looks, anyway, or you wouldn't have received three offers." I grinned. "Four, if you count mine."

"Yours doesn't count! You and Mary are destined for each other if any two ever were!"

"I hope you're right."

"I know I am! You're two halves of the same soul."

"I can't ask her if I'm not commissioned. Then what becomes of your halves?"

"Quit fretting yourself! Somehow it will all work out. And all at once."

"You're sure?"

"Absolutely! Beyond doubting."

I felt relieved to hear faith expressed by an outside voice. Then I turned to comfort her distress.

"But about your mind, now."

"It's divided. I know what I wish, but the other is what I should. Not that he's … wanting … in any way, of course, but—"

"But you don't love him."

"Except as a Christian ought. I could make all my vows but that, without being untruthful, and hope I could learn to love him." Her expression turned desolate and resolute at the same time. "We're called upon in Scripture to deny ourselves, and take up our cross and follow Christ!"

"I'd hate to see you ruin your chances for life itself."

"You're resigned to do just that, to obey God."

"It's different with me. Are you sure it's God's call, and not merely Stone's idea?"

"No."

"There you are, then. You don't have to do it."

"But I should."

"If so, need you marry him? An Indian mission must have a place for a maiden."

"Only if there were other ladies. I can't march away a thousand miles, alone with three men!"

"It would help to learn more about the way the mission's planned before you decide. And of course pray to learn God's will about it."

"Yes. I will. And you pray, too, and I'll pray about you and Mary, and we'll tell each other anything God reveals to us."

"Done!"

So was the waltz. I escorted Nannie to Vogelsang's side. She looked saved from peril to be with him.

"Must I call him out for frightening you?" he teased.

"No, Gerhardt, no! It's not him, it's Indians."

"*Sag alles mir,*" he comforted, as he led her into a polka.

* * *

Because it was the last dance and Miss Mary so precious, and because my love might be hopeless, I clasped her closer than was proper. I allowed emotion to saturate my being and imagined that hers sensed it and responded. Breast to breast, wordless, we reassured each other while we sharpened the dagger of uncertainty. The sun was rising during the walk back to the hotel. I drew her as close as I could without endangering her reputation. We were sober and still silent till only a few paces remained.

"I'd hoped to be brighter company," I said.

"You're the best company ... because it's you."

"You have the dearest heart on earth! I can never desire another."

"Nor can I."

In the hotel lobby, other young ladies were parting with their escorts. Amid the crowd whose eyes were only for each other, I could steal a kiss unobserved, but I won't put that knife to her heart while our future is in such doubt. I walked her to the foot of the stairs while she removed her gloves. I raised her hand and pressed it to my heart, then kissed the soft palm, folded her dainty fingers over it, and kept her hand in both of mine. Her dear little face turned pink, and her sweet smile was tremulous.

"Good night, little dear. I'll be here just after seven to escort you to the wedding."

"It's been a lovely time. Thank you for so much pleasure. Until tonight."

She dropped her first kiss to me onto my knuckles, released her hand, and hastened up the stairs. I watched her out of sight around the landing at the top. I got outdoors before I heaved a deep sigh and hurried back to duty.

I used all the privileges of a first class man to visit her. I'd have plenty of time to instill healthy dread in the Rats, and advise and direct my junior officers, afterward. The MacHughs left on Friday, taking with them the treasure of my heart.

* * *

At the summer encampments, yearlings had ever pulled Rats from their tents, dragged them on their bedding through dirt and wet grass and underbrush, and finished the performance by dousing each with a bucketful of water. The subs and officers made rounds once or twice after Taps, but the yearlings posted lookouts and knew when we retired. They delighted in dodging us and did it very well. They tormented the Rat sentinels and kept all the Rats from sleep at night. During the day, they napped by turns. Those awake kept the Rats too busy to sleep, till the end of the encampment.

I shared a tent with Bouleau and Vogelsang. In leisure between drills, military instruction, roll calls and parades, I wandered aside to pray, especially about Nannie's decisions.

Responsible for Company A's discipline and guidance, I intended to bring them to the superior level I'd built my squad in the Regulars. Custom decreed that first class men don't black our shoes, polish our brass, sweep our tents, arrange our bedding, carry water, or clean our muskets, but only order Rats to do it. Behind aloof gaze and faultfinding demeanor, I observed and rated A's Rats while they did my work, pondering how to bring forth the best in each. Through my junior officers, I assigned extra duty for the sake of practice to those who needed to improve their drill or their tempers.

Bouleau and Vogelsang's strengths were familiar. In the corporals, my face-to-face agents, I found varying usefulness. I assigned my laggards to supervise the extra duty I ordered for the Rats and kept sharp watch on their methods and effectiveness. By precept and example, I brought each up to the mark. By the beginning of August, I could see evidence of the spirit I intended to arouse.

The lone artillery piece in camp was fired for ceremony. I joined the gun crew as No. 2. I asked Colonel Ship, the artillery instructor, for all possible practice with the piece and more instruction than in recitation: battlefield usage beyond formal tactics, and unusual maneuvers that brought victory. At the Battle of New Market, he said, some of the artillery moved closely with the front ranks of the infantry, for greater firepower to the advance. I was determined to fight Uncle James's guns, so my real need carried conviction. The distinctions I'd earned prevented any accusations of currying favor.

The night before our practice march to Rockbridge Alum Springs on August 7, I inspected my company to insure preparedness, warned them I'd allow no straggling, and convinced them they could meet my requirements. I outlined those to my lieutenants and corporals and assigned each to oversee a specific task.

Each cadet carried his musket and bayonet and a cup for drinking water—or whatever else he might be able to forage along the way! The Midland Trail to the Rockbridge Alum, about fifteen miles distant, passed farms and tunneled through woods. We stopped at every good spring for water to combat the effect of the scorching heat.

I kept the company together. Through Bouleau and Vogelsang, I assigned corporals to take turns as file closers. Uncle James marched cavalry by stopping about once an hour, and changing the pace. I adapted it to infantry, slackening the pace as often as necessary for the weaker ones. At the next spring, I ordered them all to soak leaves and grass and put them under their caps to prevent sun stroke, then led at a brisker pace for half a mile. At a spring farther along, I bandaged a Rat's bleeding foot.

I goaded them all to endurance and determination by dares masked as rebukes, prodding them to defy my predictions that they'd faint by the wayside. Turning my back but intending to be overheard, I ordered, "Lieutenant Vogelsang, have inquiry made, whether any of the children wish to ride in the wagons." A steeper stretch brought Company A to the crest of Alum Spring Mountain. Weary, footsore, and aching, but proud they'd made a good march, being so close to their destination revived their spirits and energy.

Thibault had ridden over yesterday to locate and prepare the campground. I spotted it when we reached the foot of the mountain. Under the eyes of the visitors who'd turned out to watch us, but out of their hearing, I put the company in formation.

"Look smart for the ladies! Make every step echo!"

I marched them to the camp as if on parade. Each morning, we had inspection and drill and then were free to enjoy the resort.

The Rockbridge Alum was second only to the White Sulphur in size, elegance, and popularity. Famous for its luxury and gaiety, it attracted flocks of the fashionable from all over the South. It was said that military encampments were invited to provide beaux for the young ladies, since the War had thinned the ranks of Southern gentlemen. We were introduced to belles from Baltimore to New Orleans, Memphis to Charleston, with whom we played croquet or strolled the grounds. We joined them in impromptu entertainments and partnered them at the frequent balls. I wandered aside when I could, to explore, to pray, and to write letters and draw pictures for Miss Mary.

My heart's already given, but the young ladies had noticed me at the head of my company. My constancy to my little dear challenged the heartless belles who liked to lure their admirers to fall in love and propose marriage, and then count them only as conquests before discarding them. I'm not so mean as to play the game back on them—nor too dull to tease them! I called some of the reigning belles by the names of others less fair, like I'd forgotten their self-importance. Pretending to be quickly ensnared, I entreated the affections of others—as sisters! I introduced Carter to Miss Latimer, a rich, persistent girl, and withdrew, hiding a smile, to see which would conquer the other.

Taught to live simply and use material gain in service to others, I found the manners and pursuits of visitors at the Springs artificial and self-serving. As a first classman, soon to enter Virginia society, I was introduced by Institute faculty to some of the professional men who favored the Alum above other watering places. To men of seasoned wisdom who stood aside from much of the frivolity, I listened deferentially: doctors, judges, and professors from all over the South, from whom I learned much. Unhampered by anxiety about life's major concerns, my mind was free to drink from the pure founts of knowledge. I discovered I have a thirst for them.

These elders condescended to take an interest in my learning and experience. My mind took fire from deep, give-and-take intellectual conversation. Discussions of effective medical treatments, practical application of law, a feast of academic specialties, new ideas, and new levels of thought and analysis satisfied the hunger that military debate with Uncle James began. I was inspired to continue learning, to partake farther of such delight.

* * *

Back in Barracks after the summer, I wrote Nannie that I'd received no new insight about her future course, but repeated that she needn't serve as a missionary without a specific calling from God. To Miss Mary and Uncle James, I related impressions of the fashionable world and my keen intellectual pleasure.

Miss Mary

I asked all about the amusements of the Springs and the ladies' fashions and manners. I don't want to be left out of my dear one's mind, but I've no hunger for the intricate reasoning that delights him. Abstractions are beyond me. My interest is personal: loving care of others. I care so warmly about the human and spiritual qualities of my life and those whose lives touch mine, that I want to make them blessed if it's in my power.

MacLeod

My son's toying with Society amused me. Pointing out that he might sometime be called upon to move in such a world, I recounted some of my experiences in the national Capitol during my Topog days. Showing my pleasure in the flowering of his intellect, I unleashed my own. I'd offered milk before, but now I gave rich meat to one grown able to appreciate it. We volleyed speculations on politics and business, literature, history, and science back and forth.

Torquil

Delighted to be admitted to the depth and breadth of Uncle James's mind, I revealed my thoughts with freedom I hadn't had since Da was alive. In trust, ever closer in mind and spirit, we delved into each other's minds and pasts until we knew one another better than we ever had.

My first class year was the busiest of all. I devoted long hours to study. Access to a large book collection would end with graduation, so I borrowed from the library and pursued the subjects that had intrigued me at the Springs.

As company captain, I was in charge of a division of Barracks and bore responsibility for managing and correcting cadets' behavior. I was busiest as Officer of the Day, administering Barracks. I put on sash and sword first thing in the morning and was stationed at the Guard Room from thirty minutes after Reveille, till Taps. I received and relayed orders from the Officer in Charge, posted the sentinels and made rounds, superintended the parades to recitation rooms, and suppressed all irregularities in or near Barracks. I had to visit the rooms of all cadets absent after Taps every fifteen minutes till all returned. At the end of my tour of duty, I wrote the guard report, signed and certified it, and went off duty relieved that it wouldn't be my turn again for a while. I was detailed an assistant instructor in Latin, which consumed much time in preparation. As Loudoun had helped me, I visited some of my students in their rooms to help them.

I attended prayer meetings as often as duty allowed, read my Bible faithfully, and spent time in prayer, in rich communion with my Maker. I prayed often for guidance to shape my future.

Letters kept me connected with the country outside of school. Gunn and Ashland wrote of railroads and politics, which oriented me in Virginia's new economic and political condition. Boyhood friends' letters told that in Abercairn, some farms were being divided among new owners, crops looked promising, a new tannery was operating along the river, and everyone was speculating on who'd run for election next year. Nannie continued convinced that Miss Mary and I would wed someday. She hadn't received clear direction from God whether to join the mission to the Indians. I hadn't, either, but I tried to dissuade her with mention of massacres, hardships, and risks.

I wrote of all I learned and did, and of insights received from God, daily to Miss Mary, and read of her every day's activities, musings, and thoughts with sweet pleasure. We laid the foundation for a life together without knowing whether we'd ever build upon it.

* * *

Rewards for four years' hard work and strict discipline were in view. When the first class received final settlement of our accounts with the Institute, I was elated to be in charge of my own money for the first time in four years. I promptly wrote to Mister Ogilvie to request funds to cover expenses for graduation festivities, entertaining friends, and tailor's bill for citizen's clothing.

When the MacHughs brought Nannie for farewell visits before she left with the mission, I assigned much of Vogelsang's responsibility to others, including myself, to give him more courting time, but, by the end of the week, no engagement had been published. On the last Saturday evening, I pre-empted her. I bought her a small revolver, taught her how to use it, and instructed her how to meet perils. I don't think she'd seen me so stern since the War. She promised to write.

> Fort Liberty, W. T.
> May 9, 1872

My dear Son,

A little leisure tonight allows me the pleasure of writing a longer letter than the press of duty has permitted for some time. We nearly lost Captain Parnell, but he has recovered at last from typhoid pneumonia, and Major Jennings returned from leave, so we have more officers present for duty. I am also making increasing use of Rush's and Porter's talents as the requirements from Division increase.

The mail escort under Sgt. Mularky of the 14th Infantry was attacked near LaBonte Creek a week ago, with the loss of one enlisted man killed. The relief detachment had to gather mail scattered by the hostiles from bags they tore open. Paper was not the plunder they hoped for! There have been smaller skirmishes at intervals.

I have received three months' leave, my first since before I was assigned to the Intelligence Service in '63. It begins the last week of June, so, <u>Deo volente</u>, I shall be in Lexington to attend your graduation exercises.

The Board of Examiners convenes the first Monday of September in Washington City. When I have ascertained who are sitting this year, I shall introduce you to as many as I can, and to others who may prove helpful in advancing your interests. Colonel Hale has written to friends prominent in political circles. We shall see whether any one may have the influence to bring the legislation which will nullify your political disabilities.

Miss Gilchrist has consented to cast her lot with my nomadic one, in matrimony. She informs me that I need abide within the bounds of the congregation during the course of the banns being read, so I trust I shall have time to visit at length. We are hoping to spin out the blissful deception yet a little longer before we spring the surprise on our friends, though all our families are informed.

In joy looking forward to seeing you soon, with a father's affection, I remain,

> Your obedient servant and Uncle,
> James MacLeod

Virginia Military Institute
Lexington, Va.
May 16, 1872

Dear Uncle James,

Your most acceptable letter arrived today. May I be first to congratulate you! I've heard no word of it from Abercairn. I smile to think of the speculation they've indulged in, about the source of your lady's happiness. May I also be first to wish that it will continue for both of you, all your lives.

Please make Glenlochie your home while you are in Abercairn. It will be an honor to us all to entertain you. Please invite your family members, from me, to make their home with me for the happy occasion and as long as they wish to stop. I shall write in this post to ask them to make ready to receive you. In tomorrow's post, I shall relate the news of your visit—but not the wedding—to your old friends dispersed over the State, in case any are able to fare to Abercairn while you are with us.

It begins to seem real that I am soon to be graduated and take my place in the larger world. General Smith and our professors are applying the "nudge out of the nest" that eagles are said to use. They talk to us about positions we might fill and offer us introductions and letters of recommendation. We might even share in the government at Richmond or farther afield, or find places on college faculties. Some, of course, will be returning home to their families' plantations or businesses. I shall use my advantages to become the most useful soldier I can. I hope, somehow, to contribute to Virginia wherever I may be stationed—perhaps, as you do, in making useful contributions to scientific knowledge.

Speaking of knowledge, examinations are only a month away, and I should like to stand first. Competition for that honor is more in earnest this year. I look forward to seeing you and exchanging the rest of our news in person.

> God bless you and guard you on your journey,
> Your affectionate and respectful son,
> Torquil Drummond

Nannie's letter said the men did the preaching, but the women were relegated to domestic work. She'd hoped to be active in evangelizing, but thought she might find a way to do more. I wrote back commending her service and warning her against danger.

I studied every minute I could till the June 17 examinations. The questions given me allowed me to make the best showing of what I'd learned. I completed arrangements for my guests' accommodations, designed a coffee service for a wedding present for Uncle James, and sent the order to a silversmith Carter recommended in Richmond. I went to the tailor for final fitting.

Uncle James, in perfectly tailored citizens' clothing, arrived on Friday in time for the cadet presentation of "Julius Caesar" that night. Saturday evening, we welcomed the Abercairn party to their lodgings at the National Hotel. Besides William driving the Murrays' landau—laden with family, the Ogilvies, and guests—the caravan included Captain Murray on Sachem, Jemmie driving the Abercairn wagon with everyone's trunks and baggage, and Grieg riding Nightfire and leading Flora. We shared an early supper before I had to return for parade.

CHAPTER 27

RITES OF PASSAGE

The lines are fallen unto me in pleasant places; yea, I
have a goodly heritage.
—Psalm 16:6

Torquil

On my last day at the V.M.I., standing with the thirty-four,
out of eighty-eight who'd started, I was fifth in my class for the
entire four years, for which I'd be reported to Governor Walker.
After the band played "Auld Lang Syne," I was relieved of duty

The culmination was a shock. In one moment I finished the
preparations of youth and entered upon the privileges and obligations of manhood. I had only that moment to absorb the new
reality before I was surrounded by loved ones and friends, but it
came with confidence that I was ready.

Uncle James was first. His long legged stride put him ahead
of the crowd.

"Mere congratulations are too small an accolade for your triumph, Son—your several triumphs." He clasped my hand with a

grip like a vise and held but didn't shake it. His gaze glowed his pleasure.

"Thank you, Uncle James." I released neither handclasp nor gaze. "I wouldn't have arrived at this day if it weren't for you."

Captain Murray enveloped me in a bear hug, rumbling heartfelt sentiments, and Mrs. Murray patted my shoulder. I gave Miss Mary my arm. Grieg and the Ogilvies joined us.

"This is more symbolic than complete," said the dry, precise old voice. He handed me a legal document. I broke the seals and read the heading: *Deed of Release of Trust.* Speechless, I shook his hand and reached for Captain Murray's.

"We must, of course, execute and record this and many other documents—"

He broke off when Mrs. Ogilvie squeezed his arm. Grieg, in his Sabbath Day clothing, offered his hand. I handed the deed to Miss Mary, to grasp his hard, rough hand in both of mine.

"Mrs. Greig and I are proud o' ye, Young Drummond. She sent ye this, and weel tell ye the story of it at home."

He handed me an old-fashioned ring. I forebore inspecting it closely, to give him all my attention.

"I cannot say enough to praise your care, and Mrs. Greig's, or to give you both the thanks you deserve, for making this day possible."

* * *

Uncle James and I paid a call on General Smith. Still in awe of him, I left the conversation to my elders. They reminisced about their days at the military academy and the whereabouts and careers of mutual friends.

"I had hoped for, and thus am glad for your presence, Captain, since your care has had so large an effect." General Smith turned to me. "Mister Drummond, your record here is commendable. I have been asked by the Board of Visitors to request that you consider taking the position of sub-professor of Latin and Military Tactics, the coming academic year."

I hadn't had to scramble for words for years, but I did now, and finally used a well-learned response. "You do me too much honor, sir."

"You may think of it, rather, as an opportunity for useful service. Nor need you return a definite answer without sufficient time for consideration."

That night, I danced till dawn, with Miss Mary as often as she'd allow me. Carter escorted the rich girl, Miss Latimer, from the Rockbridge Alum, and Bouleau brought Miss Woodhurst. The Thibaults joined us, and Gunn appeared with the pretty New Orleanaise, Miss LeBrun, who'd attended Aidan's bride at the wedding. Vogelsang entered with his parents and a young lady whose dark beauty rivalled Ellie Thibault's: Miss Brandenberger, a sister-in-law. The elder Vogelsangs were as forthcoming and energetic as their son. We admired the vitality and precision of their dancing.

* * *

Wisdom is good with an inheritance: and by it there is profit to them that see the sun.
—Ecclesiastes 7:11

The first night along the way to Abercairn, I expected a business discussion when I asked Mr. Ogilvie to confer. Being graduated made me his employer rather than his ward. It shocked me to imagine an elder being subject to my direction. In deference, and in gratitude for his diligent care, I hoped to soften my position by treating him as a colleague.

"I've studied your reports carefully, sir. You have more than fulfilled the faith my father reposed in you. I must depend upon the same, since my vocation may place me at some distance. I shall make myself familiar with every detail while I'm home, so I can do my part intelligently. You must have identified what the primary concern is now." I waited respectfully.

Mr. Ogilvie

Preparing quantitative summaries, drawing conclusions, and making decisions based upon them, are my forte. I am not at ease discussing less straightforward matters.

"The primary concern … is lack of a master. Glenlochie is in want of your presence and attention. The heart will go out of it—and out of those who serve you—if you are too much absent." I warmed to my topic. "Despite the calling you profess, these seven years have had an atmosphere of expectation, of waiting for the family to be restored. With your reception of the inheritance, all expect to take part in continuing the Drummond custom of life, which we have upheld during your minority.

"You began to follow Drummond custom by defending the county. More particularly, and without knowing previous generations' works, you continued by asking that what exceeded our requirements be expended for those in want. Three generations before yours have spurned excess and luxury, in favor of generosity and service. The cohesion, and the freedom from want and financial bondage that bless and distinguish the county, result from following the Drummond standard.

"You are the head of Glenlochie and its benefactions, where ever you may go, but only at home can you be the equally needful heart. If you continue receiving its proceeds without being present to exemplify and preside, Glenlochie might as well be an agricultural manufactory." I saw his expression turn austere. "I tell you only the truth."

"I expect naught else from one so faithful. You've brought a vital matter to my attention, sir, and I shall give it prayerful consideration."

Torquil

Dear and familiar, scene of thousands of happy boyhood days, my house seemed to stand forth in welcome, promising years of the same contentment for manhood and posterity. I walked Nightfire from the bend of the drive, looking long at it. Uncle James, on Flora, matched the pace.

Mrs. Grieg gave us welcome-home. She had my favorite hot bread, new butter, and strawberry preserves on the scarred, polished old table and brought fresh coffee from the big black cookstove. I wouldn't sit till she agreed to join us. We exchanged news till she came to the point.

"Noo—aboot a' this company we're readying for?"

"I hope you can keep a secret," Uncle James teased.

"If ye can, your own self!"

"The guests are my parents, siblings, and families. They'll be here for the wedding."

"Who weel be the blessed couple?"

"Myself and a lady." He grinned.

"Weel?"

"Miss Gilchrist."

She didn't lose self-possession for a second. "'Tis an honor to the hoose, thrice welcome!"

"Naught will be wanting, I know." I grinned. "But I reckon we'd better loose him to go see her!"

Uncle James was too ardent to look abashed. Mrs. Grieg was never caught unprepared.

"Greig weel have ye a fresh horse. Your chamber is prepared. I weel send up hot water."

She called instructions to a maid before she turned to me. "Young Drummond, know ye how many souls weel be wi' us?"

I gave my best estimate before I gave her my left hand with the engraved gold circlet on the little finger. Her expression grew tender as she turned the ring to see its designs again.

"Greig said you'd tell me the story of this."

"'Twas your mother's. She lay breathin' her last when she slippit it off her finger.

"'Gie this to my bairn,' quo' she, 'wi' the love I would hae gi'en him.' She knew ye were a laddie before she was awa', ye ken."

She wiped away a tear and clenched her fingers on my hand while she regained composure. I gripped her hand gently and tried to swallow past a lump that hurt my throat.

"She was a liltin', smilin' lass, the light o' the hoose when your faither brought her home. Ye were such a dour wee bairn, 'twas like ye knew what a sweet mother ye'd lost. I loved ye not only for her sake. Ye came to my heart with love all your own, and I brought ye in to keep."

More tears escaped. Mine almost did. Keeping her hand in mine, I rounded the end of the table, embraced her shoulders respectfully, and kissed her cheek.

"You still keep me, and I am forever in your debt."

> Hope deferred maketh the heart sick: but when the desire cometh, it is a tree of life.
> —Proverbs 13:12

MacLeod

At the manse, I approached as one in a dream. She stood to greet me, a tremulous smile curving her rose-pink lips. As one, we opened our arms and walked into each other's embrace. We clasped hands then, and drew back to drink in each other's faces.

She dropped my hands and laid hers lightly on the sides of my face.

"James."

"Elizabeth."

* * *

> Virginia men did not cease to regard one another with the familiarity and frankness, friendship and feeling of their youth.
>
> —William Ellery Channing, D.D., *ca.* 1850

Torquil

Mr. Ogilvie produced a sheaf of documents conveying Glenlochie from the trust to me. With Captain Murray, we rode to the Court House to sign and record them. I was famished when I got home. In the kitchen, Mrs. Grieg set a plate of bread and cheese and a pitcher of milk on the table.

"This cheese is the best I've ever tasted."

"'Tis a receipt o' Mrs. Murray's, she and Miss Mary began making after the War. They've dairy maids they've trained noo, but their cheeses are so prized, they still have custom waiting.

"Speaking o' waiting, there's Mr. Kendrick and Mr. Murdoch in the library."

My moustache had been growing since General Smith permitted first class men to turn out whiskers; it was long enough to arrange. In the passage, I smoothed it and my hair and straightened my cravat at the hall-tree mirror. Robbie was putting one of the landholding farmers at ease.

"Lieutenant, I'm Murdoch, from over MacKnight's Run." He stood.

"Sergeant in the Rifles, I recall, sir. Won't you be seated."

"Yes, sir, I was. Brought my men all the way through till ... then brought 'em home. None of 'em deserted, neither. They didn't have to sneak home to keep their wives and little 'uns from want."

"You made a proud fight. The county's the better for men like yours. How can I serve you?"

"It's my boys. They're talkin' of goin' to the city to work, and it'd like to break my wife's heart. They're fine strong young fellers and hard workers. The missus and I was hopin' you know their characters well enough to hire 'em for some work."

"Your name stands well with us. There must be things in particular you've taught them to do."

"Well ... they do a right smart o' things around the place. Jerry's a wonder with his tinkerin', keeps everthin' fixed an' useful. Dan's mighty good with critters, got a real fine hand with the cows. I wish you could see some o' the calf crop this year, so big an' healthy they right near shine."

"That's the kind of stock you need in these times. I'll ride by one day and see them."

"We'd be proud to see you."

"Your sons must be looking to do something different from the general run of farm work."

"I don't know, so much's they're wantin' a taste o' city life, an' that's what's got the missus nigh distracted. She's afeared they'll get in with bad company. It don't comfort me, neither."

I made my first independent decision as master of Glenlochie. "Let's offer them an interest here. We can use a man who can work with machinery. Jerry'd like the implements.

"We keep beef cattle. Captain Murray and Master William breed lines for dairying. They may still have a Jersey I remember. She's a fine cream producer, but she had trouble dropping her first couple of calves. Dan might know some things to do for that. I'll be seeing the Captain tonight. I'll speak a word for him. If they have all the hands they need, I'd like to see what he can do for my beeves."

"That's right kind o' you, Lieutenant."

"We'll all benefit, Mr. Murdoch. I'd like them to be here in the morning. I'll know by then where Dan's wanted."

"I sure do thank you, sir."

> In the multitude of people is the king's honor: but in the want of people is the destruction of the prince.
> —Proverbs 14:28

"It'll be well if the county can keep those boys."

"Families like that are our backbone." I grinned, grasped his hand and clapped him on the shoulder. "I hear of your fame, Kendrick *Esquire!*"

"Middling frog in a little puddle. The judge teaches me something new every day."

"I expect Mr. Ogilvie'll do me the same. I trust your gracious wife and the children are all well."

"And increased. We've a new boy, since the first, instant. William Carmichael."

"Congratulations! You'll be patriarch of a tribe! Miss Mary wrote that you have commodious quarters to fill."

"Too commodious before long, I'm afraid. 'Judge Gram-paw,' the little ones call him, hasn't been strong for a couple of years. He never misses a Court, attends to everything he takes in hand, but he doesn't take as much as he used to. He hasn't lost a speck of his wit. Still the sharpest mind in the District, on the law. I'm blessed to learn from him."

"We owe a lot to our preceptors. You know Uncle James is here now."

"I saw him at the Court House. He looks full of something, as an egg is of meat!"

"All will be discovered. But about Abercairn. What do you see as the greatest threat here?"

"Making a living. Bringing the land back into heart. Keeping up our spirit to fight for it. I wrote you how Dominie Gilchrist preached 'Be strong. Acquit ye like men.' We're doing all we can, but many can't do all they used to. What you just did to keep good blood in the county is what we need. It's hard enough to prevent being reduced to a Yankee colony as it is, let alone losing strength.

"Beechams and Fromers going to the city are no loss, but it weakens us if men like Murdochs go. Families like theirs—and yours and mine—are the foundation of public life. It'll go to ruin without them. A few of the infantry left their land and went to the territories because debt and the re-destruction were too burdensome. The long haul they have to make, is weighing mighty heavy on some others. They're thinking about selling to Yankees. They're the only ones with money now. "

"I hope they can see far enough to know if they lose their land, they're lost, themselves, without a homeplace! Any sum they receive will enable them to live for a time, but the land will make them a life if they can hold out. I'd like to see progress in local manufacturing, to take care of as many of our own needs as we can, and I'll support it. But working the land keeps our society whole."

"They don't want to leave, but they need encouragement. Your setting an example would help."

"If only God would put me here, I would. But I'm called to the Army and can't disobey.

"With your concept of the law—manifest the country's virtue and embody our moral sense—you're already setting an example. Captain Murray said justices will be elected next year."

"They haven't asked me. They're working the way they used to, to gain a consensus, so we won't have a bitter contest and many men disaffected afterward.

"Jock Menteith's been proposed for representative in Richmond. He'd argue well for county and District interest, like a better road to Culpeper—the short way through Griffinsburg's worse than a cowpath! He's been approached by some who want to buy us up, but he doesn't like the idea of outsiders having any handle on us. Neither do I."

"There used to be enough resources in the county so outside finance wasn't wanted. I'm sure our elders know if there still are. We also have kin and connections. I'd rather call on them."

"If everybody would pitch in, we could build a toll road to Culpeper. Men who can't put in money could contribute labor for their share."

"Or right-of-way across their land would be worth something. There'd be less investment initially than if we tried to build a rail-road spur. The iron's a demand for money, and so's the rolling stock, but men could contribute labor for the roadbed."

"The Tredegar's building locomotives and producing rails again, but I doubt they'd want to trade for farm products, unless they're still housing and feeding their workers. During the War, they hauled food all the way from Georgia."

"I have to go to Washington City for the army examination. I could come home by way of Richmond and sound them out on such a proposition."

"Your heart's home already."

"It never left."

* * *

Mr. Ogilvie and I rode over the eight thousand acres. Production of wheat, oats, corn, and hay was proceeding smoothly. Working hand in hand with the Creator concerning all that sprang from the soil satisfied my soul and kept me reminded that all food and life, for man and beast, depend on God's gifts.

The soil itself is a gift. A man would be a fool not to acknowledge it. I re-immersed myself in the annual rhythm of the crop cycle, with thanks to God.

But I won't be here to savor it.

I had to set matters in order against my departure for the Army by the beginning of September, when the results of the army examinations would dictate my future. I began by reviewing the returns from the tenancies. Mr. Ogilvie still accepted rent in cash, labor, or farm products. I visited all the tenants. The Griegs' son, Iain, whose family was still increasing, said he'd soon be a landowner himself.

"Aye, Lieutenant, Mr. Kendrick drew up papers so's we could agree with auld Missus Gordon. Ye remember Mr. Gordon was never well after the War, and their daughter married and moved to Nebraska. He died last winter. We'll pay to Missus Gordon and care for her till she's awa', too—she don't want to leave Abercairn—and send the rest of the price to her daughter."

"A blessing for all of you. I'm glad, but I hate to lose you. You do well with land."

"Well, I begot me some help." With a proud smile, he jerked a thumb toward the children weeding the garden. "They and the Missus all pitched right in so's I could work off the farm and earn the cash to put down on the new place."

"May you all prosper! Have you any thoughts who'd want to be here after you?"

"Well, Jems and his family have a good place with Captain Murray—and Jemmie with you—and Bill found some land in Madison. But Davie's barely scratchin' a living over in Warren. His wife was sick a long time. She's well now, but even with both of 'em workin', they ain't got the bills paid off."

"I didn't know they'd had such a hard time. Is he coming back to Abercairn?"

"Soon's they can. He went over to work on the railroad, but they don't need so many hands now. He's been odd-jobbing."

"I recall he used to out-do everyone at harvest. He had a way of … getting more done with every motion … is the best I can describe it."

"Still does, last I saw."

"Let him know he has a place here if he wants it. And his wife. Your mother might need more help with the company we're expecting."

"I'll write him tonight."

"Da!" cried all the little voices at once.

"Reckon I best see what the bairns run up against. Proud to see you home, Lieutenant."

"Proud to be home."

* * *

I'd learned a lot since Mr. Ogilvie began teaching me after Gettysburg. The price we received for wheat depended upon drought in France or prolonged winter in the Ukraine as much as on the quality of the grain, and when and where sold. In any given year, would the cost of storage be repaid by the higher prices of February or March? Receipts at the port of Alexandria were generally higher; from Culpeper, by railroad, it arrived there in less than a day. But the previous day was consumed by hauling it in wagons to the depot, and, through heavy mud in spring, two days were the minimum. Some years, it was better to take the lower price at harvest.

Improved farm machinery was necessary to till, plant, and harvest the greater acreage we had to keep under tillage to maintain sufficient income and pay the ruinous taxes. Remembering what a race against time it was in my boyhood, to save our crops, I liked the increased harvesting speed, and Mr. Ogilvie's policy of hiring out implements and machinery to other farms, when they'd otherwise have been idle.

I liked the machinery itself. Jerry Murdoch and I spent half a day examining every belt, pulley, and blade, cog, shaft, and lever: how each was linked, where it was lubricated, and its sequence of operation. While he was gone to Murchison's forge with repairs to be made, I hitched up a team and taught myself to operate every machine. That night, I asked Mister Ogilvie about replacement parts

"McCormick's agent in Culpeper sells them. However, when one machine is beyond use, we salvage parts for repairing others. Labor costs about the same as in the past few years. It's worth expending to prevent waste.

"We've bought from several manufacturing companies, according to *Southern Planter*'s test reports and what best suits our soils and terrain, which latter requires a certain size and conformation to fit the gradients and constricted spaces. Complications arise when parts don't fit from one to another."

"Can Dick Murchison make parts as well as repair them?"

"Yes. He's taken on an apprentice who does much of the routine work, so he's free for more sophisticated tasks."

"I'll visit with him."

> Clan chiefs were expected to be open-handed, generous and ... 'a river to their people.'
> —Alastair Moffatt, The Highland Clans

> He must be the prop upon which they may lean, if need be, and his spirit the reservoir upon which theirs may draw for refreshment.
> —Captain Robert C. Richardson, Jr., Second Cavalry, United States Army, *West Point*

Discussing management policies, I learned other aspects of my family's history besides Da's record of our heroes.

"Your earliest forbear in this country was careless of money. Two generations' strict economy were required before your grandfather could manage Glenlochie on a cash basis. Your great-grandfather saw the way tobacco exhausts the soil as a squandering of God's gifts, first of all, besides creating unfavorable business terms, so he turned to grain, hay, and horses. Glenlochie solidified its economic position by selling grain during the wars of Napoleon, when prices were very high.

"We have stayed debt-free since. Watching the ebbs and flows of commerce and the financial world, and proceeding according to what they indicate, sometimes entails swift changes of plan, for which we keep resources on hand. Thus, we have kept the entire original land holding. Thus, risk and reward are our own, not subject to creditors' dictates. Thus, neither financial panic nor the catastrophes of the War brought us to ruin.

"Since the Revolution and your great-grandfather's wise policy—which I learned from your grandfather in the ripe autumn of his experience—it was he who began raising pedigreed beef cattle—we have pursued sufficiency and service, rather than excess and luxury, in stewardship of the Lord's gifts. He has graciously blessed our efforts and made Glenlochie useful to the county."

"I hope to build well upon that foundation, sir. I'm steward of such resources, and a servant for the public benefit, where ever that may lead. The War taught me our strength is in our citizens, so I'm working to keep them with us. We must lift up those in need by helping them keep their homes here, and keep up Christian morale."

"Well and good. But you must correctly estimate the opposition. The current mode militates against such a high-minded stance. It's mercantilism: production and sale of manufactured goods, and greed for profits. It seeks to focus human desire upon acquiring *things*. It cares nothing for human benefit or Godly ideals, and leads to unscrupulous business practices. Our agent in New York describes the marts of commerce as 'populated by thieves who take mean advantage of the fair-dealing man.' He adds that we couldn't conceive of the depths to which some of them stoop."

"I shall not allow the quality of their behavior to dictate the quality of mine!

"Now, in the April report, you gave the figures for sheep, cows, horses, the mill, the ship, and lending, besides the crops and rents, as our income."

"We also trade in small quantities, such as seed in exchange for temporary labor at harvest or hog killing, or food or cloth in exchange for domestic help at busy times. We house, board, and pay the permanent help, of course. We trade beef to the Murrays for milk and cream, butter and cheese.

"Both Nightfire and Nightstorm stand now. Their services are prized and well paid for. The draught breed is increasing, especially since Grieg and Jemmie have been training some for both draught and the saddle. Grieg is seeking to identify a likely stallion among them. When he finds and develops him, he'll stand also. The demand for our colts, fillies, and mares exceeds the supply."

"I expect the new bull is on his way by now?"

"The manifest was dated the eleventh, instant, per cable from our Glasgow agent. He should be on shore at Richmond before the end of the month, and aboard the cars two days later. Our agent sent a handler with him. We'll have to send the man back unless he wants to emigrate."

"I hope he will. We need men. We might request our agent to send any he considers worthy.

"The sheep appear to be thriving, no matter how high we pasture them. Put me in mind again of how the weight of wool compares to last year's."

"Three hundredweight increase. Mrs. Gordon sold us her flock of Merinos when she couldn't care for them anymore. She made such pets of them that they're the largest I've seen. They're improving our strain."

"Though lending isn't bringing good returns, I'd like to do more, so the neighbors can all keep their land. What point have you reached with the mill?"

"It will serve Abercairn, but any profit will be negligible."

"I don't want to give it up. Mr. Regis's living depends partly on how much wool he can manufacture."

* * *

I mulled over the possibilities. Was Glenlochie using all the pasturage available for sheep? Did anything prevent me from expanding it? Scouting for pasture would be a hospitable occupation while entertaining Uncle James's family. I could shift all the production uphill ... sheep at the highest elevations ... then orchards ... hay below ... crop fields as high up the slopes as equipment permits. The change would span the years ... be continued by my sons.

But I'd never have sons, if I had to enlist.

In the cool of the evening, I walked in the woods. Keir saw me, but, as always, he read my demeanor. He didn't approach.

Manhood's decisions were mine alone to make, but they'd affect a circle of others. Most important, I won't disobey God. He called me into the Army to protect Southern people.

Can't I do it better from here? Aren't there ways outside the Regular Army to protect Southrons? Temptation assailed me on every side.

It was tempting to rationalize that the V.M.I. battalion was Virginia's own military body, and I could still be a soldier if I were sub-professor there. By preparing its graduates to lead in rebuilding the devastated South, the Institute protected Southrons much more directly than the Regulars did! And I'd have a gentleman's life to offer Miss Mary.

Other temptations included that bliss, too. Gunn wanted me for the railroad and Loudoun for the mines, which would help the Southern economy. Ashland wanted me in Richmond to help the Conservatives restore Virginia's true leaders to power, to protect Virginia and the South politically

Declining to serve with Uncle James would be worse than ingratitude after his sacrifices. But I could never be one of the West Point brotherhood, whose ties had weathered even the storm of war. Jealous voices to the contrary, they were the elite of the officer corps. I'd be an outsider in the Army because I'm a Southron. And I'd lived how it is, not to be commissioned at all.

Mr. Ogilvie's plea for my presence at Glenlochie resonated with my own dearest wishes. Riding about my homeplace drew me to it with iron thread. Its future usefulness can go beyond mere philanthropy, to protect and sustain Abercairn citizens' interdependence.

Entering the family cemetery, passing the tombstones of those who'd held Glenlochie before me, I came to the newest row. The cypress behind Da and Douglas's graves had grown tall, and my infant brother's earthen cradle looked tinier than ever. I turned my mother's ring on my finger and was grateful to know her better now. I took off my hat and knelt. Did they know I was home? I almost thought 'for good.'

Da told me long ago my duty is to Abercairn—serving, to keep citizens safe in their property and persons. He'd quoted the Bible verse: "Unto whomsoever much is given, of him shall much be required." Abercairn had nurtured me. In the Army, I'd be deserting her.

Abercairn …

Haven and new beginning for the Scots who founded it.

Cradle, matrix, nourisher of her sons' spirits ever since.

Home-place, heart's home, dearer than life to her defenders.

Where I hoped my bones would rest with my family's.

I reviewed receiving my vocation. I'd made a reasoned choice to join M Company, to protect Southern people moving west. Protecting Southern people was the crux. Serving in the ranks was the only way I could accomplish it, then. Now there were several means. But set against obeying God, they were no choice. Commissioned or enlisted, I'd follow His will in the Army.

Surely He has some reason. …

I bowed my head, folded my hands, closed my eyes.

'Dear God, here am I, your servant. I owe my life and eternal life and all I am to You. I have believed, these seven years, You called me to be a soldier. I've made myself ready to obey that calling. Now my father's call returns to mind, of service to your people here. But You are the holy, the highest, my heavenly Father. How best can I serve You? Dear God, what would You have me do?'

I opened my spirit to my Maker and Savior. The idea of being of more service to Southrons here at home was only newborn, suspect, a temptation to lure me from obedience.

In answer I received, "Wait upon the Lord."

* * *

Army examinations were the first week in September. I had to review my college notes and make the best marks possible. I wrote a grateful letter to General Smith, explaining my Army calling. I couldn't in conscience accept the Board of Visitors' offer.

I'd known and been known at the V.M.I., where strict sub-ordination and military order were achieved by regulations enforced. Here, in the freedom of my home county, I could help to shape the order. Only now was I in the one place where I could know and be known throughout generations.

But I can't stay here!

I told the household we'd gather for morning devotions as we had when Da presided.

MacLeod

At the kirk on Sabbath morning, Torquil and I joined the men visiting outdoors. Robert Kendrick, Sr., met me with right hand outstretched.

"Captain MacLeod, I'd hoped to meet you some day. Thank you for my son!"

"For all our sons!" Aidan Mor agreed. "Your warning spared them to us, a further goodness of your shepherding them."

"No man could have done otherwise, they were doing their duty so nobly."

"Donald's coming to see you while you're here." The man's black hair and eyes proclaimed him a Loudoun. "He's leaving the mines to engineer themselves a bit, and bringing Amelia for a visit, too."

Mr. Airlie added, "David's here for the summer, to apprentice with Doctor Gask."

"I had the pleasure of meeting them on the road Friday. They were full of the new discoveries of the microbial origins of disease."

No one seemed to think twice about it when I escorted Elizabeth into the kirk and sat beside her, until Dominie Gilchrist read the first banns. The marriage could take place when the banns had been read on three successive Sundays.

"Two weeks from tomorrow?" I whispered in her ear.

One peculiarity, though, must not go unmentioned. No matter how small this house is, it is never full. There is always room for one more in it; and, on special occasions, such as a wedding or a Christmas frolic, the number of feather beds, straw beds, shuck beds, pallets, and shakedowns which this old house produces is literally incredible.
—Dr. George W. Bagby, Virginian

Torquil

The New York MacLeods and their servants arrived at Culpeper the Thursday before the wedding. Uncle James introduced his parents, brother Andrew and sister-in-law Lucretia, and sister Joan and brother-in-law Pieter VanDeBruick, and eight children. I introduced three generations of Griegs with honor that surprised the visitors.

Mrs. Grieg

Before my last lad returnit, I'd had the maids air and turn a' the bedding, launder and iron the linens, shine the silver and crystal, and scrub and dust and polish every surface and cuddy o' the hoose and its furniture. The hired men cleaned the outside o' the hoose and redd up the gardens and lawns. Mr. Grieg and Jemmie dressed saddles, harness, and tack, and called in Mr. Murchison's assistant for the shoeing.

Wi' the hoose full o' company, Glenlochie kept holiday. I set oot tableware, ornaments, and vessels that had no' seen daylight since before the War.

Torquil

"This is the best cheese I've ever tasted." Uncle Pieter's girth showed him a gourmand. "I'd like to arrange for a supply to use at home. Where is it made?"

"Next door." Uncle James enjoyed his surprise

"You don't say! It has the robust flavor of some Scandinavian cheeses, yet it's brightened by the perfect dash of Stilton tang."

* * *

Our cavalcade next day included not only my new uncles, but all five of their sons. On the way down the drive, we plucked little Robert—Wobbet no more!—from the Carmichael carriage bringing Emily and the children to visit with the MacLeod ladies. Uncle James took him up before him on Flora. From Chieftain's Hill, my uncles learned the lay of the land. I assessed potential sheep pasture. Doing business as we progressed toward the Court House, I bought two prime heifers from Murdochs.

"Judge Gram-paw!" Robert shouted.

Judge Carmichael was driving himself today. His gig was as ancient as his carriage, but his horse was only a six-year-old. Robert introduced his new friends.

"It's a pleasure to know all you gentlemen, and especially because of such a happy occasion."

"We're faring at DeVique's, sir," I said. "I'd be honored if you'd join us."

"I'll be pleased to. I'm meeting one of the governor's aides there. He wrote that you'd been recommended because of your class standing and hoped to talk with you while he's here. His primary purpose is to investigate a case that's come before the Supreme Court."

As we rode through the Court House, the village looked much the same. The new tannery was downstream and the sawmill now produced barrel staves as well as planks. Mr. Mitchell's store displayed a wider variety of goods than it had before the war. Mssr. DeVique greeted us and was introduced to the visitors. We met the aide from Richmond.

"What's *du jour*, that smells so good?"

"Boeuf Bourguignon, with new vegetables and hard rolls. Madame has also baked strawberry tart."

"She must have known I'd be here!"

"But of course! Young Jemmie's *grand-mère* sent him to give notice of so many."

"These gentlemen are my guests."

After dessert, Judge Carmichael took an appreciative swallow of the rich coffee. "I would have thrown it out of court, except that we were under such suspicion at the time."

"The case is so old I wonder it's been continued this long," agreed the aide, "especially since it's patently based on personal pique."

"I suppose the Freedmen's Bureau agent is like 'Bermuda Hundred' Butler, with vocal friends in high places, to keep it alive."

"No doubt. It was probably dropped to the bottom of the docket repeatedly, in hopes the plaintiff would be discouraged from pursuing it. I believe we're all united in our intention to spare Mr. Murchison any more annoyance. I'll take depositions, and try to get it dismissed once for all."

At Mitchell's store, I bought the little boys crackers and pickles and cheese to stay their stomachs till supper. Mr. Mitchell gave them a sack of maple sugar pieces to share. We went on to the forge.

Dick Murchison's a Baptist, so he hadn't seen me at kirk. I made introductions as we dismounted.

"Pleasure to meet you gen'elmen. Good to see you home, Lieutenant!"

"It's good to be here. I stopped by to see your improvements. Mr. Ogilvie tells me you're doing machine work now."

"Got to keep up with the times. But it ain't much of a jump." He led toward forge and anvil, scooping up a few horseshoe nails.

"Iron's iron. She works the same, long's it's the charcoal iron from the Valley." He pumped a treadle to operate the bellows, making the forge glow and shoot sparks.

"I'm glad they have furnaces in blast again. Can they get the same ore?"

"Good brown hematite." Murchison took a nail with his tongs and thrust it into the coals. "Only one with enough stretch to count on." He put the nail to the anvil and with a few deft hammer strokes bent it into a ring, which he quenched in a trough of water.

"Now, which o' you chil'ren will this fit?"

While he made each of the little boys a ring, he pointed out casting boxes to form replacement parts, hardened dies for machining them, welding equipment, and a stock of replacement teeth to bolt into a hay rake. "If you'd tell Jerry Murdoch his universal's ready, I'd be right obliged."

"I can carry it now and spare him a run in the morning. It looks like new."

"Stronger than new. Ought to last till the thresher gives out."

At the mill, the little boys met the Regis children, who led them to the lookout heights of the tall building. Mr. Regis and I talked about ways to prevent the great wheel from standing idle.

"I want to be useful to the neighbors, so they can get their grain ground close by, but I don't care to see your living decrease. You'll have all our custom, of course, but our flour can't compete with the big mills in Richmond.

"Could we manufacture more wool?"

"Lot o' folks lost a lot o' creeturs by the War. They're using their land for crops, not graze. I'm not sure we're makin' enough fleeces hereabouts. Had to shut down on wool sooner than usual, after shearin' this spring."

"I suppose there's no trouble disposing of what you make."

"No. I deal the way folks want to. Some take out their fleeces in finished goods. Others take the goods and sell 'em and pay for my work. I sell my share at the Court House or in Culpeper."

"You'd be willing, then, to increase woolen manufacture?"

"Yes, sir, if there's wool to do it."

Miss Mary

Abercairn all turned out for the wedding. Captain and Mrs. James MacLeod left next morning to visit other friends and relatives on their nuptial journey. The rest of the family stopped a few days, receiving and returning calls and gathering Abercairn products to carry to New York. Mr. VanDeBruick—Uncle Pieter—arranged for a supply of our cheese for his own household and told Mama he had a market for as much as Mount Murray could produce. She promised to talk with Papa about whether to enlarge our dairy.

The MacLeod ladies made happy hours for us at Mount Murray. They're so congenial that Mama and I shared the secret knowledge of our hearts. Now that Torquil Dhu is home, our hopes just can't not come true! They fondled the silk for my wedding dress and pored over the design. They promised to shop for lace and trimmings in New York, send samples, and express the ones we chose. We invited them to the wedding.

Torquil

Miss Mary's sweet company soothed my cares, and I rejoiced in Uncle Pieter's promise of a wide market for their cheese, but preoccupation with the mill hampered my conversation. Exercise might clear my mind, so I invited her to come for a walk.

"I'll change my shoes."

She put on a light shawl, too. We stepped briskly down the drive.

"You're thoughtful tonight."

"It's nothing to trouble you, little dear. I have business decisions to make."

"Many, I'm sure."

"Not all so troublesome as this one. Mr. Regis doesn't want to move from here, but custom is less than it was, and he has a large family to feed. There weren't enough fleeces this year to keep the woolen mill running as long as usual."

"If you made thinner cloth, could you make more of it from the same amount of wool?"

"I expect so."

"I'm thinking of this." She showed me a corner of her shawl. "It's called challis, and the threads are very fine. You can see, here in the fringe."

I rolled a single strand between my fingers. "I wonder if thread so fine can withstand the traction of the machinery."

"It must, somehow, or it couldn't be made."

"Most people want good, thick, durable cloth, especially for blankets and winter clothing."

"You could write to Mr. VanDeBruick, and see if people want lightweight wool cloth in the city. I like this shawl because it's warm but not heavy."

"This year's fleeces are probably all manufactured by now, but I'll look for some. It would help to have a specimen to show him."

* * *

I didn't have many words to pray during the train ride to Washington City. I'd prayed them all, over and over. In obedience, I waited on the Lord.

I'd be leaving Abercairn soon. What to have ready for either course my life would take? From my tailor: shirts and collars and warm undergarments only—or lieutenant's uniforms also? Restock my medical kit completely in any case. What weapons? I wasn't about to trust my life and others' to a single-shot breechloader! Would I need Da's saber, or not? Arrangements with Mr. Ogilvie to transmit enough money to live decently—for only myself or for my wife, too?

'Let it be unto thy servant according to thy will!'

* * *

At the offices of the examining board in Washington City, a clerk showed me into a cubbyhole where I took the written examination. None of the questions seemed difficult. During the oral portion, I answered questions and solved tactical problems with assurance born of education and Army service.

"The last thing is the test oath." The clerk handed me a printed paper.

The Ironclad Oath!

"I ___, do solemnly swear that I have never voluntarily borne arms against the United States."

"I cannot swear that oath, sir. I fought to defend Virginia."

An official told me my political disabilities made me ineligible for a commission.

* * *

Keeping stringent control of voice and expression, I dined with Uncle James and Aunt Elizabeth that night. "I'll be joining you to enlist in M as soon as I set matters in order at—"

I couldn't say home.

I'd never have home.

I'd tasted of all my heart's desires and the cup was dashed from my lips and smashed forever. This must be the final measure, the bitterest measure, of punishment I deserved for vengeance and hatred.

I felt like railing at God for alluring me into wasted preparations for a life I could never live. I felt like getting stinking blind drunk. I felt like picking a fight with some bully-boy in the streets and beating him down with my bare fists.

But trust in God took hold. In my room at the hotel, I knelt beside my bed. In faith, in humility, and in genuine sorrow for years of sin, I repented, and renewed my surrender.

'Dear God, be it unto thy servant according to thy will. Do with me as You please.'

* * *

Next morning I entrained for Richmond, where I presented the proposal for trading with the Tredegar Iron Works, bought medical instruments, and took the next cars toward Culpeper. I caught a ride with some waggoners returning with goods taken in trade for Valley products, over the "cow-path" through Griffinsburg to Abercairn Court House. Would my friends ever get that good road built?

I wouldn't be here to use it.

> The planters did not trim honor to fit law, place courtship in the hands of lovers alone, or divert education from its association with true character.
> —Steven M. Stowe, *Intimacy and Power in the Old South*

I was as silent at home as I'd been after Da and Douglas were murdered. I bathed, shaved, and rode Nightfire through the lane to Murrays' that night.

Miss Mary and her parents were in the porch. One look at my face set gloom upon theirs.

Captain Murray sought relief in action. His kilt quivered with the impact of his heels as he paced the wide boards of the porch. After a couple of turns, he glared at me.

"Tell us, the noo, and have done!"

"The Ironclad Oath. I'm going to enlist. I can not say what I want to."

I looked long at Miss Mary. Her face was dead white.

"We must part. I release you from any obligation you've felt towards me." I bowed my head in sorrow.

Captain Murray

We grieved, we who love her. None thought to disobey the calling o' God. But—by begetting and guardianship, I'm faither to both these bairns!

"I am nae mair in authority o'er ye, Torquil Dhu, yet I maun speak—as Robert Bruce's friend. Ye are come to a point o' choosing pathways, wi' life's duty before ye. Ye have a broader station noo, where auld things are passed awa', wi' new to take their place.

"Ye are enlarged beyond the point where a private soldier's duty would make use o' a' the moral improvement and knowledge ye possess. To waste them would be naught but sin!

"Begone, the noo!"

Torquil

I descended the steps unseeing. Nightfire sensed my heaviness and didn't prance, but stepped his foxtrot all the way to the public road.

"Naught but sin!, naught but sin!" echoed in my mind.

I couldn't take it all in at once. Could there be Divine assignment to live the life I long for? I jumped off Nightfire, dropped to my knees by the roadside and opened my questioning spirit to God.

In immediate answer, Truth confirmed that protecting Southern people is my calling, and I was now equipped to take a larger part than one enlisted soldier on the frontier could accomplish. It would indeed be sin to waste my education.

But—wherever God directed me, I'd have the position I needed to offer Miss Mary! I was instantly so happy I thought I'd explode. Nannie was right: fulfillment of my heart's desires all came at once.

Too late tonight to tell Murrays. On fire to share my heart-full, I galloped Nightfire home. There was one I would tell first of all.

Mrs. Grieg

I was setting the candle o' welcome-home in its chimney when I heard braw leaps take the front steps three at a time. My last lad raced in, took my hands, whirled me in a circle.

"I'm getting married! I'm getting married, Mrs. Greig!"

Words tumbled oot. Tale o'ercame explanation, and my nods o' perfect kenning.

"I'm getting married! I must be halfwitted, not to understand till Captain Murray told me!"

Torquil

My eyes opened at first light. I dressed with extra care. Grinning, I slid down the bannister rail as I did when a boy. Old as it is, it's too solid to creak, so I surprised Mrs. Grieg in the kitchen.

"Good morning! I'm going to cut roses. May I have a basket?"

"A sma' one! Would ye please leave some for the hoose!"

"Yes, ma'am!"

* * *

Nightfire broke to a canter in three steps and his spirited gallop in six. Up the lane to Mount Murray we flew, his mane aloft on the wind of his going, and sunrise breaking over Chieftain's Hill.

Captain Murray was for a ride, himself, when we thundered up to him.

"Ye're early abroad!"

"I couldn't wait, sir!"

"I doot I'm the reason!"

"You're the first reason."

"Aye weel, are ye come to the point?"

"Yes."

"Leave the flooers in the porch, then, and ride wi' me."

He took Sachem from Young Grieg. We rode over the home meadows, observing the progress of the second crop of hay and scaring up a fallow doe who'd bedded there over the night.

"My position does her the honor she is due. If I have satisfied you, sir, may we have your blessing?"

On a winding track with a gentle gradient, we ascended a steep-sided knoll above the meadows. Captain Murray kept silence to the summit, where we looked out over the pastures and crop fields of both our lands. Unhurried, his observation roved among the coverts and tops of the glens and hills. He raised a hand in worship.

"'Tis passing fair, dear Laird." He turned to me. "Ye have kept us all long in doot."

His look chided. I met it head-on.

"Could I have hastened the day, I would."

He laid his big hand on my shoulder as though in condolence. Keeping to doleful tones, he continued, "That none o' us be burdened the more ... let us awa' ..." His grin leaped out, white teeth amid luxuriant beard "... son-to-be!" He turned Sachem and led the way, laughing for joy.

Miss Mary

From my chamber window, I saw Torquil Dhu gallop up the lane, greet Papa, and ride off with him. Eileen brought me the roses. Red and white combined signified unity, and coral, passion and desire. My heart beat faster. My love had brought roses before. Riding with Papa at sunrise was nothing unusual. But he was transformed—not the unsettled youth of two years ago, not the too-careful beau of last year, nor sorrowing in obedience, like last night. The set of his jaw and determination in his bearing gave me a flutter of trepidation before the might of this new male creature. Rising up within myself to overcome the qualm and meet the essence of him, I, too, was transformed. I made a careful toilette and put on my prettiest dress.

Torquil

In the dining room, I bowed to Mrs. Murray and William before I took Miss Mary by both hands. Her touch, and the sight of her sweet form and face, drove all elaborate words from my mind. I knelt on one knee and said what had lain long awaiting within.

"I love you, Mary, with all my heart. Will you marry me?"

Miss Mary

I'd imagined this moment over and over. I'd seen myself giving gracious acceptance … calm consent … joyful affirmation. But his humility kept me from displaying the womanly daring I'd summoned up. He is still my own dear Torquil Dhu.

As pure in love as he, I simply answered, "Yes," and our future on earth was sealed.

Torquil

Awed by the glory of being no more alone, I whispered, "We are so blessed."

"When we didn't know … if we'd ever have the most daily of joys."

CHAPTER 28

"REJOICE WITH THEM THAT DO REJOICE ..."

Every heir or young chieftain of a tribe was obliged in honour to give a specimen of his valor before he was owned ... leader of his people.
—Colonel David Stewart, *Sketches of the Highlanders of Scotland*

Torquil

We were to wed on Thursday. All my friends had arrived except Vogelsang, by Wednesday night. Uncle James and Aunt Elizabeth were at the manse, Mount Murray was full of relatives, and the New York MacLeods were with me.

While the ladies and girls gathered at Murrays' to celebrate the bride, Uncle James collected the men for a supper at DeVique's. Aidan Beag looked brim-full of news. A forthcoming heir or a success for his firm? Not a clue did he speak. Robbie presented the first toast.

"To the once and future Chief ... gentlemen, the bridegroom!"

"The bridegroom!"

I rose to respond. I made the expected speech with gentle irony, ending it with the second toast.

"With deepest admiration and respect, I acknowledge debts which may never be possible to repay. Concerning most of you: we gave as good as we got. To one, I owe my life, the freedom of my soul, and much of whatever understanding I may possess. For his patience—sorely tried—and his wisdom—sometimes bestowed in vain—and, most of all, for his daily and dangerous sacrifice on my behalf, I honor the man who is a father to me. Gentlemen, our host ... Uncle James!"

"Uncle James!"

As one, the Rangers sprang to their feet and raised their glasses high, followed in a heartbeat by all the others.

MacLeod

Shifting my goblet from right to left hand, I gave a solemn smile and rose up.

"Gentlemen, there were days when, if told, I wouldn't have believed this occasion possible. You of Abercairn shared many of them. We fought together, bound up each other's wounds, and 'drank from the same canteen.'" I mentioned in turn the contributions the others had made.

"Gentlemen ... the company!"

"The company!"

Torquil

"The company" invited any choice of honoree. Carter stood and raised his glass.

"To absent friends."

"I am present as soon as I could!"

"You're a present from first to latest, you tardy Dutchman!" I smiled to take away all sting.

Smug grin on his face, Vogelsang handed his hat and cane to a waiter. He strode one long pace to me and shook my hand before he stopped next to Aidan Beag. Mssr. DeVique appeared as if conjured out of thin air. He placed a chair while the waiter set another bottle and glass on the table.

"Will you dine, sir?"

"I am fed to the full, but, thank you, I will drink!"

Carter continued suavely, "With the pleasure of there being one less among them, since he is among *us*, let us drink to those who remain … our absent friends."

"Absent friends!"

Carter took his seat. Aidan Beag stood, grinning.

"Gentlemen, I am greatly relieved to present my newest brother, Gerhardt Vogelsang, who, after years of keeping us in suspense, is now husband to Nannie." He raised his glass. "To Mr. and Mrs. Vogelsang, long life and God's blessing!"

"God's blessing!"

Airlie was on his feet before the echo died away. "To the secret of your success, Vogelsang!" He raised his glass. "Let's hear it!"

"Let's hear it!"

Vogelsang emptied his glass before he stood. The observant waiter refilled it.

"The secret? Do not permit 'No'! My liebchen required three months to try with the Indians. I appeared for her answer. She was 'not sure in her mind.' I would bring her home. She would not travel alone with a man. I said she would—with her husband. We were married by the minister there." He gestured an end. *"Das ist alles!"*

My friends all told stories to my credit, and to my embarrassment. To honor God, my betrothed, and tomorrow's holy vows, I drank as little as good comradeship allowed, but Vogelsang and Bouleau waged a good-natured, unspoken contest over who could hold the most.

It was nearly two in the morning when Uncle James nodded to me. We both rose.

"It's a long time till tomorrow night! We've just started!" Airlie protested. "We haven't got to when we bagged that company of Yanks … present company excepted, of course, asking you all's pardon." He nodded to the MacLeods.

"Exception not accepted," Uncle Andrew grinned. "We're part and parcel of 'you all' tonight!"

Keir

Grieg and I headed the horsemen escorting The Drummond to his marriage. We came oot the lane and stopped befair the company o' guests. As his ghillie, 'tis my honor to announce the Chief.

"Friends … I present ye … Drummond!"

He put Nightfire a length forward, took off his hat, and bowed. "Your servant."

MacLeod

Mount Murray is built on as generous a scale as its master. From a spacious central passage opened parlor, dining hall, and office. The staircase swept upward to private chambers. Dominie Gilchrist used the bottom stairstep for a chancel. Torquil and I stood on the main floor and Mr. Dunnachie beside the staircase to our right. The passage was great enough for the pipes, so the skirl resonated but didn't overpower. Dominie Gilchrist nodded, and he piped the glorious strains of "Azmon": "O for a thousand tongues to sing, my great Redeemer's praise!"

Nannie

I walked, to the measure, in advance. The congregation rose in honor of my best friend. Captain Murray wore up-to-date

Highland full dress. Only the guests from afar looked long at him. All other eyes were on Mary, her bridegroom's most of all.

Her gown was pale golden silk, flowing skirt trimmed with lace in garlands tied up with bows of ribbon. A gathered over-skirt was caught becomingly at the back and flowed into a train. No veil hid her face. Her hair was dressed with white roses worked into the simple corona that's so perfect for her. From its rim flowed a headdress of matching silk voile. She carried a bou-quet of white roses and deep green laurel leaves and walked with her chin up, the sheen of the silk accenting the grace of her step.

Miss Mary

So happy I must have glowed, I gazed at my beloved. His face looks fairer than ever in contrast to his new black clothes. Almost too fair. Does he feel the same sacred awe I do? He met my gaze, his face lit with a smile. I could almost see his heart springing forth to embrace mine. From the perfect security only he inspires, I poured out my heart's love over the intervening distance.

Torquil

The years of unknowing were dissolved like drifting moun-tain mist. She was come to be all my own at last. The time was now, yet also the future I'd scarce dared hope for. I didn't know I was white with tension until, giving the tender smile that's only for her, I felt it break.

Captain Murray gave her hand to me. Dainty, graceful, lying warm in mine, it signified she was giving all her being to me and trusting me with her whole life. I swallowed hard and prayed silently,

'Dear God, grant I may never fail her!'

Miss Mary

I saw him turn pale and felt his hand turn cold. I shivered inside at the eternal significance of the oneness we were pledging. He's mine to feed and comfort, mine to cosset and cheer, mine to live for and bear a new generation for and to bless in every way I can.

'Please, dear Lord, may I never disappoint him.'

Torquil

"... ye promise to cleave to each other ... to love, honor, and cherish each other ... by every kind, affectionate, and faithful office, to lighten each other's cares, relieve each other's sorrows, promote each other's joys, and support each other's duties; and in all the scenes of life, whether prosperous or adverse, joyous or afflictive, through which, in divine Providence, ye may be called to pass, ye promise to fulfill to each other the offices of husband and wife.

"Ye, Torquil David Drummond ... solemnly promise before God and these witnesses that ye will love and honor her, and in every regard prescribed by the Word of God ... prove to her a faithful and affectionate husband till ye are separated from her by death. Do ye thus promise?"

"I do," I declared it in firm tones.

"Ye, Mary Jennet Murray. ... Do ye thus promise?"

"I do."

"In accordance with the Word of God, I pronounce ye husband and wife."

I put the wedding ring on her finger.

"What God hath joined together, let not man put asunder!

"Let us pray.

"Most holy and almighty God, be pleased to accompany thine own institution with thy blessing." He raised his hand over our bowed heads. "The Lord bless ye and keep ye."

While Mr. Dunnachie stepped to the fore to pipe us to the feast, I gave my new wife a chaste embrace and kiss.

"My own dear love," I whispered.

She returned our watchword. "We are so blessed!"

We followed Mr. Dunnachie and the triumphant, swelling "Nicaea": "Holy, Holy, Holy!"

Mrs. Mary

I was too inundated by the flow of well-wishers to do anything but respond with full heart. When the last dear guest was gathered in, I pointed out the decorations to … my husband.

Wreaths and garlands of laurel … tall branched silver candelabra on the head table … gifts … serving table, every inch covered with carved meats, tureens of vegetables, pies filled with game birds, venison, mincemeat. The bride's cake crowned the head table. Above it, given pride of place, were the flags of the Abercairn Shield and the Caledonians.

"Papa says they're the blood of the men who died for them."

We were sobered by the memories when David came up to us.

"You both look like you got the worst of the bargain! Cheer up! It's only for this life!"

Torquil

Surrounded by warm support, we began to make our new place in the matrix of Abercairn. After the feast, Uncle James stood to propose the first toast.

"Ladies and gentlemen, I present to you the son of my heart and my first daughter. Let us continue to pray God's blessing upon them, upon their marriage, upon every scion of their house, until time becomes eternity. To the bride and groom ... God bless them!"

"God bless them!" Hundreds of voices made hall and passage ring.

Captain Murray erupted to his feet. "The distaff side o' this union weel noo be heard from! From bairn to man, hath this lad"—he clapped a mighty hand on my shoulder—"been under my eye. A worthy son to his father, a brother to my perished lad, and noo ... my lass's own true man, son to us.

"My heart is full satisfied!" He raised his glass. "My friends ... twa hooses joined!"

"Twa hooses joined!"

I rose, drawing Mary up with me, and raised my glass. "To you all ..."

I gazed long and affectionately at her to honor Mrs. Grieg before I caught the eyes of the whole company of those I'm called to serve.

"... whose affectionate care, whose teaching and example, and whose unfailing friendship and loyalty brought us to this happiest of days ... to ABERCAIRN!"

"ABERCAIRN!"

Finis